"Have you never seen a naked man before?" Rorik asked.

"Of course!  n brighter shade of er, and sometimes se s, as a hostess should. ed and looked away.

"Never so prepared to do honor to your beauty?" he supplied with a laugh. Then the laughter left his face abruptly. "Is it maidenly modesty that sets your face aflame? Or fear that I will discover the way has been opened by another? Are you a virgin, Alaine?"

She regarded him with amazement. "Of course I am virgin!"

"Then you will not labor under that burden much longer."

Before she could cringe or dodge away he picked her up in his arms and laid her gently on the bed...

&

Also by Emily Carmichael

Autumnfire
The Devil's Darling

Published by
WARNER BOOKS

Emily Carmichael
Surrender

WARNER BOOKS

A Warner Communications Company

WARNER BOOKS EDITION

Cover illustration by Doug Gray

Warner Books, Inc.
666 Fifth Avenue
New York, N.Y. 10103

 A Warner Communications Company

Printed in the United States of America

First Printing: June, 1988

10 9 8 7 6 5 4 3 2 1

NOTE: Historians believe that the battle at Val-es-Dunes took place near the beginning of the year 1047. For the sake of this story I have pushed it back a few months into the autumn of 1046.

CHAPTER 1

Alaine de Ste. Claire sat among the frost-rimed leaves, knees drawn up to her chin, watching the first molten sliver of the sun climb above the eastern hills. Ruddy rays of light speared out over the valley, touching first the western meadows with their dots of grazing sheep and cattle, then advancing through the village huddled on the far bank of the River Ste. Claire. Sparks of the sun glinted off the brass bell in the spire of the parish church. Alaine sat still and silent, her eyes following the progress of the morning flood of sunlight as it poured across the valley. When the rays finally touched the towers and battlements of Castle Ste. Claire and danced along the swift-moving waters that flowed at its base, she rose stiffly from her cold seat and brushed the clinging damp leaves from her cloak. She cocked her head slightly, the better to catch the sound of the brass church bell ringing Prime. As the clear tones of the bell rolled over the valley, Alaine knelt beside a mound of freshly turned earth. The morning sun turned her neatly plaited hair to molten gold as she bowed her head and made the sign of the cross, trying dutifully to pray.

Seven days had passed since Sir Geoffrey had been laid in the cold earth, and every morning Alaine had greeted the dawn beside his grave. Her father had been a hard man to love, but she had loved him nonetheless. His harsh words and brusque manner had wounded her often, but the wounds were salved by the knowledge that if he demanded more of her than of anyone else, he also loved her more than anyone else. She was his only child, his heir, and much as it sorrowed him to pass the lands and villages of St. Claire to a mere girl, he had been proud that she was, as he often boasted, as good as any man.

The last echoes of the church bell faded, and still Alaine had not gathered her thoughts into a proper prayer for her father's soul. With a stab of guilt for her lack of discipline, she gave up and rose from her knees, hoping at least that her good intentions would make her father's rest a bit easier. In a tender gesture she reached down and brushed away the brown and brittle leaves that the wind had blown across the grave.

"Rest well, Father."

Her words seemed to echo in the stillness of the morning air. Rest well. Rest well. Heaven knew there would be no rest for her this day, Alaine thought bitterly. What an untimely demon was death, to snatch her father from her now, when the whole land was aflame with war and rebellion and the harvest was so poor it seemed that nature itself had turned against them. For all that Sir Geoffrey had tried to mold her into the image of the son he had craved, the fact remained that she was a mere girl of seventeen years. Ste. Claire was hers now, but she could keep it only if she could hold it; and how was an unwed maid to hold a castle whose walls were as broken down as her remaining men-at-arms and whose villagers were starving because the ground had yielded no decent crops for two years? How indeed? The land was torn by rebellion and savagery, and the lack of a strong lord at Ste. Claire would beckon every landless adventurer and ambitious lordling in Normandy.

There were no answers to be found, she realized sadly, by standing vigil at a grave. She said a silent farewell to her father and turned to walk back up the slope toward the castle. Sounds of the valley coming to life were dancing through the crisp morning air. Even at this distance from the castle she could hear the ring of metal on metal as Ste. Claire's smith began his day's labor, and the honking of geese and an occasional bleat of a ewe proved that the goosegirls and herdsboys were awake and about their business. The smell of fresh bread baking in the huge ovens in the bailey set Alaine's empty stomach to rumbling.

She paused for a moment to regard her home, wishing it were as strong as it looked. Across the orchard to her left the mighty Ste. Claire flowed wide and deep, passable only by way of a bridge that spanned its width where the orchard road met the river. In case of attack, one section of that bridge could be drawn back to create a gap in the middle. In the distance off to Alaine's right ran the faster, shallower Reve, fordable most of the year in only one narrow spot where horses or wagons could cross single file. If the walls were manned with skilled archers, a whole army could be picked off at leisure as they tried to wade the treacherous stream.

Where the two rivers joined there reared a steep hill of solid granite. On that hill sat the castle of Ste. Claire, glowering guardian over the rivers, fields, and villages below. It was approachable only from the south, where the triangle of land formed by the rivers' confluence sloped gradually down to orchard and field. And on this gentle slope a wooden palisade and two stout stone walls, each with a deep dry moat, discouraged unwelcome visitors.

To a stranger's eyes Ste. Claire might seem a glaring stone gargoyle crouched on its cliff of granite, but to Alaine the keep was home. Every vault, passage and chamber, every foot of the walls, every corner of the bailey was an integral and beloved part of her world. As she stood at the edge of the orchard watching the line of morning sunlight crawl down the towers, her breath caught with the same love and pride her father had felt for this place. But love didn't blind her to the places where the stones of the walls were crumbling, or the pitiful number of men who stood guard on the batttlements. Once again she wished that the fortress were as strong as it looked.

As she crossed the road onto the exercise grounds a familiar voice hailed her.

"Ho! Alaine!" Her father's senior squire Garin de Longchamps grinned and waved from where he stood with several of the younger squires and pages of the household.

Alaine smiled and changed course to join the group.

"I thought you'd be at Mass with Lady Joanna," Garin remarked as Alaine walked up.

She grimacèd as she realized she had managed to miss Mass once again, the third day in a row. Her stepmother Joanna would not be pleased.

"But then again"—the squire's tone bantered with easy familiarity—"I see you're not exactly dressed to attend one of Father Sebastian's services."

He surveyed her wool tunic, chausses, and leather boots with a cockily raised brow, but the male attire that would have scandalized any proper Norman woman didn't even bring a blush to Alaine's face.

"Even Joanna has given up trying to make me look like a lady, though she'll not admit it." Alaine grinned mischievously. Garin's sunny smile put light back into her world and made her problems seem far away.

"It's as I thought." Garin laughed. "I'd lay odds on you against Joanna any day." He shrugged his right arm out of his enveloping cloak. "Care to go a few rounds, as long as you're here and already in trouble?"

Alaine's eyes lit with friendly challenge. It was tempting to put aside her cares and pretend she was back in the days when she was free to spend her hours practicing at arms with the boys and young men. But regretfully those days were gone.

"Not this morning. Later maybe."

"Later, humph! Once Joanna gets her hands on you she'll have you sewing and spinning and some other such trivial work for the rest of the day." He swept her attire with a critical eye. "Especially if you let her catch you dressed that way!"

Alaine shrugged. Garin's impertinent scrutiny didn't bother her. He had first come to Castle Ste. Claire when Alaine was only four. He was the brother she'd never had. They had grown together, fought, argued, romped through the keep, bailey, and surrounding woods like two ragamuffin villein children. And when Alaine was old enough she had followed Garin onto the practice field. Her father had not denied her. He'd encouraged her, in fact. It had been easy for Sir Geoffrey to succumb to the temptation of transforming his motherless little daughter into the son he would never have. At five she could control a horse as well as any boy, and at seven she began her training in swordplay and archery. At ten she was introduced to the lance and spent as many hours as the young pages and squires being bruised and battered by the quintain, that insidious jousting target that would flip around and deliver a stout rap to the back of anyone clumsy enough to deal it a less than perfectly placed blow.

Only since her father had taken Lady Joanna to wife had Alaine been forced to endure a woman's tutelage. Garin had teased her unmercifully about her growing awareness of her role as a noble lady, but their friendship hadn't dimmed. This past week, with her world turning topsy-turvy, his familiar teasing and warm smile were like a balm to her wounded spirit.

"If you're afraid to let these young fellows see me trounce you at swordplay, I'll be generous and let you outdo me with the bow." Garin's eyes sparkled with mischief. He gestured to the end of the field where targets were set up for archery practice. No one in the castle could best Alaine with the short bow. It was not a knight's weapon, and the pages and squires spent only minimal practice on what they considered a yeoman's skill. But Alaine had developed an uncanny instinct for the complex variables that went into an accurate bow shot, and she'd been fascinated with the weapon since she had first held one in her hand.

"Let me beat you?" She laughed incredulously. "The

day hasn't dawned when I couldn't beat you at this game blindfolded!''

"Rashly spoken, milady! Let's just see how . . .''

"Oh no you don't, you two!''

They both looked around in surprise as a new voice entered the fray. Alaine's stepsister Mathilde had come onto the field unnoticed. She looked at Alaine and shook her head. She was doing her very best to look sternly disapproving, but the gleam of mischief in her velvet brown eyes gave lie to the intensity of her glare.

"You're in trouble now, Alaine,'' Mathilde warned with saucily lifted brow. "Sir Oliver saw you from the gate tower and told Mother you're down here on the practice field. She was already vexed that you didn't show up for Mass. She sent me along to fetch you.''

Alaine shrugged and grinned at Garin, but Garin, it seemed, had eyes only for her short, buxom, chestnut-haired stepsister. Mathilde modestly lowered her gaze before the onslaught of Garin's eyes, but to Alaine it looked more like a coy fluttering of the eyelashes than proper maidenly modesty.

"Garin!'' Alaine nudged him ungently in the ribs with her elbow.

"Huh? Oh! Right! I guess we'll have that contest later.'' With difficulty he tore his eyes away from the tentative smile that curved Mathilde's generous lips. He turned back to Alaine. "I'll have that blindfold ready,'' he said with a grin.

"You do that!''

Alaine cast a last longing look back at the practice field as she walked toward the outer wall with Mathilde. She felt the problems of her existence closing in around her once again.

The chamber that Alaine shared with Mathilde and her other two stepsisters, Gunnor and Judith, was icy. The sun's warmth couldn't penetrate the twelve-foot-thick stone walls even in the summer, and in the damp, dreary months of winter the chamber rivaled the outdoors for cold. Alaine could see her breath as she tugged off her tunic and unlaced the cross garters binding her chausses. She wondered irritably why the scullery maid assigned to light the fires in the mornings had passed by this chamber.

"God in Heaven above! What are you doing in here with no fire on the hearth?" A short, plump woman with hair of dingy gray pushed through the door without knocking. Hadwisa had been Alaine's nurse and the only mother she had known since the noble Constance of Ducey had died giving her birth.

"Lord above!" the old nurse muttered, sticking her head out the door. "Lizzie, you useless slattern! Get wood up here for a fire! Do you want the young mistress to freeze to death in her own chamber?"

"It's all right. I'll be gone in a moment." She rolled her eyes dramatically. "Joanna wants to see me."

Alaine smiled as a harried kitchen girl loaded with wood pushed through the door. The servants might take their time when she or Joanna asked for something. But every last one of them jumped when Hadwisa started shouting. She'd been known to jump pretty quickly herself when she had earned her old nurse's displeasure.

"Here, baby, let me help you with that." Hadwisa took the linen chemise from Alaine's hands and lowered it neatly over the girl's golden head. Then she stepped over to the wardrobe and chose an elaborately embroidered gown.

"Not that one!" Alaine said with a laugh. "It's Joanna I'm going to see, not the Queen of France! The plain brown wool will do."

Hadwisa clucked disapprovingly, drawing an apprehensive glance from the maid laying the fire.

"Don't bother, Lizzie," Alaine told the girl. "There's no sense in wasting the wood when no one will be in here most of the day. Just don't forget to light the fire tonight."

"Yes, milady." The girl managed to bob her head respectfully toward Alaine and at the same time give

Hadwisa a surreptitious look of "I told you so" as she left the chamber.

The old woman bristled. "Disrespectful slut! Don't know what's happened to the people around here since poor Sir Geoffrey met his end! Half the men-at arms going off to God-knows-where just because they didn't get their few pence worth of pay, and now the servants growing bold. I don't know what's . . ."

"You can go too, Hadwisa." Alaine practiced what she hoped was a polite but authoritative voice. She pulled on wool stockings under the loose folds of chemise and gown. "Tell Joanna I'll be along soon."

Hadwisa raised her brows at Alaine's tone. She was still not used to the fact that her charge was growing up and was now mistress of this castle and its surrounding lands and dependent peoples. "Well, you'd best not keep the lady waiting too long," she sniffed. "She has a right strange look in her eye this morn, and I'll wager she's up to something."

As Hadwisa shut the door behind her, Alaine moved to the polished metal mirror that Joanna's older daughter Gunnor had installed in the chamber. Her hair needed replaiting, she decided, and Joanna certainly wouldn't like the hint of windburn that reddened her cheeks. But then, Joanna seldom liked very much about her appearance or manners. She would rather Alaine simper like Gunnor or be demure like Mathilde.

Remembering the way Garin had looked at Mathilde on the practice field, Alaine looked into the mirror and experimentally fluttered her eyelashes as she'd seen her stepsister do to such devastating effect. After only one or two flutters she gave up in disgust. It was hopeless. What looked winsome on Mathilde looked ridiculous on her. No wonder men never looked at her as they did at her stepsisters. As Joanna had so often told her, her manner was much too bold, too honest and open—entirely unflattering for a young maiden. She didn't know how to flirt, and being coy was completely beyond her. Her directness made most men stutter in embarrassment and most women look at her aghast.

Her father had liked her that way, though. Alaine smiled at the memory of a jongleur who had tarried at Ste. Claire last Christmastide. Most songsters who plied their trade in return for the hospitality of the great hall fastened on her stepsisters as subjects of their ridiculous lays. But this one had woven a song just for Alaine, naming her eyes the blue of the summer sea and her hair the color of warm sunlight on a springtime afternoon. Alaine had been amused, suspecting the man had seen her father's fond looks and was hoping to please the old man by praising his favorite daughter. But instead, the jongleur's song had drawn only a frown of impatience from the lord of the castle, for her father, if he could not quite think of Alaine as a son, at least preferred to regard her as some sexless being who had been sent in place of that much-coveted gift. Alaine laughed again at the memory. Her clear blue eyes sparkled into the glass. She was what she was. Let Joanna fuss and fume all she wanted. It was too late to change.

The Lady Joanna awaited her in the solar with impatiently tapping foot and an irritated furrow in her brow.

"I must say, Alaine, you took your time. Did it take this long to change from those . . . those men's garments?"

Alaine shrugged. She refused to argue. Her stepmother looked tired and worn, she thought. Now twice widowed, Joanna was an attractive, slim woman whose hair was only a shade paler than the dark chestnut of Mathilde's. No gray flecked the thick locks that were neatly coiled at her nape and peeked through her simple linen wimple. But this morning, Alaine noticed, Joanna looked old. Her shoulders lacked their usual square set, and lines that had not been there a week ago creased her forehead.

"You know how I feel about you cavorting with the young men." Joanna's usually gentle voice was sharp with disapproval.

"We weren't cavorting," Alaine said mildly. "We were merely talking. "Besides, my father . . ."

"Your father is dead, Alaine."

Joanna's eyes met hers, and Alaine's conscience twinged at the grief that clouded their usually clear gray depths. Her stepmother also had suffered the pain of loss this past week, yet Alaine had given her no thought. She had thought only of her own sorrow.

"I'm sorry, Alaine," Joanna said in a softer voice, "but you must face reality. There comes a time in every person's life when he or she must put aside the privileges and joys of youth. This is your time."

"What would you have me do?" Alaine asked sharply, not able to quell a flare of resentment.

"I would have you act like a woman who is responsible for the lives and welfare of all the folk who depend on Ste. Claire."

Alaine looked at the floor in tight-lipped silence.

"Yesterday I went over the accounts with the bailiff. He says you know the books better even than Geoffrey did. I would like to know why the taxes and imports from the serfs have not been collected for these past months."

Alaine looked up, confident of her ground now. Her father had insisted she know how to run his estate as well as how to fight for it. She knew the accounts backward and forward, knew every rent that was due and every payment owed to every knight in service. Not a denier left or was added to the Ste. Claire treasury that she didn't know about. She knew every bushel of grain and every single pig or sheep the serfs and free tenants gave to their lord in return for land and protection.

"Father and I agreed," she said stiffly. "The serfs and villeins are starving as it is. Poor crops and raids by de Prestot's men have nearly wiped them out. Father agreed that it wasn't to our good to press them so hard their children die and the men grow too weak to provide for their families."

"All very well and good, but the vaults are mostly empty. What are we to do if . . . ?"

"Joanna, you can't take from them what they don't have!"

Joanna pursed her lips thoughtfully. "I suppose you're right. We'll just have to make do and hope that we have no need for reserves of food—a feeble hope with the countryside in such turmoil as it is. Which brings us to the other subject we must discuss."

"What subject is that?"

"Finding you a husband."

Alaine was silent for a moment, then moved to the window of the solar and looked out over the sere brown fields and meadows to the village clinging to the bank of the Ste. Claire. She could see the brass church bell winking in the morning sun, make out the herdsboys prodding the cows along the river trail. Sounds from the bailey drifted to her ears—the steady clanging of the smith's hammer, the shrill voices of the village wives gathered around the huge bread ovens, the rough laughter of the men-at-arms as they honed their skills in the small practice yard just inside the bailey wall. The same sights and sounds had greeted her since she was a small child looking out this same window. Nothing was changed. And yet somehow everything was different.

"Must we talk about that so soon after . . . after . . . ?" Her lips tightened in a spasm of sorrow. "My father is scarcely cold in his grave."

If Alaine had turned away from the window she might have seen the spark of sympathy in her stepmother's gentle gray eyes, but Joanna allowed no awareness of her stepdaughter's plight to soften her voice.

"That is all the more reason why you must have a husband. Your father is no longer here to defend us. Half the men-at-arms have drifted off to find a more generous master. You are without even a lawful overlord to defend your rights, since your father could never bring himself to do proper homage to Fulk of Brix."

"Fulk of Brix is a usurper," Alaine said contemptuously. "Father could not do him homage without breaking his oath of fealty to the lawful lord of Brix."

Joanna snorted, her woman's practicality disdaining her late husband's notions of honor. "So your father always said. But the fact remains that Geoffrey neglected to provide you with a strong man who could defend these lands we call home, and also left you without the protection of an overlord."

Alaine sighed and turned away from the window. Joanna was right, of course. Unless she wed, and quickly, all she loved might be lost to her. News of her father's death would bring the scavengers swarming. She could choose for herself, immediately, or have her and her holdings become a prize to be fought over by the dogs of war that ravaged the land.

For generations Ste. Claire had owed fealty to the vicomtes of Brix as overlord and suzerain. In another, more ordered time, feudal law would have required the lord of Brix to protect the rights of Ste. Claire's orphaned heiress. But the rightful vicomte was dead, murdered long ago when Alaine was but a child, and her father had stubbornly refused to do homage to his murderer, Fulk, who now called himself Vicomte of Brix. And the young Duke William, barely out of childhood, was too occupied defending is own life and ducal throne to come to the aid of a minor barony on the far-flung western edge of his dukedom. Alaine was painfully aware she was on her own in a vicious and savage world, and her only course was to barter herself and her holdings to some man who would defend her home and her people. "If only your father had seen fit to arrange a betrothal before he died!" Joanna sighed, lamenting that fact for what must have been the hundredth time in the past week. Geoffrey's refusal to acknowledge his daughter's vulnerability would be the death of them yet, Joanna thought. Even now she could hear his laughing assertions that his daughter could fight as well as most men and that his men-at-arms would follow her down to the last man. What need had she of husband? he had boasted. She is more of a man than any of the milksop barons who sued for her hand. Sir Geoffrey had been so wise in some ways, and so stupid in others!

Alaine grimaced in distaste. "Whom would you have had my father betroth me to, Joanna?" She shared her father's contempt for the men who had come seeking her hand and secretly delighted in the fact that at an age when most girls had been married several years, she was still free.

"Gilbert de Prestot is a strong knight with lands adjoining Ste. Claire. I vow in the last two years he's petitioned your father at least five times."

"Gilbert de Prestot asks for my hand and at the same time sends his men to raid our farms and villages. He abuses his serfs and mismanages his fields. Would you want me wed to such a man?"

"What about Sir Robert St. James?" Joanna offered. "He is not only wealthy, but he is also reputed to be a kind and fair man."

"The last time Sir Robert paid a visit to Ste. Claire he was so fat he could barely sit his horse. He has given up fighting in favor of eating. Is that a man you would have defending Ste. Claire?"

"Rannulf, Lord of Carentan?"

"He certainly never asked for my hand!"

"He wasn't free until only six months ago. If he knew the situation here, I'm sure he would be eager to offer his protection. He would jump at the chance to have Ste. Claire and your lands in the Isles. He's a powerful knight, Alaine. I watched him in the melee that your father hosted only last year. No one could stand against him. He is in the prime of his strength and skill. Rannulf would be the solution to all our problems."

Alaine sighed in exasperation. "Rannulf took a dislike to his last wife and locked her in a chamber for the duration of their marriage. I've heard the gossip that her screams could be heard nightly when he beat her. Is that the kind of man you want me to give myself to?"

"Don't be a fool! Adela was a shrew and stupid into the bargain. I don't blame Rannulf for locking her away. You wouldn't make her mistakes."

"How do you know?" Alaine asked stubbornly. "What do I know about pleasing a man? Nothing!"

"A man would only have to look at you to be pleased, Alaine," Joanna insisted more gently. "You may have some irregular notions and habits, thanks to your father, but basically you're a sweet girl. And you're a beauty. These last two years you've grown up and filled out. Much as your father tried to keep you hard as a man with all that riding and training, you've softened into a woman. No man could look at you and not be moved, daughter."

Alaine looked away, embarrassed.

"Alaine!" Joanna stood and placed her hands on her stepdaughter's shoulders. "You must make up your mind, girl, or risk having it made up for you. Think of your stepsisters and me. If Ste. Claire should be taken, you might be married off to the victor, but what would become of Gunnor, and Mathilde, and little Judith? Your goodwill is their only defense, Alaine."

Alaine sighed in helpless resignation at the fate she saw creeping up on her. Had her stepmother blustered and demanded, she might have met her demands with stubborn refusal. But Joanna's eyes held not only concern for Ste. Claire but love for her as well. She had been a kind stepmother in the two years since she'd married Sir Geoffrey, and if she had frustrated and exasperated Alaine by her demands that she learn to be a lady, she had always done what she thought was best for her stepdaughter. Now Alaine must do what was best for Joanna, her stepsisters, and Ste. Claire. As a child running and training with the pages and squires, she had fancifully entertained the notion of not marrying, of herself donning hauberk and sword and acting the lord of her castle. And if she had to marry, she'd once bragged to Garin, her husband would want her for herself, not her castle and vast fields and pleasant villages. But those were childish dreams, and in the face of reality the fantasies of childhood must be put aside.

"Send a message to Rannulf, Joanna," Alaine conceded in a quiet voice. "Tell him my father has died and Ste. Claire is at risk. Tell him his suit would be welcomed."

Joanna smiled broadly, proud of the look of mature purpose in her stepdaughter's fact. "That should bring him."

"Your pardon, my ladies."

Joanna turned in surprise at the sound of the old seneschal's voice. The men of the castle rarely invaded the solar, which being the brightest and warmest room in the keep, was where the women came to sit with needlework, carding, and spinning.

"What is it, Sir Oliver?"

"News, my lady. Not good, I'm afraid." The old warrior pulled uneasily at the stringy gray hair that fell to his shoulders, an affectation Alaine had always found curious in a land where men generally wore their hair clipped close. "There's an army coming up the eastern road. Doesn't look much like a friendly visit."

Alaine's heart seemed to freeze in her chest. News of her father's death couldn't be out yet. The men-at-arms who had quit their walls would carry the story with them, but surely seven days weren't enough for those men to have spread the news abroad.

"Who is it?" With effort she schooled her voice to calm.

"Can't see the banner as yet, my lady."

"How far away are they? How much time do we have?"

Sir Oliver sighed. His post of seneschal of Ste. Claire had been a sinecure, a gift from Sir Geoffrey to a friend who had grown too old to sell the services of his sword arm. While the lord had been alive, Ste. Claire needed no seneschal to oversee the security of the castle and fief and keep the men-at-arms in hand. Now that Sir Geoffrey was dead—curse the sudden fever that had taken him—Sir Oliver knew he was no longer warrior enough to defend what was in his charge.

"We've not enough time, my lady." His voice was dark with resignation. "If we had a week's notice, nay, a month's notice, we still would have not enough time. The outer palisades are weak and not even worth spending the lives to defend it. The bailey walls are crumbling in places and the battlements are undermanned. As you well know, the serfs and peasants have had difficulties seeing to themselves this season, and the work levies were dropped this year. The work to the walls was never done. The only thing worth defending is the keep itself.''

"And the keep's vaults are mostly empty," Joanna reminded them.

"The river bridge must be pulled back at once," she directed.

"Already done, my lady," Sir Oliver acknowledged. "But the Reve is what they must cross, not the Ste. Claire, and that won't hold them long. The river is at low ebb, and a determined and stalwart army will not hesitate to cross in force."

Alaine strode impatiently to the window. The view was to the north. All she saw were peaceful fields and a quiet village, all unaware of the danger closing from the east.

"Is there time to send for the villagers to come in?"

"I'm afraid not, my lady."

Feudal law required seven days' notice of private war—plenty of time to herd the vulnerable villagers and their livestock inside the protection of the bailey walls, but in these sad days the law was mostly ignored. The villagers would have to stay where they were and hope for the best.

"We have to put on at least a show of resistance," Alaine told the old seneschal in a heavy voice. "If they think we're strong they may not think a seige worth the effort. If they persist..." Her mouth drew into a grim line. "If they persist we'll just have to take what comes. Don't spend lives unnecessarily. If we can't put on a show that will drive them away immediately, we'll have to surrender."

The old man's face tightened with pain. Surrender was a word he'd never had in his vocabulary. Until now.

"I'll change and join you on the battlements," Alaine concluded.

"No you will not!" Joanna grabbed Alaine's arm as she started to follow Sir Oliver out of the solar. "You are the lady of this castle. Your place is in the hall, not on the battlements. You let Sir Oliver direct the men.''

"The men will follow me.''

"No doubt they will. But would you have our enemy see you covered with the blood and sweat of battle, or would you put yourself in the path of the spear or arrow and thus end our last hope?''

"What would you have me do? Cower in the safety of the hall while men spend their lives in our defense?''

"You'll put on your richest gown and wait with me and the girls in the hall as befits your station. There's much to be said for maintaining dignity even in the face of defeat, Alaine.''

They stared at each other in tense silence, Alaine defiant and Joanna determined. A clattering and clumping on the stairs from the great hall broke their contest of wills.

"My ladies! Your pardon.''

Garin sketched a hasty salute as he strode through the archway. His usually merry eyes were clouded with grim purpose.

"The enemy's banner is in sight,'' he told them in a dark voice. "It is Sir Gilbert de Prestot!''

CHAPTER 2

"You black-hearted yellow-haired spawn of a toad! Your years have made you slow. We'll see who comes out on top this time!''

The tow-headed giant laughed at the younger man's words as they faced each other across the cleared space between the tents. The ring of onlookers—foot soldiers, villeins, and knights alike—smiled at the arrogant confidence in his mirth. "You young whelp!" he answered in a booming voice. "The ladies might not like you so well once I've redesigned your face. Didn't the drubbing I gave you last time teach you to mind your manners with your superiors?"

A savage grin split the younger man's face. Ruddy light from the cook fire flickered across swelling muscles in his bare chest and arms. His broad-shouldered torso gleamed with sweat from the just-ended first round of their contest. Cropped black hair fell in damp spikes across his forehead and curled at the nape of his neck in short ringlets.

"Having second thoughts, boy?" The giant's pale gray eyes gleamed with challenge. "Want to concede my victory so early?"

"You've seen your last victory over me, you great dull son of an ox!"

The younger man stepped forward into a tense crouch, waiting for his opponent to spring. His face was study of concentration, the sharp, strong features rigid and set. The firelight played games with the fine looks that had won him the devotion of many ladies who should have known better. It outlined the square strength of his jaw and made the sensuously curved lips, now pressed together in a grim line, seem a mere slash in the granite facade of his face. It swept along the bold planes of his cheeks and shadowed the deep recesses of his green, glinting eyes. He could have been a god, or a demon. The eerie gleam of the fire made him seem more than mere mortal man—bone and sinew and muscle holding a power reserved for the immortals of a lost mythology. But the aura of menacing power that exuded from his gleaming body didn't deter the pale-eyed, pale-haired giant who stepped forward to meet him in the center of the clearing.

A communal intake of breath from the ring of spectators signaled the beginning of the second round of the contest. The two men grappled. Necks corded, muscles bulged and strained. Like two trees rooted to the spot, neither man would give way. Finally the giant's grip slipped on sweat-slicked skin. The younger man shifted and drove his elbow into the giant's midsection. The huge blond bared his teeth in a grimace of pain as he toppled backward and hit the ground with the force of a felled tree. Snickers and calls of "Hai! Dragon!" rippled through the audience.

"Give up yet?" the black-haired demon asked.

"Give up to a young pup like you?" The giant laughed hoarsely and pushed himself to his feet. Before the words were completely out of his mouth his foot lashed out in a vicious kick. His opponent caught it on his hip rather than in the groin where it was aimed, but the force of the blow sent him sprawling to the ground. The giant followed up his advantage by launching his considerable bulk onto the younger man's supine body. The two men grappled and rolled, coating themselves with dust that was smeared in places with crimson as the stones littering the ground took their toll of flesh. Finally, in a feat of mutual acrobatics, both men managed to spring to their feet. They drew apart and panted, regarding each other with wary eyes.

The spectators were delighted with the sight of blood. Calls of "Go, Northman!" and "Hai, Dragon!" were becoming a steady din. Green eyes glinted in the firelight as the younger man grinned audaciously at his older, heavier opponent. The tow-headed giant's mouth twitched in reply. He suspected what the other was planning. A booted foot shot out, aimed at the older man's knee. The giant twisted with a nimbleness that defied his great size. He grabbed the younger man's foot and twisted with all his might. With a howl of pain that truly might have come from a demon, the black-crowned head made jarring contact with the ground, followed by shoulders and hips. Stunned and dizzy, the downed man turned onto his back just in time to see his opponent lean down with deadly intent, the light of malice in his eyes. The huge fist was balled into a killing hammer that could crush the skull of a fighting destrier. The crowd was silent, breath held in anticipation. The fist descended, opened, and delivered a painful blow of comradeship on the younger man's shoul-

der. A beefy hand covered with pale yellow hair grabbed
the defeated challenger's arm and yanked him to his feet.

"Trying to teach a fox how to kill chickens, are you,
you lily-livered pansy?" Sihtric Olafson's fierce grin bared
teeth that were white and strong as a wolf's. "Who taught
you that little trick, now, just tell me that!"

Rorik Valois cocked an arrogant black brow. "You did,
you toad-faced bastard. And it seems you didn't teach me
very well."

Sihtric chuckled. "Always keep a few tricks to myself.
Can't let the younger generation know all your secrets."

Rorik snorted. "Next time, old man."

"You'll not live long enough to best me, you young
cockerel!" Sihtric laughed and clapped his erstwhile opponent on his blood-streaked back. "After all these years I
can still whip you in a fair fight! Though I'll wager I'm the
only man who can. Your father would be proud—of both
of us."

"What's this here?" A young man scarcely more than a
stripling shouldered his way unhesitatingly through the
crowd of burly spectators, who were noisily settling their
wagers and calling for a third round. He fixed both Rorik
and Sihtric with a jaundiced eye. "Have my two best
knights nothing better to do than spend their time beating
each other to a bloody pulp? Did you two not have enough
fighting this past day on the field at Val-es-Dunes?"

Both men nodded respectfully to the youngster. "My
lord duke," Rorik explained with a gleam of humor in his
eye, "it's an old contest."

"Aye," Sihtric added. "Settled now."

"Hardly!" Rorik denied with a grin.

"You young pups never learn," Sihtric shrugged.
"Begging your pardon, my lord." He winked at the young
Duke William. "But I could beat him with one arm tied
behind my back."

William glowered darkly at the two men who had been
with him through every crisis of his turbulent youth. He
had always regarded them with the affection of a younger
brother, depended on them for protection, companionship,

loyalty, and most of all, friendship. But tonight he was feeling neither young nor brotherly. The mantle of the recent victory at Val-es-Dunes was weighing heavily on the shoulders of a youth who had to grow much too rapidly to manhood.

"Why is it," he remarked acidly, "that while all my advisers constantly remind me I am barely out of the crib, tonight I feel years older than you two ancients?"

"Some men grow in body only," Rorik replied with a sidelong glance at Sihtric.

"I'll agree with you there," William said with a meaningful look at Rorik. "Though it is no harm done, I suppose. Better the men should be watching you two flailing in the dust than chasing every female in yonder village. I have enough to worry about without irate fathers demanding compensation for their daughters' torn virginity."

Sihtric snorted. "No need to worry about that, my lord. There's not a female in that village over the age of six who hasn't already had the deed done to her before we arrived."

"Aye," William said with a grimace. "They live like swine and breed like rabbits."

They walked together to Rorik's tent, where they were met by the worried and puckered face of Timor, Rorik's painfully adolescent squire. The senior squire who had stood at his back the last four years, every since the day he'd been knighted, had taken a sword in the throat in the previous day's fighting. Now only Timor was left to see to his needs, a fact that didn't rest well on the boy's mind.

"My lord!" The boy's eyes grew large when he saw his master was accompanied by none other than the duke himself.

"Begone," William ordered, not unkindly. "I wish to have a word in private with your master."

Timor bobbed his head and took off without a word as the men ducked into the tent.

"That's a nasty gash on your back," Sihtric told Rorik as they moved into the lantern light. "You'd better let me dress it before a festering sets in."

"Leave off," Rorik frowned. "It's nothing."

Sihtric chuckled with good humor. "Don't try your dark looks on me, boy. I'm not some shy maid you can send scampering with one of your evil scowls. I've been patching you up since you were still walking on all fours."

William sat himself on the sleeping pallet and watched as the giant Norseman picked at the grime and gravel embedded in the ugly gash in Rorik's back. Sihtric was the only man he knew who could get away with calling Rorik a boy, and probably the only man in camp who could beat the black-haired knight in a fair fight. That was only right, William mused, since the blond giant had taught Rorik to wrestle, to hold his own with a sword, mace, and lance, and to sit a horse as if he were glued to its back. He had also taught William a fair number of those things. As a result, at the tender age of nineteen years, William was already renowned for his fighting ability.

"It's amazing to me, Sir Rorik, how you survived a whole day's fighting just one day past without so much as a scratch to show for your valor, and here tonight you let your own man fling you about to be torn upon the rocks." William's eyes sparkled with mischief, and suddenly he looked as young as he really was.

Rorik grinned. "The great ox cheated." The grin tightened abruptly to a grimace as Sihtric splashed cold water over the raw wound.

"Aye, you pup, I cheated. How long have we been having these little scuffles? And how long have you tried to whip me? I keep telling you, the day you beat me is the day I'll be so weak that I'm one step out of the grave."

Rorik grunted as the older knight slapped a passably clean wad of cloth over the gash and secured it with a crude bandage.

William, never able to sit in one place for long, stood and started to pace the limited confines of the tent. "It was a telling battle yesterday, my friends. I'm grateful for the part you played in my victory. You'll be suitably rewarded, of course."

Rorik shifted impatiently. "I've lands and keeps enough granted by your generosity, my lord."

"Aye," Sihtric agreed. "And I want none. I'm content enough to serve this impudent cub, and yourself, my lord." He gave Rorik's bandage a tug to make sure it was secure.

Rorik saw William was still in need of reassurance. The young duke had few enough friends, it was true. Few men followed him without thoughts of personal gain and power uppermost in their minds. "We're your loyal men, sire." Rorik searched for the right words, for he was not a man to whom words came easily. "We serve you out of love. You've already rewarded us generously, and we're well content."

"Aye, you are both my loyal men. That's right enough. I suppose I am still unaccustomed to such loyalty."

William sat again, regarding both men assessingly. His eyes were hard as flint, contrasting with the youth of his face and the still-boyish lines of his body. They had grown hard during a childhood spent running from murder; a childhood watching those who were loyal to him pay with their lives, one by one; a childhood full of uncertainty and treachery, never knowing when another of his family would act to wrest from him his ducal throne, or his very life.

"You should never have cause to doubt us, my lord," Sihtric assured him readily. "Why such a gloomy mien this evening?"

"Am I gloomy?" William asked. "I suppose I am. Winning sometimes does that to me. But I'd be a good deal gloomier if we'd lost."

"Indeed!" Rorik agreed, pulling a clean shirt and tunic over his battered back.

"Those rebel scum got exactly what they deserved," William commented. "They should be grateful I didn't kill those that the River Orne didn't drown in their fleeing."

"Generous of you," Sihtric agreed, thinking that if William disposed of every mother's son who plotted rebellion in his fractious dukedom, he would have very few men left to rule.

"They'll all do proper homage to me on the morrow,

and I'll make every last one of them pay in lands and men for raising their swords against me. All except that scum Guy of Burgundy, who should pay dearest of all for seeking my throne. He's nowhere accounted for among the survivors, and the devil is too clever to have been drowned in the river.''

"You've broken the back of his rebellion," Rorik commented. "He'll trouble you no more."

"No one will trouble me more," William added with a bitter smile. "No more will these barons of Normandy regard me as a mere pawn to be pushed here and pulled there for their own profit. Normandy is mine! Every baron in the land will acknowledge my rule now they've seen what I can do with my loyal men behind me. Next time I won't need Henry of France to fly to my aid when some upstart threatens my rule."

"Most likely that's true, my lord," Rorik said with a quiet sigh. His muscles were beginning to stiffen from the drubbing that Sihtric had given him. And a thorough drubbing it had been, he admitted. Ever since he had come into the full strength of manhood he'd been testing himself against the good-natured giant. He would probably never win, but he'd go on trying. The periodic contests kept him humble, he admitted with a smile to himself, and sore. He wished William would stop gloating and leave so he could lay his tired body down on his pallet and let sleep soothe his hurts. But William was looking at him in a most peculiar way, and he suspected his duke had not yet said what he had come into the tent to say.

William regarded his two liege men with undisguised affection. He had no more loyal man, and no more capable knight in his service, than Sir Rorik Valois, who had always been like an older brother to him. Not only was the black-haired knight a superb warrior, but he was also a natural leader. He was as loyal to the men he led as he was to William himself, and in turn his men would follow him into the gates of Hell and beyond.

The Stone Dragon, the men had dubbed him, partly for his emblem—a blood-red dragon on a field of black—and partly for his often stonily grim manner. Rorik accepted the title with good humor, seeming to find it appropriate confirmation of the unyielding purpose that ruled his life. The emblem well represented his ferocity in battle and his absolute refusal to accept defeat. William wished he had a hundred knights just like him, but he was unique. The young duke hoped that what he was about to do was not a terrible mistake.

"You look tired, Rorik," William commented. "Perhaps this will teach you to use our days of rest to truly rest."

Rorik grinned. He had used the same words to the energetic duke on several occasions in the past.

"Hard to believe," William continued, "that it's been ten years since you joined me. Two days after my uncle the Archbishop of Rouen died you appeared in my palace to offer your services. You were a mere boy, looking starved and ragged as those sorry men who were your followers."

Rorik grunted irreverently. "You weren't long out of swaddling yourself."

William chuckled. "So I wasn't. Quite a lot has happened in those ten years. We've both become men, you and I, and now Normandy has bowed its head and accepted me as its ruler. Some day the world will know me as something more than William the Bastard."

Rorik sighed. Sihtric didn't bother to hide his boredom.

"All right, gentlemen," William smiled. "I can see you grow impatient with my rambling. I've got a mission for your, my friends—one that I think will please you well." He paused for effect, knowing he had piqued their interest. "What say you, Sir Rorik, to marching with a troop of my good men and taking back what was once wrested from your family by treachery?"

Rorik's eyes narrowed slightly as he observed William's delighted grin. It wasn't William's way to tease, but he was dangling a tempting bait in front of his eyes.

"Don't look so shocked, my friend. Did you think I don't know the desire that rules your life? I know you won't be at peace until what once was yours is again securely in your hands.''

"My loyalty is to you," Rorik affirmed. His face had set itself in stony intensity.

"I know that," William answered. "But now my need to have you at my side is not so desperate. You can have your heart's desire and we can both profit from your victory. I'm releasing you, Sir Rorik and Sir Sihtric—nay, I'm ordering you as your liege lord—to go from here with an army of fifteen knights and one hundred footmen. You will do anything you must to secure the castle of Brix, which is your lawful patrimony. Once Brix and its lands and vassals are under your control you will act as my man in the western lands. You will subdue the rebellious western lords and make the Cotentin secure for my rule.''

William held up an imperious hand for silence as Rorik and Sihtric both surged to their feet. "Hold!" he ordered. "There's more. If you can do this, my good and loyal friend, I will make you a comte with the upper half of the Cotentin under your rule.''

Rorik stepped forward and bowed his head to the boy-man he had followed and fought beside for ten years, and who tonight had given him his heart's desire. "I'll serve you up the Cotentin on a silver platter, my lord, with no reward necesssary other than the chance to kill Fulk the Usurper.''

"Just as I thought." William smiled cannily. "But you will have your reward, and so will Sihtric. You are the only men I would trust not to be seduced by that western nest of vipers. Though for the life of me I wish I could keep you here with me.''

"You won't regret this, my lord duke," Rorik assured him grimly.

Looking at the bloodlust in Rorik's face and the cruel light that glowed in the Norseman's pale eyes, suddenly William was very glad he was not Fulk of Brix.

For hours after William left, Rorik and Sihtric squatted on the floor of the tent drawing maps in the dirt floor and discussing strategies and approaches. All thought of sleep had fled, and all trace of weariness was gone.

"It'll not be an easy task, this," Sihtric commented grimly. "Brix is well planned and well defended. Even with vermin like Fulk and his men, the walls could be held for many days, and the keep could withstand an assault for months. And it's not a large number of men that William is giving us."

"Aye," Rorik agreed. "Like a rat in his hole, Fulk will be hard to dislodge. He's clever, that one. But he'll find that I'm cleverer still. William has set us a task that my heart has longed for these ten years, and no man can now keep me from what is mine."

Rorik looked at the rough map of walls, towers, and fortifications that they had traced in the dirt. Brix. It had never been absent from his mind and heart from the day he left it, fleeing like a rabbit before a ravening wolf. Even now it seemed he could smell the sea wind as it swept up the rugged coast and swirled around the great square keep. He could feel the pounding of the breakers as they thundered against the granite cliffs. The thick stone walls and deep ditches, the ramparts and palisades, the hidden exits and secret tunnels—all had been his playground when he was a child. No one knew the castle of Brix better than he did, and no one would be better able to take it back from the vermin that infested it. When the castle was in his hands and the wrongdoers had been called to account for their sins, then maybe he would know the peace of an untroubled sleep. Dreams of that day ten years ago would no longer haunt him.

Ten years ago. Had it really been that long? It seemed only yesterday he had been a whelp of fifteen, sleeping beside his two older brothers in that cold loft overlooking the sea. He and his brothers had been close companions ever since he could remember. There was no jealousy that Thurgood, the eldest, would receive the bulk of Brix as his patrimony. The two younger brothers knew that they would each receive one of the lesser estates held by their father. And all three boys judged that they had the fighting skill to increase their holdings if they so desired. The mad duke Robert the Devil had recently died, naming his bastard son, a mere lad of seven, as his heir. Chaos had erupted throughout the dukedom in war and lawlessness, and Rorik and his brothers knew that the situation was ripe for a bold warrior to win fortune and power. Anarchy was regrettable, their father had told them, but only a stupid man or a coward would not take advantage of such a chance.

But in a twist of fate Brix was the victim and not the benefactor of the situation. One cold morning as the sky was just beginning to lighten in the east, Thurgood shook Rorik from sleep and bade him arm himself. Shouting from the walls broke the early morning stillness. He could hear the commotion in the great hall below as his father's knights gathered.

Rorik had jumped from bed with the pleasant anticipation of action warming his blood. At fifteen he was already taller than most grown men, but his lanky body had yet to put on the bulk of muscle and sinew that was to come in later years. With sword and lance he was almost as capable as many of the household knights, and he was anxious to prove himself in his father's eyes.

He donned a clean shirt and woolen tunic, leathern hose and cross garters, shoulder sword belt, and then the fine mail hauberk his father had given him the year before. The ring-mail armor covered him from neck to knees and reached down his arms to below the elbow. It was split from the hip down to accommodate the scabbard and hilt of his sword and to allow him to sit a horse. He left off the heavy mail hood and ventail that would protect his head, neck, and chin when he rode into battle, but tucked that and his conical helm under his arm as he descended the narrow stairs to the great hall.

The household knights were milling around the fire hearth, chewing on hunks of bread and cheese and washing it down with the fine beer that Rorik's mother Theoda brewed. There was no sense of urgency, but the talk was animated and loud, and Rorik could tell that the men were anxious for a bit of action after a long winter of dreary cold days with nothing to do.

Thurgood thrust a sizable hunk of bread and a thick slice of cheese into Rorik's hands as he approached the hearth. "Come on! Let's be off to the battlements. There's some good sport promised for today. A runner from Gauchemain stumbled in an hour ago with news of an army slinking through the woods." His grin grew wider still. "None other than the bastard Fulk is at its head."

"Fulk!" Rorik exclaimed around a mouthful of cheese. "The man's lost his mind!"

Fulk's envy of his neighbors was common knowledge, but his holdings were pitifully small, a sop tossed him from a father whose wealth and power fell to his legitimate sons. No army raised by Fulk could possibly threaten a fortress as strong as Brix.

They reached the battlements on the outer wall just as Fulk's army was emerging from the woods to the east. It was a larger army than they had expected to see. Fulk must have enlisted aid from one of his half brothers, or promised a mercenary band rewards from the spoils of their victim. But Brix could withstand an army much larger than the one that now gathered beneath its walls.

The boys stood at the battlements and watched as Fulk drew closer. Their father, Stephen, Vicomte of Brix, and one of the household knights joined them as Fulk separated himself from his army and rode boldly toward the barbican, stopping just out of bow shot of the twin towers that protected that outermost gate. Even watching from the walls, Rorik could tell how arrogantly he sat his horse, almost, Rorik thought, as if he were a king and not a minor baron who couldn't even claim his father as his own.

"Always thought Fulk was mad as a loon," Stephen commented. "Now I know he is." In a louder voice he hailed the figure who pranced in front of the palisades. "What want you, Fulk? Do you come to pay a call with this ragged army of yours?"

"You know what I want, Stephen. For the insult you paid me when last we met, I say we two are at war."

"War is it? It is custom to grant seven days' notice, sirrah. Already you have broken your honor."

"Notice be damned! Are you afraid to fight me, old man?"

Stephen chuckled. "Does the eagle fight the rat? Go back to the dank pile of stones you call home, Fulk. You'll not lure me out to be shot in the back by your archers."

Rorik imagined he could see steam venting from the challenger's helm. He delighted in the calm and scornful way his father addressed the other man. Still, the unlikelihood of a real fight was a disappointment, and he could see the letdown in Thurgood's face also.

Fulk, stiff-backed and fuming, returned to his army. Stephen, accompanied by his eldest and youngest sons, continued his tour of the battlements, insuring that none of the men were taking their duties lightly in the face of this puny challenge. All were convinced that Brix was unassailable. The outer walls were twelve feet of solid stone, and the walls shielding the inner bailey were just as strong. And if the unthinkable happened and both walls were breached, the great square keep was nearly impenetrable and could withstand a siege of many months without hardship.

But the unthinkable and more came to pass. What could not be taken by force was taken by treachery. Even now, many leagues and ten years removed from the deed, Rorik felt his face burn with anger as he brought that treachery to mind. The one he'd trusted most had brought disaster on them all. And if that one was still alive after all these years, Rorik would finally see swift and terrible justice done.

The army that had looked so puny outside the walls had become a deadly foe once inside the inner bailey. No hint of the traitor's perfidy had reached those dining in the great hall that same evening until Fulk and his minions burst through the doors. Then blood had flowed like fountains. Crimson pools collected on the stone floor and stained the rushes. Shrieks and curses were drowned in the clatter of steel on steel and the grisly sound of knife-edged weapons hacking through flesh and bone. Thurgood had been one of the first to fall, a knife slicing through his back. Stephen had been not long in following along the road of death. He fought back-to-back with Osgood, the middle brother. They fell together, wallowing in their own lifeblood.

Rorik came upon the scene late, having excused himself from the hall to wishfully polish and tend his armor. The unexpected sound of chaos had drawn him from the loft, sword in one hand, knife in the other. A cry of agony swelled in his throat at the scene that met his eyes, but before that cry could pass his lips and call his enemies to him, Stephen's faithful seneschal Sihtric had shouldered him into the shadows.

"All is lost, boy, unless you escape. You are the last of your family to live. So follow!"

They had collected a tired and bloodied band of men-at-arms as they slipped into the chapel and out the hidden door that exited from behind the altar. The inner and outer baileys were quiet as death, and death was all that they saw there. Silently the little band had made their way to the postern gate in the eastern wall. They tumbled down the ditch, ran swiftly across the open lists, then used the ropes Sihtric had thought to bring to lower themselves over the palisades. One man fell and broke his leg. They carried him into the woods where Sihtric attempted to set the bone whose ends protruded jaggedly from his shin. They gagged the poor man so his screams wouldn't alert their enemies to their escape, but he'd been brave, not making the smallest sound. He had died two weeks later, Rorik remembered, from putrefaction of the wound.

"Well, boy, what do you think?"

Rorik's bitter memories of ten years past faded once more into the back of his mind at Sihtric's words. "Sorry. I wasn't paying attention."

"I can see that!" Sihtric snorted impatiently. "The chance we've been waiting for taps us on the shoulder and you're off somewhere woolgathering. Now look here. We can approach Brix overland from here"—he pointed to the area of rugged hills and rocky cliffs he had squiggled on the dirt map—"or we can use the flatter country along the River Ste. Claire and approach it from the south. Which will it be?"

Rorik studied the map and called up pictures of the two routes in his mind, remembering the country he had roamed as a boy. "The flatter country will be best, even though there's this in the way." He pointed to the spot on the map that represented the well-defended confluence of the Ste. Claire and the Reve.

"That shouldn't be so much of a problem," Sihtric commented. "Sir Geoffrey's a good man and might even lend us aid. And if not . . ."

Rorik nodded his head in agreement. In order to take Brix then, they were agreed that they must first take Castle Ste. Claire.

CHAPTER 3

Alaine fixed her eyes on the gold crucifix fastened to the chapel wall behind Father Sebastian's head. Her knees ached from the cold stone floor, and her whole body was stiff from tension. The little priest was deliberately being slow, she thought, and blessed the man for his concern. But nothing could save her now. Father Sebastian's slow and halting recital of the marriage service, along with his silent prayers for delivery from their troubles, would not call down a miracle from Heaven.

Alaine let the priest's words flow over her unheeded as

her mind tumbled back over the events of the last few hours. What mistakes had she made to bring her people to this sorry fate? She had known the castle was doomed from the moment she saw Gilbert's army of knights, pikemen, and archers ranged before the walls. The small show of resistance by her men-at-arms had only whetted the enemy's appetite for the victory to come. They had smashed the portcullis and gate with a battering ram and surged into the bailey, cutting a bloody swath through the pitifully few defenders. Gilbert's men had been at the entrance to the keep before it could be barricaded. At that point Alaine had instructed a distraught Sir Oliver to surrender. More fighting would be a useless waste of life, and she was not willing for her men to die to no purpose.

Following Joanna's advice, she had hurried to her chamber and instructed Hadwisa to dress her carefully in her best garments. The chemise was heavily decorated with gold and silver embroidery around neck, hem, and lower sleeves. A gown of blue silk complemented her hair and eyes, and the elaborate embroidery around the wide three-quarter-length sleeves, the deep V neckline, and the three-quarter-length hem repeated the design on the chemise. As the newest fashion demanded, the gown was laced tightly in back to conform to the contours of her body, showing off her slim waist and high breasts. As Hadwisa added the finishing touches to her hair and adjusted the graceful drape of the gown, Alaine had felt every inch a proud and noble lady. She would find some way, she vowed, to rob Gilbert of his victory. She would not lose her inheritance to this paltry strutting lord.

So with head held high she had met the victor in the great hall, standing proudly with her stepmother on her right and her three stepsisters on her left. Her anger left no room for fear as Gilbert boldly walked the length of the hall, looking around him with possessive satisfaction. The loathsome knight spared not a word of courtesy that was due even defeated ladies as he strode up to the dais and stripped off his helm and mailed hood. His men, their swords rattling against their mail, dropped behind respectfully as he stepped onto the platform and faced the women. His eyes passed contemptuously over Joanna and her three daughters and then came to rest on Alaine.

He smiled unpleasantly as he noted her proud stance and haughty gaze. "You wear defeat well, my lady. Glad I am to see it. A spirited woman is more to my taste than some simpering maid who droops in the first harsh wind."

She frosted him with an icy glare. Gilbert was a handsome man with a tall, powerful build, a lean hawklike face, and thick hair of silver gray. Most women would find him attractive, Alaine acknowledged, but something about the cruel set of his thin-lipped mouth and coldness in the depths of his eyes had always repulsed her. She had not been lying when she'd told Joanna that Gilbert managed his lands poorly and mistreated his serfs, but those had not been the primary reasons Alaine couldn't abide the thought of taking him as husband. He reminded her of a poisonous snake gloating over a helpless rabbit—herself. The fine clothes and ladylike airs that Joanna had urged her to don wouldn't help her with this man. The only way to deal with a vulture like Gilbert de Prestot was to hold to her rights. He couldn't have Ste. Claire without her, not lawfully at least. And she wouldn't have him. He could rape her, beat her, and throw her out into the cold, but she would never say the marriage vows with him beside her.

"You may find that this maid has more spirit than you can stomach, Sir Knight. Ste. Claire may have fallen to your lawless attack, but I have not."

Gilbert raised a peremptory hand for silence. "Hold your peace, woman! I came to bargain once again with Sir Geoffrey, but after meeting several of your former men-at-arms on the road and learning of his death, I decided I would take what I came to bargain for."

"You have no right!" Alaine accused in a furious voice.

Gilbert lifted his bloody sword before her face. "This gives me the right, my lady! Don't prattle to me of right and wrong. You must take a husband and I will be that man."

Alaine opened her mouth in vehement protest but shut it

abruptly as Gilbert grabbed her chin in his hand, bringing his face close to hers. She could smell the sweat of his body and the fresh blood on his clothing. His breath was foul, and she attempted to turn her face away, but his hand tightened until she thought her jaw would break.

"Send for your priest, Lady Alaine," he said with deceptive quietness. "Send for your priest to marry us here and now, or I will put every knight and villein and serf in your service to the sword."

So now she was kneeling on the cold stone floor with Gilbert beside her. Her firm resolve not to be dragged to the altar had not counted on Gilbert using her people as whipping boys for her stubbornness. He had but to raise his bloody sword to one man—an aging household knight who had served Ste. Claire since Alaine was a child—and she had capitulated before the blade could complete its deadly arc. She had accompanied him meekly to the little chapel off the hall and in the presence of Joanna and Sir Oliver knelt with him before poor flustered Father Sebastian.

From the beginning of the ceremony the little priest had tried to delay the inevitable, but not even that saintly man of God could halt the flow of time and events, and Gilbert was stirring impatiently at the priest's halting and repetitious delays.

"Get on with it, Father," Gilbert finally interrupted the little priest. "Get the job done or I'll consummate the marriage right here and now without the benefit of your blessing."

Father Sebastian's eyes grew wide and his face flushed.

"Would you desecrate the sanctity of . . . ?

"You can be sure that I would," Gilbert stated flatly.

As the priest's intonations speeded up considerably, a shaft of light speared through the chapel's one narrow window slot and fell full upon Alaine's face, turning her hair to spun gold and gilding the thick, long lashes that were lowered against her cheeks. Gilbert felt his impatience build to a throbbing urgency. He was about to achieve his goal of the last ten years, joining the rocky hills of Prestot to the wide and fertile fields of Ste. Claire.

And as a bonus he would get the lands on the Channel Isles that his bride held through inheritance from her mother. But right now all he could think about was the woman who was about to become his wife. She had always been secondary to her land in his mind, a small added benefit to the expansion of wealth and power. But seeing her kneeling in that shaft of sunlight, looking like an angel at prayer, his body throbbed to possess her and drive every remnant of innocence from her soul. He longed to bury his face in that golden hair and crush those sweet childlike lips with his own. Most of all he wanted to drive himself into her until she cried for mercy, until he felt her body fold and crumple like a wilted flower.

Gilbert stirred uncomfortably, his musings producing an urgent arousal that certainly wouldn't be satisfied by continued kneeling before this addlepated priest. He was about to demand an end to the ceremony as a knight clattered through the archway into the chapel.

"Sir Gilbert!" he panted. It was evident he had run the entire way up the stairs.

Gilbert turned in annoyance, a scowl darkening his face. "What in Hell? How dare . . . ?"

"We're being attacked! An army comes from the east and is nearly upon us!"

Gilbert rose to his feet, his face flushed red with frustrated anger. "Who?"

"I don't recognize the banner, sir. A red dragon rampant on a field of black."

Gilbert swung around to glower at Alaine, who had gratefully risen to her feet. "Do you know such a banner?" His tone implied she might have summoned the newcomers out of thin air just to annoy him.

She lifted her chin proudly, enjoying his dismay. "No, I know no such banner."

Joanna, who was standing in a corner wringing her hands, gave him the same answer, as did Sir Oliver and the priest. No one knew who the newcomer was, but, Alaine thought, if he managed to drive off Gilbert, she would have one thing at least to thank him for, even if her fate was worse with him than it would have been with her present conqueror.

Gilbert fumed, cursing the fates that let this happen. And now, of all times! He could still feel the pressure in his loins that now must wait for its easing. And that arrogant little bitch was secretly laughing at his discomfiture. He knew she was! But he would make her pay when at last he got her under him. Indeed he would!

"Sir!" the knight reminded him. "The portcullis and gate were smashed in our attack, and the gate tower on one side is crumbling. We have not enough time to . . ."

"I know, I know! Concentrate the archers on the wall above the gate, with the pikemen inside. I'll be there directly."

He turned to Alaine as the knight rushed out with his orders. "Ill fortune, my dear. But don't let this little delay distress you. We will finish the ceremony when this intruder is driven off." He gave her a brief bow and a gloating smile. "Be assured, my lady, that before the sun has set this day you will be wedded and bedded. No one shall be in doubt who holds Ste. Claire . . . and its heiress."

Without another word to them he turned on heel and left, calling for his squire to bring him hauberk and arms. Alaine stared after him balefully. Sir Oliver, looking grimmer than ever, followed him out.

"I hope he gets a length of steel in his guts!"

Father Sebastian looked at her reprovingly. "Alaine, my child! What have I always taught . . . ?"

"Don't prattle to me about mercy and kindness and long-suffering, Father!" Alaine said stubbornly. "You weren't about to be forced into bed by that villain!"

"Alaine!" Joanna said sternly. "Mind your manners! Shame on you for speaking of such things before a man of God!"

Father Sebastian merely chuckled and shook his head. He had been Alaine's tutor and confidant since she was a tiny child, and by now he was accustomed to her brash and impetuous manner. She was straight and forthright as an arrow, no matter whom she was talking to—a trait much admired in a man but more than little disconcerting in a woman.

"Aye, my child, you have much to be angry at." He smiled at her fondly. "But as good Christians we should at least hope Sir Gilbert is driven off without hurt, or at least," he conceded with a twinkle, "without mortal hurt." His familiar impish grin made Alaine smile in spite of herself.

"At least Gilbert is an enemy we know." Joanna began to pace with worry. "Who can guess what this newcomer will demand of us if he overcomes Gilbert's forces?"

A rustle of silk heralded the arrival of Joanna's three daughters, Gunnor the eldest in the lead, as they crowded hastily through the archway into the tiny chapel.

"What's happening?" Gunnor demanded. "There's a whole new army at the walls and fighting around the outer gate. The only men left in the keep are the guards at the outer door."

"We know!" Alaine snapped, impatient at the sulky indignation on her eldest stepsister's face. One would think Ste. Claire's misfortunes were contrived only to create inconvenience for Gunnor.

Mathilde pushed around her older sister and took Alaine by the arm. "Are you all right?"

"Yes," Alaine answered, her voice softening. "I'm all right."

"Are you . . . are you and Gilbert . . . ?"

"Wed?" Alaine finished the thought. "No. And we won't be, either. Not if I can help it!"

"Oh, Alaine!" Mathilde frowned in worried suspicion. She knew her brash stepsister too well. "What are you going to do?"

Judith started to cry. The events of the day had been too much for a seven-year-old girl. Joanna held out her arms and let the little girl run into them. "There, there, baby," she soothed. Events were getting too much for her also.

Alaine surveyed the scene with grim purpose in her eyes. "I'm going to fight! That's what I'm going to do!"

"You're going to what?" Joanna handed Judith to

Mathilde and followed Alaine as she swept out of the chapel and crossed the great hall. Alaine paused only to waylay a boy in the hall and send him with a summons to Garin. Then, ignoring the stepmother and stepsisters who trailed fearfully after her, hurriedly climbed the stairs to her chamber.

"Just wait a minute, young woman!" Joanna ordered in her most authoritative voice. While that voice had always been effective with her own girls, it had never impressed Alaine. And it didn't now. She pushed into the chamber after Alaine, her daughters close on her heels. "Just what is it you plan to do?"

Alaine motioned to Hadwisa to unlace the fine silk gown. "I'm going to do what I should have done to begin with!" She stepped out of the gown impatiently, throwing it aside with contempt. "I should have known no good would come of trying to handle this like a woman!" She pulled off the embroidered chemise, stepped into heavy leather chausses, and pulled a linen shirt and plain woolen tunic over her head.

Joanna tapped a foot impatiently. "This will do you no good, Alaine. I know your father—may God grant him peace—treated you like a man, but you cannot further our cause by putting up a hopeless fight against both Sir Gilbert and this new army storming our walls."

Alaine didn't deign to answer as she bent over and wound the cross garters around her calves.

"You're making a fool of yourself!" Gunnor added her support to Joanna. Her voice was strident with fear. "Our only hope is that whoever wins out there is honorable enough to marry you and let us retain our places here. If you go traipsing along the walls like an ill-bred ruffian, no one in his right mind would take you to wife. Whoever wins the day will have us all killed!"

Alaine snorted with contempt. "You are overly generous in surrendering my inheritance, sister!"

"Fool!" Gunnor spat. "With your father dead, you will have to take a husband anyway. What matter who it is as long as he can manage the lands and defend the castle?"

"Gunnor, be silent!" Joanna commanded. "Take Mathilde and Judith and go back to the chapel. Pray for our deliverance from both of these armies."

Gunnor huffed indignantly but did as she was told.

Alaine went to the corner chest and laid out the light leather hauberk her father had made especially for her. Chain mail was too heavy for her slender body, and the leather had afforded her adequate protection on the practice field, where even the opponents who defeated her had never seriously tried to hurt her. Beside it she laid her sword, still gleaming from a recent polishing, her knife, and a beautifully carved short bow and quiver of arrows.

Joanna watched the care with which Alaine laid out her weapons and armor. Stephen hadn't done the girl a favor, she thought, by treating her as he would a son. He had filled her with false aspirations and pride, and denied her the resignation and humility necessary for a woman to survive in this world of arrogant warriors.

"Gunnor is right, you know," she said softly. "Our only hope lies in your assets as a woman. No matter who is the victor in this battle, it will be much easier for him to claim and hold Ste. Claire with you as his wife."

"The victor in this battle will not claim Ste. Claire!" Alaine returned hotly. "Ste. Claire is mine. And if it must be ruled for me by a man, it will be a man of my choice!"

Joanna sighed. "Alaine, grow up. Very few women are ever afforded a choice in matters such as this."

"I will not be forced!" Alaine insisted. "I'm tired of being fought over like a bone between the hounds. I will not end up a prize of war. Or a casualty either." She glowered impatiently at Joanna's set face. "Don't you see? We've been given an opportunity! We've been delivered just as Gilbert was about to claim his victory. He'll never have Ste. Claire now. The walls are undefendable with the portcullis and gate already down. It's only a matter of time before these new invaders are in the bailey. And Gilbert won't stay to withstand a seige. To do that he would have to leave his own castle at Prestot undefended."

"So?"

"So he'll flee, leaving us to the mercy of this newcomer."

"And what do you plan to do about it?"

"I'll leave you enough men to defend the keep and take the rest of our men with me into the forest. When we're safely away I'll ride for Brix to ask Fulk's help."

"We are no longer bound to Brix."

"Only because my father refused to do homage. Fulk might think it to his advantage to help us if he will gain my fealty as heiress of Ste. Claire."

Joanna frowned. "Fulk is an unprincipled rogue. If he manages to beat off the invaders, what makes you think he won't take Ste. Claire for himself?"

"Why should he, if he can bring it under his domain lawfully?"

"And if he won't help?" Joanna shook her head doubtfully. Alaine's scheme was harebrained and hopeless. But she could see from the light of determination in the girl's eyes that it would be useless to try to dissuade her. She was as stubborn as her father had been. And thanks to Geoffrey's spoiling of her, she thought she was as good as a man.

"If he won't help . . . well, you have enough food in the storeroom to withstand a siege of at least a few weeks. I can harass the attackers from the forest and they'll be caught between fire from the keep and my fire from the woods. We'll make it not worth their while to press the attack."

Joanna sighed hopelessly. "You're mad, Alaine. It will never work."

"What will never work?" Sir Oliver's voice came from the doorway. Garin was right behind him. Both men looked exhausted, and Garin sported a bloody and hastily bandaged gash on his brow.

Alaine explained her plan. Sir Oliver shook his head, but Garin leapt to Alaine's defense.

"It might work," he speculated. "Fulk's a clever one, and if he sees an opportunity to bring Ste. Claire under his power . . . He might come."

"It is a great risk," Sir Oliver cautioned. "Fulk is a

snake if I've ever seen one, and that son of his is no better. We'd be putting Ste. Claire in grave danger to give him power over us.''

Alaine pursed her lips in exasperation. "Do you think Ste. Claire is not at risk now?"

Sir Oliver rubbed at his brow with a grimy hand. "You've a point there, my lady." He had always admired Geoffrey's fair-haired daughter, even though she acted more like a lad than a lady. She had a good brain in her head for a woman, and an unfeminine talent for the art of war. This plan of hers was a chancy scheme, but he could think of none better.

"Then it's settled." Alaine took the uneasy silence for consent.

Sir Oliver spent the next several hours inconspicuously plucking the Ste. Claire men-at-arms from the midst of battle. Alaine left him to decide who should stay to defend the keep and who should go with her, insisting only that Garin must be among those who would leave the castle. She needed a man at her side whom she could trust with her life, and Garin, she knew, would stick by her at all costs. As she thought on it, in fact, she wondered if the cost to Garin would be greater than she had a right to ask. She put the question to him as they sat together in the solar discussing her plans, occasionally peeking out from behind the hide window covering to watch the progress of the battle. They were both hoping the gate could be defended at least until sundown, when they and their band would have a better chance of slipping out the postern gate and into the woods without drawing notice.

"You've been at Ste. Claire nearly all your life, Garin," she said during a lull in their conversation. She didn't know quite how to say what she felt she must say.

"That's so," he agreed. "My father fostered me out as soon as I was able to hold a wooden sword. I've known no other home but here."

"My father would've seen to your knighting before too many months were gone."

"Aye," Garin agreed simply. Both knew that Geoffrey's death had ended Garin's hope of being awarded his spurs in the near future. His own father had died a few months past, and his older brother, never a generous man under any circumstances, would not be anxious for Garin to be knighted and thus become eligible to claim his small portion of the patrimony.

"Perhaps"—she hesitated, afraid of insulting her friend but also afraid of letting him sacrifice his own future out of loyalty to her—"when we return from Brix, you should go to your brother. Surely when he sees you face-to-face he cannot deny you the knighting you have earned."

"Perhaps he wouldn't," Garin agreed with a marked lack of interest.

"Then you should go."

Garin looked at her directly, his gray eyes holding her blue ones. "I won't leave you, Alaine. You're like my sister, and the truest friend I've ever known. To leave you now with these hounds nipping at your heels would deny any honor I've learned from your father's teaching."

"No one could ever doubt your honor, Garin. And I'm more than grateful for your loyalty. But Ste. Claire may be a lost cause." She lowered her eyes, for the first time admitting the possibility of defeat. "I can't assure you that any of us will be rewarded with anything other than death."

He smiled mischievously and struck her shoulder a carefully measured blow with his closed fist, a man-to-man gesture of comradeship. "Now you're talking like a woman!"

A gleam of indignation lit her eyes. Then she laughed.

The afternoon wore on with interminable slowness. Garin left to assist Sir Oliver with organizing the keep for what everyone felt would end up as a siege. All the Ste. Claire men-at-arms who were not being assigned duties in the keep had instructions to gather at a prearranged signal at the postern gate with equipment and horses. Satisfied that all in the storage vaults, pantries, butteries, and kitchens was in order for the coming days of hardship, Joanna joined Alaine in the solar. Now the only thing left to do was wait.

As the interminable afternoon dragged by, Alaine alternately paced the floor and stood by the window so she could watch the progress of the battle below. The solar was high enough and far enough away from the walls to be out of arrow-shot, and she doubted that the men who were spilling their blood below would even notice a silent watcher from the heights of the keep tower.

Gilbert's men were putting up more resistance than Alaine had thought possible. Before the army was actually upon them they had managed to raise one side of the smashed gate, leaving only a small opening where the new invaders could be easily picked off by archers and pikemen as they tried to sally through. The attackers' leader was no novice at war, though, and he was spreading his attack over the entire length of the south wall instead of yielding to the temptation to storm immediately the damaged gate. Gilbert didn't have enough men to defend both the wall and downed gate and portcullis, and slowly but steadily the attackers were wearing away at Gilbert's determined resistance. The invader's casualties, from what Alaine could see, looked to be few, while Gilbert's men were bleeding their lives out on the walls. She was glad the Ste. Claire men had been safely pulled away from the bloodbath below.

Joanna made one more attempt to dissuade her stepdaughter from the plan of action. This unknown knight, she argued, might deal honorably with the family. He could not deny that Alaine was the rightful heiress, and he might marry her to one of his loyal men or might himself take her to wife.

Gilbert would have done the same, Alaine countered, and she did not count him as honorable.

Joanna knew when to give up. Alaine was a bright, sweet child for the most part, but when her mind was set on a course of action, she was as stubborn as a mule. She only hoped that in her refusal to yield, Alaine didn't doom them all.

The sun crept close to the western hills and washed the sky with a pink glow. Soon dusk would spread its shadows across the valley of Ste. Claire. Alaine knew that Gilbert was making his last desperate stand. She was amazed he hadn't given up earlier and fled, and for once she was glad of his greedy desire to have Ste. Claire as his own. His men had suffered hugely in this fight, but Gilbert had unwittingly bought her the time she needed until the shadows of dusk could conceal her departure. She took one last look out the window at her beloved home—the river, the fallow fields, the orchard that held her father's grave. How long would it be, she wondered morosely, before she could stand once again at this window and look out at the land her grandfather and father had nurtured and protected? Why was the world so unfair? And why did she have to be born a woman? She tried to ignore the savagery that raged below and marred this last overview of her home, but her eyes were drawn irresistibly to the walls. Just as she decided the time for departure was at hand, a ruddy shaft of the setting sun caught the shield of one of the figures below. The rearing red dragon on the shield seemed to blaze into fiery life, hurting her eyes with its brilliance. She remembered the description of the banner that flew before this army. This man, then, was the leader. From this distance she could discern very little about him other than he was big—very big, and swung his broadsword with amazing strength for day's end. Why had he come to Ste. Claire? she wondered. He wasn't one of the suitors who over the last few years had come to petition her father for her hand, all the while seeing not her but her rich lands. Nor was he one of the local landholders who might wish to expand his territory by strength of arms. Had news of her father's death spread so fast and so far that already the wolves were coming to claim the undefended prize?

"You're going to get a surprise, Sir Dragon," Alaine whispered softly to the figure below as the sun finally set and the dragon shield faded once again to an ordinary piece of armor. "You may think the prize a fat lamb ready for the taking. But I've learned that the only way to deal with wolves is to become one yourself. So be it."

Fifteen men and ten horses were gathered in silence before the postern gate. The desperate sounds of battle on the south wall all but drowned out the soft chant of Father Sebastian's prayer of blessing. It could not be many more minutes, Alaine knew, before the wall was lost. Gilbert and his remaining men would not be long in following them out the hidden gate, if he could find it. But by then they would be safely concealed in the forest, wet and cold from crossing the river at the base of the steep hill, but safe all the same. She tried to conceal her impatience as the priest rambled on.

Finally he finished. One by one men and horses slipped through the gate, falling, rolling, and sliding down the steep slope to the river. The crossing would be treacherous. And if any man or horse drifted slightly downstream to where the smaller, faster Reve joined the Ste. Claire, he would be lost. Alaine tried to still an inner tremor of fear, both for her men and herself. Then it was her turn.

"Go with God, my child." The priest kissed her chastely on her forehead. Then her hand was grasped in a firm grip by Sir Oliver.

"Don't spend your life helping Gilbert defend the gate," she told him, trying hard to keep her voice steady. The events of the day were wearing at her mind, and she still had much to do before she could rest.

"Don't worry about me, my lady." Alaine could feel his warm smile, even though the shadows of the coming night hid his face. "We'll all still be here when you return."

"Guard my stepmother and stepsisters well." An attempt at a brave smile turned into a grimace. She turned and slipped through the gate, rolled down the rocky slope, halted briefly to get her bearings, then silently slid into the icy waters of the Ste. Claire.

CHAPTER 4

A wet, cold fog shrouded the woods, painting every naked twig and branch, every needle of pine and fir with a ghostly rime of white. Freezing rain drizzled down from the shrouded sky, pattering softly on the carpet of dead leaves and crawling under Alaine's cloak to drip in icy rivulets down her back. The horses slogged through the half-frozen mud and rain with their heads hung low. Exhaustion was closing in like a heavy smothering blanket on both beasts and riders.

It seemed to Alaine that weeks and not just hours had passed since she'd slipped through the postern gate of Ste. Claire and rolled down into the river. She had paused in the forest only long enough to change to dry clothes. Then, instructing Garin where to set up a temporary camp, she'd taken five of her men and ridden the night through, arriving at Castle Brix with the break of dawn. There'd been no rest for them there. Indeed, they had been lucky to gain admittance through the heavy iron-studded gate that had been barred shut the moment they were sighted. Alaine had been required to wield all her powers of persuasion to convince the porter in the gate tower to summon his master. And when the great gate had finally lifted to admit them to the outer bailey, the old servant who appeared to conduct her to the keep was sullen and uncommunicative. All the people of Brix, in fact, eyed her with closed and guarded expressions. She wondered what there was about this castle or its lord that fostered such hostility. At this time of morning her own people would have been chattering noisily as they went about their business. They might have gaped in friendly curiosity at a stranger who came through the gate, and the children would have made pests of themselves by trailing along to catch any hint of news or gossip. But they never would have stared in the half-malevolent, half-fearful manner that greeted Alaine as she followed her guide toward the inner wall and the keep beyond. The silent, hostile chill of the castlefolk had made her suddenly and unreasonably fearful of the coming interview with Fulk. But in that, at least, her fears were not realized.

Now, slogging back toward Ste. Claire through the wet, cold dusk, Alaine admitted that from the beginning the expedition had been a fool's errand. She was wet to the skin and her very bones ached with weariness. She would like nothing better than to strip off her soggy clothes, wrap herself in a warm quilt, cosy up to the small hearth in her chamber, and listen to the soft snores of her stepsisters. But the warm scene that had been so often a reality during the past two years was now a part of the past. Only if she were very clever and very lucky, she reminded herself, would she ever again see the inside of Castle Ste. Claire.

The almost indiscernible game trail they had been following rounded a copse of trees and then widened abruptly into a small clearing. A glad shout greeted them as Alaine allowed her mount to amble to a weary halt. Before she could dismount, Garin was at her stirrup assisting her. It was well he was there to catch her, because when Alaine's feet made contact with the ground her numb legs refused to support her. Groans from her five companions showed them to be in similar straits.

Garin solicitously helped her to the log that served as a makeshift bench by the fire. "What news?" he inquired anxiously, unable to contain himself.

"Not good." Alaine groaned as she bent her legs to sit down.

"Fulk refused? That lowborn bas . . . !"

"Fulk wasn't there."

"Wasn't there?"

Others were starting to gather round to hear the news, and a rumble of disappointment started to build as her words fell on anxious ears.

"He rode off some weeks ago with most of his men to join Guy of Burgundy. Apparently there's some plot afoot to replace William on the ducal throne with Guy."

Someone handed Alaine a wooden bowl full of savory venison stew. She thanked him with a weary nod.

"We've been hearing nothing but plots and rumors like that for these past ten years," one of the men complained in a disgruntled mumble.

Alaine shugged and took a bite of stew. "No matter. For whatever reason, Fulk and his son both are gone. I talked to his wife, a Lady Theoda, but she wanted nothing to do with me. In fact, the lady seemed a bit daft about the head, and sometimes I wondered if she knew what I was saying. She mumbled about warning me to take care—something about Fulk coming to Ste. Claire when he returns and taking it by right of conquest now that my father is dead."

The faces around the fire grew grim.

"Looks like Ste. Claire has become an apple ripe for anyone's plucking," a yeomen muttered.

Alaine stared disconsolately into the fire. She was too tired to offer much encouragement to these men who had followed her on this wild scheme. But there was still hope, even if it was a slim one.

"The dragon won't be in Ste. Claire for long," she said with an effort to show some spirit. "The keep is shut up tight to him, and we'll hit him every opportunity we get. The land this autumn has nothing to give him to support his army. The harvest was bare. The winter cold comes early. We'll win yet."

Garin cleared his throat and looked uneasily at the ground. "The keep has surrendered."

Alaine looked up slowly, not believing what her ears had heard. Seeing the expression on her face, the men retreated in a single body, drawing away from the fire as if they had all remembered at the same time tasks that awaited them elsewhere.

"What did you say?" she asked in a quietly ominous tone.

"The keep has surrendered, Alaine. Little One-eyed George—you know him, the boy who helps Maudie in the kitchen—came in this afternoon and said the invader had been admitted to the keep and parlayed with Lady Joanna and Sir Oliver. The men-at-arms and the servants were told to accept this fellow as their new lord."

Alaine couldn't believe it. She wouldn't believe it! Joanna and Oliver wouldn't do this to her! The keep could have held out for at least a month with no one the worse off.

"Georgie said no was was hurt," Garin continued morosely, "and there wasn't even any fighting."

"Did he hear what this . . . this lord's name was?" Alaine's voice was full of bitter bile.

"No," Garin sighed. "He only hears what the servants hear. And that doesn't very often include details."

Alaine put down the bowl of stew, her appetite gone completely. "I can't believe it. Are you sure he wasn't mistaken?"

"I sent two men to the edge of the woods to see what they could see. There was no fighting on the walls or around the keep. Parties were already at work cleaning up some of the mess and burying the dead."

Alaine sighed and put her head in her hands. The urge to weep was almost overwhelming, but she wouldn't let anyone, even dear Garin, see her give in to such a womanly weakness. She didn't know what to say, and her exhausted mind couldn't think of what she could do.

This turn of events was past her understanding. Why had Joanna done it? They'd had their disagreements, their petty quarrels, but since the day her father first brought Joanna and her daughters to live at Ste. Claire two years ago Alaine had regarded them as family. With Sir Geoffrey dead they were her only family. She thought Joanna felt the same about her. Why would she betray her?

She felt Garin's hand on her shoulder, squeezing softly in an attempt to comfort.

"I'm not crying!" she denied quickly.

"Of course you're not."

"Why would Joanna surrender?" she moaned, her voice close to cracking.

"She must have had a good reason." Garin thought a moment, wondering how Alaine would take his next suggestion. "Why don't we go ask her?"

"What?"

"It's the only sensible course of action. What's the use of fighting? The keep is taken. What can we do but throw ourselves on this new lord's mercy?"

Alaine stood up abruptly, throwing off his hand. "Go crawling back there and beg for mercy? While we still have our freedom? Ask forgiveness and leniency from some arrogant bastard who's unlawfully taken what's mine?"

"Alaine . . ."

"You can surrender if you want to, Garin, or leave and go to your brother's keep. I have no hold on your service. And the men can choose their own paths, but as for me . . . !" She choked back the bitter tears that threatened. "As for me . . . I . . . I don't know yet what I'll do. But I won't surrender. Ste. Claire is mine! And I'll never bend knee to some usurper."

"Alaine . . . !"

She turned on heel and left without waiting to hear what he had to say. Not knowing whether she was sorry or glad that Garin didn't follow, she chose a relatively dry spot under a tree, close enough to the fire to feel some warmth but out of the path of the whirling smoke. Wrapping her still-damp cloak around her, she curled up in her cold nest of dead leaves and silently but despairingly let the tears flow.

Alaine woke to darkness and silence. Only an occasional rustle or grunt from the sleeping men broke the heavy stillness. Her eyes burned from the pungent wood smoke that still rose above the remains of the fire, and her nose was stuffy from crying. She remembered thinking she would never sleep, not with all the grief that weighed on her mind. That must have been her last thought before she drifted off. The numbing exhaustion had lifted a bit, and now she felt only a dull weariness.

She raised herself on one arm, searching the eastern sky for signs of light. There were none. All her companions still slept soundly. Snores and heavy breathing rose from huddled bundles grouped around the dying fire. She lay back down again and pulled her cloak more tightly around her, wondering if she could escape the miserable cold by going back to sleep. She doubted it. Her mind was already buzzing with the events of the day before and uncomfortable speculation as to her future—or lack of it.

Perhaps she should go back to the castle, as Garin had suggested. She played with the possibility briefly then discarded it. Most probably she wouldn't be admitted, unless Joanna had struck a very favorable bargain with the dragon. And even if the new lord of the castle consented to her return, very likely Garin and the men who had followed her would be hanged or put to the sword as an object lesson on the fruits of rebellion. She couldn't lead them back to that fate.

Alaine stared into the darkness, feeling her earlier despair return. The men could scatter and find other lords to serve. Garin could return to his brother's keep, welcome or not. But what could she do? All her life she had prepared to be lady of Ste. Claire, to rule over its castle and its villages. The land and its people gave her life purpose and reality. She knew nothing else. Without Ste. Claire she was nothing and might as well be dead. There was no place she could go and nothing she could do. Without a dowry, even escape to a nunnery was denied her. The convents did not welcome homeless and destitute maidens into their noble sisterhood. A woman bereft of land, money, and family, no matter how noble her birth, had no place in this world.

If times were normal, if Normandy had been ruled by a strong and able duke instead of a sorely harassed bastard child, the law would have prevailed. Alaine would have had an overlord to protect her rights and guard her safety upon the death of her father. If times were normal, Alaine thought bitterly, all this never would have happened. The anarchy that ruled Normandy since the death of Robert the Magnificent, or Robert the Devil, as some named him, had allowed many a lawless man to make his fortune. And now Ste. Claire was in the hands of one such devil and Alaine, rightful lady of the castle, was huddling for shelter on the cold, damp, dead leaves of the bleak October forest.

A tear trickled down Alaine's cheek to the musty pile of leaves where she pillowed her head. She wiped it off with the back of her hand, feeling dirt smudge across her cheek from the grime on her skin. More tears followed. She sniffed impatiently and sat up, shaking her hair to free it from the leaves and sticks that were tangled in the damp locks. She started to run her hands through the snarls and tangles but gave up abruptly. The task was hopeless. Her hair would just have to stay a rats' nest. She hated the itch of dirt and sweat that caked her body. She hated the musty stink of her clothes. How Gunnor would laugh if she could see her now, she thought bitterly. She had warned her that she would make a fool of herself.

The imagined picture of her oldest stepsister's satisfied smirk fired a spark of rage deep in the bowels of Alaine's despair. Gunnor was right, for once in her life. She was a fool! What would her father think if he could see her now, wallowing in self-pity while a stranger lorded it over Ste. Claire? He would name her worse than a fool—a coward and a quitter, that's what! Her anger grew as she thought of the dragon shield hanging where her father's shield had hung beside the huge fireplace in the hall. Despair faded, dissolving into the cold night as the fire of righteous indignation warmed her soul. She wasn't beaten! If the men would stay with her, she would give that lawless dragon something to bellow about. She wasn't some pale and helpless lady to stand by and pine while others stole what was rightfully hers.

She got to her feet and shook the leaves and dirt from her cloak. A pale light was fading the velvet darkness of the eastern sky, and she could almost make out the gray bulks of individual trees as she stomped life back into her feet.

"Need this?" Alaine turned in surprise as Garin's voice spoke out of the darkness. His tone was apologetic. "I was sleeping right on the other side of the bush there. Heard you get up."

She reached for the bag he held out to her.

"Hadwisa said you'd need these things," he explained.

Bless Hadwisa, Alaine thought. The old woman knew her inside and out. She had known Alaine, in her preoccupation with the battle and with plans for escape, wouldn't have let her mind drift to mere practicality. The bag contained a comb, some toweling, some strong soap made in the castle, and two changes of clothes—all masculine attire, Alaine noted with amusement. Bless Hadwisa indeed!

She gave Garin a smile of pure joy that glowed in the pale dawn light. "You're a saint," she said. "You and Hadwisa both. What would I do without you?"

"I..." Garin was nonplussed by this sudden change of mood. The night before she had looked ready to jump off a cliff. "I'm going to wash." She walked briskly off toward the streamlet that ran through the woods beside the clearing.

"That water's icy!" Garin objected, scrambling along behind.

"And I'm dirty as a pig!"

"You'll catch your death..." He stopped suddenly as Alaine discarded her cloak and prepared to pull off her tunic.

She curved him a mischievous smile over her shoulder. "Are you going to watch?"

Garin's eyes grew wide. Alaine had always been a comrade in arms, a buddy, a pesky little brother. She was brash and hard as a rock, and down to earth as the good, solid soil underfoot. Unlike the soft and winsome Mathilde,

who, in Garin's eyes, exemplified all that was beautiful in
Woman, Alaine was far too sturdy and independent to ever
be thought of as feminine. But the sight before him as she
stood in the frosty morning air and peeled off her soiled
clothes was distressingly female. And the most distressing
thing about it was that Alaine didn't seem to recognize the
temptations she was exposing.

He swallowed hard as the tunic came off, followed by
the linen shirt beneath. "I'll stand guard," he gasped as he
backed away.

"Good," he heard her say as he backed around a tree
and stood out of sight. For a few minutes a sound of
splashing was punctuated by muffled shrieks of misery as
icy cold water came into contact with shrinking skin. "Are
you still there?" she finally called, her voice shivering.

"I'm still here." Garin shook his head ruefully. He
would never understand Alaine's preoccupation with cleanliness. No one with a proper head on her shoulders would
go near that cold water.

"Good!" she said. The splashing stopped. "I'll be
through in a minute. Stay there. I want to talk to you about
what we're going to do to that toad who's sitting up there
in my castle."

Garin couldn't help a grin. She was Sir Geoffrey's
daughter all right! He wondered what the impossible little
ruffian was going to come up with now.

In the week following Alaine tried hard to keep her
spirits from sinking back into the pit of despair. There was
hope, she insisted to Garin. If they could delay repair of
the gate and walls long enough for Fulk to return, Brix
might yet march to their aid. The more Alaine thought of
Lady Theoda's confused manner, the more she allowed
herself to hope that the lady might have been mistaken in
predicting her husband's attitude. Fulk might yet be willing
to aid them when he returned. Especially if Ste. Claire
were still in such a state that attack would be assured of

success. And it would be if the damage inflicted by Gilbert wasn't repaired.

So Alaine saw to it that the work parties around the gate and walls were continually pricked by arrows fired from the cover of the woods. The time the dragon's men spent in pursuit of her small bands was that much time taken away from their other duties, and even bare of summer's foliage the woods were thick enough so that men who knew their way could melt into the thickets like so much elusive mist. Finally, a mounted guard was set over all the work parties outside the walls. Alaine merely laughed. The mounted warriors were of no use in chases through the brush, and if one band led the guard away in hot and angry pursuit, another band struck at the work party so deserted.

The work on the walls and gate came to a near standstill, and the sight of the gaping hole in Ste. Claire's defense made Alaine feel like crowing with delight. More and more she allowed herself to believe she would succeed. To believe anything else would be to give in to hopelessness and despair.

While most of her men dashed in and out of the forest to harass the work parties, Alaine took a small escort and toured the farms and villages. The village of Ste. Claire was on the demesne of the castle, just across the Ste. Claire River from the castle itself. It was the largest and most prosperous of the villages that looked to Ste. Claire, having a large stone church, a wealth of craft shops, and several large prosperous houses scattered among the crude hovels of the more common folk. Alaine made it a point to call there before going anywhere else, even though the village was close enough to the castle for someone, if he wished to ingratiate himself with their new lord, to run and fetch a troop of men to prevent her escape. The village was also close enough to the castle for the villagers to have had a grand view of the fighting on the walls. Alaine knew that rumors must be flying. She also hoped that there she could pick up news of the dragon lord and his plans.

The villagers knew nothing other than the new lord's name was Sir Rorik. He had visited the village, she was told, and seemed to be a fair-spoken man. He'd allowed his men no looting or abuse of women. But he did conscript several of the young men to help repair the walls. There were some fearful whines when Alaine explained her mission, but at the end they promised to hold by her as lawful mistress of Ste. Claire. Her family had held Ste. Claire for three generations and treated the serfs and peasants well. Loyalty finally overcame fear.

Five smaller villages and numerous farms owed duty to Ste. Claire. Alaine called at every one of them. At each village and farm she begged them to stand by her as the rightful lady of Ste. Claire. Pay no taxes or imports to the new lord, she urged them, and refuse the lord's call to work on the demesne lands. She and her men would afford them what protection they could, she promised, and she herself would see them well rewarded when the keep was back in her hands.

In the villages out of sight of the glowering keep she was greeted always with cheers and smiles and assurances of support, some of which, she knew, were sincere. She was well loved by her tenants and villagers. During the last two years of failing crops, she and her father had never demanded more than the people could give. No serf or peasant family had ever starved while there was food in the keep. When her people were sick or in trouble, whether serf or free tenant, Alaine had always been there to help, to nurse the sick, help with birthings, and mourn the dead. Now they were repaying her in turn, and her heart swelled with gratitude—and with fear. She hoped she could keep her promises to these good people and protect them from the wrath of the dragon that was sure to be loosed by their support of her cause.

Her confidence grew apace with her little army. Every day more able-bodied men from the villages swelled the numbers of her little band. She could keep the dragon busy enough to leave the villagers alone, she figured, no matter how angry he was with them. But at the same time she realized that unarmored yeomen and serfs were no match for knights and a trained soldiery. What she most needed she still didn't have. The runner she had stationed near Brix to watch for Fulk's return still had brought no word. She and her men could prick and poke and irritate. But they couldn't retake Ste. Claire. How long could they carry on this desperate crusade before the dragon tired of their pricks and led out his army to dispose of them?

It was a bright, crisp afternoon when Alaine rode into the little village of Briaux to exhort the only people she had not yet reached. In the best of times this was the poorest of the villages that looked to Ste. Claire. A good half-day's ride from the castle, Briaux was close to where the Reve started its climb into the hills. The soil was poor and sandy, the fields were strewn with rocks, and the rains here, it seemed, were not as gentle and much less predictable than in the rest of the valley. In the past two years of near famine the poor little village had deteriorated into a mere collection of hovels squatting on the banks of the Reve River.

Old Toby One-arm, the unofficial and self-appointed headman, was the first to see Alaine ride in. He squinted for a moment, the ax he was using to cut firewood held in a defensive stance. Then he recognized her.

"M'lady!" he mumbled, dropping to the ground in an obsequious bow and pushing his half-wit son down beside him.

"How are you, Toby?" She smiled, motioning him to rise. "And how's Thatch, here?"

Toby scrambled to his feet and gave her a near toothless smile. "Don't be soilin' y'ur eyes with the likes o' him, m'lady. 'E's naught but an addle brain. No more use t'me than th' ol' dog over there. Less." He hawked loudly and spat in the dirt. "Me ol' woman like ta take this ax ta the beast t'other day. Said 'e was but another mouth ta feed. Stopped 'er, though, I did. Ol' dog at least keeps the lord's 'awgs an' deer from t'garden, I says. If'n ye want ta ax somethin', then take a swing at this useless son y'gave me."

"It's not the boy's fault he's addled, Toby," Alaine frowned, silencing his rambling. The child stared up at her with round eyes of velvet brown. A spastic grin twitched at his mouth. She hoped little Thatch would survive the winter. If there wasn't food enough to go around, he would be the first in the village to starve. She was surprised the half-wit had lasted these last two years, in fact. She had been present at his birth five years ago. By accident she'd been in the village at the time, for at the age of twelve she had not yet begun making the rounds as she did regularly a few years later. But the birth screams of Toby's wife had started just as Alaine had ridden into the village, fresh from an unsuccessful hunting foray with Garin. Drawn by morbid curiosity to the hut where the woman labored, she had ended up staying to help the midwife through the entire day. The labor was long and difficult, and Ruth the midwife had murmured about the child taking too long. The babe that had finally slipped out from between his mother's legs had looked bluish and weak, and an ugly dark bruise had marred his soft baby skull. Ruth had shaken her head and frowned, but the infant had stubbornly clung to life.

Since that day five years ago, every time Alaine rode into Briaux she asked after Thatch, as the little boy had come to be known. The child was truly addled, as his father said. He drooled and jerked and could barely manage to walk. But Father Sebastian had told her that the mad and the lame had the special love of God. It saddened her now to think the little boy would probably be deprived of food during this harsh time to provide for the feeding of someone else the village deemed more worthy to live. She thought briefly of taking the child with her, then remembered that she had no home to take him to, and she herself might be lucky to live out this winter.

She pulled her mind back to more practical matters as the villagers were called from their huts by her men. When they recognized her face a murmur swelled among them, and some bowed low as Toby had done earlier. When they were all gathered she briefly explained her mission.

Toby scratched at his head in thought. "The snake won't git naught from us, m'lady. We got nuthin' t'give.

An' if'n 'e comes 'round wantin' us t'work, none'll be stirrin' from this village. 'Aven't worked fer y'ur father, God bless 'im, fur t'past two years. Since we be goin' hungry and the fields been givin' us not much more'n dirt, yer good father let us be. This lord'll get no more.''

Alaine smiled. It was all she could ask. But perhaps not all she could give. ''You're a loyal man, Toby. All of you are. In return I give you leave to take what you need from the deer and hogs in the forest.''

Though it was an offense punishable by death for the serfs and villeins to hunt the lord's animals that grazed loose in the woods, Alaine knew that Toby and his people were already poaching to keep themselves from starvation. Maybe it would bind them to her cause even more if she gave free permission for them to do it.

Toby looked sly. ''That be kind, m'lady.''

Alaine smiled. They understood each other.

''Are we through here?'' Garin asked, pulling up beside her.

''You take the men and go on,'' she answered. ''I want to say hello to Ruth. I'll only be a little while.''

''Don't tarry too long,'' he warned. ''We'll go slow on the road until you catch up.''

Garin grimaced as he spurred his horse down the track and out of the village with the rest of the men. He didn't like leaving Alaine behind, but there was no telling the stubborn girl what she should or shouldn't do. And she counted Ruth a special friend, though Garin couldn't fathom why a noble-born lady should honor a common midwife with her attention.

Ruth was the best midwife in the area. She served the villages and castle both with her art. Some named her witch, and Garin was ready to believe it. He had never seen an uglier face, and the old woman's glittering eyes had always reminded him of a snake's. But Alaine had attended many a birthing with the crone and claimed her to be a wise woman. Since she'd seen Ruth's mule tethered by a hut on the edge of the village, it was natural for Alaine to want to give greeting to the old woman.

Ruth acknowledged Alaine with a calm nod as she ducked through the door of the hovel. An old grandmother rose shakily from a low stool by the hearth—the only piece of furniture in the dark and fetid room—and motioned her to sit. Alaine smiled the shook her head, indicating the woman should sit down again.

"Goes it well?" Alaine asked as Ruth wiped her hands on her bloodsmeared dress.

The midwife shook her head and pursed her already pleated mouth. "Nay. The little one never saw the light. But just as well, m'lady. These good folk need no more mouths to feed."

A young woman lay on the straw pallet in the far corner of the room. Her face was turned away, but Alaine could see her chest rise and fall with silent sobs.

"'Er man died this past season," Ruth explained. "The lung sickness. Same disease that took yur good father."

Alaine made a note to come back later in the week with food and clothing before she remembered that she no longer was in a position to dole out charity. She bit her lip in frustration as she followed Ruth out of the hut.

"Wait, my lady!" Ruth held out a cautioning hand. "Riders come!"

Alaine ducked hurriedly back into the door.

"Who is it?"

"Five mounted knights," Ruth answered. "I can't see . . . !" Her old eyes squinted into the distance. "The shield of one carries a red dragon. Know you that emblem, my lady?"

"Oh God!" Alaine whispered. "The dragon himself. And here I sit like a rat in a hole!"

She listened to the hoofbeats of the heavy chargers as the riders pulled to a halt at the other end of the village. Or was that pounding the wild and frightened rhythm of her own heart? Even if they couldn't see her they would surely see her horse grazing in full sight by the side of the hut. She cast her eyes up in a silent prayer of desperation. So ends, she thought, the less than glorious rebellion of Alaine, ex-Lady of Ste. Claire.

CHAPTER 5

"Quick! Quick!" Old Ruth grabbed Alaine by the arm and pulled her out of the hut. "Toby's takin' 'em down to the meadow to see where the boy was killed. Get that great beast of yours into the hut while they're out of sight."

"Isn't there a shed?" Alaine looked around while she grabbed the reins of the startled horse.

"No shed. And no time. Many a cow's taken shelter from the weather in this 'ut, when these poor 'uns had a cow. So this beast should feel right at 'ome."

Alaine's palfrey was a bit bigger than a cow, however, and they got him through the door only by Alaine tugging at the front and Ruth prodding the behind. The feat, thought Alaine as she coaxed and tugged at the reluctant steed, brought to mind the biblical camel passing through the eye of a needle.

Whichever saint was in charge of miracles that day was minding his job well, for the whole horse had passed through the small door before Toby returned to the village with his guests. The old grandmother on her stool squawked indignantly as the broad horse's rump swung dangerously near her perch.

"Quiet, Mattie!" Ruth warned in a low tone. "That fearsome knight is 'eaded this way. Do you want our true lady 'ere to be snatched an' 'ung from the nearest oak?"

Alaine swallowed hard at the thought. She halfway wished she had run for it when the dragon had temporarily been out of sight. But there had been no time.

"Where did you say Toby took them?" she whispered to Ruth.

"Down to the meadow. A band of outlaws drove off the last of the sheep these poor folk 'ad. Killed the little 'erdsboy while they was at it."

That must be why the dragon was here, Alaine mused. Or was it? She was somehow disappointed that the blackguard who had stolen her home could be interested in the welfare of the village folk she'd always thought of as her own.

"Quiet now," Ruth warned. "They be headed this way." She left the window and went to the pallet to sit by the bereaved mother, who looked in startled wonder at this sudden crowd in her little home.

Alaine clamped the horse's muzzle with her hand and stepped over to the hide-covered window, peeking out through a tiny space between the oiled hide covering and the mud and straw wall. The group of riders stopped almost directly in front of the hut as Toby pointed out the path the outlaw band had taken. They were so close, in fact, that Alaine could make out the scowl that marked the dragon's face and the fierce glint in his eyes. He was an impressive figure of a man, she reluctantly admitted to herself. Mounted astride a ferocious-looking chestnut destrier, he looked tall and proud and straight. His ring mail gleamed in the weak autumn sunlight. Hood and ventail were down and his helm was tucked under one arm. Short-cropped raven-black hair crowned his head in tousled disarray. Though he was not quite what the court ladies might call handsome, the hard planes and uncompromising angles of his face had an intensely masculine appeal that even Alaine could not deny. Across his back, the hilt in easy reach of his right hand, hung the huge broadsword she had seen him swing with such devastating effect before the walls of Ste. Claire.

"Your sheep are probably already slaughtered, old man," he was saying to Toby. His voice was deep, with a harsh edge to it that made Alaine shiver. "But we'll bring you back what we can. And the lad will be avenged."

Toby looked sullen. "Thank'ee, lord. But we've na need of yur sword 'ere, as I said before. Our lady, good and true, will run th'dogs to ground."

Alaine ground her teeth. Toby, you stupid oaf! That's not what I meant when I sought your support!

The dragon snorted contemptuously. The pale sun caught his shield, and the red dragon's eyes seemed to look directly into the hovel where Alaine crouched with her horse. She shuddered and tried to curb her imagination.

"I am the rightful lord here." Sir Rorik's voice was somehow more fearful for its mildness. "Your lady, as you call her, will have no time to spend defending you from outlaws. She'll soon be hunted down herself, like the outlaw she is."

The villagers who had gathered around to gape at the strange knight and his men shuffled uneasily.

"In fact," the dragon continued. "I wouldn't be surprised if it wasn't that hellion and her men who raided your livestock and killed your son." The knight's scowling eyes sought out the dead boy's father, who looked uncomfortably at the ground.

"Na, my lord," the man said softly. "Our Lady Alaine wouldn't do naught ta 'urt us."

The unjust accusation was almost too much for Alaine's temper. Only Ruth's firm hand on her shoulder kept her from forgetting all reason and flying out of the hut to confront the black-hearted lying son of Satan. She could almost feel smoke rising from under her tunic.

"Perhaps not," the dragon conceded with a black scowl. "But your lady's a common outlaw in rebellion against her rightful lord. Don't depend on help from her. She'll soon not even be able to help herself."

The group of villagers scattered as a knight who looked even larger than Sir Rorik galloped up at full speed, hauling his huge mount to a sliding halt almost at the door of Alaine's shelter.

"Men sighted to the north," the big knight told his leader. Even in the shadow of coif and helm Alaine could see the newcomer's savage smile. "And an evil-looking lot they are, too."

Without a further word the dragon donned hood and helm, loosened his sword in its scabbard, and whirled to gallop down the track, his men following in his wake. Alaine's heart sank, hoping the band sighted was truly the outlaws and not Garin and her men.

Toby stuck his head into the hut, his mouth stretched into a toothless grin. "They're gone in th'dust, m'lady. You c'n come out now."

Alaine stepped out of the hut and pulled her palfrey out behind her. The horse was more than anxious to escape the confines of the hovel and almost took down the door on his way through.

" 'E's a clever one, that Sir Rorik," Toby commented, pulling at his forelock in thought. "But we fooled 'im, we did!"

He gave a chuckle that was more like a cackle, and Alaine realized he had enjoyed the whole incident immensely. Troublemaker, she thought. He probably would have enjoyed the excitement of seeing her chased down right here in his village. He could have talked about it for years to come.

"Clever," the little man continued. "An' 'ard, too. Me brother's boy says 'e 'eard from a lad in the castle kitchens that 'is men name 'im Stone Dragon."

"Fit's 'im," a woman joined in. " 'E looks like some great beast o' stone, an' when those glinty green eyes fasten on ya, it'd be easy t'think a dragon lies under all tha' skin an' muscle."

Alaine didn't want to hear any more. She remembered too vividly the look on Sir Rorik's face when he'd sworn she would be hunted down like an outlaw. Unwanted pictures flashed through her mind—pictures of her with her undersized sword in hand, trying to defend herself against that huge blade she had seen slung across his broad back, pictures of her loyal little band of brave men lying bloodied and broken before a charge of the dragon's knights.

Her stomach twisted in unreasoning fear even as she tried
to banish the nightmarish images from her mind.

"I must go." She swung to her horse's back and
adjusted the pitifully small-seeming sword that rested against
her thigh. "Toby, all of you—thank you for your support.
And Ruth." She leaned down and clasped the old woman's
arm.

The crone gave her hand a reassuring squeeze. "Take
care, my little lady. Don't ya be lettin' that great fearsome
bully scare ya."

Alaine waved gaily as she rode into the woods and left
the villagers behind. But she didn't feel gay. The dragon
Sir Rorik was not exactly what she'd expected. He was an
enemy not to be taken lightly, and a panicky voice at the
edge of her mind was screaming that this time she was in
deeper trouble than she could handle. For the first time
since she'd left the castle she was genuinely afraid.

Alaine didn't catch up with Garin and the men on her
ride back to camp, and with every passing minute her heart
sank lower as she became more and more sure her hapless
men were the band pursued by the dragon. The image of
Sir Rorik's fiercely scowling face loomed in her mind. She
remembered the deadly strength and skill he had displayed
before the walls of Ste. Claire. She pictured once again the
savage grin on the face of the huge knight who had
brought news of their quarry. Garin and her men wouldn't
have a chance against the dragon and his cohorts, Alaine
thought desperately. The hard-eyed, broad-shouldered Sir
Rorik made Garin look like a boy in comparison, and his
giant friend called to mind some ancient bloodthirsty god
come down to earth to wreak havoc on mankind. Alaine
quickly crossed herself at the thought.

As she rode into camp hearty greetings rose from the
group of tired men who sat around the fire. Feminine
voices also bade her welcome, for a few serving wenches
from the castle had sneaked out to join them, guided by
One-eyed Georgie from the kitchen, and several women
from the villages had followed their husbands when they
joined her crusade. The men laughed and teased as the

women served up warm ale purchased from the nearby Boar's Head Inn, and several of the village wives tended spitted birds that were roasting over the fire. The group that Alaine rode back to was happy to fight in her cause during the day and retire to women and good food when the sun set. But tonight Alaine couldn't share their cheer and optimism. Her eyes anxiously searched the group for those who had ridden out with her that morning. Her dark imaginings were more than a nightmare, she realized with a sinking heart. Garin and the others weren't there.

"Here, m'lady." A village yeoman who had been with their group not even a week stepped up to take her reins. "Sit yerself down ta some good rabbit stew. I'll settle yer 'orse."

Alaine numbly took the seat on the log that was hastily vacated for her. She waved away the bowl of stew that was thrust in her direction. How could she eat when her best friend in the world and two loyal men who had trustingly followed her on this wild scheme were probably lying in their own blood in the cold dark forest? She could picture the dragon gloating over the fallen bodies. She saw him take off his helm and pull down the mail of his hood. His eyes seemed to glow with an evil light of their own. They glowed red, the color of blood, the color of death.

"Lady Alaine!" The yeoman who had taken her horse hurried back from the direction of the corral. "Rider's come!"

The image of Sir Rorik still clouded her mind. Thus it seemed that she herself had conjured him up as he came riding into her camp. But this wasn't the fierce destroyer of her imaginings. The dragon shield hung loose from the pommel of his saddle, and the dragon himself was tied and blindfolded. Garin rode beside him, the reins of the chestnut destrier looped around his arm and a triumphant grin lighting his face. Behind Sir Rorik and Garin followed the other two of her little band, leading another destrier. The huge knight Alaine had seen in the village lay facedown across his saddle, legs and arms swinging limply as the horse was prodded into the clearing.

Disdaining all pretense of decorum, Alaine ran to greet the group. "Garin! Thank God! I thought you were . . . I thought you were . . . !" She swept incredulous eyes over the captives.

Garin laughed. "Whatever you thought we were, my lady, we're not. We're all safe and sound, and look what we ran across on the trail." He gestured grandiosely to the bound knight. With one hand he reached over and pulled off Sir Rorik's blindfold, then smiled maliciously as he directed the knight's gaze to the small girl standing in front of him. "Behold your conqueror, Sir Rorik."

Sir Rorik's eyes did not flash an evil red, Alaine noted. They glinted green—hard as ice, and just as cold. With a face made of stone he glanced around the campsite, those glittering green eyes taking in a myriad of details with a casual glance. Then his gaze came to rest on Alaine, and stayed. A new fire sparked in those jade depths, and Alaine shivered. Even though he was bound and helpless, she felt her heart freeze with dread—and something else she couldn't name.

"How . . . ?" Alaine started.

"We'll tell the whole story," Garin promised, "as soon as we've got some dinner in our bellies."

The prisoners were tied securely to separate trees and Alaine detailed two of the castle wenches to feed them. She wasn't about to untie the knights' hands to allow them to feed themselves. She made sure the two were comfortable, within reason, then headed back to the fire, where Garin had already begun his story. She felt the dragon's eyes bore into her back as she turned to leave, and the hair on the nape of her neck seemed to stand on end at the menace of that gaze. It was all she could do to keep from breaking into a run to the warmth and security of fire and friends.

"Aye," Garin was saying as Alaine took her place on the log by the fire. "It was a rare piece of luck. It seems our guests here"—Garin glanced mockingly in the direction of the two knights—"were on their way back from a sortie with old Jules and his cutthroats. When we saw his men go by we hid in the trees. But these two followed well behind. What a prize! we think. To bring this villain back to our lady who has been so wronged by his treachery!" He made a little bow to Alaine, and the band gave a few ragged cheers.

"We've no weapons to fight armed knights, I tell myself. But no paltry knight, I say, is a match for the men of Ste. Claire!"

"Aye!" roared Robbie, eager to share his part in the victory. He wiped the foam of ale from his mouth and gave a great grin. "I hasn't a lance to prick that mail, so I grabs up an 'efty stone and takes my aim. Ding! I ring his bell! My brave stone bounces off his 'elm and the great knight ends in an 'eap of tin on the ground."

Alaine risked one quick glance at Rorik. His dark scowl cut through her nerves like a knife.

"The big one gallops to his lord's aid!" Garin continued the tale, thoroughly enjoying the look on his captives' faces. "But Gurney, lowly pigherd, thwacks him in the face with a mighty tree branch."

"So falls the great one like a felled tree!" Gurney laughed. "The ground itself shook when he hit. It took all three of us to lift him back on t'is great steed."

Alaine laughed with the others, but she was uncomfortably aware of unwavering scrutiny from the dragon. She refused to look at him, even though she could feel his eyes burning holes in her back. The laughter died down slowly and was replaced with an uncomfortable silence. Could everyone feel the menace emanating from that bound figure? Alaine wondered. What kind of man, or demon, was this Sir Rorik that he could frighten people who saw him sitting tied and helpless and who had just been laughing at the unlikely story of him being cold-cocked by a luckily aimed stone?

"M'lady Alaine." Robbie the stone-thrower bowed obsequiously in front of her. Alaine noted that he was well into his cups already. "If you would grant me the honor, m'lady. I'll finish off t'job." He flipped a wicked-looking knife from his belt. "My good blade here will make short work of partin' their necks from their 'eads."

"Aye!" a yeoman called. "An' we'll ride back t'Ste. Claire with their 'eads on a pike!"

"Aye! Aye!" A chorus of agreement followed.

"Nay!" Alaine shouted down the others. For a frightening moment she wondered if she could keep control of her raucous band. "That would do no good. Now Sir Rorik's army pursues us with half a heart, like a horse switching at flies. But let us kill their lord and their revenge will be swift. They would not rest until we were all, every one of us, hanging from the gallows. Besides, we are not outlaws and thieves, to take lives so casually."

Alaine saw one of Rorik's heavy black brows arch in amusement—or was it disbelief? How could he sit there so calmly while his death was being discussed? She willed herself to swing around and look him right in the eye as the cries for his blood died down. How dare he make her so afraid when he should be the one fearing for his life!

"Do you think us amusing, Sir Knight? Entertaining, even?"

He looked at her out of stony eyes of jade, his expression not changing.

"Do you think us such a pitifully poor band of rascals that we are beneath your notice?"

He smiled an infuriating smile.

She returned the smile measure for measure. "Then what thinks this great and noble knight, sitting on his scrawny haunches on the frozen ground, nursing a headache from the stone thrown by this brave lad over here?"

Robbie got up and took a drunken bow to the cheer of the band.

"It seems you may have underestimated your foe, Sir Knight."

Sir Rorik raked the crowd with his eyes, then focused once again on Alaine with an assessing gaze. "Aye," he admitted. His voice was as deep and resonant as she remembered. And still it held that harsh, uncompromising edge that made her want to back away. But she didn't. "I won't make that mistake again."

"You'll not get t'chance again!" someone yelled from the crowd.

Alaine raised her hand for silence. She tried to fix the dragon with a look that was as challenging, as contemptuous as the one he had fastened on her. "What shall I do with you, Sir Usurper?"

He smiled again. "I suggest you surrender to me."

This time Alaine couldn't wave the laughter and comments down. She had to wait until they died of their own accord. She couldn't tear her eyes from Rorik's face, and she felt her own uneasiness grow apace with the rapid beating of her heart. How could he sit there so brazen and confident when she had him helpless and at her mercy?

"I've no wish to have your death dragging on my soul," she said when she could speak once again. "I just want you and your army out of Ste. Claire and off my land."

"You have no land," the dragon explained calmly, as if to a half-witted child. "Ste. Claire is mine. You and your people here are in unlawful rebellion. I suggest you surrender now or face the gallows."

"Why you . . . !" she clamped her mouth shut on the unladylike epithet that came to mind. "You can sit there and threaten me with the gallows when I hold your very life in my hands, you villain? I could raise my little finger and have one of my men slit that lying throat of yours! And your friend's too!"

The pale-haired giant behind Rorik spat his contempt. Sir Rorik just smiled that infuriating smile. His eyes looked into hers as if they could pierce her soul and see that she hadn't the heart for cold-blooded killing. His bold confidence was chilling. She tore her eyes away from his gaze.

"Ste. Claire is yours, eh? We'll see about that, my arrogant friend! Are you confident enough of your skill as a warrior to hold what you claim as yours?"

His lips twisted mockingly. "I am."

"Then I propose a contest." She smiled wickedly. "An archery contest. If you win, you and your oversized man there can leave here unharmed and free. And you'll not be bothered by us again. If I win, you withdraw from Ste. Claire."

He laughed incredulously. "A contest of archery you say? The bow is a yeoman's weapon, no knight's tool!"

"And I, sir, am no knight."

"Then name a champion to fight for your cause. We will fight to settle the question, as men should."

Alaine stuck out a stubborn chin. "Ste. Claire is mine. I am no man, but I need no man to fight for me. The contest shall be between you and me, with the short bow!"

Rorik's jaw tightened. "And if I refuse?"

Alaine panicked for a moment, not knowing what she would do if he refused. "Are you afraid to be bested by a woman?" she taunted.

"Ha!" The big blond knight barked his comment. "Rorik of Brix. Bested by a woman!"

Rorik shook his head and looked at her. His mouth curved in a wicked slant. "You cannot best me, Lady."

She lifted a mocking brow. "Then you shouldn't have to worry. Should you? We'll meet at first light." She gave him what she hoped was a contemptuous look of dismissal and presented him with her back.

First light came all too soon after Alaine spent a restless night in vain regrets—regret that Garin had put her in this awkward situation, regret that she had recklessly wagered all on a flight of arrows. When the idea had flashed into her mind it had seemed the perfect solution to her quandary. Knights held the bow in contempt. They preferred to kill a man up close with sword or lance or mace. The bow was a weapon for killing at distance, suitable for the hunt but not, they commonly declared, for the noble art of war. Few knights had much skill with a short bow. But Alaine, on the other hand, had practiced with the weapon since she was old enough to draw a bowstring. None at Ste. Claire could best her, and even her father had laughingly named her the best archer in Normandy. But as Alaine stared achingly into the night it seemed that any chance taken with her beloved Ste. Claire was too much risk. Better she had demanded the usurper withdraw from her home as the price of his life. But it was too late now.

Alaine woke to see the dawn wash the stars from the sky. Tattered remnants of nightmares clung to her mind, and a feeling of dread lay heavily on her spirit. She remembered part of her dreams. She and Sir Rorik had fought for Ste. Claire, not with bow and arrow as they would do this morning, but with swords—to the death. They were ringed by the horrified faces of her men, and somewhere in the unseen distance someone was wailing. It sounded like Garin. Her blade was puny compared to the dragon's great flashing broadsword, and as the dream progressed her sword somehow shrank to no bigger than a belt knife. A tragic ululation had risen from the onlookers as Rorik had beaten her back and back until she stood against a tree, unable to move. With face carved in granite and eyes glittering with malice he had pressed the heavy blade against her body, just below her heart. A savage grin had split his face as he drove the blade forward with a vicious twist. Alaine had been surprised that there was no blood and no pain, only a curious feeling of euphoria as he thrust with the blade again and again. She woke covered with sweat, in spite of the chill of early dawn, and with an uneasy roiling in her stomach.

Alaine unwrapped herself from her blanket, brushed the leaves from her hair, and walked to the stream. The icy water she splashed on her face didn't banish the nightmare that clung to her like a dirty cobweb. Never in her life had Alaine feared another person, not even her father, whose merest frown sent the pages and squires scurrying with dread. But she had to admit that for some unknown reason she was afraid of the dragon knight. She hoped to God her silly fear didn't spoil her aim.

The sun was sending the first rays of morning through the trees when Alaine gathered her courage to face her adversary.

"If I untie you to see to your needs will you give your

word of honor not to escape or do harm to any person in this camp?''

His twisted smile was just as mocking as it had been in her dream. ''Aye. My word of honor.''

She cut his bonds, then moved to Sihtric. The big knight bared his teeth in a snarl and growled low in his throat, then laughed unpleasantly as she jumped back.

''Behave yourself!'' she commanded in a shaky voice, ''or I'll leave you both to sit in your own filth!''

''Methinks the maid is afraid of us, Rorik,'' Sihtric laughed.

Rorik arched a cocky brow and caught Alaine's eyes with his own. ''Not as afraid as she should be, my friend.''

Alaine tossed the knife at Rorik. The blade buried itself in the ground an inch from his foot. ''Untie that overgrown dog yourself! And remember, no tricks. You pledged your honor.'' She stalked away and gave curt orders for the two prisoners to be fed.

The site of the contest was an open clearing on the other side of the stream. Frost still rimed the dead grass and coated the naked branches of the trees as two men marched halfway down the clearing with the targets. Alaine absently caressed the fine yew wood of the bow her father had given her three years ago. She tried to slow the pounding of her heart by calling to mind all her victories on the practice field. Sir Geoffrey, unlike most lords, insisted all the men training under him become proficient with the bow, but she had beaten them all. Surely she could score a victory over this one man. She looked up to find Sir Rorik's mocking eyes on her.

''Sure you wouldn't rather just surrender, my lady outlaw?''

Alaine's eyes narrowed dangerously. ''You are hardly in a position to demand my surrender, Sir Usurper. And after this contest you'll be in a lesser one.''

Sir Rorik shook his head at the foolishness of women.

The targets were in place. The two contestants took their positions. The rules of the contest were simple. They would shoot by turns until there was a clear winner. That shouldn't take long, Alaine thought. There was a wet fog settling over the field, making distances hard to judge. But she was accustomed to shooting in such weather. She doubted very much that the dragon was accustomed to shooting at all.

Rorik shot first, and Alaine was dealt an unpleasant shock. His arrow thunked into the target dead center. He gave her a chilling smile as her eyes widened in surprise, but looked at her in astonishment when her arrow flew just as true.

Two men hurried out to move the targets back. On the next shot Alaine watched her opponent with a practiced eye. The bow he had chosen was a good one. He nocked the arrow and drew back with confidence, taking only a short second to aim before sending the shaft straightway to another bull'seye. She caught sight of Sihtric grinning at her from the edge of the crowd. The big man was gloating, she knew. She refused to give him the satisfaction of looking his way. Let him gloat, she thought, and his master too. Rorik's form was not as true as hers. His stance was slightly off and he was too quick to aim. Sooner or later that would tell.

They continued to shoot while the men ran out again and again to move the targets back. The fog was lifting and a cold little breeze played around the field. It made shooting more difficult, but they continued their perfect scores.

The morning sun was resting on the tops of the trees when Rorik finally made a mistake. The targets were at the far end of the field, and Rorik was squinting to aim. Alaine was grateful for her eagle-sharp eyesight. She and the crowd both held their breath as his arrow flew and struck slightly wide of center. Alaine allowed herself to slant him a triumphant, mocking smile. He smiled in return. To her regret he didn't look the least embarrassed or chagrined. She nocked an arrow and drew back until the taut string rested against her ear. In her mind she pictured the distance and trajectory, aimed carefully, and let fly. The arrow sped on its way, straight and true. Alaine almost didn't have to watch to know it would strike dead center.

Then the crowd drew a horrified breath. An errant breeze ruffled Alaine's hair and stirred the branches of the trees. The arrow wavered, then struck the target a half arrow's length away from center.

A slow, triumphant smile spread over Sir Rorik's face. Sihtric chortled in glee. Everyone else on the field was deadly silent.

"Well, my lady outlaw," Rorik said with a grin. "It appears you have lost your wager."

It took Alaine a moment to find her voice, so stunned was she. "The arrow was flying true. It was the sudden breeze . . ." She hesitated. It went against the grain to plead an excuse. But Ste. Claire was at stake. "It would have struck true. You saw yourself."

"Ah, yes," Rorik agreed affably. "Except for that sudden, unexpected puff of wind. It seems nature is against you, mistress. Or perhaps God himself is against you."

"I cry foul!" Garin's voice rang out from the crowd. "Reshoot!"

His cry was taken up by the others of the band until the clearing clamored with their voices.

"Nay!" Sihtric answered. "The contest is won!"

Rorik looked at Alaine with glittering eyes. A faint smile twisted his lips. Suddenly he seemed impossibly tall, his shoulders improbably wide. Images from her nightmare flashed suddenly through Alaine's mind and a wave of heat colored her face and made her legs weak. Desperately she tried to pull herself together.

"This is a contest of skill, not chance. I demand a reshoot."

Sir Rorik shook his head. "Every contest is a contest of chance. The duel is won, and you pledged the terms on your honor."

Sihtric had drawn near and snorted derisively, as if dismissing any notion of Alaine having a shred of honor.

"Will you be forsworn, my lady outlaw?" Rorik's eyes held a challenge and a mockery.

"Alaine!" Garin shoved his way to her side. "Just give the word, my lady, and these lowborn scum will die where they stand!"

Alaine couldn't tear herself away from Rorik's gaze. For a moment it seemed that the rest of the world faded from around them, leaving only the two of them standing locked eye to eye in the autumn-brown field. Suddenly she was afraid for more than Ste. Claire, more than herself, and more than her brave little band. She was afraid of something she couldn't put a name to, but it was embodied in this arrogant, powerful, infuriating man. She forced her senses back to reality, mentally shaking herself for letting her imagination rule her mind.

At her continued silence Garin drew his sword, his face set with deadly intent.

"Hold!" she commanded. "Have you forgotten all my father taught us of honor? Would you attack an unarmed man?"

"He looked ready to harm you," Garin insisted.

"How can he harm me?" She laughed, but the laughter was hollow. She also felt the tensed and ready attitude of the dark-haired knight, as though he were ready to jump and carry her to the ground with him. "All right, Sir Knight. You have won the day, and you and your mountain of a companion can leave here unharmed and go on your way."

Alaine had the satisfaction of seeing a hint of surprise cross the dragon's face. So he had thought she would order him killed, though he'd shown no trace of fear. She had to admire the man's courage if nothing else.

Rorik and Sihtric were mounted on their horses, tied and blindfolded. Four of Alaine's stoutest men surrounded the two as they prepared to leave. They had instructions to deliver their prisoners to the edge of the forest where it joined the orchard outside the walls of Ste. Claire.

"Good journey, Sir Dragon," Alaine called in a mocking voice as they prepared to leave.

Rorik swung around to face her. Blindfolded as he was, Alaine could swear she still felt his eyes bore unnervingly into hers.

"Have I seen the last of you, my lady outlaw?" he asked with a twisted smile.

"Hardly, Usurper. You won the contest unfairly. So I'll continue to fight. You'll not see the last of me until there's no breath left in my body."

His answering chuckle held an element she couldn't define. It almost sounded as though he were relieved. But his voice was menacing as his escort prodded his horse upon its way. "Don't rest too well, Lady Alaine de Ste. Claire. I'll be looking forward to our next meeting."

CHAPTER 6

Hooves rang sharply on the paving stones of the bailey as the two heavy destriers clattered across the drawbridge and through the gate. The excited cry flew from the barracks to the smithy to the stables to the workshops. Lord Rorik was back, and he and Sihtric both looked as though they were brewing a storm in their path.

A groom dashed out to take Rorik's horse, his face set in a welcoming if somewhat fearful smile. One look from those fierce green eyes stopped the greeting that was poised on his lips. The poor man took the reins of both horses and faded discreetly into the background before the storm that was brewing in his master's face could break into thunder and lightning.

"My lord! Sir Rorik!" The captain of Rorik's troop of men ran to catch up with him as he headed with long-legged strides toward the keep entrance. The soldier was panting from his run up from the barracks. Impatiently Rorik stopped to wait for him.

"What befell, my lord? One minute you were right behind us, the next you weren't. It was as if you'd disappeared into the air itself. I've had three parties out combing the forest for trace of you."

Sihtric chuckled and refused to be silenced by Rorik's sour look. "What befell? A good story that! Tell him, Rorik."

"My lord?"

"What befell, Captain?" Rorik sneered. "We were kidnapped by woodland elves and taken to see the witch of the forest. That's what befell."

The captain shot his lord a curious look, but dared not question him further. Not, at least, while he had that scowl darkening his face.

"Lord Rorik!" Joanna met them at the lower keep entrance. "You've returned!"

"So I have. Were you not expecting me to, my lady?"

Joanna stuttered in confusion, not knowing how came that suspicious glint to Rorik's eye. "We were worried," she added lamely.

"I'll wager that's the truth!" Sihtric sniped. "But the question is who were you worried about?"

Joanna drew her still-slim body up to full height and skewered the pale-haired giant with a haughty stare. "Certainly not for you, you great ox! My concern was for Sir Rorik and none other."

Sihtric showed strong white teeth in a wolfish grin. "Was it now?"

Another voice joined the chorus of welcome as Gunnor hurried to join the group. "Lord Rorik! Oh, my lord! How I've prayed for your safe return!" The coy smile she gave Rorik as they passed into the hall soured his mood even further.

Joanna left off her glaring at Sihtric and fluttered anxiously at Rorik's side. "The captain said when he returned that

you slew the thieves, and those not slain were put to flight.
Did you . . . was it . . . ?''

"The band of miscreants harassing the villages was not
your stepdaughter," Rorik explained with his last shred of
patience. "We will not be bothered by this particular band
again, I think."

"My lord . . . ?" The troop captain vied with the women
for attention.

"I'll talk to you later, Captain. See that the men have
their gear in good order and their weapons oiled and
polished."

"You foresee riding out soon, my lord?"

"That I do. But right now all I foresee is being unarmed
and soaking in a hot bath. My lady," he turned to Joanna,
"if you would be so kind?"

"Certainly, Sir Rorik," Joanna replied, not liking the
look on his face. She gestured to a servant and ordered a
bath prepared.

"And food. I want a good, solid, hot meal. In my
chamber. Now."

The servants scattered to do Rorik's bidding, whipped
into unaccustomed haste by the ominous tone of his voice.

Joanna and Gunnor both followed Rorik to his chamber.
Joanna helped the knight disarm, pulling the heavy hauberk over his head and shoulders, while Gunnor hurried
the servants who were pouring buckets of hot water into
the tub that sat in front of the hearth. She swirled the water
with her finger to test the temperature, then stole a glance
at Rorik, who was divesting himself of shirt and chausses.
She was all too willing to perform the chatelaine's duty of
seeing to the lord's proper bathing. Such a pleasure it
would be to run soapy hands over the flat muscles that
banded that brawny chest and abdomen, and then lower
still. Perhaps this time, Gunnor thought, it would end as
she wanted it to end.

Joanna tut-tutted over the caked and blackened blood
that spattered Rorik's hauberk. She made a note to herself
to make sure that young squire Timor polished the armor
to mirror brightness. That boy was much too young for his

duties, she thought, and wished that Garin had been here when Rorik arrived. Surely that worthy squire could have found honorable service at Rorik's side.

The thought of Garin brought Alaine to mind and sent a sharp stab of anxiety to cut her heart. When he had ridden out, Sir Rorik had been convinced that the raid on Briaux had been the work of the same band who continually harassed his repair parties, but Joanna knew Alaine would never stoop to such senseless violence, especially against her own people. Now here he was back after a mysterious delay in the forest, admitting Alaine had no part in the village raid, and looking very much like he had something else to say. Joanna almost didn't want to hear it.

Rorik looked at the older woman as he gratefully sank down into the tub of hot water. Impatiently he waved away Gunnor's solicitous attempts to help him bathe. "Do you not wonder, madam, what kept me so long in the forest?"

"Did you find more outlaws, my lord?" Joanna asked in a hesitant voice.

Rorik smiled crookedly. "You might say that. I spent the night enjoying the hospitality of the stepdaughter you've been so concerned about—bound and laid in the dirt like some hog ready for the spit."

Gunnor gasped and abruptly stopped stoking the fire. She turned to Rorik with wide innocent eyes. "Oh, my lord. How awful! How could she dare?" Her comely face fell with a calculated weight of sorrow. "That vixen is truly wicked through and through. But you cannot hold us to blame for what my stepsister does. She's not even really part of the family."

Joanna ignored her eldest daughter. Her eyes grew wide, and she looked again at the blood spattering Rorik's hauberk.

"Not hers," Rorik said, seeing where her eyes rested. "She's in good enough health. Though I won't vouch for her future well-being."

"But . . . my lord . . . was there a fight? How did you escape?"

"I wouldn't call it a fight." For the first time his voice

lifted with a hint of humor. ''Sihtric and I were foolish
enough to allow ourselves to be ambushed by your stepdaughter's ruffians. The varlets downed me with a stone to
the head, of all things. And it took a whole tree branch to
topple poor Sihtric.''

''But how . . . ?''

''Oh, your little Alaine was very accommodating. She
stopped her band of villains from slitting our throats, as
they dearly wanted to do, and then devised a contest—an
archery contest—which she thought she was sure to win.
But the wench got a bitter surprise. I bested her, so she
had to let me go. She gave her word and stood by it. In
part, at least. It seems she has a regard for honor unusual
in a woman.''

Gunnor had been listening carefully to his account of
Alaine's high-handedness. Now she smiled with ill-concealed
delight. ''You beat Alaine in an archery contest? How
wonderful! That must have taken her down off her high
horse! The wretch thinks she can't be bested.''

''She very nearly can't,'' Rorik admitted.

His voice held a hint of admiration that made Gunnor's
eyes narrow. She sniffed with disdain. ''It's only to be
expected, my lord, that she would show some skill. Alaine
spends all her days practicing to be a man, and thinks
herself too good to learn a woman's talents. She has no
notion how to treat a man.'' Her sultry look told Rorik that
she, on the other hand, knew very well how to treat a man.

Rorik's mouth tightened in exasperation. Lady Joanna's
eldest daughter, whom he understood to be a landless
widow, was attractive enough in a full-bodied sort of way.
But her clinging manner and cloying sweetness were
enough to drive a man to violence. And even if he were
interested in what she offered, he was smarter than to
partake of her ample charms. There were enough willing
servant wenches in the castle to satisfy him without his
entangling himself with a noble-born lady. The girl was no
doubt looking for a husband. Once her charms were well
sampled she would whine and plead and demand that her
outraged virtue be appeased. And he had no intention of

saddling himself with a wife. Women were good for bed sport and for bearing heirs. Beyond that they should be approached as a wise man would approach a poisonous snake. Rorik had learned very early in life just how poisonous Woman could be.

Joanna caught the look in his eye. "Gunnor," she said curtly. "You have duties elsewhere, I think."

Gunnor's sultry look turned to a pout.

"Leave us," Joanna repeated. "Sir Rorik and I have matters to discuss."

Gunnor huffed out the door, leaving the two of them in silence. Rorik sank deeper in the tub and enjoyed the girl's absence. His sour mood was being evaporated by the bath, and the smell of the food a kitchen wench had brought up a few minutes earlier improved his state of mind even further.

"If you would scrub my back, my lady, then I would be up and about devouring that food that beckons me from the table."

Joanna took a cloth and did as she was bid. "My lord," she said in mid-scrub, "I wish you could understand about Alaine."

He grimaced. "What's to understand? The girl's an outlaw in rebellion against her lawful lord."

Rorik regretted Joanna's distress about the little witch, for he had come to have a grudging respect for Sir Geoffrey's widow. Since the day he'd accosted her in the great hall with the news that Brix's lawful lord had returned, she had shown a practical turn of mind that he was forced to admire. And she was the first woman he had ever seen stand up to Sihtric's blustering without a quiver. The verbal battles between the two of them had proved a rousing good entertainment on these cold nights when they gathered together in the hall. Joanna was a rare woman indeed, and it seemed she deserved better of her daughters, and her stepdaughter, than she got. Why the lady's wayward stepdaughter merited such concern he couldn't guess. But it was obvious that Joanna cared very deeply for the girl. She had talked and worried about her constantly since the moment she'd surrendered the keep.

"You have to understand how she was brought up, my lord. She's a good little maid, really. She only needs . . . !"

Rorik snorted in disbelief. "I'm sure your stepdaughter is a model of propriety when she's not running around the forest like some malicious little wood sprite."

Joanna sighed sadly and handed Rorik a towel as he rose from the cooling water. "I just don't understand why she continues this hopeless crusade. I was sure that once she learned she owes you feudal duty she would bring her men in from the forest."

Rorik shot her a look of surprise. "Once she learned . . . You mean she doesn't know?"

Joanna looked at him in consternation. "You didn't tell her?"

"I assumed she knew, dammit!"

"How would she know, my lord? We were in desperate straits when your army was sighted. No one recognized your banner, and Alaine was gone before we learned you were lawful Vicomte de Brix. She thought . . . all of us thought you were just another adventurer come to take her lands and force her hand in marriage."

"Force her hand in marriage?" Rorik exclaimed with a great bellow of mirth. "What man in his right mind would take to wife a narrow-hipped boy-woman who wears chausses and fights like a man?"

"Gilbert de Prestot, for one," Joanna said acidly, miffed at this slur on Alaine's worth. "The arrival of your army interrupted their wedding ceremony."

"Then Gilbert de Prestot owes me a favor," Rorik quipped.

Dressed in fresh shirt, tunic, and chausses, Rorik sat down to do justice to the meal the kitchen had sent up. He paid rapt attention to the food, but still could no keep his mind from summoning up an image of a petite, golden-haired pixie dressed in faded tunic and worn chausses. Her mouth was set in an arrogant curve, and her clear blue eyes sparkled with challenge. Somehow the thought of the tempestuous, utterly exasperating wench he had met in the forest kneeling at the altar beside Gilbert de Prestot struck a discordant note in his mind.

He and de Prestot had met only once, years before. Gilbert wasn't a bad sort—a good fighter, a worthy drinking and wenching companion. But he had a streak of greed that Rorik didn't like. He hadn't been surprised when he learned that Gilbert was the one who held Ste. Claire and fled before his victorious troops. No doubt with Sir Geoffrey's death the knight had regarded Ste. Claire as a prize free for the taking, and had sought to secure his hold by forcing Ste. Claire's heiress to the altar. Rorik couldn't too much blame him for that. But if Gilbert still entertained ambitions toward Ste. Claire, it would no doubt come to war. Not now, though. He had Brix to take and had no time for petty squabbles. Just so he could put it off until Brix was in his hands once more.

"My lord, Alaine is only doing what she was brought up to do." Joanna's voice forced Rorik's mind back to the present. "Her father raised her more like a son than a daughter, letting her run wild with the pages and squires and castle lads. He taught her how to fight the same as a man would teach his son—and instilled the same pride of possession. When her home was threatened she did the only thing she knew how to do."

Rorik scowled into his food.

"Wouldn't you have done the same, my lord?"

"What I would've done is of no consequence," he replied gruffly. The girl's upbringing was none of his concern. If she wanted to fight like a man, then she could be defeated like a man. "I am a man, and a knight. It's my duty to fight. A woman's duty is to bear a man's weight in bed and give him children. And to obey."

Joanna sighed. "I'm afraid Alaine's never learned to obey anyone."

"She'd better learn soon," Rorik said somberly. "Or she'll not be long for this world. She's a thorn in my side that needs plucking."

"My lord!" Joanna pleaded. "Don't be so harsh with

her, please. If she knew who you are, I'm sure she'd bend to your will. Alaine knows her duty and obligations.''

"Well, then, let her know, dammit! You can't tell me that someone in this keep doesn't know the location of her camp. Somehow she gets news of what's happening here. And there were boys and wenches in that camp I've seen in the keep before. Why didn't they let her know?''

"The servants don't think about who you are, Sir Rorik. They care nothing for feudal ties. They only know you're their new master."

"Then we'll find someone who knows where your stepdaughter is, and tell him to carry the... Damn! Where is my head?''

"What?" Joanna didn't like the light that was beginning to glimmer in Sir Rorik's green eyes.

"Why didn't I think of that before? Someone here knows where that little witch has her camp. How else would those castlefolk have found their way to her side? We'll find him, indeed. And he'll lead me straight to her.''

"Sir Rorik . . . !" Joanna pleaded.

"I'll teach that arrogant little wench to make a fool of her betters!'' He strode purposely over to the chamber door and called down into the hall. "Sir Oliver! Sihtric! Get up here!''

Alaine watched despondently as the morning mists curled between the trees. She sat chewing unenthusiastically on the cold, stringy rabbit that was left over from the night before. Beside her on the log sat an equally glum Garin.

Four days had passed since Sir Rorik and Sihtric had been escorted out of camp. Alaine had kept her promise to continue the fight. Her men had ridden out every day to prick and poke at the repair parties, and she'd heard from a village wife at Bethune, a village only slightly smaller than Ste. Claire itself, that the new lord's demands for a levy of villagers to work on the walls had been refused. No punishment had been forthcoming—yet, the old woman had told her. But the lord was very angry.

Alaine couldn't get Rorik's parting comments out of her head. He meant to put an end to her and her men. What had been a mere prick in his side had become a personal insult. They had twisted the dragon's tail one too many times, and now he was breathing fire.

"I'm riding to Brix today," she told Garin abruptly, deciding on the deed in the same instant as giving it voice. "I'll need two men with me. Whoever you can spare. I've no mind to ride that distance alone."

Garin sighed. "Why ride to Brix? Timothy hasn't come to say Fulk has returned."

"I think Timothy may have bid farewell to our cause. Fulk must be back by now. If not . . . well, perhaps I will try once more to convince his lady of the worthiness of helping us."

Garin just looked at her glumly.

Alaine lowered her eyes and looked away uncomfortably. "It's our only hope, Garin. We can't continue to pit our small force against Rorik. We're like mosquitoes buzzing around a giant. Sooner or later he's going to swat us."

"I guess I just made things worse by conking him over the head and dragging him in here, didn't I?"

Alaine smiled wryly. She had always thought of Garin as the epitome of knighthood, second only to her father. But in the last few weeks she'd discovered he was in many ways a green boy. He had much to learn before he was ready to take on someone like Sir Rorik. They both had much to learn. She couldn't blame Garin for being green when she herself had made so many mistakes. "You just did what you thought would help, Garin."

Alaine's mood wasn't helped by the persistent feeling that she had missed some important piece to the puzzle of Sir Rorik and Ste. Claire. Something nagged at the back of her mind, something she had seen or heard while Rorik and the giant Norseman bided here as prisoners. Whatever it was, she had promptly forgotten it because in spite of the nagging at her mind, nothing could she dredge out of her memory.

The other inhabitants of the camp were beginning to stir. The first two men who arrived at the fire for their breakfast were detailed to ride with Alaine to Brix.

"What if 'e says no, m'lady?" one of the yeomen asked.

"If he says no," she replied glumly, "then you and the other men should look to find a new master before the new lord of Ste. Claire has all our heads on pikes outside the south gate."

"And what would you do, Alaine?" Garin asked. "Surrender?"

Alaine shot him a smile that held a hint of bravado. "You know me better than that, Garin. I never surrender."

Alaine had just downed the last of her breakfast when the crack of dry branches heralded the stumbling arrival of George Tanner, a village lad from Ste. Claire who was standing the morning lookout.

"My lady!" he said breathlessly. "Riders come! The dragon shield is at their head!" He dropped to his knees to try to regain his breath, then gave a strangled cry as he looked behind him.

The dragon shield materialized out of the mist, looking for a moment like it was suspended in the fog like a symbol of doom. Then through the swirling haze, the man and horse behind the shield became visible. And on either side of the dragon shield, men and horses stretched out on both sides to form a deadly ring around the camp.

For a moment time seemed suspended. The mounted men stood like menacing ghosts on the margin of the camp. Alaine's men and women, most still groggy from sleep, stood stunned and silent, facing their doom. Alaine's heart seemed to stop beating for long breathless seconds. They were all dead, she thought. All her faithful, brave men, all their wives, all the loyal servants who had deserted Ste. Claire to follow her cause. They were all dead, and she would die with them with the dragon's sword against her breast. The nightmare had come to pass.

One of Alaine's men moved to draw his sword. Metal rasped against the scabbard. The deadly silence broke. The knights pushed forward. Women screamed. Men bellowed their wrath and ran for their weapons. Alaine stood where she was, unable to tear her eyes from the dragon emblem that seemed to come to life in the eerie fog. It seemed to claw and rend, rearing in anger, snarling in bloodthirsty intent.

"Move, for God's sake!"

Garin grabbed her arm and almost pulled her off her feet before she could break her trance and get her legs to move. The mounted troop was plunging through the camp. Shouts of pain and anger and the clash of metal on metal filled the little clearing.

"Run!" Alaine screamed to her people. "Don't fight! Run!"

Some had already run, as she and Garin were doing. But the mounted men were braving the brittle thickets and the dense weave of branches to pursue.

"We need horses!" Garin shouted through the chaos.

"We can't!"

Now Alaine was doing the tugging. Rorik himself was between them and the corral. Every corner of Alaine's mind screamed the desperate need to flee. She could feel the dragon's eyes swing in her direction. He sighted the bright banner of her hair through the milling men and horses. She saw him press forward. His face was shadowed by mail coif and helm, but her imagination provided the deadly intent of his expression.

"Move, Garin!"

She pushed the squire toward the nearest thicket and followed hard on his heels. No one opposed them. Every man seemed busy with his own private duel with no attention to spare for two more fleeing outlaws. Only Rorik pursued. They faded into the maze of thickets and branches and hoary tree trunks. Here the brush was too thick for a horse to follow. But Rorik tried. Alaine heard him curse. A crashing behind them indicated he was following on foot.

His progress was clearly marked by the sound of snapping branches and crackling dead vegetation, as was theirs.

Garin pulled her through a particularly thorny coppice, down into a stream cut, and under a shadowed cutbank. He motioned her to silence as Rorik continued to crash toward them. She closed her eyes and breathed a silent prayer to every saint who she thought would hear her plea. The crashing stopped, punctuated by a frustrated curse. He started to move again, and Alaine buried her face against Garin's shoulder, willing herself to not even breathe. But the sounds of his progress were growing fainter. He was going back to the camp.

They stayed in their cubbyhole for long moments after the sound of Rorik's passing had faded. It was Garin who first spoke.

"He's given up," he breathed quietly.

"Not him," Alaine denied. "He'll not give up until he finds us. Mark my words." She knew Rorik better than their short association might allow. Something in his eyes had burned its way into her soul. The intense nature of their few hours together had left her with the feeling that she knew the stranger knight better than she knew the close friend who was crouched beside her. The dragon Sir Rorik was not a man to give up until he had gotten what he was after. And he was after her.

"Then we must flee," Garin said, believing her. "We'll circle around to the back of the camp, to the corral. If we're lucky we can slip two horses out and be on our way. They won't be paying any mind to the mounts until they've rounded up all the stragglers."

Alaine gritted her teeth in frustration. "I can't just leave all these people to their fate. They followed me. They trusted me."

"What do you think you can do for them?" Garin asked with a touch of cynicism that was new to his young voice. "Do you think he'll spare their lives if you give yourself up? Why should he?"

Alaine buried her face in her hands. Something inside her wanted to give herself up and share her people's fate.

But logic told her it would be an empty gesture, a useless waste.

"Those people love you, Alaine," Garin insisted. "They knew what might happen when they followed you out here. Even the castle men-at-arms. You gave them a choice. They came anyway. If you give yourself up now, you're wasting their lives."

She dabbed at the tears that welled from her eyes, cursing her womanly weakness. "You're right, of course. I'm sorry for weeping like a woman. We'll go."

"Good!" Garin clapped her on the back. "We'll ride to my brother's keep at St. Pair. He'll give you refuge. And perhaps once we're safe you can apply to the young duke for justice."

Alaine didn't reply. She doubted Garin's brother would be happy to see them, but he would probably take them in. And as for appealing to William, if what the addled Lady Theoda had said was true, William might be cold in his grave by now, with Guy of Burgundy sitting on the ducal throne. In the long run it made little difference, though. She couldn't picture either William or Guy concerning himself with the troubles of an insignificant heiress from the wild western marches of his domain.

The mist had turned into freezing drizzle, and the ground was slippery underfoot as they cautiously circled around toward the corral. The soft patter of the rain covered any noise they made, but it would also drown out noise made by any of Rorik's men who might be searching through this section of woods. Alaine could hear the heavy pounding of her heart as they dodged from thicket to tree toward the corral. She was sure if the enemy were nearby he could hear it too.

They crouched together behind the thick old dead stump that formed one corner of the corral. Cautiously Alaine peeked over the splintered top of the stump, hoping that with her cloak hood over her head she blended in with the dreary gray forest. She expected to see the ground littered with the bodies of the men and women who had followed her on this impossible crusade, but instead she saw her ragged group trussed up and bunched together in the center of the campsite. Four mounted soldiers stood guard over the glowering crowd and exchanged threats and insults with the men and made ribald suggestions to the women. Alaine breathed a prayer of thanks that her people hadn't been cut down to lie unshriven upon the cold, wet ground. In this, at least, the dragon was more merciful than she had expected.

Garin tugged at her sleeve, then silently pointed to two horses ambling toward their side of the corral. None of Rorik's men were looking their way, and to Alaine's relief she didn't see the dragon himself anywhere in sight. She hoped maliciously he'd fallen and broken something vital—like his neck—on his way back to camp from pursuing them.

"Let's go," she whispered.

They crawled slowly toward the horses, judiciously making use of the little cover available in the corral. Garin had grabbed two lengths of rope that had secured one of the rails to a post. They were close, almost close enough to loop the rope over the horses' heads, when they were spotted.

"Over there!" a voice rang out.

Everyone's attention focused on the corral, prisoners and soldiers alike. They scrambled back under the rail of the corral, oblivious to the scrapes and cuts the rocky ground dealt to their hands and knees. Garin pulled her to her feet and they flew toward the cover of the forest. The heavy drumming of hooves pursued them, overlain by victorious cries of several voices. One voice she recognized. Rorik—damn him!—had been in the clearing after all. And now he was going to ride them down. The forest by the corral wasn't thick enough to much hinder the passage of his big destrier, but it was thick enough to slow him down. Maybe they had a chance—a slim one.

"Come on!" Garin grabbed at her arm and veered to the north, where the brush was thicker. The voices were more distant now, and fewer. Only one horse crashed through the trees behind them. Garin hesitated and glanced over his shoulder.

"He's sent his men back. The bastard wants to make this a private war, I think."

Images flashed through Alaine's mind—Garin, her true friend, her brother in every way but birth, going down in a fountain of blood before that huge flashing broadsword—herself living out the nightmare of seeing that deadly blade come to rest against her breast. Her heart beat faster. Her legs worked harder. Her mind screamed for her to flee, but like in a terrifying dream, the rain, the mist, the slippery rocks, the thickets, the air itself all conspired to hold her back.

"Hurry!" Garin urged desperately.

"I'm coming!"

A rock turned under her foot. She heard something tear as pain speared up her leg. Wet rocks and leaves and dirt came up to meet her face.

"Alaine!" Garin was kneeling beside her, brushing the dirt from her cheeks and forehead.

"Go on!" she ordered, gritting her teeth to keep back tears of pain. She didn't want him to go. She didn't want to be left alone to the dubious mercy of their enemy. But he had to go.

"No!" he insisted. "It's only him that's coming. Only one. I can beat him."

"Don't be a fool!" she cried in a harsh voice. "Maybe ten, fifteen years from now you might beat him. But now he'll cut you to bloody pieces. And if he leaves you alive you'll end on a gallows."

Garin looked up anxiously. The sound of Rorik's pursuit was drawing rapidly nearer.

"Garin! In Christ's holy name! Don't spend your life on a useless cause. Rorik might spare me. But for you there's no hope. Now go!"

"I'll not give up till you're rescued!" He brushed her forehead lightly with cold lips. "I promise you I won't give up." Then he was gone.

Alaine pounded the ground with mingled frustration and

pain. She wanted to scream curses at her fate. But she didn't. Instead she started to pull herself into a thicket, ignoring the pain that shot up her leg at every move. So hard did she concentrate on the task of reaching a spot to hide that she didn't hear the crash in the brush behind her.

"What have we here?" Rorik's voice was infuriating, mocking, dark with black humor.

Alaine looked back with a gasp. The chestnut destrier stood heaving for breath in the rain. Rorik urged him forward until his great hooves thudded to the ground next to her head. She didn't move. She didn't breathe. Death was mere inches away.

Gracefully the dragon swung down from his saddle. Even with his face shadowed by coif and helm she could feel the cynical smile that twisted his face. She knew in the recesses of those shadows, green devilish eyes were glittering fiercely. With one economical motion he pulled his broadsword from the scabbard on his back and laid it against her breast. She closed her eyes, waiting, reliving the terror of her dream. But the death stroke didn't come.

The point of the sword lifted and flicked her cowl from her head, exposing her face and hair to the cold rain. Even in the dingy light her hair gleamed gold.

"My Lady Alaine," he said. She thought she heard a hint of laughter in his voice. "Well met. I've been looking forward to the day you and I should come together again."

CHAPTER 7

Alaine pounded her fists against the feather ticking of her mattress, flailing with frustration as much as with pain.

"Ow! Owwwwoooow!" she complained sharply. "Go

easy there! Do you think me a horse or hound to be handled so?''

"Stop whinin' like a babe!" Hadwisa surveyed the neatly wrapped ankle with a critical eye then set herself to apply one more layer of bandage. "It's not like I 'aven't been patchin' and salvin' you since you was a skinny little tot, what with you ridin' and fightin; and cavortin' with those lads out on the practice field. I always said paradin' around like a man was goin' to be your downfall, and see what it's brought you to now." Hadwisa clucked like a disgusted mother hen as she gave the bandage a final tug.

"Well you needn't be so rough! And I'm in no mood for one of your scoldings."

"Rough, is it?" The old nurse scowled. "Why, I've been gentle as a lamb with you, and you mewlin' like a babe in arms. I tended Sir Rorik just after the keep was taken. Nasty cut on his thigh 'ad to be seared with the 'ot knife. Didn't 'ear 'im cryin' and carryin' on. Never uttered a sound 'e did. And thanked me proper like a true-born knight."

"You should have let the wound fester," Alaine commented with a curl to her lip.

Hadwisa shook her gray head. "Lord above but you're in a fair snit. You'd best mend your mood, my lady, before the Lady Joanna mends it for you. She's done nothin' but faint for worry of you these last weeks. She'll be of no mind to listen to your complainin' now."

"I've a few words to say to Joanna myself! And to Sir Oliver! What were they thinking of to surrender Ste. Claire behind my back before I'd even gotten back from Brix? And here I am dragged in a prisoner by this upstart usurper and my stepmother doesn't even bother to greet me or say a word on my behalf! Where is Lady Joanna anyway?''

The answer came from an unexpected direction. "Your lady stepmother has been plaguing me with pleas to see you and tiring my ears with excuses for your behavior."

The deep voice brought Alaine's heart into her throat. How long had the dragon been there, leaning against the arched doorway to the chamber? And how could a man so big move so quietly?

She hastily pulled the sheet up over her bare legs. "How dare you sneak up like a thief when we're having private conversation!"

Rorik's mouth lifted in a mocking smile. "The privacy of a captured rebel, traitor, and outlaw is very limited—a sad fact you'd best learn."

"Traitor? Rebel?" Alaine sputtered so with indignation that the words nearly stuck in her throat, but the target of her anger wasn't listening in any case.

"How is the prisoner's foot, Hadwisa?"

The old nurse cast a worried look at the knight's rock-hard countenance. She feared for her little mistress, who was hardheaded and quick-tempered and brash as a young gamecock. She wouldn't have the sense to back down before the superior force of this man, nor the guile to use the feminine arts to wile him out of his displeasure.

"The ankle's not broken, my lord. But she's torn 'erself good. It'll take some 'ealin', but she'll not be crippled long."

"Good," he said. "She won't need you any longer." He motioned toward the door with his head.

Hadwisa fixed Alaine with a look of stern warning, then gathered her poultices and ducked out of the room. When she closed the chamber door behind her the room suddenly seemed to Alaine to shrink in size. Rorik's presence made the chamber far too small, and she fought the urge to leap from the bed and fly out the door as the walls seemed to push in around her.

"So, little outlaw. It seems you will heal." He still leaned against the arched entrance, tall and straight and dark-hued, his shoulders seeming to fill the doorway. The sight of him made her smart anew at the humiliation of her capture in the forest, pinned to the ground by an ignominious injury, unable to lift a sword to her own defense. Never had she felt so helpless and vulnerable as at that moment when the dragon had swung off his huge destrier and strolled toward her, contempt evident in every casual stride. He'd mocked her, damn his black soul to Hell! The insolent villain had laughed at the sight of her sprawled wet and bedraggled and helpless on the icy ground.

At the memory her fury rekindled. The ignoble cur! He might at least have had the grace to kill her honorably rather than dragging her back to Ste. Claire to be humiliated in front of her people. But no! The grinning varlet had to drag her up onto his horse and parade her before both his men and hers on the long ride out of the forest. She remembered every detail—the sound of the cold rain pattering on the cloak he had wrapped around them both, the feel of his mail pressing into her back as his arm had drawn her tightly against him, the warmth of his breath in her hair, the disturbing feeling of intimacy as the gait of the destrier had rocked them together in the saddle. Now, sitting helpless on the bed, watching him watch her, she shivered anew at the memory. His green eyes were glacial as he stood there in silence, watching her as a bird of prey might regard a tasty morsel to be leapt upon and devoured. Her heart beat a rapid tattoo in her chest and her breath came in short quick gasps. Never in her whole life had she quailed before any man. Even her father's quick furies which had sent the whole of Ste. Claire into hiding had never daunted her. But there was something more imposing about this man's silence than another man's angry tantrum, and Alaine had to struggle to keep her eyes from falling before the onslaught of his gaze.

"I am neither rebel nor traitor, sir," she choked out. "And outlaw only by your own definition." The words bolstered her courage, and she lifted her chin higher. "By my way of thinking, I and the men who followed me are defenders of our rightful fief. And you are outlaw and usurper and traitor to invade my domain."

He smiled unpleasantly. "Like most women, you have a way of twisting the facts to suit your own pleasure."

"Twist the facts? I?" Anger was beginning to dull the edge of fear. Alaine struggled with her temper, which was perilously close to breaking. She hit the mattress with both fists. "I have no need to twist facts in order to justify my actions!"

"Indeed?"

"Yes! Indeed! And you! Prancing around claiming to be the lord of Ste. Claire! Telling my villagers that I am a thieving outlaw and you are their rightful lord!" Her voice grew intense. "Only the lowest of the low would take advantage of a lordless fief to gain a holding for himself—like a stray cur, snatching up a juicy bone while the noble hound is crippled and cannot fight for himself."

Rorik cocked a brow in her direction. "It seems, my lady outlaw, that you are not in a position to be honing the sharp edge of your tongue on my mettle."

"If I had a weapon at hand, you'd be cut by more than the sharp edge of my tongue!"

He shook his head in wonder and smiled. "For a crippled little hen you puff yourself up mightily like a fighting cock."

She gave him a black scowl. "Just give me a sword and see if you can still laugh, villain!"

That did make him laugh, and the contempt that colored his mirth made her temper burn even hotter. "I think not," he finally chuckled. "We have business to settle between us before you manage to get yourself killed. There is the matter of your men."

"My men?" she asked in dismay. "What have you done with them? You cannot punish them for following their rightful liege lady."

"Certainly I can," he said with a patient smile. "I can do whatever I like. The sooner you learn that the more likely you are to survive." He paused to let his words sink in. When the expression on her face was sufficiently aghast he continued. "But as it is, I dislike useless waste of lives. The men and women we took from your camp are held in a pen in the bailey awaiting my orders. They don't concern me. The ones who escaped our net do concern me."

"Bravo for them!" Alaine cried with glee. "Some did get away!"

"Few enough," he assured her. He had moved closer to the bed, but even his looming proximity couldn't douse Alaine's joy that some of her band was still free.

"Enough to make trouble for you, Sir Dragon! And their numbers will grow. They are loyal only to me, those men—and the villagers too. They'll continue to fight even if they see me swinging from the gallows pole on top of the keep."

He grinned a death's-head grin. "In that case, the fight would no longer be your concern, would it?"

The thought that the knave would actually hang her quenched Alaine's glee. "You wouldn't dare!"

He leaned against the post of the bed and regarded her narrowly. "Generally speaking, women aren't worth the hanging, my lady rebel. But I'll put this to you. Call your men in. Call them in to surrender and swear oath to me as their lord, or by God I'll hunt them down every one and see the fools hang from the gibbet until the flesh rots on their bodies. And every man in the pen shall join them."

Alaine's eyes widened in horror. The dragon's face was set as if in stone, the jade eyes hard and hooded as they held her own. She had no way of knowing if his terrible threat was a bluff.

"Murdering swine!" she spat. "If you must punish someone, punish me!"

"Rest assured your punishment will be no less than theirs." His voice was cold as ice. "Now. What say you? Will you call your men in to surrender and take service with me, or will you see them swing?"

Alaine gritted her teeth and clenched her fists, wishing she could smash them into that granite face that looked down at her in such mocking arrogance. "I will call them in," she conceded bitterly.

"Wise choice." The smile that curved his finely molded lips didn't soften the set of his face. "It is well you recognize that in the world of here and now, lady, you are on the bottom, and I on the top."

The deep clear blue of her eyes darkened to an angry violet. "True enough." She gave him a malicious smile.

"As anyone can see in a quiet woodland pool in summer—scum always floats to the top."

He moved closer, until his face was a mere handsbreadth from hers. "Curb your sharp tongue, mistress shrew, or I'll change my notions about the worth of women for hanging."

"I should expect no better from a lawless varlet like you," she returned with a sneer.

He snorted derisively. "Why do you insist on playing that game? Have you no notion of law?"

"Yea! I know the law well enough to know you are well outside it!"

He leaned back and regarded her for a long silent moment, his face an inscrutable mask. "We had little conversation on the way from your camp," he said in a thoughtful voice, "for you were deep in a female sulk."

"I was not in . . . !"

"Did your woman Hadwisa not tell you the story of who I am and why your stepmother and seneschal were so ready to hand over this keep?"

Alaine's heart skipped with foreboding. Something was coming, she sensed, and she wasn't going to like it.

"I know you are the knight Rorik, called the Stone Dragon by your men. I know you unlawfully made war on my . . ."

"I am Rorik, son of Sir Stephen Valois of Brix."

"Sir Stephen . . . of Brix. . . ." Blood rushed to her face. The missing piece of the puzzle—the piece that had eluded her since she had first taunted Rorik in the forest—dropped painfully into place. The giant Norseman had called him Rorik of Brix. How could she have missed it? How could she have let such a vital piece of information pass through her ears without lodging in her mind? Her stomach knotted as the enormity of what she had done finally dawned on her.

"Aye, my lady. As I said, you are rebel and traitor against your rightful overlord."

"It can't be!" Her voice quavered. "You're dead. All

of Sir Stephen's sons are dead. My own father told me of
the slaughter.''

His mouth twisted into a cynical smile. ''All dead but
one, my lady. All but me. I escaped with Sihtric, and
though yet a beardless boy, lent my arm to the duke's
service. I have been the duke's man ever since. But now I
come to reclaim my rightful place, and Ste. Claire lies in
my path.''

She sat in stunned silence, her mouth drawn into a tight
line.

''So you see,'' he continued mercilessly, ''you have
forfeited any rights you had. I would be well within the
law to hang you for a rebel, or bury you alive, seeing that
is the usual punishment for women.''

She stared straight ahead, recognizing the truth of his
words. But she would let him do his worst before begging
for mercy. Ste. Claires did not beg for mercy, no matter
what the circumstances.

Rorik watched a parade of emotions march across her
features—disbelief, anger, embarrassment, then finally a
stoic acceptance that froze her young face to an immobile
mask. She had borne much more than most women would
bear without flying into a frenzy of tears. He almost had to
admire her courage. It was an attribute he had not often
seen in women. Such nerve and determination was rare
even in men, and here was this girl, hardly more than a
child, determined to face down her fate without so much
as a quivering lip. Her spirit, along with that abundance of
golden hair and the wide blue eyes, would be enough to
bring many a man to kneel at her feet in admiration. Well
it was that he was safe from such weakness, Rorik thought.
Rorik the homeless, Rorik the bitter, Rorik the betrayed,
would never fall for the transparent charms of a woman.

Growing impatient with her stubborn silence, he took
her chin in an ungentle grasp and turned her to face him.
''What, my lady? No pleas for understanding? No pretty
tears to curb my vengeance?''

''I spit on your understanding!'' she hissed, her eyes
burning violet with contempt. ''What right have you to

claim the rights of seigneur after having left us to the mercy of Fulk and our rapacious neighbors all these long years? My father Sir Geoffrey was loyal to your family all this time, refusing to swear oath to Fulk even though he thought all of Stephen's sons dead by Fulk's sword. But instead of marching against Fulk and shouldering your rightful responsibilities, you were off licking your wounds and ingratiating yourself with the bastard duke, who is so busy defending his own hide he has no time to maintain law and order in his own land! No! I owe nothing to you, and nothing to your bastard master!''

Rorik's eyes narrowed ominously. "Guard your malicious tongue, little rebel. My patience stretches only so far.''

"Bah!'' she spat. "Do your worst, villain! What kind of a man would wait ten years to avenge the murder of his father and brothers?''

He glared down at her from the side of the bed. A muscle twitching in his jaw was the only thing that moved in his granite-hewn face. "Someday, foolish maid, to your regret, you may find out just what kind of man I am.''

They scowled at each other in silence for a long moment. The smile that finally spread across his face sent a chill racing down Alaine's spine.

"What punishment should be meted out to a little hellion who rouses her people against her lawful lord and pridefully denies him his rights even in the face of defeat?''

His words were deceptively soft, but Alaine could sense the steel underneath. It took all her determination not to flinch away as his hand went to the hilt of the sword that rested on his hip, a sword not so big as the great broadsword he carried into battle, but certainly big enough to hew her in half.

"You goad me well to anger, Lady Alaine—perhaps to invite the clean edge of my sword to end your troubles? That would suit your pride well, I think—to be sacrificed on the alter of my villainy. Do you imagine your villagers would mourn and cry out that you were a saint, a warrior maid cut down in defense of her land and people?''

Alaine sniffed disdainfully. Perhaps some such thought had crossed her mind, but he wouldn't have the satisfaction of knowing he had read her so well.

His smile broadened and he leaned closer. She could swear she saw a gleam of almost youthful mischief light up those forbidding green eyes.

"I think I have a punishment more fitting for such a prideful maid, and much less wasteful of young flesh than the hungry edge of my blade."

She waited, and challenged him with her eyes. Whatever he did to her, she swore, he would never cow her into submission. She, Alaine de Ste. Claire, had been raised by her father to be as strong, stoic, and as proud as any noble knight. Had Rorik treated her with the respect she was due instead of mocking contempt, she might have yielded him his lawful rights. She might have bent knee and sworn oath to him, and instructed her people to regard his word as law. But as it was, she swore she would die before bending a single inch. If he wanted to see her quail in anticipation of his terrible revenge, he would have a long wait!

His smile didn't fade as she lifted her chin higher. "No curiosity, my lady, about your fate?"

She lifted a disdainful brow. "Speak on, Sir Dragon. But if you wait to see me tremble in fear you are bound for disappointment."

"I'm sure your loving stepmother will appreciate my mercy in simply giving you a lesson in humility rather than the hanging you so richly deserve. We'll see how long your pride lasts when acting the part of a drudge in the kitchen."

"What?!" she shrieked. Her eyes flew to his face, hoping to see that he was joking. His infuriating grin just got wider. "I am a noblewoman—rightful lady of this fief!" Once again the unfortunate mattress bore the fury of her fists. By now the feather ticking was threatening escape through the straining seams. "What's more," she continued, lowering her voice to an intense pitch. "I am knight in all but name, and sex! I fought you honorably and bravely as a warrior should! You can't do this to me! You can't make me into a . . . a serf!''

He laughed, not at all daunted by her fury. "Can I not, little rebel? Who's to stop me?''

"My people will never allow this!''

"Your people are now my people. I am a fair and just lord, and they will soon learn that they are as well off with me as with your late father. Your people will get used to seeing you in rags and soon forget how they once thought that ragged urchin a brave and noble lady.''

"You can't do this! How dare you treat me as if I were a . . . a mere woman!''

With a cry of anger Alaine came off the bed, forgetting her injured ankle and state of dishabille. She threw herself at Rorik, lunging for his sword, but her ankle gave way and she stumbled against him. Only the iron grip of his hands closing on her shoulders kept her from ending ignominiously sprawled on the floor.

"Lesson number one!" He grinned, looking almost as if he were having a good time. "Servants are not allowed to attack their masters.''

She screeched with frustration as he effortlessly picked her up and tossed her back onto the bed. He smiled down at her from what suddenly seemed to Alaine to be a terrible height.

"Now curb your temper, wench, before I am tempted to teach you how masters deal with pretty kitchen maids when they become troublesome. Perhaps it is time you learned that you are . . . as you put it . . . a mere woman.''

He raked her with insolent eyes, and she gasped with fury as his meaning came clear. "You . . . !''

"Ah!" He held up a hand for caution. "Don't tempt my anger, little one. Or perhaps I will begin your lessons by giving you to the men in the barracks. I've no doubt they would enjoy themselves hugely, but I doubt that you would.''

She opened her mouth in astonishment, but nothing came out. For once in her life Alaine was speechless.

"I see I've finally silenced that runaway mouth of

yours. Maybe you'll learn faster than I thought.'' He turned toward the door, throwing her a stern scowl over his shoulder. ''I'll leave you here to think on the merits of proper behavior. For your own sake I hope you learn your lessons fast and well.'' Closing the door hastily behind him, he flinched at the sound of the heavy candlestick she'd thrown splintering against the heavy wood, then shook his head and smiled in reluctant admiration.

Sihtric, meeting his leader on the stairs that led down to the hall, stared at Rorik in surprise. He hadn't seen that devilish youthful grin on the younger man's face since their happier days at Brix. He raised a brow and looked curiously at the closed door of the chamber above.

Over the next ten days proud Alaine de Ste. Claire, apple of her father's eye and once mistress of all that met her gaze, served as maid of all tasks. She scrubbed the tables and the floors, set the morning fires and tended them all through the day, helped to turn great hunks of meat and fat carcasses roasting over the huge hearth in the kitchen— all under the command of old Hilda, a woman who in happier days she'd barely even spoken to, much less had to obey. Hilda had commanded the army of household serfs and servants at Ste. Claire since before Alaine was born, and though she was uneasy and embarrassed at being given her former mistress as a serving wench, she saw clearly that it was to the girl's own good to keep her too much from the gaze of the new lord of Ste. Claire. So she set her at tasks that kept her away from Rorik and his men, and away from Joanna and her daughters, also, for she guessed the girl's embarrassment at having to face her family in her current humble station.

After a long day of work Alaine would find her resting place on a hard pallet by the kitchen hearth with the other scullery maids. At first some of the girls tried to tease her about her downfall, but they were quickly silenced by a cold imperious stare that left them in no doubt about their fate should their victim ever be restored to her former high position. Most of the girls were shy and silent, though, discomfited to see the laughing, golden-haired girl who they'd respected as their true lady wearing a ragged gown no better than their own and with hands and face as smudged with dirt and soot as theirs were.

The old lord's daughter had never been much around the hall, so the servants didn't know her well. She was always busy outdoors, hunting or romping with the lads on the exercise grounds. But she had never spoken sharply to a servant, and often on the holy days she had distributed gifts of warm clothes and the tasty delicacies that those who served in the kitchen and hall got to smell and see, but never got to eat. So it was with sorrow that most of the servants saw Alaine join their lowly state.

Alaine managed to bear herself with her accustomed pride, even with dingy hair hanging in limp strands and dirt under her fingernails. Hard work and constant humiliation didn't quench the fire of anger burning inside her, and even the proud knights of Rorik's retinue hesitated before they demanded some service of her. Most had felt the cutting edge of her tongue, and few dared to repay her cheekiness as they would a real servant. They all knew who she was, and most suspected that though Rorik had declared she was a serf and should be treated as such, it was only he who was granted the privilege of battering down this wench's pride. The one brave knight who had thought to avail himself of a taste of the winsome curves that lay beneath Alaine's ragged gown found himself staring down the length of his master's sword and stammering hasty apologies and denials. No man since had touched her, and Alaine was not above taking advantage of the situation by baiting them mercilessly, knowing that Rorik had reserved revenge for himself and that any man who dared to punish her transgressions would answer to the dragon.

One by one the days passed in a haze of anger, hurt, and exhaustion. Alaine was accustomed to hard work on the practice field—riding, swordplay, and archery—not the bending, stooping, and scrubbing demanded of a lowly kitchen drudge. Her back ached, her hands were raw and bloodied, and she loathed the greasy feel of her hair and the griminess of her body. It was all she could do to hold up her head in the presence of other people, especially her family. Fortunately, she saw Joanna and her stepsisters only when she served in the hall at the evening meal. Joanna couldn't meet her eyes, and from the looks her stepmother cast at Rorik she could guess the words that had flown between them at his treatment of her. Gunnor came as close to gloating over her fate as she dared in Joanna's presence, and sweet Mathilde kept her eyes glued to the contents of her trencher whenever Alaine was in the room. Poor little Judith only looked confused at her stepsister's new status.

Always when Alaine was in the hall she could feel Rorik's eyes on her, brooding, heavy, like a weight she had to bear whenever she was in his presence. He had said not a word to her since he'd condemned her to this lot, and her fears that he would carry out his threats had eased somewhat; though at night on her hard pallet she would toss and turn with dreams of the threat—or was it a promise—she had seen in his eyes when he'd warned her it was time she learned what it meant to be a woman. She always woke from her dreams shivering with dread, wondering if there would come a day when he would carry out that threat.

She knew what it was to be a woman. She had grown up being treated like a younger brother by the men of the castle, hearing their talk of lusty adventures and the poor wenches they used for their pleasure. She was well-versed in the ways of men with women, and wondered if there was anything in it other than pain and degradation. No doubt if she pushed the dragon too far he would make good his threat. If it was her fate to be taught more pain and humiliation than she had already been dealt these past few weeks, then undoubtedly the vile and black-hearted Rorik was the man to teach her.

* * *

Rorik and Sihtric sat on the wide bench in front of the fireplace that took up much of the wall between the great hall and the chapel. Their feet were outstretched to be toasted before the flames, and beside them sat a tray with steaming meat, bread, and dried fruit. They had missed the evening meal, and now, after spending a cold day in the saddle, they were happy to sit before the fire and thaw the stiffness from their bones.

The day had been spent riding to several of the villages and persuading the people there that continued contempt of the lord's work levies were not to the villagers' benefit. It had been a nasty day's work. Rorik didn't enjoy seeing peasants cower before him, but somehow they had to be brought to heel. With only his own men to work, the repairs to the gate and wall were proceeding much too slowly. Ste. Claire was vulnerable to attack from any greedy neighbors who cared to cast eyes in their direction. For the peasants' safety as well as his own, their defenses must be in good order.

His frustration grew with every day he spent at this moldering castle. He had no time to deal with recalcitrant peasants and the problems of defending a broken-down keep. He needed to be honing his forces and planning his strategy for the taking of Brix in the springtime. But he had a responsibility to Ste. Claire that he couldn't dodge, and he needed Ste. Claire's people behind him if he was to accomplish his mission. Damn Sir Geoffrey for dying and leaving a troublesome spitfire daughter in his place!

Never before had he faced this problem. The people who served him, whether knight, soldier, or serf, had always given him ready respect. But in the villages beholden to Ste. Claire—he had never seen such stubbornness! Except for a few timorous souls, they refused to accept his dominion, though he suspected if an enemy were to appear they would be ready enough to take shelter behind his walls and let him drive off the foe with his sword. And the problem wasn't getting better. It was getting worse by the day.

There was little doubt in Rorik's mind about the source of the problem. It was the silent shadow of a maid who drew his eyes each time she passed through the hall. Even now he could feel her wary gaze upon him as she brought fresh tankards of beer to quench their thirst. As she stopped to set the mugs before them he caught her eyes with his, noticing her flinch before drawing herself up to give him her usual glare of contempt.

Sihtric watched Rorik follow Alaine with brooding eyes as she passed out of the hall toward the kitchen.

"The wench is still a haughty creature," he commented casually.

"So she is," Rorik agreed quietly, watching the spot where she had disappeared.

"You're too soft on the girl, you know. She parades around the castle as if she owns it. None of the men dare touch her for fear of your wrath, though why I can't guess. Seems you'd be amused to see her taken down a notch or two." He watched Rorik with knowing eyes, seeing the frown that drew the thick straight brows together in a line over his darkening eyes. "If you don't want the wench for yourself, why not let the men have a go at her? After all, she's naught but a rebel. Let her reap the rewards of rebellion. I'll wager she'll not be so proud after spending a couple of nights entertaining the barracks."

Rorik regarded his friend sourly. "She's not for the barracks, or for the knights either. She's a noblewoman, for all that I've thrown her in among the servants."

Sihtric chuckled, amused and somehow relieved to see Rorik trapped in a fuddled dither over a virgin maid. It gave him hope for the boy after all.

"It's a cold night." He smiled slyly. "A warm wench in bed tonight would go well."

"Aye." Rorik smiled, well aware of his giant friend's aims. But the thought of Alaine stretched out beside him in bed, or spread out under him ready to receive his loving started a painful ache in his groin. "A warm wench would go well tonight,'' he agreed. "Mayhap I'll summon that dimpled milkmaid—what was her name?—Gerthe, I think. When scrubbed up she's a sight to behold. And well-padded to pillow a man in bed.''

Sihtric scowled. "Why settle for coarse bread when that delightful pastry is at your command?'' He nodded toward the door through which Alaine had disappeared.

"Piercing the well-guarded maidenhead of a noble lady is sport for men braver than I,'' Rorik said with a crooked grin. "The wise man does not treat a noblewoman like a serving wench, even though she may be forced to play the part. There are enough lowly wenches in the castle eager to ease my needs, and one woman is much the same as another when they spread their legs. I've no yen to entangle myself in the virtue of that fair maid and have her stepmother and her priest flailing about me to say the marriage vows.''

"Aye,'' the Norseman said with a grin. "The good Lady Joanna would not be pleased, though in truth she'd do better to look to herself. Now there's a hearty piece for any man. I'd wager the fire in that woman is far from burned out!''

Rorik frowned. "The lady is under my protection. So you can just forget about scratching that particular itch. Besides, that one would snatch you bald if you so much as laid a finger to her.''

"Ah, boy,'' Sihtric said with a lazy grin. "What you don't know about women! It's shameful in a lusty lad such as yourself. Time you took a wife and bred some heirs.''

Rorik's face darkened. "You know me better than that. I do womankind a favor by not marrying. The woman who had me to husband would be sorry indeed.''

Sihtric snorted again, but declined to answer. He wondered whom Rorik was trying to convince, his longtime friend or himself.

The Norseman finally pushed his bulk off the bench and stretched the heavy muscles that had stiffened in his back and arms. "I'm for bed.'' He yawned mightily. "There's a little chambermaid keeping the fire stoked in my room, and I've a mind to stoke a few fires myself."

Rorik sat gazing into the flames for long moments after Sihtric had left. The image of Alaine's face rose in his mind. How many different women had she been before his eyes? In the forest, confident and sure of victory at their contest, looking like a slim gamin of a boy-child dressed in chausses and tunic and handling a bow as if she'd been born with one in her hand. And again on that icy day of his attack, desperate and hurt, eyes clouded with fear and defeat but trying valiantly to meet him with a brave face as he stood over her, sword in hand. Then in her room, flinging angry accusations to hide her dismay at finding out the truth of who he was. And now, proud and coldly angry in her humble rags. The fireplace soot and grime of her drudgery couldn't hide the fairness of her face and form, a beautiful face and alluring body he couldn't drive from his mind. Damn if he wasn't letting the witch get to him!

"Hilda!" His angry voice echoed through the deserted hall. "Hilda! Get in here!"

In a very few moments a scrambling from the buttery at the far end of the hall heralded the little woman's entrance, looking like she'd been pulled from her bed.

"Aye, my lord!" she panted.

"Tell Gerthe to be ready in my chamber!"

"Aye, my lord!"

"And for God's sake make her take a bath before she comes."

"Aye, my lord!"

"That's all."

"Aye, my lord!" she breathed in relief and backed out of the hall.

"Aye, my lord!" Rorik mimicked. "Would that everyone around here were so compliant!" he muttered, thinking of one in particular. He scowled into the flames and tried to convince himself that the eager Gerthe would soothe the fire in his loins. Finally, in disgust, he threw the dregs of his beer into the fire and in a spurt of anger threw the empty tankard against the stone wall, finding some satisfaction in the sound of the pottery exploding into shards.

"Women!" he spat, and stalked up the stairs to his chamber.

CHAPTER 8

"Watch what you're doing, you clumsy wench!" Sir Gillaume grabbed up a cloth and ineffectually dabbed at the spreading stain of beer on his tunic. "This is a new tunic! Now look what you've done, you wretched female!"

Alaine lifted an unsympathetic brow. New tunic indeed! And sewn by the industrious hands of her women of Ste. Claire.

"It was your overindulgence of the brew, Sir Knight, that caused the spill. Not my clumsiness. So cease your whining."

After a day spent inventorying the stores with Hilda and discovering how much food and drink was consumed by a full complement of fighting men, Alaine was in no mood to put up with the bullying of one of Rorik's knights. Of course, had her father still been alive and had Ste. Claire a like number of its own defenders, a similar amount would have been used. But that knowledge didn't improve Alaine's humor one bit. She resented every morsel of food and every drop of drink that went into the mouths of these strangers.

"You've a mouth on you that will bring you to grief someday," the knight grumbled resentfully.

"Not by you it won't." Alaine shot him a saucy smile. She knew full well these men dared not touch her. For some reason Rorik reserved to himself the privilege of causing her grief. And he was nowhere around. One of her chief delights had become baiting his men-at-arms and watching them squirm in frustration. It was small enough revenge for having been robbed of her property and position. And even though these men were not really the cause of her troubles, she could think of no way to even the score with the dragon himself.

She walked behind the tables that were set below the dais for the seating of the lesser knights, squires, and pages of Rorik's retinue. She had no care for the beer that slopped from her pitcher every other step, wetting the hapless lads she served, and she ignored the grumbles that came her way. The meat she set before them was cold. Of that she made sure. The soup had an added portion of grease, rendering it almost inedible. She hoped they were enjoying their meal as much as she intended them to.

But in one thing she could not help but afford her victims pleasure. Every few feet she was required to lean forward to refill a tankard of beer. In spite of her attempts to preserve her modesty, the overlarge bodice of her servant's garb gaped temptingly away from her bosom. The expressions of the men were full of gleeful malice as their eyes ignored the plain fare she had set on the table and feasted instead on the delicacies revealed in such a disconcerting manner. Alaine's frayed nerves screamed in outraged modesty at her unintended bold display, even though a tiny part of her savored the reddening faces and tight-lipped frustration of her enemies when she rewarded their lustful looks with dollops of spilled gravy and sprays of cold beer. Any other serving girl who was so deliberately saucy and so temptingly revealed would end up in the laps of those she tempted, enduring the rough pawing and lewd laughter of the wretches, and perhaps even be dragged off to be spread beneath some lusty soldier to serve as appetizer for the meal she served. But Alaine was safe from all save the master. And Rorik was away chasing another outlaw band who was making life miserable for several of the villages. While the tyrant was away, she would get some small measure of revenge from these invaders who dared to sit in her hall, glut themselves on her food, and take from her her pride and independence.

Joanna gave her a pleading look from the high table on the dais, but she continued her game of making the meal as unpleasant as possible for those she served. Unfortunately, the men at table were more interested in her gaping bodice than her misbehavior, and she could not carry the pitchers and platters with one hand and gather in the bodice with the other. She had to content herself with seeing the frustration on the faces of those who ogled her charms but knew they could never do more than look.

Two lads carried their frustration to a fighting pitch. Timor, Rorik's pimply young squire, and Miles LeBlanc, an older youth about to graduate into knighthood, almost came to blows over her imagined favors. Alaine was surveying with jaundiced satisfaction the threatening glares being exchanged between the two young men when a movement on the dais caught her attention. To her dismay she saw that Rorik had entered from the back of the hall and was now sitting in the lord's high seat. How long had he been there? she wondered with a guilty twinge. Abruptly she turned away as his gaze swept the hall and the diners. As inconspicuously as possible she slid in among the other servants who were seeking their meal near the warmth of the fireplace.

"Alaine!" Rorik's deep voice rang above the din in the hall. "Come serve me my meal."

Alaine sighed and grimaced. But she obediently set aside the bowl she was filling for herself. With chin held high and hooded eyes that hid the trepidation that was making her heart pound like a battering ram in her chest, Alaine picked up a platter of meat and moved to the dais. Gunnor smirked and Mathilde averted her gaze in sympathy as she approached the dragon, who did this evening appear to be in an exceptionally surly mood. Joanna managed to give her an encouraging look as she went by.

She set the platter in front of him, stiffening her shoulders in an attempt to hide from his eyes the view that had set so many of his men to squirming. But his gaze unerringly traveled to the soft valley revealed by the ill-fitting gown. At that moment more than any other in her life Alaine hated the fact that she was a woman.

"Methinks I see a feast more appetizing than the one set before me." He smiled roguishly and set one of his hands firmly on her buttocks. She jumped back in alarm and surprise. The avidly watching men laughed uproariously and her face flamed hot scarlet.

"You forgot the beer, wench. I have a thirst after spending all the day chasing through the forests after the mangy human wolves that prey on this land." He gave her rump a playful slap as she turned to fetch a fresh pitcher of beer. Laughter rang out again and seemed to echo through Alaine's head in a never-ending cacophony of humiliation. It was bad enough to be forced into the role of servant, but to be openly pawed for the entertainment of these brutish louts was beyond bearing! At that moment if she'd had a knife she would have willingly driven it into Rorik's heart up to the hilt.

She returned and set the pitcher before him with a resentful thump that sloshed some of the contents over the lip and onto the table. The hall grew hushed and gleefully expectant. Every man expected to see the cheeky wench finally get her well-deserved comeuppance. She pricked like a venomous mosquito at all of them, and they were eager to see the mosquito swatted by the lord's heavy hand.

Alaine held her breath. She was treading on very thin ice, she knew, and she certainly hadn't meant the beer to spill. Her spine tingled as Rorik's glacial eyes swung from the mess on the table to her guiltily blushing face. Something in that look told her he was all too aware of her little stabs at his men and her spiteful little attempts at revenge when she thought he wasn't looking.

With a crooked smile that didn't melt the ice in his eyes, he slid one arm around her waist and pulled her onto his lap. A little gasp escaped Joanna's lips, but Rorik ignored the lady's dismay at his treatment of her stepdaughter. His arm held his squirming, indignant victim in place while the other hand suggestively traced the low-cut gaping neckline of her bodice. Alaine's face flamed with mortification as she felt one callused finger traverse the soft upper swells of her breasts. The hungry eyes of every man in the hall followed the progress of his hand. Somewhere beneath the green ice of those eyes, Rorik was laughing at her, Alaine was sure. She hated him all the more because she knew, deep in her own conscience, that she deserved the humiliation he was heaping on her head. She had been caught out in her petty little schemes, and this time she'd pushed her tormentor too far.

Abruptly he slid one large hand under her bottom and propelled her from his lap. "Bring more bread, wench, then go light the fire in my chamber." His eyes lingered blatantly on the curve of her breasts under her gown, then traveled down to the soft swell of her hips. He made no attempt to hide his heated perusal from those who watched. "Wait for me there. I think you and I have more business between us this night." The leer on his face let no one doubt what that business was.

Her eyes narrowed and her breathing grew ragged and tremulous. Was there to be no end to this nightmare? She was sorely tempted to pick up the nearest platter and throw it, meat and grease and crockery, into his infuriatingly calm face. They stared at each other for a moment suspended out of time. His wide mouth curved into a slow smile that served to add fuel to the already white-hot fire of her fury.

"Or perhaps," he offered with a lift of his brow, "you would rather we tend to that business right here. I'm sure the men would be entertained."

Alaine gritted her teeth and speared him with an ice-blue gaze of pure hatred. Stiffly she turned to grab the platter of bread from near the fire. She slammed it down on the table in front of him with barely controlled venom, then stiff-backed and head proudly erect, swept up the stairs to the lord's chamber.

* * *

Alaine paced back and forth in front of the hearth in Rorik's chamber, the chamber that had once belonged to her father and mother. Her mother, the noble Lady Constance of Ducey, had died in this chamber, bleeding out her own life in giving life to Alaine. In the years following, Sir Geoffrey had occupied the room alone, except for the times when his small golden-haired cherub of a daughter had tiptoed from her own chamber to slide herself beneath the covers of her father's bed and wake him in giggling mischief with the shock of her ice-cold little feet against his back. He had always roared in a most satisfactory manner, like the great maned fearsome lion she thought he resembled.

That sort of play had ended long before Joanna had appeared on the scene to occupy the chamber with Sir Geoffrey, but Alaine's memory still harbored warm images of herself cuddled up to her father in that huge bed. Now this chamber of such dear memories was tainted by the dragon. And here she awaited his vengeful pleasure like any common serving wench summoned for a bit of sport in the lord's bed. At least, Alaine thought in resentful embarrassment, that was what every man and woman below thought was her role in this room, thanks to that insufferable, arrogant, foolishly grinning jackass who occupied the lord's high seat.

Alaine added another log to the fire. Hours had passed since she had climbed the stairs in silent anger and humiliation and closed the door to the lord's chamber behind her. The sounds from below had dwindled as the night grew older. The stars wheeling through the cold sky had traveled a quarter of the heavens' arc since she'd first lit the fire on the hearth and shivered in both cold and fear, expecting Rorik to immediately burst through the door.

Now she paced from window to hearth and back again, occasionally glancing toward the door and listening for sounds from the silent hall. No longer did she quiver from fear. Her initial terror was gone. Reason had calmed her mind and told her Rorik was simply playing a game. He'd been angered at her behavior and sought her humiliation in front of her family and his men. He had accomplished his aim. Her punishment was over, and when he finally came to seek his bed he would dismiss her to seek hers. He had no need of her in the way he'd threatened.

No need indeed! Much to Alaine's disgust, Rorik had the castle wenches clamoring to warm his bed. She had observed more than one comely serving girl climb the stairs late at night at his summons, and the giggling in the kitchen when the chosen one returned was always laced with sighs of envy from those not so honored. The summons did not come often, and there were many girls still longing to try their charms for the new lord's pleasure. Surely, Alaine thought, with the number of eager, well-padded, and thoroughly experienced young wenches willing to entertain him, Rorik had no need to press himself on a skinny unschooled virgin such as herself. Unless, she thought uneasily, he really wanted to take revenge to the limit and exert the ultimate masculine power over a girl who had nettled him past the point of bearing. She dismissed the frightful thought. Rorik didn't seem to be the sort who needed to prove himself by force of strength over someone smaller and weaker. Unlike most men, the arrogant tyrant seemed so sure of his own talents that he didn't need to see others cower before him to confirm his own power.

Alaine continued along this same line of thought as the night crept into the small hours of the morning, convincing herself that the worst was certainly over. Rorik was probably in the hall with that great hulk Sihtric, drinking himself into a stupor and trading compliments with the big blond Norseman about their prowess in the day's fight. When he finally sought his bed he would have forgotten all about her. Probably the best thing for her to do would be to quietly leave the chamber and tiptoe to her own rough pallet in the kitchen. With the morning's light the little incident in the hall would be forgotten.

Several times Alaine started toward the chamber door only to stop in doubt and turn once again toward the fireplace. She almost had convinced herself to leave when the great wooden door swung open and Rorik appeared in the portal. One look at his face told Alaine that all her reasoning had been a fool's dream.

Rorik slammed the heavy wooden door behind him and looked at the ragged maid who stood staring at him out of wide, apprehensive eyes. Her chin was tilted at a defiant angle, and the stiffness of her spine told him she was in no way cowed by his presence. He had spent the last two hours gazing into the flames of the fireplace, seeking the answer to the problem named Alaine in tankard after tankard of strong beer. But the beer had no answer hidden in its dark depths, so he had given up and climbed the stairs to face the problem in person.

"You've been drinking," was the first thing Alaine said. She wrinkled her nose in disgust.

"Indeed I have!" He glowered. "You're enough to drive any man to overindulgence."

She postured innocently, forgetting the need for caution. "How could a mere serving maid trouble so great a lord?

His eyes narrowed dangerously. "If you were in truth a mere serving maid I would let you take the consequences of your own childish actions! You bait and prick at my men until they quarrel among themselves or grind their teeth in frustration. You seek your revenge in the most petty ways possible—not very noble behavior for one who claims to be rightful mistress of Ste. Claire."

"You leave me very little choice in my methods of battle! I fought you honorably like a man would fight and in defeat you heap humiliation upon my head!"

He scowled at her. "My men are not your enemy, I think. Yet you try to strike at me through them. You would know far more humiliation than you have so far did my men not fear that I hold you in special esteem."

"And do you, Sir Villain!" Her delicate lips curved in a cynical smile. "Do you hold some regard for the rightful heiress who should by rights be guarded in your tender wardship?"

His stony face relaxed a bit and he chuckled. The wench was an exasperating twit, but he had to admit, she was never dull. She backed away as he moved closer to claim part of the warmth of the fire for himself.

He regarded her with exasperated amusement. "First you cry that I have no rights, that I have forfeited my family's overlordship of Ste. Claire by—how did you put it?—running off to lick my wounds and curry favor with the duke. Now you claim I should hold to my duties and regard you as my noble ward, even though you've denied me any loyalty and been in open rebellion against my rule. Your reasoning is typical of a woman. You shift your words and thoughts to suit the moment's needs."

She glared at him with tight-lipped hatred.

"Still. . . ." He smiled crookedly. "Perhaps I do hold you in some . . . special esteem."

More than the warmth of the fire glowed in his eyes as he stepped toward her and began to finger the wilted ruffles that haphazardly decorated her ill-fitting bodice. Angrily she slapped his hand away.

"You play the put-upon damsel very well," he said softly. "And you confidently bait my poor helpless men and laugh at their quarrels and frustration. But I am master here, and there is no one to tell me I can't take a troublesome wench over my knee, or perhaps teach her the use of those charms she so saucily flaunts. Perhaps, my grand proud lady, you need to learn the fate of kitchen wenches who stretch their master's patience too far."

Alaine's eyes narrowed as she backed away. She didn't bother to deny the charge of deliberately flaunting herself. He wouldn't believe her, so why lower herself to give excuses?

"You wouldn't dare!"

"Don't tell me what I would or wouldn't dare!" His eyes glittered in sudden anger. "You could be food for the crows upon the gallows if I so chose, and no man would fault me. But there are less gruesome ways of bringing a troublesome bitch to heel, I think. Who would blame me for taming a shrew who's been such a trial to my hard-pressed men—silencing her sauciness as men have always silenced such?"

"No!" Alaine didn't like the smile she saw on Rorik's face. Who would think that her spiteful little games would make him this angry? And why couldn't the man be decent about it and give her a sound beating instead of what he was obviously planning? "Don't you touch me!"

He came closer, stalking her like a hunter might stalk a sharp-toothed, mean-tempered she-wolf. "You're hardly in a position to be giving orders."

"You'll regret this!" she promised wildly. She gave a little gasp as she felt the bed behind her. Holding one arm extended in front of her to ward him off, she cautiously edged along the barrier. Of all places, the bed was not where she wanted to end up.

"Regret it?" He chuckled, a deep, resonant sound that made shivers race down her spine. "I don't think so."

He lunged. She dodged, not fast enough. His arms closed around her like iron bands. She tried desperately to push him away as he pulled her up against his chest, but it was like pushing against an immovable mountain of iron.

"Swine!"

The word was smothered as his mouth came down on hers. She stiffened and clenched her jaw, compressing her lips in a tight line of disgust. But he was patient. Where his first assault had been rough, now he became insidiously gentle, infiltrating her senses with a slow but irresistible flood of warmth. One arm still clamped her tight against his hard body while the free hand roamed, breaking down her defenses with practiced skill. His fingers brushed her neck, floated over her shoulder, lingered lovingly on the soft mound of her breast, traced the indentation of her waist, then finally cupped a firm buttock. She gasped as he pressed her hard against his loins, leaving no doubt as to the state of his arousal. As her lips involuntarily opened, he thrust deeply with his tongue, conquering her mouth in rehearsal for the sweet battle that his body strained to begin.

Alaine melted against him. She was overwhelmed by the taste of him, the scent of him, the feel of his iron-hard body straining against hers. Suddenly it was as though she were inhabited by another woman entirely, one who wanted nothing more than to be one with the male creature who held her in such close captivity. As though someone else were guiding her actions, her arms slipped down to encircle his waist. Every fiber of her body seemed to flow into his. She was lost in a warm black cavern of strange desires and stranger sensations.

Thus when she found herself suddenly pushed away she felt strangely bereft of the very source of her being. She shook her head to rid herself of the unaccustomed longings that still clung to her senses like cobwebs.

Rorik looked at her in wary distrust. His chest heaved, laboring to drag in enough air to clear his brain and body of the heady spell the little witch had cast. He had merely thought to scare the wench into behaving herself. And maybe, he admitted reluctantly, he had been curious about what it would feel like to taste of that winsome mouth. But his body's instant and insistent response to the feel of her sweet flesh pressed against his caught him unaware. If he hadn't thrust her away when he had, he swore he would have tossed her onto the bed and had the deed done and well finished before she could have cried out her objection. Well that he caught himself. He didn't need to entangle himself with a lady of noble birth, no matter how troublesome, infuriating, and tempting she was.

Alaine's breathing slowly returned to normal. She searched her mind for words bitter enough to tell the arrogant tyrant what she thought of him, but her mind was a blank. She stood mute and steaming, watching as flashes of emotion, none of them readable, crossed his face.

"Go to your bed, Alaine," he finally said in a strangely quiet voice.

She gave him a last look of loathing and turned to go.

"Remember," he warned as she opened the door. "Next time you use your claws on my men, I'll not only clip them, I'll yank them out."

* * *

"He is very handsome, don't you think?" Gunnor smiled thoughtfully.

"Who?" Alaine asked with an exasperated sigh. She had not been pleased to see Gunnor stroll into the hall while she was cleaning away the remains of the morning meal. The trestle tables had been scrubbed and set aside, the hounds had efficiently cleaned the scraps of meat and bread from the floor, and Alaine had been about to make a trip to the storeroom for fresh scented herbs to scatter among the stale rushes when Gunnor had appeared. Much to Alaine's frustration, her stepsister seemed inclined to stay and talk.

"Who?" Gunnor repeated. "Why Lord Rorik of course!"

"Rorik?" Alaine chuckled, pointedly omitting the honorific. "Handsome? I never thought about it."

Gunnor raised a carefully sculpted brow. "Well, I think he's very handsome."

An image leapt unbidden into Alaine's mind. The face was distressingly familiar. It had haunted her dreams for the three days and nights since she had been so curtly dismissed from the lord's chamber. Short-cropped black hair contrasted with startling green eyes. Features were sculpted into harsh, ascetic planes. The aristocratic nose was straight, narrow, and prominent, the lips full and framing a wide mouth that was usually set in a narrow grim line. Thick dark brows drew an angry slash above deep-set eyes. All in all it was a forbidding face, Alaine thought, but she supposed it was also an attractive face, if one found that sort of harsh masculinity appealing. And of course Gunnor had undoubtedly been the recipient of fewer scowls and frowns than Alaine. No doubt she had seen Rorik's better side. No doubt also Gunnor had been spared the wretched experience of having that grim mouth— the one Gunnor thought so handsome—press down on hers in suffocating possession.

"I suppose he's handsome," Alaine conceded, "in a brutal sort of way."

Gunnor shook her head in pity. "Poor Alaine," she

sighed. "I suppose you think Lord Rorik has been harsh with you."

Alaine didn't bother to answer. Instead, she busied herself wiping down the three great carven chairs that stood on the lord's dais.

"Myself, I think you're amazingly lucky to have escaped the gallows, or at least a sound whipping at the post."

Alaine snorted in contempt. "For what should I meet such a fate, Gunnor? For trying to defend you and your sisters and mother? For trying to preserve my land from invasion?"

Gunnor shrugged. "I don't think that's the way Rorik looks at it."

"How would you know what Rorik thinks?"

"Oh, well. . . ." The older girl smiled dreamily. "We've become close, you know."

"Don't tell me you're bedding that oaf!"

Gunnor's brows rose in shock. "For Heaven's sake, Alaine, guard your coarse language! Certainly I'm not . . . granting Rorik any favors. I'm a lady. I don't warm a man's bed until the vows are spoken. But I've seen the way he looks at me."

"Bah! I vow he looks at you no differently from the way he looks at the swine in the fields or the hounds in the kennel. He considers everything and everyone on Ste. Claire to be his property, to be reaped or plucked or disposed of at his pleasure!"

Gunnor sniffed disdainfully. "What do you know about men? You wouldn't recognize the signs of a man smitten with a fair maid. You've always been so busy playing a man yourself. If you'd spent more time being a woman, Alaine, you wouldn't find yourself in the mess you're in now."

Alaine sighed in exasperation. "Is there some reason you're tarrying in the hall and keeping me from my work?"

"I was going to tell you that when I'm lady of this hall, I'll see to it that Rorik sets aside this cruel game he's

playing with you. I thought it might make you feel better.''
She smiled graciously.

"Lady of this . . . !" Alaine swallowed her laughter.
"I'm grateful for the kind thought, sister, but you should
look to your own welfare, not mine. I think this Rorik will
not be as easily twisted around your finger as other men. If
you bait a trap with your womanly charms, he's the man to
snap up the bait and leave you caught in the snare. So look
to yourself, Gunnor."

"Tch!" Gunnor clucked in pity. "Poor Alaine. You
decried the lot of women and insisted on fighting like a
man. But look at you, scrubbing your hands raw while we
poor ladies take our leisure in the solar. You're slow to
learn, sister."

Alaine made a face as her stepsister left the hall.
Gunnor's purpose, she knew, was to goad her, not to offer
comfort. She had been at odds with her eldest stepsister
since they'd first met. When Sir Geoffrey had married
Joanna, only two of her daughters had moved in with the
new lady of Ste. Claire. Six months later Gunnor had
joined them. For three years Joanna's eldest daughter had
been wed to the wealthy, powerful Osbern Caronne. They
were wed in Osbern's sixtieth year, and in his sixty-third
year the groom succumbed to a malady of the bones and
joints. Childless, Gunnor was returned to her family, and
Osbern's family retained his vast estates and the dower
lands he had granted Gunnor upon their wedding day.
Gunnor had come to Ste. Claire a woman with a bitter
memory of the past and a sour view of the future. Her sole
occupation seemed to be dampening the lives of those
around her with her bitter tongue, and Alaine had quickly
become her primary target. The injustice of Alaine being
heiress to the fertile lands of Ste. Claire in addition to her
mother's rich lands on the Channel Isles was too much for
Gunnor to bear, and the satisfaction she took in seeing her
stepsister reduced to slaving in the kitchen was impossible
to hide.

Alaine knew all this, and understanding the source of
her stepsister's misery, she found it impossible to hate

Gunnor too much for her jibes and taunts. Most of the time she simply dismissed her as a person with a small heart and a petty mind.

So why did the thought of Gunnor luring Rorik into her bed send such a sharp stab of pain through her heart? Rorik would never wed Gunnor, who had no dowry and no land to bring with her to the marriage bed. Her bitter stepsister would never take Alaine's place as lady of Ste. Claire, as she fondly imagined; and if she allowed Rorik to take his pleasure of her charms, she would someday soon be discarded when another caught the dragon's fancy. Just payment for her scheming, Alaine thought. And if Rorik fell for her wiles and took that thorny female to his bed, then he deserved exactly what he would get—a whining, carping shrew who would surely make him pay dearly for what little pleasure he found in her body. Then why did the image of Gunnor sighing to Rorik's caresses and pillowing his hard bulk with her soft plumpness rankle so?

"She can do whatever she pleases!" Alaine muttered to herself.

She was still muttering ten minutes later when Hilda found her polishing the chairs on the dais.

"Mercy, child! You'll have those chair arms rubbed into nothing if you don't let up!"

"What?" Alaine started, jerked from her dark imaginings of an appropriate fate for both Rorik and Gunnor.

"Give me that rag and fetch some herbs to freshen these rushes," Hilda said, not unkindly. "This floor smells as sour as your face looks."

"Yes, Hilda."

"Then go check the fire in the solar. Gunnor told me it's burning low."

"She would," Alaine sighed.

"Tell Sewell to fetch more wood if you need it."

Alaine caught up with Sewell in the kitchen and sent him on his errand. He gave her a quick wink as he trotted down the stairs to the woodpile. She winked back, feeling her mood lighten. Sewell had been with her in the forest and had come in only a day or two after her messenger had made the round of the villages. Quickly the word had passed that any of her band who had escaped Rorik's net were to present themselves at the castle to be pardoned and swear oath to their new lord. Slowly the remaining men of her brave little band had trickled in, and Rorik had been true to his word, taking the men-at-arms into his service, sending the villagers back to their homes, and setting the castle servitors once more about their work. All but a very few of Alaine's men now belonged to Rorik by oath of loyalty. Only Garin and a handful of others remained in the forest occasionally harassing Rorik's patrols and exhorting the villages to rebellion.

Sewell deposited an armload of wood by the solar hearth as Alaine placed a few especially dry pieces on the fire and blew vigorously on the coals to make them burn hotter. Joanna sat in the corner with her sewing, and several other castle women busied themselves at their work, one at the loom and two others at their wheels. All studiously avoided looking at Alaine as she went about her task.

Alaine cast a surreptitious glance at Joanna and caught her stepmother in a sympathetic stare. Wordlessly she turned back to the fire. She wanted no one's sympathy. She simply wanted Rorik's head.

"My lady! Come quick!"

It wasn't until Sewell's alarmed call that Alaine noticed the racket coming from the bailey. She rushed to the window.

"For the love of God!" she cried.

At the tone of her voice, the other women in the room left their work and moved to the window.

"That's Tobrik from Briaux and Uther from Bethune!"

Rorik, Sihtric, and three men-at-arms had clattered into the bailey dragging eight soiled and bloodied men behind them. The prisoners were bound together by a length of rope, and they stumbled and cursed as they were driven forward.

"Those are all good men! True loyal men from the villages!" Alaine growled ominously. "What is that tyrant up to now? Oh! This is too much! Too much!"

Startled eyes followed her as she stalked from the room, a look of grim determination on her face.

CHAPTER 9

Alaine pushed her way through the crowd of curious castlefolk that were gathered around Rorik and his hapless prisoners. Few of the crowd recognized her in such lowly garb, so she had to use her elbows to good effect to make her way through the press of bodies. Finally she managed to reach the forefront.

Rorik sat astride his great chestnut destrier and regarded the pathetic wretches he had herded into the bailey with a mixture of pity and disgust. He was tired of playing useless games with the people of Ste. Claire. Patience, never one of his superior virtues, was at an end. Still the villagers refused to pay him their duties, either in work or produce. Stragglers from Alaine's former band of ruffians skulked in the forest under the leadership of some jacka-napes who fancifully called himself the Guardian of Ste. Claire, and now these eight village varlets actually dared to attack one of his hunting parties.

"Lash them to the post one by one," Rorik ordered in a dark voice. "Let them taste the bite of the whip, then see how eager they are to set upon good men going peaceably about my business!"

The crowd of castlefolk grew quiet, and Rorik surveyed them with a harsh sweep of his eyes. It would do every one of these sullen folk good, he told himself, to witness that his hand was not forever stayed in the face of treachery and rebellion. Mayhap it would save him from dealing out harsher punishments in the future.

The first man to be bound to the post and have his shirt stripped from his back was the one Sewell had identified as Uther of Bethune. He was young—not long into manhood— and his face drained of all color as Rorik's men tied him to the upright. Despite the chill in the air his bare torso gleamed with sweat.

Rorik turned to the seven who waited. "Watch his pain with care, for every one of you will be dealt the same. This is much lighter punishment than you merit, as well you know. When you go back to your villages with your backs burning from the whip, remember that next time you raise a weapon against me or mine, your lives will be forfeit."

He turned to the castle smith, who doubled as executioner, and gave the order to begin. With a grim set to his face, the smith shook out the whip, then raised his arm to deal the first blow. But before the cruel lash could fall to take a bite of Uther's flesh a small whirlwind flew from the watching crowd and grabbed the braided length of hide from the executioner's hand.

The crowd drew a collective breath and held it. A wide-eyed, gasping Alaine stood facing the surprised smith, the whip trailing from her hand. Every eye was on her, but one pair of eyes seemed to bore through her with special intensity. She turned slowly to face Rorik. He was gazing at her quite calmly, almost as if nothing she could do had the power to surprise him any longer.

With determined effort she stopped the shaking that threatened to set her whole body aquiver. She returned Rorik's gaze with a steadiness she didn't feel. They stared at each other for a long moment. Then at the press of his master's knee the chestnut destrier moved forward until Alaine could feel the warmth of his breath on her face. She resisted the urge to back up, and instead stubbornly held her ground.

"You can't punish these men!" Her words were not

loud, but they sounded like a shout in the expectant silence
of the crowded bailey.

Rorik lifted a sardonic brow. "And why not, mistress?"
Alaine had expected him to rage, but a hint of sharpened
steel in his quiet voice convinced her she was indeed in
trouble. She lifted her chin staunchly and clung to her
cause.

"They're good men," she insisted in a determined
voice, "true to the cause they believe is right."

Rorik smiled coldly. "They are not true, however, to
their lawful lord. With no provocation they attacked a
hunting party of my men seeking game to supply our
larders."

Alaine felt the prisoners' pleading gaze on her back.
They had been her men. They fought in outrage at what
had been done to her. She couldn't let them down.

"They fight for me," she said simply. "Punish me. Not
them."

Rorik stared at her with narrowed, suspicious eyes.
"Did you tell them, by messenger or signal, to attack my
men?"

"No," Alaine answered. "I told you I would call my
men in, and I did. But there are those who will not put
aside their loyalty to me."

Some of the tension eased out of his voice. "Well it is
that you can deny a part in this. Otherwise your back
would also feel the sting of the whip. As for them," he
gestured to the fearful prisoners, "no man can raise his
hand against his lawful lord and escape punishment." His
green glittering eyes bored into hers. "You of all people
should know that."

She detected a softening of his face that could have been
a hint of sympathy, but she couldn't believe that compas-
sion could be numbered among the Stone Dragon's emotions.

He held out a hand. "Give me the whip."

She hesitated, her fingers clenching spasmodically around
the whip handle. The crowd was hushed, and a palpable
shimmer of tension seemed to quiver the air between the
mounted knight and the stiff-backed, tight-lipped girl. His

outstretched hand beckoned, commanding her obedience. Finally, moving as though each step were a battle, Alaine stepped forward and placed the handle in his hand. Her face was a study in determined scorn.

The tiniest of smiles pulled at Rorik's mouth as his long fingers closed around the whip. He threw it to the smith, then bent down and, placing his hand on Alaine's shoulder, turned her to face the whipping post.

"Since you feel you should share in these fools' fate, you may stand and watch them take their punishment. And when you bind their wounds, you will tell them that the one they fight for has surrendered. Convince them well, Alaine. I want to bloody the backs of no more misguided men who think they are fighting out of loyalty to you."

She stood miserable and sick at heart as the lashes were administered, but Rorik's hand held her shoulder in an unshakable grip. At first out of pride she refused to close her eyes. Then finally, giving in to her sick heart and weak stomach, she tried to hide the scene behind tightly closed lids. But there was no way to escape the sounds of the lash and the screams of the victims, and they bit through to the very core of her. When the last of the hapless eight had been untied and carried away for his wounds to be cleansed and salted, she was covered with sweat and her stomach was threatening rebellion. She wondered how it would look for the former lady of Ste. Claire to heave up her last meal before the watching eyes of all the folk gathered in the bailey.

The hand that had gripped her shoulder gave her a gentle shove in the direction of the stable, where the eight villagers were being tended.

"Go see to your comrades, Alaine," Rorik ordered in a gruff voice. "And see to it they know who they serve from this time forward."

His eyes followed her thoughtfully as she started toward the stable, visibly staggering under the weight of her emotions. With obvious effort, she squared her shoulders, stiffened her spine, and firmed her step. Damn her to Hell! Rorik silently cursed. She was every inch as proud and unbent as the day he had first faced her in the forest. What was he to do with the twit?

The crowd had dispersed, revealing Sihtric leaning against a stack of baled hay, regarding him with knowing eyes.

"You've got to admire her guts," the Norseman commented casually.

Rorik merely grunted in reply.

"And you can't blame these folk for being loyal to such a one. They'd do anything she asked, you know, down to the last man."

Rorik glanced back again to the stable door where Alaine had disappeared. "Just what are you getting at, my friend?"

Sihtric grinned wickedly. "You know what I'm getting at, boy."

Rorik didn't bother to deny it. He tossed the Norseman a dark scowl that only made the blond giant's grin stretch more widely across his face.

Rorik's scowl slowly faded and was replaced by a look of pensive speculation. For a long moment his thoughtful gaze rested on the stable. His brows drew together in a frown, then abruptly he chuckled.

"I just might, Sihtric. Would that surprise you?"

Sihtric snorted. "Nothing you could do would surprise me!"

Rorik laughed softly. But his humor was directed inward. His decision was made, for better or worse. There were some challenges too great to ignore, some gauntlets that were meant to be picked up, no matter what the cost.

"It would be an apt answer to our problems here, I think, at little cost to me." He grinned conspiratorially. "There's more than one way to win a castle, and certainly more than one way to tame a shrew."

"Aye," Sihtric agreed with a wink. "You have the right of it."

The Norseman chortled softly to himself as Rorik summoned a groom, dismounted, and strode with a confident gait toward the keep. For certain there was more than one way to tame a shrew—or a dragon. He wondered which of the pair of them was going to end up tamed.

Alaine headed toward the keep, a small storm brewing in her path. With every brisk step she cursed Rorik Valois, supposed Vicomte de Brix. The moans of the men she had left in the stable still sounded in her head, and she knew she would be haunted forever by the crack of the whip as it prepared to bite again and again into the cringing flesh of its victim. Rorik could have taken their lives, but he'd chosen their pain instead. Alaine supposed it was a mercy, but at the moment it didn't seem so.

She hoped that through their pain the men had listened well to her words and would carry her plea for peace back to their villages. She wanted to see no more backs stripped of skin because of her people's loyalty to a lost cause. And especially she wanted no corpses hanging from the gallows. Rorik wasn't a cruel man, as men went, but even now his tolerance was stretched to the breaking point.

Alaine doffed her cloak as she entered the hall. The trestle tables were being set up for the evening meal, and the fire in the huge fireplace had been stoked to a roaring furnace to ward off the chill of the dreary winter afternoon. Her entire family were warming themselves before the hearth, and Alaine supposed that the solar, with its two big drafty windows, was too frigid now that the sun was so low in the west.

Gunnor gave her a sharp look as she approached the fire to thaw her frozen hands and feet. "Are you satisfied with what you've done?" she queried in an acid voice.

"Gunnor!" Joanna warned.

But Gunnor was not to be silenced. "I'm tired of her putting herself above all the rest of us. We have a precarious existence here at best, and she never fails to do her part to see that we all get thrown out into the cold."

"Lord Rorik has never threatened to throw any of us out," Joanna reminded her.

"No," Gunnor sniffed. "But he will soon, I vow! When he's had enough of Alaine's sauciness he'll rid himself of the lot of us! Did you see that nasty smile he had on his face as he came in—after she—after she made a fool of herself and pushed herself in where she had no right to be?"

Alaine gave her eldest stepsister a contemptuous look. "What did you expect me to do? Those were my men out there feeling the bite of his anger."

"You have no men!" Gunnor shot. "You have nothing! You're naught but a slave because you refuse to accept that Sir Rorik has every right to take over wardship of this moth-eaten castle and demand that its wretched people do his bidding! You have no rights! You are nothing!"

Alaine turned her back to the fire and lifted her skirts a bit to let the heat flow under them. She schooled her face to an impassive mask. Gunnor's spiteful words stung all the more because there was a modicum of truth in what she said. But it wouldn't do to let her stepsister know that her vicious barbs had scored a hit.

"Those men were fools in any case!" Gunnor continued, unable to halt the flow of spite once her mouth had opened. "Rorik was generous to give them only ten lashes. He should have plied the whip until their miserable souls were driven from their bodies. I only hope he doesn't hold us accountable for their actions, or the pranks of those other fools who sneak around causing trouble with that so-called Guardian of Ste. Claire."

This was too much for Alaine's temper to bear. She turned to her stepsister with a calm face, but her ice-blue eyes glittered with fury. "Shut your mouth, Gunnor, or I will shut it for you! You defame the courageous acts of men who sacrifice themselves out of loyalty to me! Yes!" She advanced a step, making Gunnor fade back in uncertain trepidation. "To me! Rightful lady of Ste. Claire! The Guardian of Ste. Claire, whom you take for a jest, is my father's most trusted and loyal squire. Garin holds by a promise he made to me in the darkest of hours, for all that I would release him from it if I could. I honor Garin for his loyalty. But I suppose loyalty to anyone but yourself is something you know nothing about!''

"Loyalty to a lost cause is an idiot's game!'' Gunnor shot back, still carefully staying out of Alaine's reach. "Those pigheaded villains simply try Rorik's patience with their pranks and assure that eventually we will pay for their stubbornness. All because of you and your cursed pride. Why can't you admit your defeat and surrender?''

"I did surrender, Gunnor,'' Alaine declared with head held high. "I just can't convince some of my people to do the same.''

Joanna sighed and stepped between the two girls. "Did you really surrender, Alaine? Or are you still fighting, just in a different way?''

Alaine looked at her stepmother in surprise. She hadn't expected Joanna to support her petty-minded daughter.

"Gunnor,'' the older woman continued in a calm voice, "I think you've said too much. Alaine has duties to see to, and dinner will be served soon. I think we'd all best go get ready.''

Only Mathilde lingered when the others swept out of the hall. She cast Alaine a shy look that was almost an apology.

"Don't pay Gunnor any mind, Alaine. She thinks she's practicing to be a great lady. But for all the cow eyes she makes at Lord Rorik, he only gives her scowls in return.''

Alaine snorted. "A scowl is the only expression that man knows! His face is cast in an unbreakable mold!''

She moved to help the other serving girls distribute trenchers of dry bread on the tables. Mathilde trailed in her wake.

"He's not so bad, Alaine,'' Mathilde said softly. "He's been kind to me and Judith, and to Mother. And he told our lady mother that when he's settled at Brix he'll give us dowries and find us husbands. He says it's his duty toward Sir Geoffrey's daughters. Though we're only stepdaughters,'' she added hesitantly.

"I'm the true daughter,'' Alaine said bitterly, "and I'm reduced to serf and toil all day in the kitchen.'' She turned from her task abruptly. "Would you really wish to wed some lout that arrogant tyrant forced upon you?"

Mathilde shrugged, but there was a hint of sadness in her voice that Alaine found suspicious. "A maiden must wed or spend her life serving the Church in a nunnery. Rorik has lands and keeps that William has given him. He has need of loyal castellans to hold his properties. What better way to bind a good man's service than to give him a well-dowered wife who owes her loyalty to Rorik? Gunnor and I, and Judith also, when she comes of age, should consider ourselves lucky to have such a protector."

"Protector! Bah!" Alaine spat. "Some protector! I think our Rorik has little use for the fairer sex unless they can further his own designs. He will use you and Gunnor and Judith for his own purposes with no regard for your wishes or happiness."

Mathilde shrugged again. "It's so for all women, is it not?"

Alaine gave the younger girl a disgusted look and hurried to the kitchen to help with the platters of meat and tureens of soup. When she returned to the hall Mathilde was standing by the hearth, gazing into the flames with a wistful look on her face. Alaine felt a stab of pity for her stepsister, who, though only a year younger than she, seemed so much more fragile and vulnerable than Alaine herself ever had. She began to regret her harsh words of moments earlier and walked over to the hearth to place a friendly hand on the girl's shoulder.

"What ails you, sister? Why aren't you with Gunnor and Judith preparing for the meal?"

Mathilde sighed. "Alaine?" she ventured timidly. "Is that fellow who keeps causing trouble in the forest—that Guardian of Ste. Claire—is that really Garin?"

Alaine raised a brow at the concern in Mathilde's voice. "Aye, it's Garin," she answered softly. "I'm sure it is. He must know I've sent for all my followers to swear oath to Rorik, but it's just like him to refuse to give up the fight. Dear, loyal Garin."

"He'll be killed, won't he?" Mathilde's voice was

heavy with the weight of unshed tears. "Rorik will catch up to him and kill him."

"Nay, Mathilde," Alaine comforted. "Soon Garin must realize how hopeless the fight is. He'll leave our forest and go to his brother. He has no other sensible choice."

"I'll never see him again," Mathilde sighed. "I'll be married to some stranger of Sir Rorik's choosing. And I'll never see Garin again."

"It's the way of all women," Alaine whispered sadly, echoing Mathilde's earlier words. She slipped one arm around her stepsister's plump waist while the girl laid her head on her shoulder. Mathilde's cheeks, made rosy by the fire, were wetted by a single miserable tear that slipped unheeded from her eye.

"My Lady Alaine!"

Old Sir Oliver hobbled up to her as she struggled to hang a full kettle of water over the fire. His joints had grown stiffer as the weather had grown colder, and of late his gait was slow and halting. But now he bustled along almost gleefully.

"Lady Alaine!" he repeated as he limped to a halt in front of the hearth.

She raised a brow at his use of the honorific, for when he'd done so in the first days of her servitude Rorik had rebuked him soundly.

"What is it, Sir Oliver?"

"I bear a message from Lord Rorik, my lady!"

"What sort of a message?" She wondered what trial Rorik had planned for her this day. Her mind had still not settled from the trauma of the day past; and though in the early morning all eight of Rorik's victims had left for their homes in fairly high spirits, grateful to still be in possession of their lives, she continued to smart from the memory of the lash.

"Rorik bids you be rid of your rags and have your

serving women dress you in your best raiment. He orders you to dine at table with the gentlefolk this evening.''

Alaine looked at the old man in surprise, then a bitter smile crooked her mouth. "What's this? Serving maids to wait on a serf? Rorik to dine with a dirty kitchen wench? You must be mistaken, Sir Oliver."

Oliver frowned. "No mistake, my lady. Sir Rorik is smiling today. I suggest you quit this bitter role you've cast for yourself and take advantage of his good mood."

Alaine placed her hands on her hips and looked at Oliver warily. "What reason did he give?"

"No reason." At her continued scowl he shifted uneasily. "Come, child. Take the lord's change of heart with a trusting soul. Perhaps he's decided your punishment has come to an end. Be happy."

"Trusting soul indeed!" Alaine muttered, turning back to stoke the fire under the kettle. Whatever Rorik was planning, she was sure it would bid no good to her.

"Hilda!" Sir Oliver summoned the pudgy little housekeeper as she came into the hall. He would be grateful to foist his recalcitrant lady off onto someone else. "Come see to our lady. She's to dine with the lord tonight."

"So I've been told." Hilda showed a mouthful of half-rotted teeth in a happy grin. "It's about time that great beast came to his senses. It'll be good to see you back in your place, my lady."

Alaine sighed with exasperation at both of them. "He but plays a game. He'll heap some humiliation upon my head at table tonight, then when he's had his fun I'll find myself back on my pallet in the kitchen."

Hilda cocked a saucy brow. She thought it much more likely that Alaine would find herself bedding on Rorik's pallet this night, from the way the big knight had been looking at the girl these past days. But who was she to upset so innocent a child?

"Nay, my lady," she answered. "Sir Rorik was bound to restore your place someday." She grinned another black-toothed grin. "And if you don't mind my saying so, you've not the makings of a decent serving wench. Glad I will be to see you back on the dais where you belong!''

Alaine was hustled to the chamber she had formerly shared with Gunnor and Mathilde. While Rorik still resided at Ste. Claire, the chamber was occupied by Joanna and Judith as well. But none of the others were present as Hadwisa directed the efforts of a bevy of girls who prepared a bath and brushed out the chemises and gowns that had hung unused in the wardrobe these past two weeks. Alaine's brushes and combs were laid out on the table by the big bed, just as she had left them on that day a lifetime ago when she had risen in the cold dark morning to visit her father's grave. That former life seemed a world away, a dimly remembered dream that fled with the morning's cold reality.

Hadwisa experimentally sniffed at a selection of fine oils, trying to decide which one to use in her mistress's bath.

''Which do you prefer, my lamb?''

She offered the oils to Alaine, who brushed them away impatiently.

''I won't be oiled and scented like some offering to his high-and-mightyship. If he doesn't like the way I smell he can send me back to the kitchen.''

Hadwisa ignored her protestation and poured a rose-scented oil into the water. ''Be sensible, my girl,'' she advised. ''When in the dragon's den it is best to soften up the beast however you can.''

''This beast is made of stone, remember?'' Alaine scoffed.

What was the use of this charade? What cruel scheme had Rorik devised now? He had said nothing to her since he'd dismissed her to tend her poor hurt men. No threats had he sent her way for interfering in their punishment and no scowls for spending most of the afternoon in the stable seeing to their hurts. But his anger must be great if he was going to all this trouble to spring some new hurt upon her.

The bath did feel delicious though, despite her protestations, and she enjoyed it as she had rarely enjoyed any-

thing in her life. The swirling hot water almost lulled her
to sleep, and the delicate rose scent of the oil nearly made
her forget the smells and dirt and toil of life in the kitchen.
She had begun to wonder how angry Rorik would be if she
skipped dinner altogether and simply spent the rest of the
night in this wonderful steaming bath when the sweet
voice of Mathilde woke her from her reverie.

"Oh, Alaine! Isn't it wonderful? I knew he wouldn't be
so cruel as to keep you in the kitchen forever!"

Alaine opened one lethargic eye and regarded her stepsister with something less than welcome. She wanted to
enjoy this respite while she could, not listen to the chatter
of Mathilde, dear as the girl was to her.

"Hilda told me you were up here, so I came to help you
dress, and do your hair. Oh, I'm so excited!"

"Mmmph!" Alaine sank deeper into the tub.

"Oh Alaine! Your hands! That's so disgusting!" She
picked up one of Alaine's hands from where it rested on
the lip of the tub and exclaimed with horror over the dirt
ground under her fingernails and into her skin. "Oh! We
will have to do something about this! And your hair!
Ugh!" she shuddered. "I'll be surprised if you don't have
fleas!"

Alaine sighed in resignation. Apparently her time of
relaxation was over.

"Hadwisa," Mathilde asked with daintily wrinkled nose,
"where are the clothes she was wearing?"

"I burned 'em," Hadwisa replied. "No telling what
sort of vermin were nesting in 'em."

"Oh, stop, you two!" Alaine ordered. "I washed every
day in water I hauled from the well myself, which is more
than I can say for most of the kitchen girls. They hardly
have time of their own to eat and sleep, much less indulge
in bathing. See how clean you'd be after working in the
kitchen for a few days!"

In answer Hadwisa pushed her head under the water,
then commenced to scrub until every golden strand of her
hair squeaked with cleanliness. Thus rudely roused from
her lethargy, Alaine finished the job herself, taking a brush

to every square inch of skin until she tingled and glowed with a rosy sheen.

"Much better!" Mathilde exclaimed as Alaine stepped from the bath and allowed herself to be wrapped in a towel by one of the army of girls Hadwisa kept scurrying in and out of the room.

She reveled in luxury as the old nurse brushed her hair dry in front of the fire while Mathilde clucked and commented on the gowns a serving girl had laid out.

"Is this all you have, Alaine?" she finally asked.

Alaine shot her a devilish grin. "I prefer tunic and chausses."

Her stepsister frowned in exasperation. "Well I guess this one will have to do." She held up the finely embroidered chemise and gown Alaine had worn to greet the conquering Gilbert, the one that had almost become her wedding raiment.

"Not that one," Alaine said with finality.

"None other is so fine," Mathilde admonished. "Don't be difficult."

Alaine shook her head, tangling Hadwisa's brush in her thick locks. "You might as well throw that one in the fire. The memories that cling to it are worse than any vermin that nested in the rags you just burned."

Dinner was a festive affair. Word had gotten out that something special was afoot this night, and everyone came dressed in his finest. The men of Rorik's retinue were surprised to see Alaine dressed as a fine lady and seated on their lord's right. Compared to the other ladies on the dais, her gown was plain, and she wore no adornment other than a simple band of gold that secured a gauzy headrail over her bright locks. All the same, many a man who during the last weeks had been ready to throttle her for impertinence now wondered how he could have become so annoyed with so fair a creature. Young Timor especially couldn't keep his eyes from the one he swore must be the fairest lady in all of Normandy. His food went ignored, and he stared in such moonstruck raptness that his dinner companions snickered and guffawed, elbowing him in the ribs and reminding him unmercifully of a thorough set-down Alaine had given him just the week before.

Up on the dais, Alaine wanted to squirm uneasily under the weight of the stares that were directed her way. Rorik, seated on her left in the high seat, was being a model of propriety, selecting the choicest morsels from the platters as they were passed and placing them in her bowl. His conversation was sparse but polite and gave no hint of his intentions in suddenly raising her from serf to lady. She refused to ask him directly and settled for fixing the big knight with a suspicious eye that let him know she wasn't fooled for one moment. His consideration and gentlemanly conduct were a mere facade designed to put her off her defense. She didn't want him to think her dumb enough to fall for such a ploy. He was planning something rotten and she knew it.

The dinner was done and a sweet cake with candied fruits was served as dessert—a rare luxury at Ste. Claire. Tankards of beer were refilled, and for this special occasion, Rorik had ordered several fine wines brought up from the storeroom for those who preferred a more refined beverage. Such unaccustomed festivity made Alaine even more wary, and the knot of suspicion twisting her gut drew even tighter. She raised a brow at Joanna, who was sitting on Rorik's left, but her stepmother simply shrugged in ignorance, and Alaine settled back unwillingly to watch Rorik play the game out. She almost wished she were back in the kitchen. At least there she knew the extent of her troubles.

The dessert was consumed along with several tankards of cold beer. A chalice of wine sat untouched in front of Alaine. She had no appetite for either food or drink. But when Rorik stood and motioned for silence she suddenly had an urge to down the entire draught in one gulp.

"Hear me! All of you!" he said without preliminary, his strong voice carrying to every dark corner of the hall.

The diners grew hushed and expectant, with the exception of those who were so far into their cups that curiosity was no longer a possibility.

"All of you gathered here—my own men and the men of Ste. Claire—know why I am here. As rightful Vicomte of Brix and overlord of Ste. Claire, it is my duty as well as my right, on the death of the faithful Sir Geoffrey, to assume wardship of this castle and these lands and villages until a husband can be found for the heiress—the lovely Lady Alaine."

He turned to smile at her, emerald eyes sparkling with laughter and with something else she was certain boded no good. Her hands gripped the arms of her chair with spasmodic intensity. No doubt he had decided to marry her off and thus gain some minor baron and his men to his service. She should have guessed. Her heart sank, but she willed herself to maintain a serene and dignified face. She would not disgrace herself in front of this vile man and give him reason to laugh all the harder. She tilted her chin at a proud angle and looked out at the crowd, waiting with dread to hear Rorik's next words.

"It is my responsibility to see that Sir Geoffrey's daughter is wed to a man who will guard well both this land and her own person. With such a fair lady under my care"—there were a few snickers here from some of Rorik's men, who had seen Alaine at her thorniest, but a lowering of Rorik's black brows brought respectful silence once again to the hall. "With such a fair and gracious lady under my care," he repeated firmly, "the decision was not hard to make."

Not a cough or a titter broke the expectant hush. A shiver of pure tension raced on icy feet up Alaine's stiff spine.

"The banns will be posted tomorrow morning on the door of the parish church. Three weeks from now the Lady Alaine will become my wife."

CHAPTER 10

"Marry you?! Marry you?! I'd rather rot in hell! I'd rather have demons pull out my fingernails one by one and set fire to my toes!"

Alaine threw the words like missiles, each one more explosive than the last. But all she elicited from her target was a crooked smile and a shake of the head.

"Calm your temper, my lady. I'm well within my rights to take you to wife, as well you know."

"I'd rather toil in the kitchen! I'd rather bed with the swine!"

A devilish smile pulled at his mouth. "It's my thought that the swine would rather have you bed with me. They're somewhat choosy about their companions. And you've a temper that might put a wild boar to flight."

Her face darkened ominously. "I'll swing from the gallows before I crawl into bed with you," she spat. "So do your worst! Call your executioner! I'd rather sleep in my grave and be food for worms than mate with vermin."

Rorik chuckled, a warm sound that rose from deep in his chest. "You've a curious turn of the phrase for a woman gently reared. I'm almost tempted to believe your stepsister's stories about your waywardness."

"Then marry my stepsister if you want someone to marry!" Alaine snorted with disgust. "Marry Gunnor! She'd be glad to play your little games, I'm sure!"

"Your stepsister is not the one I've chosen, Alaine," Rorik explained, a hint of exasperation entering his voice. "And your feelings will not sway my decision. But put your mind to rest. I'm not such a monster. The women I've taken to my bed have been well enough pleased."

Alaine's eyes grew wide. "Oooohhh! You are vile!"

She headed for the door of her chamber, where he'd followed her after she had flown in a fit of anger after his announcement. The chamber, it seemed, was no longer a sanctuary, and she wanted nothing more than to be away from his infuriating presence. He caught her arm as she turned to stalk out.

"Don't try to run away, little rebel, because there's nowhere you could go that I wouldn't find you. You have no choice, so you might as well accept what you cannot change." He ignored the ice-blue glare that speared from her eyes. "The banns will be posted with the morning light, and three weeks from tomorrow you will become my wife before the sight of God and all your people and mine."

She whirled on him in a fury. "Why do you do this? You've no fondness for me! How many times have you named me traitorous, treacherous, spoiled, and childish? More times than I can count you've threatened my very life. How can you think to take me to wife?"

"Your faults are no greater than any other woman's," he conceded generously. "At least you've a straight tongue in your head and attack from the front instead of sneaking around a man's back. I can learn to put up with you."

"Put up with me?" she shrieked. "You arrogant swine! You oafish lout! Suppose I can't put up with you, you villainous knave?"

"Then you'd better learn to put up with me, sweet lady," he mocked. "If you'll use the few brains God gave you you'll realize how lucky you are. I could have given you to anyone, or shut you away in a nunnery and let the good sisters worry about your waywardness. I could have even hanged you and no one would have said me nay."

"Why don't you?" she taunted. "That would be a kinder fate than having to bear with you!"

"Because by marrying you myself I secure the loyalty

of your people, and I need your men to help me take Brix in the spring.''

Alaine regarded him with narrowed eyes. She should have known it wasn't she whom he sought. It was her people. The surprise was the amount of hurt his words inflicted.

"Why not marry me to one of your loyal men?'' she offered in an acid voice. ''That would have the same effect.''

"Ha!'' he almost shouted. ''Do you think I'd trust a viper like you to the care of one of those innocents? Just the sight of you had half of them swooning in their tankards tonight. You'd wrap any of those poor doting louts around your finger and before I knew it Ste. Claire would be doing homage to some other lord.''

"Are your knights such simpletons that they can be swayed by a mere woman?'' she sneered.

He smiled cynically. ''You underestimate your own allure, my lady. When you try, you can present quite a pleasing picture, though it hides the soul of a she-wolf.''

"And of course you are much too strong a man to succumb to such a lure!''

He gave her a condescending smile that set her temper to flaring even more hotly. ''Strong enough,'' he assured her. ''My soul is proof against the fairer sex. I've seen their true colors revealed, and none has yet changed my opinion.''

She fumed, but desperately struggled for once to control her temper. It seemed that the madder she got, the wider the smile stretched across his insufferably arrogant face. The way to handle this situation was with brains, not with ire. She'd outsmart the rogue yet.

"Suppose,'' she said in a strained but passably civil voice, ''I promised that in return for my freedom I would deliver my people's loyalty of my own will.'' The judicious retreat stuck in her throat, but the people of Ste. Claire could do much worse than have Rorik for protector, infuriating though he was.

He smiled cynically and shook his head. ''Promises are

empty things. I trust few men, and no women. I've said before that I will have Ste. Claire in no hands but my own, at least until Brix is mine. Lands and lives have been taken from me before by treachery. Then I was just a green boy. Now I am a man, and what I name as mine remains mine. Ste. Claire is mine. You are mine."

So much for being reasonable with the beast. Alaine's temper reached the end of its frayed rope. She balled both her small fists and sent them driving into the rocklike hardness of his chest. "You, sir, are an ass!" she said, breathless with fury.

He grabbed both her wrists and clamped them in a viselike grip before she could twist away from him. Holding her at arm's length, he bored into her eyes with his own. "Hear me well, little spitfire maid!" he warned. "I bear you no special ill will. Your courage and audacity have even won for you a place in my regard. I am honoring you above all other women, and if you act the proper wife and behave yourself you will receive from me the respect due your position. But if you cannot tame your mouth and act the shrewish bitch, I'll deal with you as any other man treats a saucy wife."

Alaine grimaced and twisted to be free of his grip, but he held her firmly, giving her a little shake.

"Stay! And heed me well, my stubborn little rebel." Here his voice grew dark with a grim promise. "Sauciness and hot words I can bear with, like any other man. But if you are given to treachery, beware. For if you ever betray me by word or deed, I will make you wish you were never born. Do you understand?"

"I understand," Alaine ceded hastily. She was overwhelmed by the intensity of hatred she glimpsed in those glittering ice-green eyes—hatred not of her, but of someone or something he saw in her place. She wondered what woman had betrayed him so badly in the past and set loose the bitter bile that ate at his soul.

"You cannot keep yourself from me, my lady, so don't try. I am stronger than you, and infinitely more ruthless. Don't make me prove it."

He released her, gave her a final scowl, then turned on his heel and left the chamber without a word. She stared after him in dismay for a moment, then shook her head angrily. What irony that she, who had refused to become a woman, should be finally wed to a man who seemed to despise the whole of the fairer sex.

The afternoon was cold and gloomy, matching Alaine's mood. A mist had rolled in from the sea and shrouded both forest and meadow, clinging to the stones of the keep like some damp and dreary spirit. The fire in the solar, though crackling and lively, failed to drive the damp chill from the room. Alaine shivered and motioned Sewell to add another stick to the flames.

"I'll go for more wood, my lady," he offered. "This damp is enough to chill a body to his very bones."

Alaine nodded and smiled, then went back to her stitching. Joanna regarded her from a chair on the other side of the hearth.

"That looks like fine work, Alaine. I can remember when two years ago you couldn't take a straight stitch to save your very life."

Alaine mumbled a reply. She was in no mood for female chatter.

"Who would have thought, back then, that you'd prove your talents working on such a grand trousseau."

"Indeed!" Alaine replied caustically. The five other women seated in the room were also working on her trousseau, and Mathilde, who of all the women of Ste. Claire had the most talent with a needle, was stitching away at an especially fine gown to be worn at her wedding. The cloth and trim—satins, silks, fine wools, linens, miniver, squirrel, black sable, and even ermine—must have cost Rorik dearly in coin, Alaine thought. She knew the merchant from whom he had purchased the goods, and the man sold top quality for top price.

Alaine's acid tone was not lost on her family. Gunnor,

who had been clench-jawed and hot-eyed since Rorik's announcement a week past, scowled moodily into her stitchery, and Mathilde looked up with a little frown creasing her ivory brow.

"You've not told us, sister, how it feels to be finally back in your rightful place."

"She's not said two words to any of us," Gunnor sniffed disdainfully, "since she's now such the great lady."

Alaine ignored her eldest stepsister and turned to Mathilde. "For the price I must pay, I'd rather be back toiling in the kitchen. That's how I feel!"

"Oh, Alaine!" Mathilde looked hurt. "Sir Rorik seems a decent sort to me. He is young and a strong warrior— and not at all bad to look upon. What other maid would not be satisfied with such a man?"

"Alaine thinks herself the equal of any man," Gunnor sneered. "Thus no man is good enough to be her master. Did you not tell me once that you would have no husband save one you chose yourself? Now where are your high-and-mighty words?"

Alaine sent a dark scowl in Gunnor's direction while Mathilde sighed wistfully. "No maid can choose for herself. Would that it were otherwise. But I think being betrothed to such a man would make many a maid smile."

Alaine snorted. "I'd rather wed a pigherd!"

"You go too far, Alaine!" Joanna's voice was sharp with exasperation. "Rorik is a just man and an honorable knight. Has he not proved it?"

"Just?" she asked with a sneer.

"Yes, just! Generous, in fact! Marriage to a vicomte is much more than we could have expected, especially under these circumstances. Even putting your criminal misbehavior aside, you are still merely Sir Rorik's ward. He could look much higher for a bride."

"He can wed with a princess for all I care!" Alaine returned hotly. "In fact, I wish he would! I have no wish to become the dragon's lady. He's cold and unfeeling and cynical, and he wants me only to secure Ste. Claire for himself!"

"True," Joanna agreed, making Alaine's frown etch more deeply into her face. "But still you should be grateful to have him to husband. He will make Ste. Claire a good lord, and he's highly placed in the duke's regard. Even the knights who follow him—with the exception of that hulking Norse brute who guards his back like some faithful hound—were most of them detailed to his command by William, a sure sign that the duke regards him as one who has earned his favor."

Alaine answered with tight-lipped silence, ignoring Gunnor's smirk and Mathilde's tender look of concern.

Joanna gave her stepdaughter a long measuring look. "It is time to grow up, Alaine," she finally said. "You can be a sweet and sensible maid at times, and I have hopes of you growing into an extraordinary woman. But thanks to your father, you can also be a spoiled little terror. It's time you stopped thinking only of yourself and thought of your people, who need you desperately."

"I am thinking of my people!" Alaine contested with a black scowl.

"Are you?" Joanna shook her head. "When you become Rorik's wife, your people will stop their useless fight and accept him as lord. He's a strong man, a good protector, a just lord. Ste. Claire will prosper. Your sisters and I will be well settled under his protection. And you will bear Rorik a son who will insure that the blood of Ste. Claire still rules here."

"I don't want to bear any man a son! Especially him!"

Alaine threw her sewing aside and stalked to the window, staring angrily out at the damp and gloom. When she turned once more toward the fire, Joanna was gazing at her half in exasperation, half in sympathy.

"You're not a child anymore, Alaine," she said softly. "You'll soon be a woman, and wife to a strong man who will put up with little nonsense, I think. Time to grow up."

In the days following Alaine was almost too busy to brood. A week passed, and more. Only a few days were left until the wedding, and preparations became frantic.

The trousseau was nearing completion, and even Alaine was moved as she saw the beautiful gowns and warm fur-lined cloaks, the fine soft leather shoes made especially for her feet, and the richly embroidered chemises of fine linen and silk.

The castle servants were assiduously scrubbing and sweeping and polishing every corner of the keep under Joanna's stern direction, and the bailey was being swept free of refuse and clutter in preparation for the great day. Hunting parties rode into the forest every day to stock the larders for the multitude that would be at Ste. Claire to see its heiress wed, and the kitchens were kept busy dressing and preparing their offerings—deer, rabbit, and game birds of every kind. Swine and sheep were butchered, and little One-eyed Georgie and the other cook's assistants were kept busy scurrying to Maudie's orders, fetching herbs, spices, and dried vegetables from the windowless ground-floor storerooms.

Rorik and Sihtric most often rode out with the hunters, grateful to be away from the feminine bustle and dither that prevailed in the keep. So Alaine did not often have to bear the presence of her prospective bridegroom. For that she was grateful, for his presence often made her squirm with uneasiness. When he was in the hall his eyes constantly followed her, watching, brooding. She suspected he looked for signs of rebellion on her part, so he could settle some humiliating punishment on her head. When they met face to face every evening at dinner, he was polite, proper, and reserved. But she could feel something behind his cool manner and sense a fire hiding in his hooded eyes. But the fire could cool rapidly to ice, and sometimes he regarded her almost as if he expected a two-headed monster to appear in her place. And Sihtric, Alaine observed, watched Rorik as closely as Rorik watched her. The big blond Norseman's eyes twinkled with laughter as he observed Rorik's manner, and frequently he chuckled into his beer in a way that made Rorik look as though he might dump his entire tankard over his friend's head to cool his amusement.

Alaine for one could find nothing funny in the upcoming nuptials. She thought long and hard on Joanna's words, and finally admitted to herself with characteristic honesty that she had been acting like a self-willed, spoiled brat. But it was difficult to accept such a fate, even for the sake of Ste. Claire. It had been far easier to endure the rigors of the forest and the uncertainties of their little hit-and-run skirmishes than to resign herself to having Rorik as lord and master. She would far rather wield a sword or a bow in battle than to be forced to accept the cold-eyed attentions of the man who now ruled this hall. But Joanna was right. Dreams of independence, and of love, were for children. For Ste. Claire's sake she would try to make Rorik a good wife, impossible as that task seemed.

Gunnor's malicious tongue didn't make Alaine's mind rest any more easily. Alaine tried to avoid her eldest stepsister whenever possible, but too often they were thrown together in the solar without Joanna's presence to make Gunnor guard her words. The young widow delighted in regaling the innocent Alaine with horror stories of the pain and indignities a woman must bear in a man's bed; and though Alaine told herself that Gunnor indulged in spiteful exaggeration, she still couldn't suppress a growing anxiety about the part of marriage she had thought the least about up until now.

"My Osbern was not a man to dally long over his husbandly duties," Gunnor confided to Alaine one afternoon as they sat by the solar hearth with their stitchery. Joanna was absent and the other women in the room were out of earshot of their low-voiced conversation.

"With him it was slam it in and take it out. Then the unpleasantness was over, thank Heaven! But of course Osbern was old. I imagine a bold man like Rorik would want his pleasures to last a bit longer." She smiled knowingly. "Much longer. . . . But I'm sure you'll learn to endure."

Alaine raised her brows in disbelief. "It can't be that bad, Gunnor. Elsewise why have you been drooling after Rorik from the minute he showed himself at Ste. Claire?"

"I have certainly not been drooling!" Gunnor huffed indignantly. "I make no secret about wanting to remarry, since marriage is the only way a woman can be secure in this world—marriage to a man or marriage to the Church." She breathed a little martyred sigh. "I suppose security is worth having some oaf crawl between your thighs every once in a while. I just didn't want you go to your marriage bed unprepared, as I did."

Alaine suppressed a snicker with difficulty. "Kind of you to think of my peace of mind."

Gunnor shot her a malicious glare. "You can laugh now, but we'll see how long you laugh once you've a man in your bed every night. I thought Osbern was killing me when he stuck that awful thing in me. It felt like a knife jabbing up into my innards. And he was a smallish sort of a man. I can imagine what Rorik was hanging between his legs might well split you in two, little sister."

Alaine swallowed uncomfortably, but she threw brave words back into her stepsister's face. "You're just trying to scare me, Gunnor. How can something that's natural and meant to be cause pain? Does the mare scream when mounted by the stallion? No. I've seen does and bucks at play in the forest and they show no signs of such agony. I think you're trying to put goblins in my mind."

Gunnor smirked. "Woman is not a mare or a doe. God declared that all women must suffer for the sins of Eve, and thus we must bear the pain of a man's rutting. Believe what you want, sister. When mighty Rorik climbs atop you on your wedding night you'll see the truth of my words and you'll thank me for letting you know what's to come."

Alaine tried to push Gunnor's words aside, but they swarmed around her mind like annoying gnats. She caught herself looking at Rorik and wondering what indeed was in store for her when she became his wife and he claimed her as his own. Likely he would be cruel, and all men were crude when it came to dealing intimately with women. She'd learned that well enough from her association with her father's men-at-arms. But if there was pain to be borne she would bear it without a squeak, she vowed. A Ste.

Claire did not snivel at a little discomfort! All the same, she couldn't quite suppress a shudder at the thought that soon she would belong to this big, black-haired, frowning knight, and for the hundredth time since she had first laid eyes on the man she cursed her fate at being born a woman.

As the great day approached fearfully close, more and more demons beset Alaine's mind. She attempted to soothe the pricks of her uneasiness by losing herself in work, but in that she was foiled. Preparations for the wedding were drawing to an end. All was nearly ready. Of her trousseau, only the finishing touches on the wedding garment itself was left to be done, and when the bride offered to help, Mathilde good-naturedly shooed her away, declaring that Alaine's hands were shaking too much of late to be of any help at stitchery. The cleaning and polishing were complete, and long-unused chambers on the level of the keep below the hall had been opened up for the noble guests to use during their visit. Invitations had been sent out to every baron and lord within a two-day ride. Even William was coming to see his liege man succumb to the matrimonial trap. The guest chambers were all prepared. The only thing left to do was to light the fires on the hearths and spread the beds with fresh linens and soft furs.

Shooed away in all her attempts to join in the last-minute preparations, Alaine returned to the solace of her favorite pastime. On a bright morning two days before her fate was to be sealed, she donned chausses, cross garters, woolen tunic, and a sturdy cloak and made her way to the exercise fields beyond the outer wall. Well did she know that these few days before her wedding would be her last hours of freedom.

There were few men working out on the field, as the morning was icy cold and many preferred to work on the smaller practice field inside the bailey, close to hot drink and warm hearth should the cold start to seep through to the bones. Of the few men-at-arms, knights, squires, and pages who had braved the frigid morning air, most of the faces were unfamiliar to Alaine, who during her childhood had known every one of her father's men. She recognized a few pages who had served with her father, and Timor, Rorik's inept squire, was on the field with Miles LeBlanc, who served Sir Guillaume.

As she was recognized, mock battles stopped and heads turned her way. One of Rorik's younger knights was so startled to see the long golden hair coiling from under her hood that his attention was diverted in the midst of a charge with lances. His opponent's lance struck squarely on his shield, and, unprepared, the hapless young man toppled ignominiously from his horse, landing on the ground with a hard thud and a whoof of painfully expelled breath. His opponent laughed, then looked to see what had drawn the other's eyes with such disastrous results. As he spotted the object of everyone's attention the smile left his face.

Alaine squirmed uneasily. She was not used to meeting with so much attention. The men of her father's forces had always accepted her as a rightful member of their group, and the squires and pages had been like so many brothers. But Rorik's men stared as though she had grown an extra head or sprouted a tail.

The young knight who was still ahorse with his lance left his companion sitting in the dust and rode over to where Alaine stood. He doffed his helm and respectfully touched his forehead in salute.

"My lady," he smiled with a hint of condescension that set Alaine's temper on edge. "What may we do for you this day?"

Suddenly she felt that the world had turned and she had remained still in one place. She realized belatedly that this was no longer where she belonged, but she wouldn't give this young snip of an arrogant knight the satisfaction of seeing her discomfort.

She lifted a contemptuous brow. "I require nothing, Sir Robert. I merely come to work up a fair sweat, like the rest of you."

The young knight's brows lowered in disapproval, but Alaine ignored his frown.

"Would you care to have a go with swords, Sir Robert?" she asked icily.

"My lady . . ." he started, not sure what to say. "I don't think . . ."

She swung her eyes to poor Timor, who had abandoned his bout with Miles and stood a respectful distance away.

"How about you, good Timor?" She smiled sweetly, aware that the boy was smitten and taking unmerciful advantage of the fact. "I think you could use some practice to better guard my lord's back. Will you go a few rounds with me?"

Timor's eyes grew large and round. His mouth dropped open to reply, but no sound came out. She smiled at him again and a slow blush crawled up his face.

"Mmmm . . . my lady?"

"You'll oblige me, won't you?"

"I . . . I'd be honored, my lady."

Alaine allowed herself to toss a smirk of victory in Sir Robert's direction and, taking the stunned squire's arm, guided him in a direction away from the group, where they would have room to battle.

Swordplay with Timor turned out to be more frustration than exercise for Alaine. She knew the boy had skill, for she had seen him score victories over opponents who would far outmatch her with a sword, in spite of his usual bumbling awkwardness. In fact, when Timor took a blade in his hand his adolescent gawkiness usually disappeared and he became a whipcord-lean package of energy, grace, and skill. It was the reason, Alaine was sure, that Rorik kept the boy as squire and put up with his bumbling wrong-handedness in all else.

But now Timor was naught but a bundle of thumbs. His parries were inadequate and his feints were completely lacking in finesse, or even in strength. He was terrified to raise his blade against her and too bemused by the sight of her to effectively defend himself against her attacks. Alaine pressed him hard, hoping to give him no choice but to come at her in return. She didn't want a rout. She wanted a workout.

Always more than willing to see one of their own made the fool, the little circle of men surrounding the bout chortled and howled with glee at Timor's lack of success. The boy's face reddened with shame while trying inadequately to fend off Alaine's offensive. Suddenly Alaine felt a stab of pity. She had taken advantage of Timor's puppyish tongue-tied devotion and made him disgrace himself in front of his friends, all because she had felt hurt and out of place and wanted to prove she still belonged in this haunt of her childhood. There was no reason poor Timor should suffer for her troubles. Abruptly she lowered her blade, leaving Timor looking at her in ill-concealed relief.

"That's enough," she said. "Thank you, Timor, for trying to make me look good."

Timor looked at her in startled surprise, then grinned and poked out his scrawny chest as though what she'd said were really true. Their audience scoffed and called loudly for them to continue the battle. Then all sound abruptly died.

Alaine turned to see what caused the sudden uneasy silence and fell into the trap of Rorik's green eyes looking down at her from the intimidating height afforded by his chestnut stallion. All other eyes were diligently studying the ground, leaving the two of them suspended in a world of their own.

Rorik's voice was calm when he finally spoke, but Alaine detected a sharp edge of steel that made her heart thud with apprehension. "What do you here, my lady?" he said politely enough. The frown that lowered brows over deep-set eyes belied his easy words.

She tilted her chin at a stubborn angle. "I merely take some exercise with these good fellows, my lord."

A glacial green glance swept her apparel and the blade in her hand. Then his gaze moved to Timor, who, red-faced and breathless, was trying hard to lose himself in the sparse crowd. "Kind of them to accommodate you in your play." His face was blank. "If these men have nothing better to do than to battle with women, I'm sure Sihtric can relieve their boredom."

The onlookers hastily took the hint of dismissal and disappeared toward the outer gate. Rorik swung down from his charger. He advanced toward her until he was standing uncomfortably close, but Alaine refused to give ground.

"Perhaps, since you insist on acting like a child, you should be punished like a child." Rorik raised an inquiring brow and flexed a hand.

Alaine's eyes grew wide. She could imagine that his large callused hand, landing with force on any part of her body, would surely crush bones and flesh like fragile porcelain. She glared at him defiantly, forgetting her recent resolve to become a good and biddable wife.

"You don't dare touch me!" she challenged.

"Don't I?" he asked. "I surely will if you even once more engage in such a display of childishness. I think you are in rare need of a hand across your backside."

"You are not man enough to deliver it, villain!"

He chuckled and lowered his hand. "You will soon discover what I am man enough to deliver. I would give you a well-deserved beating, but I've no wish to ruin the pleasures of our wedding night by bruising your nether parts unnecessarily."

Her eyes grew wide as he unknowingly added fuel to Gunnor's well-laid fire. "You are an animal!" she gritted from between angrily clenched teeth.

He smiled. "That may be true, my lady. But it's a fault I've oft made use of, and never regretted."

She was speechless with anger and turned her back on him, staring with a fixed frown into the distance. He picked up the blunted blade Timor had dropped, then looked at the similar blade still clenched in Alaine's hand.

"You should choose a more worthy opponent than poor Timor, little rebel. If you've a need to vent your temper through battle, try your mettle against me. These timid lads wouldn't dare to smite you a goodly blow."

Alaine sniffed in disdain. "I've no wish to fight you."

"You've been doing nothing but fighting me since we

first met, my lady. Perhaps for once we should fight with weapons other than words. The outcome may be instructive.''

She snorted contemptuously and turned to face him. ''You think to gloat just because you can best me with a sword? A poor knight you would be if you couldn't best a woman half your weight and strength. What kind of a contest is that?''

He chuckled and hefted the light sword in his hand. ''Seems we once did contest with your weapons, and even then you cried unfair. You claim to be knight in all but name, yet you are afraid to fight me with a knight's blade. You brag of your skill yet will fight only boys who are bedazzled by your winsome face.''

That was the last straw. Alaine lifted her blade and faced him across the scuffed ground where she and Timor had fought. At the moment she wanted nothing more than to bring the grinning jackanapes to the ground in ignominious and thoroughly shameful defeat.

But of course, it was not Rorik who was brought to the ground in defeat. He played with her for a time while he accustomed himself to the light blade and felt out what skills she had at her command.

''You fight like a woman.'' He laughed after easily fending off her most furious attack. ''You let your temper do your thinking.''

His taunt brought her fury to a rolling boil, and she proceeded to prove out the truth of his words, made even angrier by the fact that Rorik looked like he was having a good time, as in fact he was. He brought the mock battle to a swift end, though, and Alaine found her sword flying from her hand and Rorik's blade hovering lightly above her breast. A sudden unreasoning fear gripped her, not so much of the blade but of the hand that held it and could thrust it mercilessly into her heart. She threw herself back, lost her balance, and ended her fall ignobly against the hard trunk of a tree at the edge of the orchard.

Rorik cast his blade hastily aside and knelt beside her as she ruefully rubbed the slight lump that was sprouting where the tree had taken its toll. Carefully he parted her hair and examined the injured spot.

"It's naught but a little lump," he proclaimed, then shook his head wonderingly at her behavior. "Silly maid. Did you imagine that I would actually hurt you? Haven't I pledged to wed you in two days' time? Do you think I want my bride spitted on my own sword?"

She answered with a surly silence.

"I but wanted to show you who is truly master here, and the foolishness of this game you play. You should concentrate on being a woman, Alaine, instead of trying to be something you can never be. A woman's use is in her lord's bed and seeing to his home, not fighting with his squires."

Alaine frosted him with an ice-blue glare. "I've no wish to grace your bed and bear with your swinish rutting!"

Rorik threw back his head and laughed. "Is that what's bothering you, my surly little demoiselle?

She wanted to spit in the face of his laughter, but wisely restrained herself.

"It's but a part of marriage, Alaine," he said, not unkindly. "You must bear my heirs, and so put up with the attentions of my body. And I, likewise, must beget heirs to carry on my bloodline. So it seems I must be satisfied with having a skinny little boy-woman beneath me in bed."

Her eyes narrowed as he pulled her to her feet and swept his gaze assessingly over her slender frame. She missed the twinkle in his eyes as he lifted her to the back of the big destrier and mounted behind her.

"It seems, my lady," he said, smiling as he felt her stiffen at his touch, "that we both must make the best of a bad bargain."

CHAPTER 11

"Wake up! Wake up!" Mathilde sang in a merry voice. "Out of bed! It's your wedding day!"

Alaine ignored her stepsister with determination. Joanna had allowed her privacy on the last night of her maidenhood, taking herself and her daughters to make their beds in a chamber on the lower floor. Father Sebastian had dutifully advised Alaine to fill the dark hours of solitude with prayer. He seemed to think she might need divine help to attain the blessed state of a good and dutiful wife. But prayer had not assuaged her dread of the day to come, and sleep, coming only in fitful moments plagued by nightmares, had afforded little escape. Mathilde's voice brought her only groggily awake. The ragged remnants of uneasy dreams lingered in the back of her mind, making her even more reluctant to emerge from her bed and face the dreaded reality of the day.

"Go away!" she mumbled as her stepsister pulled open the heavy bed curtains. Stubbornly she turned her face into the pillow.

Mathilde would have none of it. "Rise and face the day, lazypuss! Water is being heated for your bath and Hadwisa is on her way up with hot bread, honey, and spiced wine."

Alaine's eyelids creaked reluctantly open. Giving Mathilde a hard time was one thing, Hadwisa quite another. If she weren't up by the time that good soul came through the door, she was quite likely to find herself urged to move by

a sharp slap to whatever part of her anatomy was closest to
the old nurse.

"You've got to get up and bathe and dress," Mathilde
admonished. "Do you want to leave such a handsome groom
standing at the portal of the church?"

"Yes!" Alaine declared. "I'd like to leave him standing
at the portal to Hell!"

Mathilde smiled indulgently, and Alaine sighed. There
was no satisfaction in baiting someone who simply wouldn't
fight back. She experimentally stuck a toe out from beneath the thick furs on the bed.

"It's cold out there."

"Not for long," the unceasingly cheerful Mathilde assured her. "Gwyne was up to tend the fire while you were
still fast asleep. See how it blazes on the hearth? Soon it
will take the chill from the room."

A determined Mathilde ignored her stepsister's grimace
and moved to open the heavy shutters that blocked out the
sunshine. In contrast to Alaine's mood, the morning was
bright and golden. The cheerful yellow square of sunlight
that fell across the bed did nothing to cheer the reluctant
bride, however, and it was with studied reluctance that she
emerged the rest of the way from her fur cocoon.

The steamy bath felt good, and even Hadwisa's less
than gentle scrubbing was welcome, for it was something
Alaine had endured since she was a mere babe. It reminded
her that some of her old life would still surround her after
this dreadful day was done. At least the dragon was not
carting her off to some unfamiliar keep in a land where
everyone she met would be a stranger. Her life would be
different, yes. She would go to the big chamber and sleep
in her father's bed with a man she must call husband. The
heavy ring of keys would go from Joanna's belt to hers,
and she would have duties and responsibilities to occupy
her every hour of the day. No more sporting around the
exercise grounds. No more long walks alone in the
orchard. No more greeting the sunrise at her father's
grave. But she would still have Joanna, Mathilde, little
Judith, and dear, familiar Hadwisa. That at least would

remain the same. She tried to take comfort in the thought.

The bath was finished and she was wrapped in a soft linen robe while Hadwisa brushed her hair dry in front of the fire. She drew a frown from that good woman when she refused to eat a morsel of the bread, honey, and dried fruit the old nurse had brought from the kitchen.

"Wedding day nerves!" the old nurse complained, plying the hairbrush with more than necessary vigor. "You'll do yourself better to be eatin' a few bites. Or at least take some of the spiced wine to settle your stomach."

Alaine adamantly shook her head, and Judith, who had climbed up on the bed to watch the preparations, puckered her little face in a frown.

"What's wedding day nerves, Haddie?" she piped.

The nurse laughed. "That's the fluttery stomach that silly young maidens get when they're bound to be wed. Like a skittish filly not yet broke to 'arness."

"Why?" Judith inquired innocently.

"Because being a woman is different from being a maid. And maids gently reared give too much importance to fearing the things they cannot change."

"Are you fluttery, Alaine?" Judith grinned mischievously.

"No! I'm not!" Alaine snapped, then immediately regretted her sharp tone. "I'm sorry, Jude," she apologized. "I guess I am a bit fluttery. I didn't sleep too well last night."

Hadwisa snorted. "Well, I'll wager you'll not be sleepin' that well tonight, either, if I've taken proper measure of Sir Rorik."

"Haddie!" Mathilde frowned. "Poor Alaine. You're not being much help!"

"Tch!" Hadwisa clucked. " 'Tis not so bad, my lamb. Before morn you'll be purrin' like a kitten and wonderin' why you tried to dodge this marriage. 'Tis beyond me why young maids go so pale and goosey at the thought of a man doing what comes so natural. When I was a young girl we'd be just grateful to get an 'usband. Sir Rorik's a good man. He'll treat you proper like a man should treat a woman."

"I think Sir Rorik is beautiful!" Judith added dreamily. "When I grow up I'm going to marry a knight just like him—strong and wonderful and very brave! And he's going to make me a great lady, just like you're going to be, Alaine. And he'll have black curly hair and green eyes just like Sir Rorik.''

Alaine snorted. Judith was carrying her silly hero-worship entirely too far.

The hours of the morning flew away with breathtaking speed. Alaine was pampered and oiled and combed and was begged once more to eat. The sky-blue chemise and lighter blue gown that Mathilde had labored over was a perfect accent to Alaine's golden hair, blue eyes, and soft ivory skin. Her hair was left unbound and trailed gloriously over her back and shoulders in soft gilt waves, covered only by a gauzy headrail of matching blue. Examining herself in the polished silver mirror, even Alaine admitted she looked every inch a vision of loveliness. Mathilde and Hadwisa had outdone themselves. She had never thought of herself as anything but quite ordinary looking. And here they had somehow created a swan out of a common ordinary goose.

Joanna smiled broadly when she came into Alaine's chamber to inspect the bride and give her blessings.

"You look lovely, dear. Sir Rorik will be so pleased."

Alaine frowned at the reminder of who she was meant to impress. "Yes. He'll be surprised, too, I'll wager." She still smarted from him naming her a skinny boy-woman just two days before.

Joanna lifted her brows at the hint of rebellion in her stepdaughter's voice. She reached out and, taking her hand, patted it. "Remember why you are doing this, Alaine. And remember, you're not a child any longer."

"I remember," Alaine confirmed in a tight voice. "I'll make the dragon a good wife. He won't have reason to bellow." Or at least not much reason, she added silently to herself. She would have to be dead to be that perfect.

The wedding procession was glorious. Or at least everyone but Alaine thought so. The bride was benumbed and allowed herself to be handed from one attendant to another, told to sit here or stand there. She was mounted on a beautifully groomed white mule outfitted in a harness of gold and trappings of scarlet samite. The same trappings had been used for the weddings of Ste. Claire women for generations, and after the ceremony they would be once again tucked neatly away in the *chambre de tapisserie*. The ladies who rode with Alaine to the church were also mounted on mules. They crowded close behind her as the procession wound its way through the bailey to the outer gate, through the far exercise grounds to the road that bordered the orchard.

Rorik had declared the day a holiday for all who owed duty to Ste. Claire. The villagers and castle folk were dressed in their finest and crowded about the procession with enthusiastic clamor. Some threw dried flowers in her path, some pelted her with grain they had pilfered from the storehouses. All wished her a good and fruitful marriage with shouts and songs. They knew a hefty feast would be awaiting them when bride and groom finally emerged from the church as man and wife, and that added to their merry spirits. Rorik had seen to it that all of the serfs and peasants would remember this wedding well. He wanted no grumblings that he had not done proper honor to his bride, and no more complaints from the villagers and castlefolk about his treatment of their precious lady.

The procession was slow as the mules made their way through the cheering crowd, but Alaine was in no hurry to meet her fate—this final ceremony that would seal her life and her lands as Rorik's, forever. She let her mind slip back to the day before, to an equally important ceremony where she had been required to swear her oath and allegiance to Rorik as his vassal and do homage to him for the fief of Ste. Claire. The words they had spoken had been familiar to her, a cornerstone of feudal law. But as she'd spoken them they had taken on a new and ominous meaning, making her realize how trapped she was, making her want to get up and flee from where she knelt before Rorik's chair. She could see the scene again in her mind, and hear the words with which she finally and irrevocably admitted Rorik's lordship over her.

"Sir Rorik, I, Alaine de Ste. Claire, enter into your

homage and faith and become your man, by mouth and hands, and I swear and promise to keep faith and loyalty to you against all others, and I swear to guard your rights with all my strength."

And he had answered her in his strong voice. "We do promise to you, vassal Alaine, that we and our heirs will guarantee to you the lands held of us, to you and your heirs against every creature within our power to hold these lands in peace and quiet."

Placing her hand on the tiny box containing, Father Sebastian told her, splinters from the true cross, Alaine gave voice to the words she had memorized, but only now taken to heart.

"In the name of the Holy Trinity and in reverence of these sacred relics, I, Alaine, swear that I will truly keep the promise that I have taken, and will always remain faithful to Sir Rorik, my seigneur."

Then Rorik had given her the kiss of lordship, a chaste brush of the lips that had nevertheless set her nerves to vibrating. With that kiss he had officially given her Ste. Claire, and today, with another sort of kiss, he would take it away again.

Finally they crossed the bridge over the River Ste. Claire and moved into the town itself. The lane leading to the church was decorated with colorful streamers that waved in the breeze. One waved too close to Alaine's mule and sent the beast skittering over the paving stones and against the mule next to it, threatening to pile them both against a masonry wall. A guard hastened to grab the bridles of both animals until they were calm once more.

"Sorry, my lady," he said with an embarrassed grin. "Guess they're a bit skittish, with the crowd so close."

The mule wasn't the only one feeling skittish, Alaine thought as they drew close to the church and she saw the crowd gathered before the portal. Duke William himself was mounted somewhere in the retinue of noblemen, along with the important barons of the west, and some not so important. Gunnor had told her the day before that Gilbert de Prestot was here. She had flown to Rorik and demanded why the knave had been invited. He had merely shrugged, saying the man was no enemy to him, and he would keep it that way a while yet. Then he'd had the nerve to inquire why mention of the man threw her into such a state.

"He tried to take Ste. Claire from me and force me to the altar!" she'd replied hotly, thinking that was surely enough reason to never want to see the varlet again.

Rorik merely smiled. "I have done much the same deed," he commented. "And yet you show no such agitation with me."

He had looked at her suspiciously, wondering if there weren't more to the incident with Gilbert de Prestot than he thought. Gunnor had hinted that Gilbert had been a favored suitor. She insisted that Alaine's reluctance to wed the man was but a show for the benefit of her people, who despised him as a longtime enemy who regularly raided their farms, destroyed their homes, and killed their livestock. Was Alaine agitated now because she truly hated him, or was this but another show to hide her true feelings? A sudden surge of possessive outrage had surprised him.

Alaine had mistaken the jealousy that fleetingly darkened Rorik's features for a look of anger, and merely turned away in a huff, wondering what made men so damnably obtuse.

Rorik and his attendant noblemen met the bride and her party of ladies as they halted before the church door. The noble guests were all mounted on fine graceful palfreys whose smaller size and gentler temperament made them more suitable than the high-strung destriers as mounts for this peaceful occasion. Only Rorik was mounted on his great warhorse, and Alaine took good note of the fact. She wondered if her groom was making a symbolic statement. Did he regard this marriage more of a war than a truce?

Both parties dismounted. Rorik lifted Alaine from her mount and escorted her wordlessly to the church portal, where Father Sebastian greeted them with a paternal smile. The priest made the sign of the cross and uttered a short prayer, then, there on the stone steps that led to the church door, the couple knelt before him and said their vows before all the gathered people, villager and noble alike.

Rorik's voice was strong and clear as he repeated the sacred words. Not to be outdone, Alaine also attempted to make her words ring out in a clear and confident tone. But her throat was tight. Her voice faltered and her bumbling tongue seemed to be tied around her teeth. Disgracefully, the hand that was clasped firmly in Rorik's started to tremble. She felt Rorik's fingers tighten in a gentle squeeze. Did he intend encouragement, she wondered, or a threat?

After an eternity had passed, the vows were finished. In loud and ringing voice the priest proclaimed the worth and extent of the dowry that the bride brought to her marriage, and then detailed the dower that the groom was bestowing on his bride. The crowd made appropriate sounds of appreciation of the wealth of the couple, as they were expected to. Only then were the bride and groom allowed off their aching knees. They stood, and Rorik grinned down at her with the devil's own light in his eyes as the priest invited him to kiss the bride and seal the vows. Alaine stood benumbed as Rorik with one hand tilted her chin up to meet his mouth while the other hand slipped behind her head, holding her steady under the caress of his lips. It was not much of a kiss—a light and lingering brush of flesh on flesh. But all the same it left Alaine breathless. She felt surrounded and possessed by the power of his hard warrior's body—a not altogether unpleasant sensation, she discovered. When they parted it was as though cold water had been dumped on a new warm blossom that was unfolding in her soul, and she drew back and looked at her husband in startled confusion.

"Smile, my lady," he whispered softly. "Your people are cheering for you."

Indeed they were, though until that moment Alaine had not heard the din breaking in waves around them. Mechanically, as if in a slow-moving dream, she turned and waved, and Rorik did the same. The cheers were still growing in volume when Father Sebastian signaled them to follow him into the church.

The marriage Mass that followed was long and elaborate. Father Sebastian seemed determined to make up for the hasty ceremony Gilbert had labored to make him perform. Alaine knelt and stood and sat on cue, giving no thought to the Latin chants and prayers that the priest intoned in endless succession. She was mesmerized by the imposing physical presence of the man who knelt and stood and sat next to her, and her mouth still burned from that brief and gentle contact with his. Her mind kept wandering to what the night would bring, though she thought it a very unholy thing to be thinking on in God's sacred house. She hoped that under the circumstances God might understand her distraction.

After the Mass was completed Rorik and Alaine rode together back to the keep, only on the return trip Alaine was mounted not on a mule but on a splendid mare whose fine breeding showed in every graceful line and every spirited toss of her beautiful head. She was a wedding gift from Rorik, and Alaine had been hard-pressed to contain her excitement within dignified bounds when Rorik led her to the gentle-eyed mare. For a moment she forgot the circumstances of the gift. She even ignored Rorik's half-amused remark that the mare was a more appropriate mount for a gentle lady than the destrier Alaine was wont to ride. Like her father, Alaine had always admired fine horseflesh. Ste. Claire bred horses that were known as the best in western Normandy, and Alaine's discerning eye immediately recognized that the mare would add beauty and soundness to their stock. She wondered that Rorik could have guessed that this gift above all others would be treasured by his reluctant bride. Had it been a mere happy accident, she wondered, or had Rorik actually looked to please her on this day?

A feast of rare proportions awaited them in the hall, and as the newly wedded couple and their noble guests sat down to table, they were pleasantly assaulted by aromas of spitted quail, roast lamb, pork, and venison, soups of cheese, fish, watercress, and cabbage. Hard cider, wine, and beer were in plentiful supply, along with serat, a drink of fermented buttermilk boiled with onions and garlic and cooled in a closed vessel. Maudie and her kitchen drudges had been laboring all the week long and had done themselves proud.

Tables were laid for the villagers and castlefolk in the bailey, and they were served a similar fare. After two long years of poor crops and sparse victuals, the common folk laid to with gusto and did justice to Rorik's hospitality. Alaine fervently hoped the next season's harvest was plentiful, for surely the castle storerooms would be near to cleaned out by this sumptuous feast.

In spite of the tempting dishes laid before her, Alaine found that she could force very little down her throat. She smiled at her guests and played the proper hostess, but assiduously avoided the eyes of the man sitting beside her. The fact that this fierce knight, this harsh stranger, was now her husband was an idea she couldn't yet bend her mind around. And a casual comment by Gunnor that she would feel more like a wife once the night was done made her feel no better.

Rorik also said little and seemed to brood into his beer. Sihtric gave him no respite and pricked at him sorely with chortled speculations about the married state. The new master of Ste. Claire would so much enjoy the pleasures of hearth and home and a comely wife, Sihtric chortled, that he would forget about Brix. The Norseman ignored Rorik's black looks and, as his tankard was emptied and refilled and emptied again, his guffaws grew louder and his jests more bawdy. More than once a sternly disapproving Joanna had to avoid the caress of his hand, which seemed to have a propensity for landing on her thigh. Rorik finally gave his friend up as a lost cause and set about the task of ignoring him. From the black scowl on her husband's face as he endured Sihtric's teasing, Alaine wondered if Rorik, also, had his doubts about this marriage to which he had bound himself.

Everyone was well sated by the time dessert was served, but somehow most found room in their already stuffed bellies for the baked pears, peeled walnuts, dates, and dried figs. As the dessert disappeared and the guests sighed in contentment, Alaine and Joanna, as the senior ranking ladies of Ste. Claire, passed around the tables with baskets to collect leftover food for the poor. Today the peasants and serfs were as well fed as the barons and their ladies, but on the morrow beggars would still come to the gates. As Father Sebastian said, the poor and starving were always with them, if only to afford noble ladies the opportunity to exercise the virtue of charity.

As the afternoon wore on, the diners in the great hall adjourned to lively celebrations in the bailey. The day was warm for the season, and many of the noble folk made mellow by beer and wine were quick to join with the villagers in games of hot cockles, ragman's roll, and guilles. Several of the more staid barons and their ladies and a few of Rorik's older knights elected to remain by the fire and indulge in the more genteel entertainment of chess and backgammon. Rorik remained in the hall in conversation with a minor baron who, Alaine knew, had small holdings close by her lands in the Channel Isles. Those lands as well as the fields and forests of Ste. Claire were now her husband's to administer in her name, she thought ruefully. Suddenly wanting to be free of her new husband's disturbing presence, the bride followed the guests out of the keep, across the small courtyard, and into the bailey. Mathilde immediately latched onto her arm.

"How does it feel, being a married woman?" The younger girl had a gleam of mischief in her eye.

Before Alaine could answer with some casual inanity, Gunnor joined them and put her acid tongue to work. "How would she know how it feels?" she said. "She is not truly the wife yet. Ask her in the morning how it feels to be under a man's power and be slave to his base desires."

Mathilde flung her sister a disgusted look. "I didn't notice you cringing away when Rorik offered to find us husbands. You decry the woes of marriage and wail about what rutting beasts men are, but you don't hesitate to enter

into that state again. I think you are merely trying to upset
Alaine!''

Gunnor sniffed haughtily. ''Marriage is woman's lot in
this world. I bear with it as every Christian woman should.
That doesn't mean I like it. And as for Alaine, she's made
of stronger stuff than to be frightened by what every
woman bears without complaint. After all, she—with her
men's clothes and her men's ways—is so much stronger
than we mere women. Aren't you, sister?''

Alaine gritted her teeth and wished Gunnor would drop
into a hole and stay there for the rest of the afternoon and
evening. The older girl was trying to get under her skin,
and succeeding admirably. No matter that Gunnor was a
bitter and small-minded shrew, her barbs were finding their
target.

Joanna, also, well-meaning though she was, added to
the tightly strung tension pulling at Alaine's nerves. She
found myriad different ways throughout the afternoon to
remind Alaine that she must do her duty by her new lord
and seek to please him well. Remember Adela, she cautioned,
Rannulf de Carentan's foolish wife. What happened to her
could happen to any shrewish, stubborn woman.

So Alaine's afternoon was not a festive one. Her gut
roiled and her stomach knotted, and as evening shadows
threatened the celebration, she fled to her chamber to lose
what little food she had managed to eat. She contemplated
the wisdom of simply remaining in her chamber when a
sudden commotion in the bailey below drew her attention.
She peered out the window, straining to see through the
failing light what tumult caused this sudden interruption in
the gaiety. A knot of men were moving toward the outer
gate. She could make out Rorik's tall form and the shorter,
stouter frame of Sir Guillaume. The other three with them
she couldn't identify at this distance. Another group of
about ten men were advancing to meet them. This larger
group was surrounded by guards from the gatehouse. The
tall, lanky figure in the front almost looked like—no! it
couldn't be! Garin! It could be no other.

Alaine snatched up her cloak and flew from the chamber. She was breathless by the time she reached the bailey and pushed her way through the crowd. Heedless of raised brows that followed her bold passage, she hurried toward the little conclave of men. Garin and Rorik were staring at each other wordlessly. Garin was unarmed, she noted with relief. Rorik was fingering the hilt of his sword but, right now at least, did not seem to be actively threatening the younger man.

"Garin!" she said as she pushed into the group. "Oh, Garin!" She could think of nothing else to say.

"My lady." Garin regarded her assessingly. If he expected to see bruises or other signs of abuse he was disappointed. But the signs of strain were there for him to see. There was a pallor about her that hadn't been there before, and a new sad maturity that didn't fit well with the impulsive child-woman he knew so well. "News of your marriage finally traveled to the far reaches of the forest. I came to hear it from your own lips."

"It's true." Alaine lifted her chin a notch, hoping he would accept what she said and understand why she had to let events happen as they had. "Sir Rorik is my lord, and the new lord of Ste. Claire." Oh, Garin! she cried in her heart. Foolish, foolish Garin! Why did you not come sooner?

A shadow of resignation darkened Garin's face. He turned back to Rorik. "It seems my cause is lost. I thought to defend the lady, but it seems she no longer needs my sword in her service. Therefore I and my men come to beg your amnesty, and to enter your service if you will have us."

Rorik's face was set into unyielding lines, and Alaine's heart thumped with apprehension.

"The time for amnesty is long past, Sir Guardian of Ste. Claire." He regarded the youth with cold eyes that revealed none of what he was thinking. "Your lady long ago passed the word that her loyal men were to surrender to me. Did you not hear it?"

"I heard," Garin admitted in a tight voice. "But I didn't believe. I thought she was acting under duress."

The hard planes of Rorik's face eased a bit as he lifted one brow in amusement. "It is very difficult to get the Lady Alaine to do anything under duress."

Garin's mouth twitched in a nervous smile.

Alaine moved forward and placed her hand on Rorik's arm. "Sir Rorik, please."

The hard muscle of his arm jumped beneath her touch, and she fought the urge to pull back as though she'd laid her hand on a hot stove. Her eyes pleaded with him in silent appeal. For herself she had never begged a thing. But Garin was her true friend, her brother of the heart. For Garin she would beg.

Rorik sighed. "What name do you go by, Sir Guardian."

"I am Garin de Longchamps, my lord."

"Well, Garin de Longchamps, since it seems my lady puts so much value on your life, and seeing that this is a day of celebration, I grant you your amnesty, and all your men with you. I have a need of good loyal men, and if that's what you prove to be, then we may both yet profit from this."

The stiffness in Garin's frame eased a bit as he bowed his head to his new lord. Alaine breathed a sigh of relief, drawing Rorik's eyes to her.

"I give you this man's life as a wedding present, wife. If he proves unworthy, I may take it out of your hide as well as his." But his mouth curved up in a smile that belied the harshness of his words. "Is this the same Garin that your stepmother has so often lauded as squire to your late father?"

"Garin was my father's senior squire, my lord."

Rorik looked at the tall youth with an assessing eye. "You seem overage for a squire's post, good Garin, and if the trouble you caused me is any proof of your ability, you should have your spurs. There is a tourney a week hence to end the celebration of our wedding. What would you think to ride that day and prove your worth to be a knight? If you fight well, in Sir Geoffrey's place I will gift you with a good horse and arms and see you knighted."

Garin's eyes glowed, but his words had an edge of

doubt. "You are generous, Sir Rorik. But I would rather earn my own way."

Rorik grinned. "You will, Garin. Never doubt that you will."

Alaine suppressed an unladylike whoop of joy, but her eyes brimmed over with gratitude. "My lord . . . I . . . thank you . . . I . . ."

For a moment Rorik's smile seemed to hold an answering warmth, but then, as though he had caught himself in error, his face became stern again. "We have guests to see to, my lady." He gestured for her to precede him back to the waiting crowd.

Sihtric watched the two as they disappeared into the crowd that was drifting toward the keep, whose warmth beckoned now that the shadows of evening had merged into a chilly gloom. The stern visage Rorik had turned on his new lady hadn't fooled the Norseman one bit. He shook his head in wonder, thinking that the unassailable Stone Dragon had cracked at last.

The warmth and light of the great hall was welcome, and the guests set about once more draining the keep of the wine and beer and hard cider stored in its vaults. Alaine was almost happy. She found it easy to forget her own doubts and fears in the joy of seeing her husband's leniency—nay, generosity—toward her dear friend. So it was like a flood of icy water on her glowing mood when she caught sight of the tall, silver-haired form of Gilbert de Prestot across the hall. He saw her at the same time, and as their eyes met he gave her a smile that brought loathsome memories racing into her mind. He immediately broke off his conversation with the group around him and moved toward her. Desperately Alaine tried to think of a way to flee without causing an embarrassing scene.

"Congratulations, Lady Alaine," Gilbert said smoothly, as though nothing untoward had ever happened between them. "It seems you've made quite a conquest."

Alaine saw Rorik glance casually toward them and wished he would come to her rescue, but he seemed content to observe from a distance.

"You play the winsome wife well, my lady," Gilbert commented into her frosty silence. "But then, you don't really know this man you've taken to husband, do you?"

Alaine glared at him. "I know him well enough to know he suits my taste much more than you, Sir Knight."

Gilbert merely chuckled. "Don't be so harsh on me, my sweet. After all, you've not yet tasted the dregs of the cup you've been given to drink. Sir Rorik is well known to hold women in contempt. He'll not treat you gently, my little dove."

"What would you know of gentleness, Sir Gilbert? You are naught but a knave in my eyes!"

Gilbert shook his head as if in pity, eying her with an unwarranted spark of heat in his gaze. "I would have treated that delicate body of yours as it deserved, little Alaine. You cannot expect the same of him." He glanced over to where Rorik stood. Only Alaine could see the contempt in his eyes.

"I think I've heard enough of your prattle!" Alaine turned to go, not caring if she appeared rude. There was a limit to how long one could speak to a toad and not get warts.

But the toad grabbed her arm. A smile spread across his face—a slimy smile, Alaine thought as she backed away from his touch.

"Don't despair, little love," he assured her. "I have not yet lost hope of having you—and your lands—as my own. You and your lands, and maybe more."

He raised her hand and pressed a kiss to her shrinking skin as Rorik watched from across the hall.

CHAPTER 12

The night hung heavy and black on the land. Not even a sliver of moon softened the darkness that wrapped the forests and meadows in its chilly embrace. Alaine stood at the window looking out at the stygian gloom and feeling that it had somehow slipped in through the stones of the keep to invade her heart. Gone was the warmth that had filled her at Garin's good fortune. The nervous energy that had buoyed her through the day was fled with the sun. Now the night had come, and her time of reckoning was near.

"Would you cover that window, Alaine?" Joanna's voice seemed to shiver as a draught of cold air set the flames of the tallow lanterns and candles to dancing. "Come back over here and let Hadwisa do your hair. It would be a disgrace to not be properly ready to meet your bridegroom."

Numbly Alaine refastened the thin-scraped skins that covered the window and closed the shutters. Then she obediently sat before the fire and let the soothing strokes of Hadwisa's hairbrush ease some of the tension from her small frame. Joanna had helped her remove her wedding finery and now, she had on nothing at all. Her eyes roved unwillingly to the huge bed that seemed to squat in the middle of the chamber in obscene threat. The curtains hung open and the linen and furs were turned back. Some hours earlier the bed had been strewn with rose petals and blessed by good Father Sebastian, who was now in the hall well and happily into his cups. The scented dry petals beckoned like a bait to lure the hapless victim close. Soon,

Alaine thought, she would be lying in that bed, and Rorik would be lying close beside her. Her mind went black at the thought. She couldn't imagine how she would survive the night locked in that harsh knight's embrace.

"Stand up and let me look at you," Joanna ordered brusquely.

Alaine did as she was bidden.

Joanna frowned momentarily. "Such a shame it's not spring. A circlet of wild flowers would go well on your brow, or perhaps a string of blossoms wound through your hair. But you look well enough, I suppose. You really have grown into a beautiful woman, Alaine, for all that your hips are a bit narrow and your breasts on the small side. Rorik should be well pleased."

Alaine grew a shade paler. At the moment she cared nothing about whether or not the dragon was pleased by his prey. She felt like a fat pig being prepared for the spitting. Her only hope was that she could keep her courage through the night and not disgrace herself before the beast who had forced her into this. That would please him well, she thought, to see her broken and cowering as some weak-willed goose of a girl. "Ye're lovely as a queen, my lamb," Hadwisa added, beaming with pride.

Alaine allowed Joanna to lead her to the bed and settle her in it so she was sitting decorously with her back against the pillows and the furs over her lap. Her stepmother smiled encouragingly as she noted the ashen color of the bride's face. "Remember that all girls must become women someday, my dear. Just do your duty and please your husband. Everything will work out fine."

Hadwisa kissed her cheek and chafed one of her cold hands between her large warm ones, as if willing life back into her numb body. "Don't fret, my lamb. No man could resist the likes of you. You'll 'ave that surly dragon actin' like a tame lapdog before the night is out. You mark my words."

Alaine managed a smile for her old nurse. "I'm quite all right, Haddie. When have you ever known me to be afraid of anything?"

"That's my girl." Hadwisa smiled and patted a pale cheek.

Then she was left alone to await the coming of her husband and his attendants. The room suddenly seemed colder without the presence of her stepmother and her nurse. Alaine shivered and pulled the furs up around her shoulders.

Long minutes passed and the groom didn't come. The sounds of merrymaking in the hall carried up to Alaine's ears and made her wonder what was delaying her husband from his duty. Was he deliberating delaying to make her fear all the greater? Or did the thought of spending his passion on a skinny boy-woman, as he had called her, sit ill on his gut?

With irritation adding to the nervous roiling of her stomach, Alaine flung off the furs and stalked to the wardrobe. Her clothes and possessions had all been moved to the lord's chamber earlier in the day, but their order had been mixed up in the process. It took her a long moment to find what she was looking for, but finally she pulled out a long woolen cloak and wrapped it around her shoulders. It covered her from neck to toes. With a defiant look on her face she pulled the cloak more tightly around her and moved to sit by the fire. She had no intention of freezing herself stiff, sitting on that bed like some virgin on an altar of sacrifice while Rorik reveled below in the warmth of the hall.

Her defiance was short-lived. Before many more minutes passed heavy boots rang on the stone stairway that led to the chamber. Masculine voices lifted in song and ribald laughter accompanied the dreaded footsteps.

"Your dove awaits, good Rorik," one unfamiliar voice slurred. "Need you help in plucking the soft little bird?"

"Nay, he'll need no help!" another offered. "The hunt is over and the quarry neatly snared. And our Rorik was always one to end the hunt with shaft sunk deep and true."

Drunken laughter and the sound of someone stumbling heavily against the door made Alaine flinch.

"Likely the poor maid will find herself sprouting with child on the morn, so well does this knight wield his weapon!" Sir Guillaume's voice guffawed in overly loud tones.

More laughter followed along with a call from the hall

below. "Beware, Sir Rorik. Once the chase is done the
sport loses excitement and the blood cools. Best make
your mark while your weapon still has its edge!"

The laughter rose in volume as the chamber door opened.
A scuffle followed as Rorik shut the door in the faces of
those who would follow and dropped the bar firmly in
place.

"Begone, you drunken sots!" he ordered with mock
severity. "This is business I can see to myself. Go wallow
in your beer or find your own sport this night."

He turned then to see his bride standing straight and
stiff-backed by the fire with a plain woolen cloak hiding
every curve and swell of her young body. It wasn't the
sight he had expected to greet him. The revelers had held
him below in the hall while his groin had ached and
swelled at the thought of her sitting warm and naked
in his bed.

He raised an inquiring brow. "Is that how you greet
your husband, wife? You look like an icicle wrapped in
wool. I expected a warmer sight to greet my eyes."

"I was cold," Alaine explained. Her chattering teeth
bore witness to her words.

"You'll not long feel the cold," he promised her with a
smile. "Let me take this."

Alaine dodged away as he reached for the cloak. "You've
been drinking," she frowned.

"Of course I've been drinking. It's my wedding day."

"You're drunk," she accused hopefully.

He laughed. "Not even close, my little bride. Rest
assured I can perform my duty as a good husband should.
And in fact, I strain at the leash to begin my labor."

Alaine's eyes dropped from his face and widened. If he
was not literally straining at the leash, he was certainly
straining at his seams. Even the tunic that draped over his
hips couldn't hide his eagerness for what was to come.

"Now end this game, Alaine." His voice was soft and
vibrated with a note of warmth she had never thought to
hear from his lips. "Come here to me."

Her wary gaze flew once again to his face and was

immediately caught by his eyes. The chill of their depths
was gone, replaced by a heated glow. Despite the gentle
tones, his words were weighted with a compelling quality
that made her yield to his command. She had no choice,
she reminded herself grimly. This was her husband who
stood before her. From now until forever she belonged not
to herself, but to him. Slowly she dropped her hands from
where they clutched the wool tightly around her and
moved to stand shivering before him.

He raised one hard-callused hand to her cheek, traced
with his fingers the line of her jaw, then tilted her head up
until he could look into her ice-blue eyes.

"Are you so cold, little bride? Or is it fear that makes
you quiver so?"

"I fear no man," she declared, but the smallness of her
voice was apparent even to her ears.

"That's good." He smiled, seeing the lie, but admiring
the pride behind it. "For there's nothing to fear here."

He reached out to unfasten the clasp holding her cloak.
At the brush of his hand, she flinched but did not move
away. "Let me see now what I have bargained for this
day."

The cloak dropped into a pool of wool around her feet.
She saw his jaw tighten and a muscle twitch below his ear
as his eyes drank in the feminine charms revealed to his
admiring eyes.

"A skinny boy-woman, as you have said," she commented
bitingly. Two spots of color burned on her cheeks as he
ignored her remark and continued his slow, heated perusal.

"I may have gotten more than I bargained for," he
murmured, half to himself. He reached out a hand and
placed it on one delicate breast. Alaine shut her eyes
tightly and gritted her teeth as the warmth of his touch and
the gentleness of the insistent caress sent a frisson of
mingled ice and fire racing down her spine. His thumb
found the peak of her nipple and gently teased until it
stiffened and tingled beneath his hand.

"Demoiselle," he said in a hoarse voice. "You have a

treasure there. Why do you hide yourself behind men's garments and dowdy gowns that do you no justice?''

She twisted away from his caressing hand. ''I've no wish to make myself alluring to men,'' she returned scathingly. ''They regard women as helpless quarry for their sport! But I won't play that game.''

He grinned and turned her toward him. ''And yet it seems a hunter has finally taken up the chase, my little wildcat. And the quarry brought to bay.'' His hands slipped from her shoulders down over the smooth rounded contours of her breasts. She shivered at the raw desire she saw spark in the deep recesses of his eyes. His voice grew low and husky. ''Even now the hunter approaches.'' His hands slipped down over her waist and hips before leaving to rip impatiently at his own clothing. His eyes never left her as one by one he shed his garments and threw them aside. When he stood and his raw masculinity was revealed in aroused glory, Alaine's face flamed with color.

''Have you never seen a naked man before?'' he asked with a throaty chuckle of amusement at her reaction.

''Of course!'' she snapped, turning an even brighter shade of red. ''I have bathed my father, and sometimes seen to the bathing of guests, as a hostess should. But...but never...'' She stuttered and looked away.

''Never so prepared to do honor to your beauty?'' he supplied with a laugh. Then the laughter left his face abruptly. ''Is it maidenly modesty that sets your face aflame? Or fear that I will discover the way has been opened by another? Are you virgin, Alaine?''

She regarded him in amazement.

''You can tell me the truth,'' he urged. ''It makes little difference. I do not value women and their innocence overmuch, but I would do my best to not hurt a virgin bride in making her a woman.''

Alaine's mouth drew into a tight, angry line. ''I would not dishonor any man by coming to his bed soiled by another man's leavings! Not even you would I so dishonor! Of course I am virgin!''

"Well enough, my little bride. I meant no insult. I know you were subject to Gilbert de Prestot before I arrived."

"Gilbert didn't touch me," she insisted. "I am virgin still."

"Then you will not labor under that burden much longer."

He smiled, not knowing why he felt relieved. Usually he preferred experienced women for this sport, not cringing virgins who cried with pain and embarrassment at a man's natural lust. But the thought of being the first with this girl filled him with an unfamiliar feeling of protectiveness. He felt reluctant and achingly impatient at the same time. More than anything he wanted to wipe away the wide-eyed fear he saw on her face and replace it with the wonder of discovered passion.

He quickly unfastened the lacing of her flimsy gown and pushed it down over her shoulders. It slipped slowly, almost caressingly down to lie pooled with the cloak. Her ivory skin seemed to glow in the candlelight as she stood shivering in alabaster perfection, but he took only a small moment to appreciate the view. His body was demanding release, and aesthetic appreciation was a poor second to the feel of warm soft flesh against his.

Before she could cringe or dodge away he picked her up in his arms and laid her gently on the bed. She reached for the furs and attempted to pull them up over her, but his hand caught her wrist in a gentle vise and he shook his head.

"Can we not at least snuff the candles and lanterns?"

"Nay," he smiled. "The sight of you pleases me. Why do you wish to hide in the dark?"

"It's indecent!" she insisted.

"Between man and wife there is no shame or indecency. Does the sight of me frighten you?"

"Nothing frightens me!" she shot defiantly. "You are no different from other men."

It wasn't quite the truth. While Alaine was no stranger to the sight of a naked male body, never had she seen one quite as magnificent as Rorik's. Broad shoulders tapered to narrow waist, lean hips, and straight muscular legs. The scars of battles past marked him in places, but they only accentuated his hard-muscled, almost animal perfection. With every movement, muscle and sinew rippled beneath smooth skin. Alaine found herself watching with fascination the play of candlelight over the ridges of his chest.

"Do I pass inspection?" he asked with a chuckle.

Alaine jerked her eyes away from him and colored with shame. She dodged the brush of his arm as he settled himself on the bed beside her, pushing herself to the far edge and eyeing him warily.

"What's this?" he frowned. "Do you fear me so much you flee before I even touch you?"

She glared at him in ashen-faced misery as she felt a tight knot of tension twist her gut. The shame of her weakness made Alaine even more miserable, but for the life of her she couldn't move from the spot. Gunnor had spoken of pain and humiliation to be endured, Joanna had lessoned her on duty, but no one had prepared her for the purely physical impact of Rorik reclining on the far side of the bed, magnificently male, disturbingly animal, regarding her like a hungry wolf might look at a fat and helpless ewe.

Her mixture of defiance and misery struck a chord in Rorik. For some reason he loathed to be the cause of this girl's fears.

"My lady," he said gently, reining in his aching passion and trying to temper his voice with patience. "It's not my wont to use force to slake my desires. If you are truly this afraid, we can wait until the time comes when you are more ready to accept your duties as a wife." He surprised himself with his offer. It wasn't like him to be merciful with women, and this one merited his consideration less than most.

Alaine met his eyes in surprise. She had expected a rutting beast who would use rape to gain his ends. If he had the kindness to offer this reprieve, then could this thing truly be as awful as she imagined?

"Nay." She labored to keep her voice firm, but it shook

just the same. "It's the waiting that eats at me. Do the deed and have done with it. I would not wait and wonder through another day."

Rorik suppressed a smile. "Then come here, wife. The deed is hard to do at this distance. And I've the notion should I advance you'd catapult yourself off the bed."

Reluctantly Alaine inched back toward her waiting husband. She flinched as he gathered her to him, but made no struggle. For a moment he simply held her, letting his warmth ease some of the stiffness from her body, but the feel of his manhood, rock hard and hot and insistent against her belly, caused great shudders to course through her body.

He sighed. "I can see the job must be done before your fears are eased."

Gently he pushed her on her back. She lay stiff as a board as his lips descended to caress hers, then trailed across her throat to fasten gently on one erect nipple. He suckled playfully while his hands traversed her flat stomach, swept down her thighs and traveled back up to massage her buttocks. A spark ignited in the pit of Alaine's belly and started a glow that warmed her stiff body. Slowly she relaxed under his expert ministrations. She willed her mind to a blank, for surely if she thought about what he was doing she would go cold with shame.

He felt the tension start to ease from her and doubled his efforts. Kneeling at the foot of the bed, he started with her feet and massaged the tautness from her calves, her thighs, her buttocks, waist, and arms. She couldn't suppress a little moan of pleasure at this careful attention, and unconsciously as his mouth once again paid homage to the perfection of her small breasts, her arms slipped around his neck and her hands kneaded the taut muscles of his back. She felt a new tension in him as his lips descended once more to hers. This time he was less than gentle, and his tongue battled its way past her lips and ravaged the inside of her mouth, claiming its sweet softness for his own. But she was past the need for gentleness. When his mouth lifted its heady attack and placed a quick kiss on the tip of her nose, she was almost sorry. Her body was wanting something more, and the glow had become a fire. His every touch fueled the flames and made her squirm with wanting.

In a quick movement his knee slid between her thighs and his hand slid to her most intimate badge of womanhood. She jumped with sudden fear and tried to clamp her legs shut, but his thigh was wedged firmly between hers.

"Don't close yourself off from me," he breathed. In the candlelight she could see the tension in his face. "It's too late now to flee, my lady. Try to relax. I would not like to cause you pain."

She tensed herself as his fingers probed where none had trespassed before.

"Relax," he urged again, and this time the full force of his manhood was poised at her entrance.

"I can't!" she cried, and tried to scramble away from that eager weapon that would surely rend her apart.

But he held her fast.

"Be brave, little rebel. You are afraid of no man, remember?" With one quick motion he buried the spear of his desire in her warm softness.

Alaine bit her lip and suppressed the cry of pain that leapt into her throat. She tasted her own blood and vowed to not utter one cowardly sound, willing the pain to end before her control broke. She lay rigid and barely breathing, listening to the rapid drumbeat of her husband's heart and wondering how women ever survived a nightly dose of this tearing agony. Then carefully and with gentle control Rorik began to move. He filled her, probed her depths with his hot rigid flesh, withdrew, then gently filled her again. Little by little the pain faded. His movements carried a rhythm that stirred something primitive in the unknown depths of her being. Her blood seemed to heat in her veins, and her heart began a heavy, quick drumbeat that marched in time with Rorik's. Of its own will her body joined in the dance of passion. She opened her eyes to find his face above hers. His eyes caught and held hers, refusing to let her sink back into her own little world.

Something built inside her with every movement, and the fire that had burned earlier became a raging furnace. His steady gaze held her captive, demanding she go further with him into the furnace, challenging her to stay with him as the heat of their desire seared them both. Her world started to swirl around in an eddy that centered on their two joined bodies. Faster and faster it swirled, until finally she was sucked into the vortex and hurled into a world of floating, soaring sensation. She heard Rorik's low, guttural cry and the ecstasy of his throbbing release drove her even higher. She clutched him close as her only life raft in this world of unfamiliar, heartstopping joy.

Alaine opened her eyes to warm darkness. The glow from the dying embers on the hearth was the only light in the room. She didn't remember Rorik snuffing the candles. She didn't remember anything after she had been swept into the storm of his desire.

Rorik moved in his sleep and pulled her closer against him. She tilted up her head where it rested against his shoulder. In the dim light of the coals she could make out the strong line of his jaw and the curve of his lips. Gunnor had been right about one thing. The dragon was handsome, very handsome. How could she ever have denied it? And kind, and patient. Alaine was not so innocent to think all men would have been so tolerant of a reluctant bride's fears and fancies. How could a man who presented such a harsh face to the world show such kindness to a frightened girl? Why would a man who professed contempt for women take the trouble to woo an ignorant virgin away from fear and into joy? Alaine raised herself on one elbow and let her eyes roam in a leisurely manner over Rorik's face. There was more to this man than she had thought. Much more. He was relaxed in his sleep and looked younger and gentler than the man she had vowed to honor and obey only the day before. She smiled to herself, wondering what his men would think to know their Stone

Dragon could crumble into a man of warmth and feelings and consideration.

The chill in the room grew as the fire sank even lower. Alaine quietly rose from the bed and padded barefoot and naked across the icy floor to put more wood on the coals. Shivering with cold, she hurried back to bed and gratefully pulled the furs up around her shoulders. But before she could settle herself once again close to Rorik's warmth, a seeking hand traveled up her ribs and with sure instinct cupped a cold and goose bump-covered breast. The sudden warmth of Rorik's hand against her chilled skin made her jump.

"Are you so anxious for my attention," a deep voice inquired, "that you must wake me in such a manner? With your cold feet against my naked buttocks?"

Alaine gasped as he suddenly pulled her under him, not sure if he was angry or merely jesting. "I didn't mean to wake you."

"Did you not?" One of his hands traveled up the inside of her thigh. She felt the now-familiar fire spark anew in the center of her womanhood. "If you were cold, my love, there was no need to feed the fire. I would be more than happy to warm you."

He proceeded to give attention to that task, and she allowed herself to be carried away on the wave of his seductive passion. This time she didn't fight being drawn into his arms. There was no fear or shame as she became one with him once again. She sighed in contentment as his mouth closed over hers in sweet demand. If this was what it meant to be a wife, she thought through the haze of desire that clouded her mind, then it was going to be more than easy to keep her vows.

The sun was high when Rorik finally descended the stairs into the hall, leaving his bride still peacefully slumbering in the chamber above. The hall was deserted except for servants, for it was another fine day outside the chill stone confines of the keep. A serving wench hastened to bring him bread, cheese, and wine to break his fast as he sat down by the fire.

"What ho?" The great wooden doors flung open to admit Sihtric, who crossed the hall with a grin on his face when he saw a morose-looking Rorik sitting before the fire. "Have you left your poor bride so exhausted she can't rise from the pillows?" Uninvited, he took a seat beside Rorik and called for beer. "I hope you went easy on the poor little maid," he chortled. "It's easy to see she's known naught but her old nurse's gentle touch. Certain it is she's never had to deal with such a surly beast as you."

"What puts you in such rare mettle this morning?" Rorik asked sourly.

"It's the crisp morning air and a hearty ride away from this dank pile of stones. Gillaume and I and two of your guests—Sir Gilbert de Prestot and Sir Rannulf de Carentan—brought down a stag this morn while you were still snoring in the furs. Worthy man, that Sir Rannulf. Seems he himself was thinking on paying suit to your lady before you came on the scene and snatched her up."

Rorik merely grunted.

"You're in a fine black mood for a sated bridegroom," Sihtric said with a taunting grin. "What brings you to this sour state? You seem to have taken your ease well enough last night. The bloody flag is flying for all to see."

Rorik grimaced at the memory of the early dawn, when Joanna and the older women guests had come to the lord's chamber to strip the bed of its linen. The bedclothes, soiled with the scarlet stains of Alaine's virgin blood, were hung from the chamber window for all to see. In this way all present could bear witness to the purity of the bride and final irrevocable sealing of their vows. Rorik thought it a barbaric custom, but Alaine had not seemed at all embarrassed. On the contrary, she'd had a definite air of being proud of herself. Quite a change from the quivering maiden who the night before had turned crimson at the very sight of him. Who could fathom the mind of women?

Sihtric chortled, undaunted by Rorik's moody silence.

"Could it be the flame-breathing Stone Dragon has been trapped in his own fire?"

Rorik shot his friend a baleful look. "You're in a rare talkative state this morning. In fact, your mouth is moving so fast your brain can't keep up."

"She's a winsome lass," the Norseman continued, blithely ignoring the other man's words. "Such a maid could make a man forget his vow to never soften his heart toward the fairer sex."

"The woman with that power doesn't exist," Rorik insisted in a determined voice. "She's a tempting wench, I'll admit, but my soul is closed to such gentle passions as other men might feel."

Sihtric raised a brow in disbelief and glanced at the closed door of the chamber above. "A burden of hate is not such a bad thing to give up, my boy. And if you can cling to old bitterness and despise such a one as this little maid, well, you're more of a boy and less of a man than I thought."

Rorik ran a hand through his short-cropped black mane, leaving it in tumbled disarray. Sihtric had come perilously close to the source of his dishumor. "Hate and despise are words too strong for what I feel. But it's a foolish man who ignores the painful lessons of the past."

"And it's a foolish man who cannot see the worth of a jewel that's couched in his own hand. This maid is different. I feel it in my gut."

Rorik shook his head in rueful admiration of his friend's persistence and ventured a grin that convinced Sihtric that still there was hope. "This one is different, all right." He looked at the chamber door and his face softened. "Half woman and half wildcat. You never know the next moment which she'll be."

Sihtric chuckled, remembering their unwilling sojourn in the forest. "The wildcat half I've seen. Poor Rorik," he snickered. "Did you feel the sharp edge of her claws last night before you found the woman part?"

"Nay," Rorik replied softly. "This wildcat, I think, is more dangerous with her claws sheathed."

He stared at the chamber door for a long moment, his brow furrowed in thought. Then, abruptly, he stood.

"Come on, you old warhorse. I've a need to work the kinks out of my mind. Today is my day to beat you, I think. Our guests will be busy with their games in the courtyard, or heaving their pickled guts into their chamber pots after emptying too many wineskins. The exercise yard will be all ours. I've not had a chance to best you since you took unfair advantage and beat me in William's camp."

"Unfair advantage was it?" Sihtric stood and flexed the heavy muscles of his shoulders and arms. "Watch your words, boy, or your pretty bride will have to piece you together before she can benefit from your attention again!"

Rorik grinned in savage delight, his pensive mood forgotten. Sihtric smiled and shook his head as he followed the younger man out of the hall. Some men just never learned.

CHAPTER 13

Alaine's plans to become a satisfied and obedient wife died a quick death. Indeed, they didn't last out her first full day of marriage.

She woke to find the bed cold with Rorik's absence. When she descended to the hall, Gwyne—with whom she'd shared a sleeping pallet in the kitchen a few short weeks ago—told her the lord had left with Sihtric an hour past. She was bemused and not a little miffed that after a night of such rapturous intimacy Rorik would leave without a word to her. As the day progressed and there was no sign of either Rorik or the Norseman, she began to worry. What would have taken her husband from his guests and his wife with the wedding festivities barely begun?

Rorik and Sihtric didn't return to the hall until just before the evening meal. They both looked like they had lost a war, covered with grime and smelling of sweat and open air. Alaine's questioning look won no explanation from her new husband, however. He merely greeted her with a polite nod and called for a bath to be brought to his chamber. Sihtric's grin and covert wink were no more informative. Neither was his admonition to comfort her husband well, for his pride had taken another licking.

Alaine's growing annoyance swelled into anger as she sat beside Rorik that evening on the dais. Their wedding guests were busily entertaining themselves with food, wine, and beer. All of her husband's attention was captured in a conversation with the young Duke William, who was seated on Alaine's right. Since Rorik was to her left, the two had to lean slightly across her in order to carry on their discussion. She felt like a pillar of stone for all the acknowledgment they gave her, and when she attempted to interject an intelligent comment into their discussion on fine horseflesh—a subject on which she fancied herself quite knowledgeable—they both regarded her with polite disdain.

"But what I say is true!" The old stubborn look flashed into her eyes. "For years I helped my father in purchasing the stock for our breeding program here at Ste. Claire, and we produce some of the finest horses in Normandy."

Rorik tried to quell her impertinence with a frown, but William gave her the beginnings of a warm smile.

"The Ste. Claire horses are indeed fine, my lady. We must talk of them sometime."

Abruptly the conversation shifted to another subject.

Alaine gave up in disgust. She was unaccustomed to being ignored—she who had been the apple of her father's eye and the pride of his life. How could Rorik treat her so coldly, she wondered, after having been so warm and gentle the night before? Had she done something to displease him? How could she have, when she'd not seen him the entire day?

Alaine nursed her injured feelings the rest of the evening, though Rorik seemed not to notice the venomous looks she tossed his way as he continued to enjoy his conversation with William. They retired to bed after most of the guests had drifted off to their own chambers and those of lower rank had settled themselves on pallets in the hall. As the chamber door closed behind them Alaine opened her mouth to give her husband a sharp piece of her mind, but found her lips immediately put to other uses.

Rorik had tried to ignore the unwanted but tantalizing images of Alaine that had drifted through his mind all day, wreaking havoc with his concentration and making him easy meat for the pummeling that Sihtric had dished out. He had thought once they were wed the little she-cat would cease to be a problem, but the passionate and gentle side of her nature that had surfaced in their marriage bed now had his mind addled beyond all reason. Why could she not be like other women, whose appeal always paled once he sampled their charms? He had tried to keep his disturbing siren of a wife at a distance all evening, but the moment the were alone together in the intimacy of their chamber, the gnawing hunger in his groin demanded attention. He pulled her into his arms before they were two steps into the room.

She pulled away in a huff of anger. "Rorik, I want to know. . ."

Her demand was cut short as his mouth came down on hers.

"Quiet, wench!" he whispered against her lips when she struggled halfheartedly in his arms. "Now is not the time for conversation."

"But . . . !" She attempted to marshal her forces when he finally released her, but was distracted as the sight of Rorik hastily shedding his clothing drew her mind to other things. In single-minded determination he drew her back to him and expertly removed her gown, and then her chemise. As he pushed her gently back onto the bed and covered her body with his own, all thoughts and all purposes but one became superfluous.

The days that followed added to Alaine's growing confusion and annoyance. At night in their chamber she basked in the heat of Rorik's passion. There were no words of love or declarations of undying devotion. But he played her body like a finely tuned instrument, taking her with him as he ascended the heights of desire and enjoying with almost cynical delight her blossoming sensuousness. There was no room for deception in the raw power of his lovemaking, and Alaine knew the intense pleasure he took in her body was real. She knew that in this way, at least, she had touched him.

But during the day Rorik was polite, proper, and cold as ice—a different man entirely from the lover who wooed her to passion in the dark hours of night. Never did he use a harsh word to her, never did he embarrass her in front of others. But if she labored to please him, he frowned. If she was impertinent, he glowered. If she was suitably meek, he ignored her. She began to realize why his men called him the Stone Dragon. His cool withdrawal made her heart ache with confusion, and the chill of their relationship frosted the just-emerging buds of her trust and affection.

Having Rorik's passion was not nearly enough for Alaine. Whatever he had awakened in her on their wedding night— the part of her that had come to life in response to the gentle humor, the consideration, and the almost-affection he had shown her that night—that part of her wanted more of him than just his animal desire.

Feeling beyond her depth, Alaine went to Joanna for advice. She received a well-meant lecture on duty and obedience and acceptance of a husband's foibles. Having failed to gain comfort from her stepmother, she tried to seek out the faithful Mathilde, but Mathilde was scarcely to be seen in the hall these past days. Alaine assumed her natural shyness around so many strangers was keeping her close to her chamber, but the one chance she had to seek her there Mathilde had taken herself elsewhere. And to seek help from Gunnor would have been unthinkable. Never would she be that desperate!

In her state of confusion, vexation, and doubt, it was only natural that Alaine should feel flattered when William, Duke of Normandy and her husband's liege lord, began to show interest in her unusual accomplishments. Alaine had spent her entire life at the rugged edge of Normandy and had rarely been off the lands that were beholden to Ste. Claire. Bastard or no, William was the most illustrious personage she had ever met. When he complimented her on the quality of the hunting birds she had raised and trained from fledglings and showed interest in her breeding program for the famous Ste. Claire destriers, she felt the return of some of the dignity that Rorik was mercilessly destroying. William, it seemed, did not think it such an unwomanly disgrace for a lady to be proficient in arms, and he was vastly amused at her stories of growing up among her father's men-at-arms and training along with the pages. When he laughingly invited her to demonstrate her skill with the short bow, she accepted with alacrity. A misgiving or two tweaked her conscience about how Rorik would feel about a display of "childishness," as he called it. But she managed to ignore her good sense, telling herself that Rorik couldn't possibly object. Hadn't William himself requested the display? And besides, she thought rebelliously, if Rorik was going to treat her like some piece of property that he could ignore at will, she felt no obligation to play the dutiful wife. If he didn't like who and what she was, he could just be damned.

So one sunny afternoon near the end of the week, William and a few other curious guests were treated to an archery display of rare skill. For the occasion, Alaine had once more donned tunic and chausses, though she was careful to choose her finest. The flaring three-quarter-length sleeves of fashionable ladies' gowns were not suited to wielding a bow, and William seemed not at all shocked by her attire. In fact, he seemed delighted by the entire showcase of her proficiency.

"By God, my lady! I've never seen one who could match your skill. When next I call for your good husband's services in battle, I'll demand he bring you with him!" he said with a laugh. "Would that only half my archers could hit a target with such accuracy!"

Alaine grinned in a most unladylike fashion and felt inordinately proud of herself.

"Ah!" William smiled. "Here comes your proud husband now. What say you Sir Rorik?" he shouted as Rorik's long-legged strides brought him into the group surrounding Alaine. "It seems you're wed to no ordinary maid, here. Never have I seen such extraordinary skill."

The few other guests that were present followed the duke's lead and murmured appreciatively. Only a few brows were raised at the unconventionality of Alaine's attire and the novelty of a noble lady using a man's weapon.

"You have a very unusual gift, my lady." William told Alaine with a delighted grin.

"Aye," Rorik agreed coldly. "Very unusual. She's only been bested once that I know of."

Rorik's untimely recall of that humiliation took the edge off Alaine's pleasure, but she refused to be cowed in front of her guests.

"I was not bested, my lord," she reminded him pertly. "It was a trick of the breeze that played me false. And my opponent, not being a sporting man, took unfair advantage of my ill luck."

"Few victories are the result of luck, my lady," Rorik said ominously. "I believe on that day the better man won."

His eyes carried a warning as she opened her mouth for another saucy retort, and wisely she decided that enough damage had been done. She had certainly gotten her husband's attention. But something told her she wasn't going to enjoy the consequences.

"If you'll forgive us, my lord"—Rorik turned stiffly to

William—"Lady Alaine is needed in the hall. It is nearing time for the evening meal."

With a nod to William and the other guests, Rorik took his wife's arm and steered her back to where he thought she belonged.

"I warned you I would tolerate no displays of that sort! What were you thinking of, disgracing yourself before...?"

"I certainly didn't disgrace myself," Alaine interrupted haughtily. "For being out of practice I was quite good!"

"You deliberately disobeyed me!" Rorik's voice sounded deep and ominously threatening in the small confines of their chamber, but Alaine refused to be intimidated.

"William asked for a demonstration of my skill. Would you have had me refuse him?"

"William wouldn't have asked had you not enticed him with your stories."

"Enticed him?" she exploded. "You make it sound like I committed some act of obscene seduction. I merely...!"

"You merely went against my direct orders to...!"

"Direct orders!" she spat. "Bah! I'm not one of your men who jumps to your command! I'm not some hound who grovels to your call."

"No, you are not," he agreed icily. "You are my wife. You took a sacred vow to honor and obey."

"And you vowed to cherish and protect. To love as you do yourself!"

"I have honored you above all other women!" Rorik gritted through teeth clamped tight with exasperation. "I raised you to a position of respect. Every night I have sought your bed and no other's."

"Is that supposed to be an honor?" Alaine sneered, anger getting the best of wisdom. "Am I supposed to be grateful to service your nightly needs while you treat me like a stranger when I'm not bearing your weight in bed?"

"Guard your saucy mouth, wench!" the dragon roared. "I am angered enough as it...!"

"You are angry?" Alaine exploded. "What about me? Have I no right to be angry? Or don't I count? God above! Are all men such simpletons?"

Rorik raised his hand. Confusion added to anger, and he longed to strike out. No man was expected to stand for such behavior from a wife, and he more than most men had little reason to tolerate such rebellion. She ignored the threat and glared at him, face pale and eyes flashing violet fire. Something inside him could not send the blow crashing down on her small defiant form. His features froze into cold immobile bronze as he slowly lowered his arm.

"Next time you defy me," he promised. "You will feel the weight of my hand. I will not have a wife who clings to her will over mine."

"Then perhaps you should have hanged me after all," she taunted.

With a curse he turned and left the chamber. As the door closed behind him, the ceramic pitcher Alaine threw splintered into a thousand pieces against the heavy oak. She got only small satisfaction out of watching the shards tinkle to the stone floor.

"I am cursed with a disobedient and headstrong wife," Rorik moaned into his tankard.

The fire in the cavernous fireplace was dying. The wedding guests all snoring on their pallets. Only Sihtric and Rorik were awake to watch the night hours away. And Sihtric was growing weary of his lord's miserable groaning.

"Why not just beat the wench?" he proposed. "Every new wife deserves beating, just to let her know who rules the roost."

"She's so small," Rorik objected illogically. "I might hurt her."

"Teach her a lesson," the Norseman declared. Engrossed in the depths of his tankard, Rorik didn't see the twinkle of mischief in his friend's eye.

"She disobeys my every word, then accuses me of being a bad husband!"

"Bad husband are you? The wench should learn how a truly bad husband would stop her sauciness."

"Aye," Rorik agreely morosely. "I'm being too patient. I've treated the witch more gently then she deserves."

"She should be grateful you don't beat her senseless. It was surely what your father—bless him!—would have done. Now there's a man who knew how to handle a woman!"

Rorik cast his companion a dark look.

"You've been more than good to her. Why should she covet a smile or a warm word—just because you're her husband? After all," Sihtric continued with a sardonic grin, "you've accomplished your purpose in wedding the maid. Why should you put yourself out to coddle her now she's your wife? She should be grateful you needed her to secure her lands and people. Otherwise she'd find herself out in the cold."

Rorik snorted with contempt. "So you also think that my behavior is lacking."

"Lacking only in guts." The Norseman shrugged his huge shoulders in casual scorn.

Rorik's scowl etched its way deeper into his face.

Sihtric laughed and shook his head. "Face it, boy. You're afraid of the little maid. She's got her hooks into you and you're making an ass out of yourself trying to keep from being landed. You're acting like a green boy who's never crawled under a maid's skirts."

No other man could have said such a thing to Rorik's face and not been subject to disastrous consequences. But though the black-haired knight frowned ominously, her merely grunted in reply. He wasn't so drunk that he couldn't see the kernel of truth in the Norseman's words.

"She's a sorceress, I swear," he declared with an alcoholic sigh. "She'd have me bedeviled by her charms if I weren't wise to the ways of women."

Sihtric snorted with contempt. "No man is wise to the ways of women. Least of all you. Only thing to do is surrender gracefully—before you make a total fool out of yourself."

But Rorik would have none of it. "My father was besotted by my mother, and look where it led him. Though he beat her more times than I could count—even locked her in her room a sennight one time—because of her shrewish tongue he said. Still she beguiled him with her witchery, and it was the end of him."

"This maid is not your lady mother. I've said as much before—though you with that thick skull of yours haven't listened. This female's a different breed of woman."

"She is that," Rorik admitted.

Sihtric rose from the bench and yawned mightily. "Go to your bed, boy. Your wife is probably cold and lonely, ready to forgive your stubbornness." He took the tankard from Rorik's hand before it could slip from his loose fingers. "Show her you're the man I know you are. Let her forgive your stupidity."

Rorik looked at him blearily. "Nay. The sharp-tongued witch can sleep alone." He sank back on the hard bench. "It is I who should forgive her." He closed his eyes and the start of a snore rumbled from his mouth.

Sihtric yawned again and shook his head. Soon, he thought. Soon that stone wall that Rorik built around himself so many years ago would come tumbling down. And about time, too.

The next day—the day of the tourney that would officially end the wedding festivities—dawned in fog and rain. The field between the orchard and the practice yards, where temporary barrier fences and seats had been erected, was muddy and cold. A hastily spread tarpaulin sheltered the seats from the rain, but nothing could keep out the cold mist. Nevertheless, the wedding guests gathered in high spirits to see their favored knights try to mash one another into the mud. Petty wars and skirmishes had been an everyday part of Norman life for the past decade, but another fight was always a welcome entertainment.

Alaine sat in the viewing stands and tried with difficulty

to play the part of the smiling hostess. Her head ached abominably and her eyes were bleary from lack of sleep. She hadn't realized how cold and lonely a bed could be. She had lain awake all night listening for Rorik's footsteps. When he didn't return she'd tortured herself with visions of him finding his comfort in the willing arms of a serving wench. Crying into her pillow, she alternately cursed him for his insensitivity and damned herself for her undisciplined temper and shrewish tongue.

It was with some satisfaction she noted that Rorik himself was not looking in top form as he rode out onto the field. As custom demanded he stopped before her seat to beg a token. At this close proximity she could see the dark shadows under red-rimmed eyes and the greenish cast to his skin. She concealed a smirk at the thought that perhaps the night had been no more comfortable for him than for her. Cheered by the signs of his misery, she graced him with a sweet smile as she tied one of her silk scarves to the end of his lance. He gave her a jaundiced grimace in return and, after a hasty salute, spurred the chestnut destrier with unnecessary vigor and galloped back onto the field.

The morning passed in individual jousts. Rorik won his contests but rode with little verve. To Alaine's delight Garin also downed every opponent who rode against him. She hoped that despite his foul humor her husband was noting the squire's skill. About mid-morning the sun broke through the overcast and began to disperse the cold mist. As the air warmed, everyone's spirits rose higher. Alaine sent a message to the kitchen that the midday meal should be set up on the field so her guests would not be required to trudge back to the keep through the mud.

Rorik appeared at the midday meal and, though he had lost most of the greenish pallor, stayed a goodly distance from the food. Alaine congratulated him on his victories and he politely commented on how well she looked. For their guests' sake they were civil, and Alaine took special care to comment on Garin's good performance. Rorik seemed sincere as he agreed with her praise of the boy's courage and skill.

The afternoon was almost warm as the guests reseated themselves to watch the melee. This mock battle was the most favored part of the tourney, and the onlookers were eager to cheer on their favored champions, and even more eager to see their kin capture prisoners for whom valuable ransom could be collected—usually amounting to a man's horse and arms.

Two groups or warriors gathered on either side of the field, one group led by Rorik and the other by one of William's most able lieutenants—Robert Fitzwater. Squires and pages crouched at the edge of the field, each ready and eager to go to his master's aid should he fall. A squire wearing William's livery shouted out the terms of the contest and extolled the leaders of the two mock armies. Then the battle was on.

What followed was mass confusion. Rorik and Fitzwater were leaders in name only, providing a pennant to rally behind and enflame the men's fighting spirit. Each knight was on his own to prove his prowess, win the acclaim of the crowd, and collect as much in winnings as he could. The result was chaos. The two groups thundered toward one another and met in a roiling mass of flying mud, churning hooves, and tangled lances. Contestants paired off and dueled with an intensity that was barely short of the blood lust of actual battle. Some unfortunates were compelled to yield the day early on and left the field knowing they were poorer by horse and arms. Some nursed injuries and trudged off to consign their cuts and bruises to the tender mercy of their squires' care. One knight with dented helm and bleeding head had to be carried off the field by his squires.

Only the strongest and most skilled managed to stay on the field to the very last. Alaine couldn't quell a twinge of concern as she watched Rorik battle his way through the mass of men and horses and deadly steel. She marveled at his strength, knowing his belly was empty of any nourishment and his head was pounding with the hammers of a hangover. One opponent after another fell to his skill, but with a worried frown she noted he didn't move with his usual buoyant energy and grace. She was grateful that Garin was fighting at his back.

Only a few knots of battling men were left to be cheered by the crowd. Two pairs dueled on foot, while Rorik, Garin, Gilbert, Robert Fitzwater, and two of Rorik's younger retainers were still ahorse.

William, who out of deference to his rank had declined to enter the field, leaned toward Alaine and smiled.

"A splendid contest, my lady. I can see your good husband has lost none of his vigor, and those still on the field with him are surely the cream of the lot. Who is that who fights at Rorik's back?"

Alaine smiled proudly. "That is Garin de Longchamps, my lord—my father's senior squire."

"He fights too well to be a squire. He should be knighted."

"Rorik has promised to sponsor him," Alaine answered.

"Good!" William replied. "If he didn't, I would myself. I need young men like him."

Alaine's eyes traveled back to Garin. The fighting had migrated very close to the viewing stand, and she could almost see the sweat running from beneath the helms of the battlers. For a moment Garin was in the forefront, and Alaine noticed with surprise a scarf tied around his upper arm. She was momentarily taken aback, though she didn't quite know why. There were plenty of young girls who would be honored to give Garin their favor for this contest. Then she tumbled to what gave her pause. The scarf was one she'd seen before. Surely no other had that color of perfect robin's-egg blue. The favor belonged to Mathilde. For a brief instant Alaine wondered if during all this week since Garin's return Mathilde had really been keeping so closely to her chamber, as she had blithely assumed. Might she have been . . . ?

Her attention was diverted from Garin and the scarf by William's touch on her arm.

"It's been a good day, Lady Alaine. No deaths, and

only one seriously injured. Perhaps we should call an end to the contest before those weary knights do themselves in. I wouldn't want to lose any such warriors. I have need of them all.''

''As you wish, my lord,'' Alaine said, trying to hide her relief. She was sure Rorik had to be at the end of his endurance, considering his condition.

William gestured to the squire who had opened the contest. But before he could pass along instructions that the melee was at an end, the crowd gave a gasp.

Alaine turned her eyes back to the field, and her heart lurched in alarm. Rorik was pinned to the muddy field under his great chestnut destrier. The great horse had lost his footing in the slick mud. He heaved and struggled to rise, but was hampered by the confusion of horses around him. Sword still in hand, Rorik worked to free his leg from under the struggling horse. His helm had come off in the fall, and scarlet rivulets ran down the side of his face from a gash hidden in his mane of black hair.

The scene seemed to hover in nightmarish suspension before Alaine's horrified eyes. She wanted to scream when she saw Gilbert ride out from behind another knight and gallop toward Rorik's unprotected back. She could tell from the set of his lance he intended to do mortal damage, not merely take a prize of war. With one leg still pinned under his horse, Rorik could only listen to the drumbeat of hooves charging down upon him.

Alaine finally found her voice as she screamed and rose from her seat in horror. Her useless shout of warning was lost in the volume of noise that rose from the crowd. The tableau of downed knight and foul attacker dragged on in dreamlike slow motion, then changed with confusing abruptness. Suddenly Garin was there between Gilbert and his helpless victim. At the same moment the chestnut destrier managed to struggle to his feet. Rorik staggered upright and swung to meet the oncoming charger, his sword held before him. But Garin, his face grim with hatred, had already engaged Gilbert, who had thrown aside his lance and met the boy with wildly swinging broadsword.

"Hold!" William trumpeted into the confusion. "Hold! I command it!"

Reluctantly, Gilbert backed off. Eyeing his opponent warily, Garin spared a glance back to Rorik, who was sheathing his sword and trying to calm his battle-fevered destrier.

Almost before William's command was out of his mouth, Alaine pushed her way through the crowd in the stands and, finding an opening in the fence-barrier, ran out onto the field. Her heart had leapt into her throat when she saw Rorik pinned beneath the bulk of his stallion, and it had stayed there. She had to find out for herself how badly he was hurt. William followed close on her heels.

"Oh, mercy!" she cried as she reached her husband's side. One side of his face was crimson, and high above his ear his ebony mane was matted with blood and dust. He held his left foot gingerly off the ground, and she culd see streaks of blood seeping through his mud-covered chausses.

At the sound of her voice he turned. His face, where it wasn't covered with blood, was streaked with mud and sweat. And it would take poor Timor hours of labor to put his mail once more into condition to use. But his mouth stretched across his face in a grin, and his green eyes were still alight with the exultation of battle.

"It's not so bad, my love," he said, seeing the ashen hue of her horrified face. "Don't concern yourself."

"Don't concern myself? You were almost killed! Where is that swine de Prestot?"

"Calm yourself, my lady," William warned. "No harm was done. Sir Gilbert made a mistake in the heat of battle. He has withdrawn, as you see." He gestured to the canopy at the end of the field, where Gilbert stood talking to his squire as though nothing untoward had happened.

"He meant no real harm," Rorik said in a mild voice.

Alaine didn't believe it. She didn't think Rorik believed it either, in spite of his words. She opened her mouth to voice a hot denial, to remind them that Gilbert had not only ignored the rules of the melee, but had exceeded the bounds of honor as well. But a frown from Rorik silenced her before the words were out of her mouth. She pursed her lips in disgust. Guest or not, the man should be punished!

Rorik turned to where Garin still sat astride his horse. "Garin de Longchamps, you have more than proved your worthiness for knighthood. I would be glad to have you at my back in battle any day."

"Thank you, my lord," Garin replied with a grin.

"Glad I am that now you will be riding with me instead of against me, lad."

"You have my loyalty and my sword for as long as you'll have them, my lord."

Alaine sent Garin a smile of special warmth. Even if no one would admit it, she knew Garin had saved Rorik's life this day. She intended to find some way to reward him. She glanced again to the canopy at the end of the field, where most of the knights had gathered with their squires and pages. Gilbert was still there, and his eyes were fixed on her with frightening avidity. She shot him a look of icy blue contempt, and dearly wished she could find an appropriate reward for Gilbert, also.

CHAPTER 14

Alaine was silent as she carefully clean away the clotted blood and dirt from the gash in Rorik's scalp. When she'd rushed onto the field her anger with Rorik had been momentarily forgotten. Fear for his safety had driven all other thoughts from her mind. But here in the quiet seclusion of their chamber, with Rorik out of danger and the excitement well past, her anger returned in full measure. No words had been spoken between them since she had urged him to come to their chamber so she could tend his hurts.

Rorik sat stoically still and silent while she washed the gaping cut that sliced his scalp. In being dragged off his head the helm had scored a long and jagged gash. She could see that in places she would need to stitch it closed for it to heal properly. She summoned the servant who was pouring steaming water into the wooden tub in preparation for the master's bath.

"Elizabeth, fetch me some fine thread and a new needle. And bring some wine."

When the servant had gone on her errand, Rorik allowed himself a doubtful look at his wife. "I think your hand would be steadier without the wine."

She laughed at the look on his face. "It's to soak the thread, my lord, so the wound will not fester. And mayhap for you to drink, if it would give you ease."

"Nay," he refused. "You seem skilled enough in these matters. I doubt you would hurt me overmuch."

"Joanna is more practiced in this than I. Perhaps you would rather that she tend to closing the wound."

He looked at her a moment with hooded eyes. Finally, a crooked smile twitched at his mouth. "You're practiced enough at pricking me with your tongue. I doubt your needle is as sharp. Besides, it's but a small matter."

The job was soon done, and the sigh of relief Rorik breathed when the last stitch was snipped was the first sound he made. Alaine suspected his silence was due more to stoicism than her skill. That would teach him to be so flippant when she had a sharp weapon in her hand!

"My thanks." He gave her a tight smile as she put away the needle and thread. His face was only a trifle pale.

"The leg will be easier."

She knelt to unwind his cross garters. The leg that had been pinned under the horse was bloodied by a wide but shallow scrape. It required only cleaning and binding, and the binding would wait until after the bath. As Alaine bent to her work she felt her husband's eyes on her. The silence between them was beginning to weigh heavily. Alaine searched for some word to relieve the tension.

"I should thank you for sponsoring Garin for knighthood, my lord." She fixed her eyes on the bloody scrape as she cleaned the last remnant of dirt from his muscular calf.

"He more than earned any favor I show him."

"All the same," Alaine insisted, "it was a kind thing for you to do, and I am grateful."

Rorik smiled cynically as her face finally raised to his. "Kindness and justice are two different things, my lady. You should never mistake anything I do for kindness. I am not a kind man."

Alaine flushed slightly under his gaze. He was mocking her, she knew, but something in his eyes told her he was mocking himself as well.

"Kind or not, I think perhaps you are a just man," she said softly. "Not many men can dispense justice without rancor to one who has offended them in the past."

He shook his head, almost sadly. "You are wrong, Alaine, if you think I am a man whose actions are not colored with rancor. Bitterness is the fire that fuels my life. You should remember that."

She frowned at his cynical assessment of himself. "I think you wrong yourself, my lord. All men of war are harsh, and at times cruel. But I think you are basically just, and at times even merciful."

"If you think that then you will be sadly mistaken," he answered. "And disappointed."

She bent once more to her work, cleaned the last of the blood and dirt from the scrape, and helped him off with his heavy arming tunic. She watched with frank admiration as he stepped into the tub of hot water. No more did she feel shame at viewing his powerful male body. After just a few days of marriage it had become familiar ground. But familiarity hadn't dimmed the spark that lit inside her every time she saw him thus.

"Would that matter to you?" she asked as he sank down with a painful grimace into the hot water.

"Would what matter?"

"If I were disappointed. Or hurt."

A flash of feeling raced across his features and was gone. When he raised his eyes to her his face was once more a cautious mask. "As I told you once, I bear you no ill will. You give me pleasure, and though you're not the most biddable of women, at least you don't hide your mischief in deceit. Given a choice, I would not see you hurt."

A sad little smile flickered across her mouth. "And I suppose, my lord, given a choice, I would please you if I could," she said, answering him in kind.

With a tiny sigh she moved to the tub, picked up the sponge, and proceeded to her wifely duties. She was energetically scrubbing his broad back when he began to work a lather through his hair.

"Let me do that," she insisted. "You're likely to undo all my careful work."

Carefully and gently she massaged the soap through the thick ebony mane, meticulously avoiding reinjury to the site of her needlework. Then, scooping a pitcher full of warm water, she poured it slowly over his head. He winced as the water washed over the cut but then lay back in the tub and sighed with contentment as it flooded down over his face and neck.

"You have a way about you that makes a man forget the travails of the day."

She smiled hesitantly, not knowing from his tone if the words were praise or censure.

"Could it be you've accepted the wisdom of this marriage, lady wife?" he inquired lightly, almost teasingly. "Did I see tender concern on your face as you ran to me on the field?"

Alaine frowned, irritated at being so transparent. "I suppose you are better as husband than some others who might stand in your place," she admitted.

His smile was full of the devil. "And I suppose if a man must have a wife, you will do better than most."

"What a loving pair we are!" she commented bitingly.

She got off her knees, shook out her dampened gown, and went to fetch the clean towels that lay on the bed.

He laughed. "Love has naught to do with marriage. If it is words of love you want, you need but cross a minstrel's palm with coin. Such nonsense has no place in a good marriage. It is better that we understand each other."

She was silent, quelling the urge to turn back to the tub and wring out the sodden sponge over his head. Understand each another indeed! She doubted he understood her and despaired of ever understanding him.

"Now be a good wife and come give me a kiss," Rorik commanded, seeming well pleased with himself.

She eyed him with distaste.

"Come now," he said with a smile. "Did you not just say you would please me if you could?"

She leaned over and gave him a chaste peck on the cheek.

"Is that a kiss?" he asked with raised brows. "I've gotten better from my dried-up great-aunt of an abbess."

"It's an awkward position," she complained. She didn't like the hungry-wolf look she saw in his eyes. She had seen it often enough over the past week to know what it meant.

"We'll see about that," he chuckled.

Without warning Alaine found herself seized and dragged down to the level of his face. He promptly covered her mouth with his in a quick but thorough kiss.

"You're right," he agreed, the light of mischief dancing in his eyes. "It's an awkward position. Let's try it this way." Before she could draw back he pulled her into the tub atop him, ignoring her indignant squeals. "This is much better."

"Look what you've done, you jackanapes!" Alaine splashed helplessly in the soapy water, prevented from rising by Rorik's firm grip. "My shoes, my clothes! All ruined!"

"I'll purchase you more," he promised.

"It's a shameful waste!"

"Nay!" he laughed. "It's worth it."

He grinned in satisfaction as her outraged struggling promptly brought her in intimate contact with the evidence of his desire. Her eyes flew to his in dismay, and she was instantly lost in the searing heat of his gaze.

"Rorik! It's daylight still!"

He lifted her skirts from under her so that they floated up around her hips, leaving her warm flesh pressed against his. "Is there an edict proclaiming a man may take his wife only under cover of night?" His voice had grown low and husky. He pulled her forward so she lay full against him. The water swirled with their movements, adding its warm caress to the brush of his hands.

"But in a tub full of water?"

He chuckled, a throaty, masculine sound that sent shivers racing down her spine. "Anyplace I like, my love. One would think you were still a startled virgin at the look on your face."

"Nay, but . . . !"

"Let us be rid of these!" With one swift movement he pulled her garments over her head and dropped them in a sodden pile by the tub. "Now come here."

She squirmed in objection as he lifted her again and with a soft sigh began to nuzzle at one wet breast. "But your injuries . . . !"

"Ache not half as much as the parts that are urging me on." His mouth found the other nipple and teased insistently. She felt the hard shaft of his manhood rear hot and ready against her thigh. Her own body responded in kind as a flower of passion began to swell open and warm the pit of her belly.

"The servants," she objected halfheartedly as he lowered her against his chest and slid his hands down the length of her back until he grasped her buttocks in a gentle grip. "What if they should come in?"

"Then they will see the lusty appreciation the lord has for his new wife."

"You're impossible!"

"And you're irresistible—at times." He held her eyes with his. They were a warm and verdant green, she noticed, so unlike the chips of green ice she had grown to expect.

He guided her hips over his and gently, carefully, pushed her down to be impaled on the hard root of his desire. She closed her eyes contentedly as she felt the hot length of him slip inside her. Instinctively she began to move, but his hands tightened on her hips.

"Be still," he said in a quiet voice. His hand moved to cup her breasts, then he pulled her down to lay against him.

"I want to . . ."

"I know what you want." He kissed the top of her head. "Just be still and let nature take her course."

She nestled her face into the curve of his neck and shoulder. His hands roamed gently over her back and buttocks and she could feel the texture of his coarse chest hair against her breasts. Of their own accord the muscles of her body tried to bring him more fully inside her. The movement of the warm water against their bare bodies seemed an erotic torture. Still he wouldn't let her move. They simply lay quietly and let the water rock them to and fro with gentle motion. She felt the aching tension between them build to almost unbearable heights as his arms tightened around her and his breathing quickened to rapid, shallow breaths. Inside herself Alaine sensed a spring coiling tightly, tighter, still tighter—just waiting for the moment of glory.

Finally, with a low cry of victory, Rorik arched against her. She felt the pulsing power of his release, and her own body shuddered in delight at the intensity of her own reaction. She buried her face in the hard, corded muscles of his neck and suddenly never wanted to draw apart. Every time he possessed her it seemed that more and more of her merged into him, making it hurt even more when he drew away from her once again and closed that rift in his defenses that their physical intimacy had opened. She snuggled closer and felt his arms tighten around her in response. Someday, she thought, she was going to go mad from these wild swings between joy and pain.

"The water grows cool," Rorik said a few moments later.

She raised her head and smiled mischievously. "And you also, my lord?"

"Not yet awhile, I think," he said with a grin. "One taste of such a feast is not enough."

He stood and pulled her up with him, openly admiring the rivulets of water that curved along the contours of her slim body.

"Yet we should go see to our guests," he said reluctantly.

"We should," she agreed, stepping out of the tub and bending to pick up a towel. As befit a good wife, she ignored her own dripping body and applied the cloth gently to his.

"Nay." He stepped out beside her and took the towel from her hand. "You're shivering."

He wrapped the towel around her, brushing against her in the process. They both hesitated, then he reached under the towel and cupped a bare goosefleshed breast.

"Our guests can wait a few minutes more," he decided. "It seems I've not yet had my fill."

The sunlight that sneaked through the shutters was showing the mellow hues of dusk when Rorik finally rose well satisfied from their bed. Alaine also was warm and content and forgetful of the annoyances of the past week. She watched admiringly as Rorik pulled on a fresh shirt, tunic, and chausses. His ebony hair was still damp and clung to his broad forehead in thick curls. The richly embroidered tunic highlighted the deep green of his eyes and the bronze of his skin. She thought she had never seen a man quite so ruggedly handsome.

He went to the wardrobe and, after a few minutes' inspection, pulled one of her new gowns from the chest and tossed it on the bed. A fine chemise of complementary color followed.

"Wear these tonight," he said. "They become you

well. I would not like our guests to think you are forced to wear the tunic and chausses they saw you in yesterday."

She raised one brow but held her tongue. Reluctantly she climbed from their warm nest and padded naked to fill the washbowl from a pitcher of clean water. She could feel his eyes on her as she sponged the leavings of their passion from her body. Those changeable windows to his soul were once again heavy and brooding, and she wondered what she had done this time to merit this switch in moods. She slipped into a flimsy shift and followed it with the fine linen chemise. As she reached up to fasten the lacings her hands were promptly brushed away by his.

"You're much more the woman than I gave you credit for," he told her, deftly lacing the chemise. He dropped the gown down over her head and, turning her around, laced it snugly in the back so it would fit the slim contours of her body. "I should have beat you for embarrassing me in front of William yesterday and here I am instead, ignoring my duties to lie abed and pleasure myself with your charms. Truly you've bewitched me."

She turned around and regarded him with an annoyed frown. He had seemed well enough content while mounted atop her not too many minutes before, and now he was prattling about being bewitched. All the irritation of his puzzling behavior flooded over her mind in a wave of anger.

"It is not I who's bewitched you," she commented acidly, "but your undisciplined desires. Most men are content to leave their wives be at least until the sun has set!"

He shook his head wonderingly. "The sight of you heats my loins no matter what the time of day, little Alaine. I can't get enough of you, it seems." he snorted in disgust. "Bah! I should ride to war with William and wipe you from my mind."

Now Alaine was truly incensed. "And why should you want to wipe me from your mind, my lord? You, who took my land, who took me to wife against my will, who treat me like a wanton when your passion burns and like a worthless stranger once your needs are eased.''

"I give you the respect a wife is due.''

"Do you?'' she queried archly. "Do you think our guests don't see through that cold exterior of respect to see how you despise me?''

"I don't despire you, Alaine. I've told you before . . .''

"Then it must be all womankind who rates your ire if it's not I as one woman who draws your contempt. Do you think as some churchmen that women are all daughters of the devil sent to tempt men into fleshly sin? Or do you simply scorn the softer minds and weaker bodies of those who had the misfortune to be born female?'' Her voice burned with acid bitterness.

Rorik's face drew into tight, harsh planes. With an ungentle motion he turned her to face him. "Stop your harping, wife! I tell you straightly I have much respect for womankind, the same kind of respect I have for the wild boar charging through the forest—wily, intelligent, cunning, and dangerous. A man without respect for that kind of creature ends with his bowels ripped from his belly and his heart torn from his chest.''

Alaine's eyes widened at the vehemence of his declaration. She had often bemoaned her state in being born female, but this gross insult pushed her solidly into the ranks with her sisters. The fact that she had actually enjoyed the intimate attentions of this man filled her with humiliation.

"You make me ashamed to call myself your wife,'' she said coldly.

"Is it so?'' he answered with a crooked smile. "Seems you enjoy your wifely duties well enough when you lie purring beneath me in yonder bed.''

Every muscle in Alaine's body coiled with tension as she tried desperately to control the temper that threatened to flare into white-hot rage. She longed to strike out at that sculptured bronze face, to pound her hard fists against him until he cried out in pain. The truth of his words hurt more than the insult. She did respond to his every caress in

passion and gladness, even though she knew no love
inspired his gentle wooing of her desire. No more could
she allow herself to be so used by one who held her in
such contempt. She was no mare to be serviced by an
uncaring stallion, no harlot to warm a man's bed in return
for title and security.

"No more!" She swept her hands before her in a
gesture of negation. "I will not share a bed with a man
who thinks me a vicious creature whose every charm is
some trap for an unwary victim. You can seek your
pleasures from the serving wenches, or from whoever will
have you. The comely kitchen maids have been cold and
lonely since first you sought my bed. Go back to them!"

"Don't give me ultimatums, wife!" Rorik thundered.
"You've little choice as to whether you welcome my
attentions. I am the husband God gave to rule over you.
Besides"—he fingered a bright gilt curl that had escaped
from the heavy coil of hair at her nape—"some parts of
our arrangement have pleased me well." The sudden
gleam of humor in his eye was completely missed by
Alaine as she jerked back from him.

"Go practice your charms on the harlots of William's
court," she snarled. "They might appreciate your merits
more than I. Didn't you say you wished to drive me from
your mind?"

"Alaine . . . !" he warned. His frown was thunderous
and might have intimidated a lesser maid, but not one who
had spent her life standing against the volatile tirades of an
ill-tempered father.

"Don't think to frighten me with your fiery looks, Sir
Dragon! I will not submit to a man who names me a
creature to be despised. I will not be used to ease your
manly needs then put aside and treated like a poisonous
snake!"

"Curb your temper, shrew!" He grasped her by the
shoulders and brought his mouth down upon hers in a
ravaging, breath-snatching, heart-stopping kiss. She fought
to remain immobile and unmoved, but a traitorous heat
began to steal through her veins, soften the rigid set of her

body, and melt her against him in the beginnings of surrender. When he released her there was the knowledge of victory in his eyes.

"You are my wife, and I will come to your bed when it pleases me. Don't put your pride between us, Alaine," he warned tersely. "If you do, I assure you it will be torn down and utterly destroyed."

Alaine steeled her heart against the magnetism of his nearness and the weak, womanly urge to simply lean her head against the broad wall of his chest and surrender everything. With a determination born of desperation she pushed him away.

"You have much to learn, Sir Stone Dragon, if you think that you or any other man can destroy my pride or any other part of me!"

She gave him her back and, with head held high, stalked from the chamber, defiance written in every line of her body.

Alaine stormed down the stairs into the bustle of the hall. The menservants were setting the planks across the trestles for the evening meal, and kitchen girls hurried in and out of the pantry, the buttery, and kitchen. There was an air of joviality, and not only among the guests who were drifting in from their pastimes in the courtyard. The serving people were smiling, the squires and pages were entertaining themselves boisterously in one corner, and some of the lesser knights looked as though they might shed their knightly dignity and join in the fun. Even Hilda looked relaxed as she oversaw the army of castlefolk who were preparing to serve the lord and his guests.

The hall had never been thus when Geoffrey was master. He had been a stern lord with a volatile temper that could explode at a joint of meat too well done or at a serving girl's nervous clumsiness. Sir Geoffrey's hall had been a place of tense industriousness. All had labored to please the lord and avoid his wrath. The servants were too busy to smile, and the younger pages and squires would never have dared to indulge in these harmless frolics when the master was soon due to appear. It sat ill with Alaine to admit that Ste. Claire was a happier place since the dragon had made it his lair. Never had she seen him raise a hand to a servant, yet since he'd taken her to wife they all strove to please him. And the squires and younger knights openly worshiped him. One chastening glance from those emerald eyes was enough to set an offending youngster back on the path of proper behavior.

Only with her did the dragon bare his fangs, she thought resentfully. She swept through the hall like a small storm cloud, stomped down the stone stairs, pushed open the heavy timber and iron keep door, and stalked through the courtyard. One man detached himself from the crowd gathering around the hearth and followed her.

Alaine sought refuge in her favorite place. In Castle Ste. Claire, the kennels were given importance almost equal to that of the stables, for Sir Geoffrey had loved his hunting hounds. Usually they roamed the keep, courtyard, and bailey at will, but with so many illustrious guests about they had been confined to the kennel, where two or three of them were quartered in each spacious straw-floored run. When Alaine pushed open the door to the low stone building and lit the tallow lamp, she was greeted with a chorus of welcoming barks, whines, and howls. She walked along the runs and greeted each hound by name, saving her favorite, her special pet, the soft-eyed bitch Mallie for last.

"There, now Mallie." Her voice lowered to a gentle croon as the young bitch jumped against the run fence. She stroked the velvet ears and ran a caressing hand down the lean, muscular back. "Soon these strangers will be gone and you and your friends here can run riot beneath the tables. Soon, my love."

"She's a fine-looking bitch."

Alaine jumped at the voice beneath her, but breathed a sigh of relief when she turned and saw it was only Sihtric outlined against the fading dusky light of the doorway.

"She has a nose the like of which you've never seen," Alaine said proudly. "And she can stay a chase longer than many of the bigger hounds."

"They're a goodly pack of dogs," Sihtric commented. "But it's passing strange that a new bride should prefer the company of the hounds while her guests and groom celebrate within the hall."

Alaine frowned, and turning without an answer, started once again to stroke the tail-thumping Mallie.

"Could it be all does not go right with yon lord and master?"

Alaine snorted in disgust. "That thickheaded, ox-brained knave?"

"Had words, did you?" Sihtric ventured.

"That jackanapes has no words worth listening to. His mind is clogged with prejudice and his head is muddled beyond all repair."

Sihtric smiled tolerantly. "Do you find him that bad?"

"Worse!" Alaine declared. "You are a valiant warrior with a good brain in your head. How came you to follow such a jackass?"

"The jackass has been in my charge since he was but a long-legged colt," he chuckled. "It was I who taught him how to sit a horse and wield a sword, how to hold a steady lance and to throw the war ax." He hefted the vicious double-edged ax that never left his side.

"And did you teach him also to hate the weaker sex?" she asked bitterly. "Did you teach him to despise those who by fault of birth are fated to have their futures held in the ungentle hands of hardened souls like himself?"

"Nay," Sihtric answered in a dark tone. "That was left for another to teach. And she taught him well."

"A lover's story?" she asked contemptuously, wondering how the Rorik she knew could ever have softened his stony heart enough to love.

"Nay," Sihtric replied. "No lover was he. But son."

Alaine left off her attentions to Mallie and turned an inquiring gaze on the Norseman. "Tell me," she said.

"It's an ugly story, my lady."

"I of all people have the right to hear."

"Aye. You do. But I think it's only right you hear it from your husband."

Alaine laughed bitterly. "That pillar of stone? The only time he speaks to me is to lash out with his tongue at what I do and what I am. Do you really think he would soften enough to speak of such things?"

"Then maybe the story should be kept buried in the past, where it belongs."

"But it's not in the past, is it? Rorik carries it with him and nurses his hatred like an open wound. How can I fight this vile thing if I never know what it is?"

Sihtric sighed and leaned against a stone pillar. "Do you want to fight it, my lady?"

"Aye," she admitted readily. "The Rorik I see in the moments when he forgets this devil who rides him is a man worth fighting for."

The dogs grew silent. Sihtric met her eyes with a frankly assessing gaze that seemed to cut through to her soul and weigh her strength, her worthiness to be privy to Rorik's pain. Their eyes held for a long moment. Then the Norseman smiled at her, a smile he might have given some comrade-in-arms before the start of a vicious battle.

"Rorik's mother was a beautiful woman," he began. "I remember her well. Tall and stately, like your stepmother Joanna. Always had her hand to some female task, and her talents seemed endless. Any stringed instrument that the minstrels brought into the hall it seemed she could play with surpassing skill. Her voice was that of an angel. With the castlefolk she was gentle and generous. Not a babe fell sick in Brix but she was there to lend her healing skills. Not a child begged for a sweet who went away empty-handed. The hall was always well ordered. The serving folk loved her. Everyone loved her."

Alaine raised a disbelieving brow. "And how did such an angel teach her son the devil's own hatred?"

Sihtric shook his head. "It is not the happy story it may seem. Rorik's father Sir Stephen loved his wife to distraction. But he was a harsh man with a violent nature. Like his father and grandfather before him, his temper was always on a sharp edge. He'd been taught that gentleness was weakness, and that a man must be harsh to keep his house in order. He did not beat the Lady Theoda often, but beat her he did whenever she showed an independence of mind he didn't like or dared to stand against his will. In his temper he injured her more than once. And slowly her gentleness turned to fear.''

"Lady Theoda?'' Alaine asked. "There is a Lady Theoda still at Brix. Fulk's wife. I begged her for help to retake Ste. Claire.''

Sihtric miled sadly. "So. I wondered what happened to the lady.''

"It cannot be the same one,'' Alaine denied. "The woman I saw was shrunken and cronelike, and her mind wandered in places normal people do not tread, I think.''

"It would be the same,'' Sihtric assured her. "Theoda grew tired of living in fear of her lord. Or maybe she just grew weary of living with a man who never showed by one word or gesture the tenderness she craved. She took a lover, it seems, and her lover wanted more than the favors she bestowed upon him. One spring dawning while her husband and three sons all slept in their beds, she opened the gates of Brix to her lover's army. Fulk had ranged his men before the walls the day before, but none had worried, because of all the castles hereabouts, Brix is the stongest and best laid. There should have been no danger. But through Theoda's treachery Stephen and his two oldest sons were slain without mercy. Rorik was but a beardless youth. He came to the battle late and saw his family cut down before his eyes. He also would have ended on a bloody sword, but I dragged him away along with what few men could still stand. The castle was lost. But on that day he grew to be a man. He vowed to retake what had been stolen, and to take fitting revenge on his betrayers.''

Alaine stood in stunned silence for a moment, bowing her head against the rough wood of the kennel partition. "It's a terrible harsh thing,'' she said quietly. "To be betrayed to death by one's own mother. Bitter, bitter. . . .''

"Rorik worshiped his lady mother,'' Sihtric continued. "In his eyes she was all that was good and true in womankind.''

"She could not have meant for her children to die by her lover's hand." Alaine mused out loud. "No woman would sell the lives of her children in such a way. No woman with a scrap of sanity. . . ."

"So now you understand, my lady, how it is with Rorik."

She raised her eyes to Sihtric, and he noted with surprise they were swimming with tears. "Men have committed equally terrible crimes. He should not assign Theoda's perfidy to all women."

Sihtric shook his head. "Thus speaks reason. Rorik was a child, with a child's understanding. Now he is a man, but on this one thing he still thinks as a child."

"Then it is hopeless," she said sadly. "He will always regard women as creatures of vile treachery."

"Nothing is hopeless where men and women are concerned." Sihtric raised a quizzical brow at her. "Should a maid so straight and true and honest as the one I see before me, should such a maid set out to win Rorik's heart, I can see the dragon being tamed by such a gentle and loving hand."

Alaine tilted her chin a notch higher. The big Norseman was seeing far too deeply into her heart, and she hastily pulled the curtain on her thoughts.

"If such a maid would dare to fight for the heart of your grim master she must be a miracle worker, I think. More likely in trying to tame your dragon she would have her own heart shredded by the claws he wields so fiercely."

"Then more's the pity," Sihtric said quietly. "More's the pity for both you and him."

He walked out of the kennel and breathed in the icy night air, leaving the brooding girl behind to talk to her dogs. No discouraged frown pulled at his face, but instead a bright gleam lit his pale eyes. He'd always had pity in his heart for the lady who would eventually marry Rorik, but he had no pity for Alaine de Ste. Claire. She was a maid who could give as well as she got, no timid demoiselle to cower before Rorik's grim moods and hard looks. He chuckled to himself as he moved back toward the keep.

Perhaps in truth Rorik was more the one to be pitied. This time he had met a female he couldn't trifle with as he saw fit.

CHAPTER 15

For the next week Rorik and Alaine put on civil faces to each other and made the rounds of villages and tenant farms beholden to Ste. Claire. Alaine kept her peace and managed to look the part of a content and dutiful wife while Rorik talked to the villagers and farmers. The people were hesitant at first, eyeing the escort of three men-at-arms and remembering their many offenses toward this fierce-looking lord. They looked toward Alaine at almost every word he spoke. She gave them encouraging smiles and nods. She wanted no more trouble to plague Ste. Claire. Rorik had Ste. Claire, and her, in the hard palm of his hand. Now was time for her people to accept that.

They talked little on these daily rounds. But Alaine had to admit a grudging admiration for the way Rorik dealt with the common folk. He greeted them fair, and spoke to them as a strong man to other strong men. He treated the women with the deference due their sex, and always had a kind word and a smile for the children who peeped at him around their mothers' skirts. Alaine marveled that this was the same man who held such bitterness in his heart. After their initial standoffishness the villagers were at pains to please their new lord and to make up for their obstinacies of the past weeks. They saw their beloved lady mounted at his side and decided in their hearts that God had decreed the right master for Ste. Claire. And who were they to argue the dictates of God?

It was in poverty-ridden Briaux that Alaine saw a side of Rorik she had never thought to see. The village was quiet as they rode through. Alaine recognized the woman whose hut had been her refuge when she'd been caught weeks before by Rorik's unexpected arrival. The child who clung to her skirt was silent and listless, and the woman herself was scarce more than a scarecrow. Alaine reined to a halt in front of the hut.

"Where is the old grandmother?" she asked the woman, remembering the lively old crone who'd squawked so when Alaine's horse had almost broadsided her with his rump.

"Dead," the woman said flatly. "Gone two weeks now."

"I'm sorry," Alaine said, thinking how hard it must be to lose both a babe and a mother in such a short span of weeks.

"Times is hard," the woman answered emotionlessly.

Alaine looked around. All the villagers looked gaunt and haggard—worse than when she had been here before. Rorik was talking to old Toby One-arm, and the sight of the old man suddenly reminded Alaine of Thatch, the half-wit with the gentle eyes and long-suffering patience. Had the boy succumbed also? She rode toward Toby and Rorik, keeping her eyes open for the small five-year-old. But he was nowhere to be seen. Her heart sank in dejection. Reason told that her feelings were out of proportion for a crippled half-wit, but the boy had held a special place in her heart ever since she'd seen him slip from his mother's womb.

Rorik remounted his horse as she drew near. "Has this village always been so bone-bare?" he asked with a frown.

"The last two years have been bad," Alaine answered, still searching. "All the villages have suffered, but up here near the hills, the soil is rocky and the rains either too hard or too light. Still, these people will not move. Their fathers were born here, and their fathers' fathers. We've tried to help, but. . . ."

"We'll be having to keep these people alive with dole from the castle storehouses before long."

Alaine could bear it no longer and turned to the old headman. "Toby," she asked, almost holding her breath. "Where is Thatch?"

Toby looked at her in surprise. "That 'un? He be around . . . there he be."

Alaine breathed a sigh of relief as the boy lurched unsteadily from Toby's hut. He grinned when he saw Alaine, that magical grin that had always captivated her heart. But the glow on his face didn't hide the pathetic wasting away of his frail body. Suddenly Alaine knew what she had to do—an unreasonable and totally senseless solution to a problem the shouldn't concern her, but she had to try. She turned to Rorik, who was watching the boy quizzically.

"Husband," she said in a low voice that carried only between the two of them. "Please, may we take the boy with us to Ste. Claire? He will die here. These people regard him as useless. I doubt he's had a real meal in two months."

Rorik looked at her in surprise, then frowned in confusion. "That boy?" He nodded his head toward the child who was awkwardly propelling himself toward Alaine's mount.

"Yes, that boy."

"He's a half-wit, a cripple. What would you do with the boy, Alaine? Surely it's a mercy that he die young before he has full knowledge of the ills that beset him."

That was what everyone said. Alaine had hoped that Rorik's understanding would go deeper. She prayed silently, then girded herself to try again. Thatch looked up at her, a curious half-smile on his pale face.

"He's not really a half-wit. He's possessed of keen intelligence—a true gift from God. I've watched him grow. I've seen it in his eyes."

"You can't drag home every stray cast-off child. . . ."

Alaine fixed her husband with an almost challenging gaze. "I helped deliver him from his mother's womb when I was but twelve. I've had an attachment to him ever since. Please, Rorik. I've not asked for much. The boy would be no trouble." It was as close as she could come to begging.

Rorik regarded her with a frown, and her heart sank. Why had she thought this rock-hard man would soften his heart toward a helpless child? She should not have asked. She should have thought of the boy as soon as she had married and arranged to have him brought from the village, as she'd long wanted to do. Her husband need not have known.

Rorik's frown slowly faded. He shook his head, a wry smile pulling at his mouth. Then he nudged his stallion forward to the curious Toby.

"I would buy your son, old man."

Toby's grizzled brows stretched toward the sky. "The half-wit? That 'un? Can't y'see, m'lord. That lad's n'good for aught but . . ."

"Still, I would buy him."

Toby's face grew sly. " 'E's but a cripple, m'lord. Still, 'e's flesh o' m'flesh. I wouldna' . . .

Rorik reached in the purse at his belt and extracted three gold coins. "This will see you and your people through this winter and several winters to come. You needn't beg at the castle, you can hold your head up at market when you buy your wares with good coin. What say you?"

Old Toby's eyes grew wide and seemed to reflect the gleam of the gold Rorik placed in his palm. Rorik dismounted and lifted Thatch onto the saddle before Alaine. The boy crowed with delight and waved grubby hands in spastic ecstasy. Ignoring the grime that covered him from head to toe, Alaine circled the boy tightly with one arm. Her throat was curiously tight as she turned to her husband.

"Thank you, my lord."

Rorik grunted, but he couldn't quite hide the spark of warmth in his eye. "See you treat him as a boy and not a pet dog,'' he warned. "Elsewise would be more merciful to leave him here to his fate.''

The week wore on, and one by one the villages beholden to Ste. Claire declared their loyalty and devotion to their new lord and filled his ears with complaints of robbers, poor crops, and near-empty storehouses. At night Alaine and Rorik would return from their day's ride silent and weary. After presiding over the evening meal at her husband's side, Alaine invariably excused herself to her chamber. Each night she would wash her face, brush out the gilt cornsilk waves of her hair, and curl herself in a chair by the hearth with mending or sewing. She denied to herself that she was listening for Rorik's footsteps, but each night she finally retired to bed disappointed. She had said in her anger that she would welcome him no more to her bed, and he had replied in equal anger that he would take her whenever it pleased him. Apparently it no longer pleased him. Not understanding her own grief, in the long lonely hours of the night she soaked her pillow through with tears.

And then he was gone. One morning she descended to the hall early, as was her wont. The servants were bustling about the fire. Two of the lesser knights of Rorik's retinue were seated at the lower table discussing loudly the merits of a horse one had won from the other. Joanna was seated on the dais taking the morning meal. Sihtric sat beside her, and from the flushed faces that both of them wore, Alaine guessed that the two of them had had words again.

Nowhere was Rorik to be seen. Alaine had missed him at Father Sebastian's morning Mass, but it wasn't unusual for Rorik to skip holy worship for an extra hour on the practice field. It was unusual for him to skip the morning meal.

Gwyne hastened to bring her bread, cheese, and cold milk as she sat herself beside Joanna.

"Has Lord Rorik already been served, Gwyne?" she asked.

"M'lord was up 'ere any of us stirred this morn, my lady,'' the girl answered " 'E took Miles and Timor, Sir

Guillaume and Sir Robert and Sir Gunnulf, and the forest-er and three hounds. They was all in here demandin' food before the sun had broke over the hills.''

Alaine sighed. Trust the servants to keep curious eyes on what everyone was doing. ''Did he say where he headed this day?''

''He'll be back in three or four days' time.'' It wasn't Gwyne who answered, but the deeper voice of Sihtric. ''He's merely ridden to the hunting lodge up beyond where Rive begins. He told me to bid you not to worry.'' He didn't tell her about the harsh words the two of them had exchanged that morning, words concerning Rorik's offhand treatment of his wife.

Alaine tried to school her face to hide the disappoint-ment and chagrin of her husband setting off on such a trip without a word to her. Unused to deception, she wasn't entirely successful, and Joanna eyed her suspiciously.

''It's a passing queer time for a hunting party, what with winter setting in so deep.''

''The days have been fine, though,'' Alaine answered noncommittally. Joanna obviously thought Rorik had left because of her. Maybe he had. Maybe he was as disturbed by these lonely nights as she was. She'd lain awake each night imagining him in the warm arms of one of the serving girls, or lying in the hay with the milkmaid who always made cow eyes whenever she passed him in the bailey. But maybe, just maybe, he had been as restless and empty as she, and now sought some relief away from the sight of her. The thought made Alaine's lips curve in a most unseemly smile.

The days of Rorik's absence stretched to a week. Alaine surprised herself by missing him. She missed the sound of his voice, the constant knowledge of his presence, the occasional touch of his hand. The excitement and vitality of her life had departed with her husband. But all the same she was glad to be able to gather all her thoughts about her in peace. Since the day she'd first seen him Rorik's presence had charged her with a coiled-spring tension— sometimes painful, sometimes exciting, but never soothing. Now she accepted the dull pallor of his absence with a kind of gratitude. She needed the peace to regather her scattered wits.

There was work to be done to make the castle ready for the deep of winter, for though the past few weeks had been exceptionally fine, any hour might bring the cold, mist, freezing rain, and fog back to their little valley by the sea. All the women of the castle were put to work at one task or another, and Alaine found herself with little time to brood on her husband's absence.

One chill but bright afternoon she sat before the hearth in the solar spinning wool from last spring's shearing. The women had been at this task for several weeks, for the fleeces must be washed and carded and spun before the worms could get to the piles in the storeroom. Joanna and Gunnor and Mathilde sat a little distance off carding piles of wool that had been picked free of straw, grass, and twigs by Judith's little hands. Now Judith was learning to card and use the drop spindle under Mathilde's patient tutelege. On the other side of the hearth sat Father Sebastian and Thatch. The little cripple had been scrubbed and combed and dressed in decent clothing. The priest, hearing of Alaine's intent to raise the boy in the castle, had attempted to change his name to John, arguing that the lad must have a decent Christian name if he was to take his place among gentlefolk. But the name Thatch, so descriptive of the wayward mass of red hair that defied Hadwisa's comb, had stuck.

But the boy himself had changed. After just a few days of good food the hollows in his frail body were beginning to fill out and his skin was taking on the rosy luster of youth. He was faithfully aping Father Sebastian as the priest drilled him in his letters, and Alaine watched with a feeling of almost maternal pride. She wondered if she would feel this way shen she had children of her own, whether they be straight and tall or crippled and bent. If she had children. If Rorik ever decided to claim once again the place she had denied him in her bed.

"It's a cold day despite the sun," Gunnor commented,

placing several loosely rolled lengths of carded wool beside Alaine's wheel. "It appears that winter is about to set upon us at last."

"Indeed," Alaine replied.

"I would've expected your husband and his friends to return 'ere this long."

Alaine eyed her stepsister suspiciously. The vicious tongue was coiled to strike, she suspected, and she was growing tired of being whipping boy for Gunnor's discontent.

"Perhaps they're having a good hunt. We could use the fresh meat."

Gunnor smiled. "You're being very brave, sister. What other newlywed maid would hold from complaint when her bridegroom tired so quickly of her company and found more sport in the forest than with his tender bride?"

Joanna looked up and frowned, but reminded herself that she was no longer mistress in this keep. Alaine had to learn to stand up for herself against more formidable foes than her sharp-tongued stepsister.

"Rorik does as he pleases," Alaine answered, meeting Gunnor's eyes with an unwavering gaze. "No amount of complaint would bring him to my side, even if I wanted him there. I suggest that you yourself learn the virtue of an uncomplaining tongue."

Gunnor raised a surprised brow. "Your mood has grown sharp of late, Alaine. Now you are truly lady of Ste. Claire, you think to raise yourself above the rest of us and forget the common rules of courtesy."

"When you soften your viper's tongue then will I guard that my words are more pleasing to you, Gunnor." Alaine sighed in exasperation. "I tire of your sly insinuations. Every day you do your best to needle me with your barbs."

"If my barbs prick then perhaps there is truth in them," Gunnor remarked with a sly smile.

Alaine frowned. "Go cautiously, Gunnor. As you say, I am lady of Ste. Claire now. You might do well to try to please me."

Gunnor sniffed scornfully. "And what disastrous conse-quences flow from your disfavor, great lady that you are."

"Nothing so disastrous," Alaine admitted with a slow smile. "I'm not a vengeful sort. But perhaps you should keep in mind that Rorik has taken on the chore of finding you a husband and providing you with a dowry. Surely he would welcome my advice on what sort of man would best suit my dear stepsister."

Gunnor paled and snapped her mouth shut on the acid retort she had prepared. The beginnings of a smile tugged at the corner of Joanna's mouth.

"Gunnor, dear," Joanna intervened, acting as though the exchange had not reached her ears. "Will you accom-pany me to the kitchen to check on the progress of this evening's meal. Maudie has been growing lax since the master is away." She winked surreptitiously at her step-daughter. "We will see you at table, Alaine. Mathilde, please keep an eye out for Judith. She's making a pest of herself at the looms."

The atmosphere in the room lightened when Gunnor left. Mathilde gave Alaine a delighted grin. "I was wondering how long you were going to put up with her drivel. She's done nothing but snipe and complain since the wedding. You think she really thought Rorik had a mind to wed with her?"

Alaine stopped her wheel and removed the full spindle. "I don't think Gunnor wants to marry anyone. I don't think she knows what she wants."

"Well," Mathilde said with a certain satisfaction, "you certainly stopped her in her tracks. It's about time."

"Maybe she'll be happy when she has a husband and can be her own mistress once again."

Mathilde's little round face tightened momentarily, and she gave Alaine a searching look. "Is Rorik anxious to find us husbands and have us out of his charge?"

Alaine sensed a note of distress in her stepsister's voice and so proceeded cautiously. "I don't think he's anxious to be rid of anyone, and I wouldn't think he'll even think about husbands for you and Gunnor before he's accomplished his purpose at Brix.''

Mathilde visibly relaxed.

"Are you so reluctant to wed?''

"No,'' Mathilde hastened to assure her. "Truly I think I am anxious to wed. It's . . . well . . .'' She ducked her head to hide the flush that was staining her cheeks. "I need your help, Alaine.''

Alaine felt a sick dread grow within her. Of all the people in the world she wanted to see happy, dear Mathilde was the foremost. She already suspected the problem, and despaired of any power to help.

"It's Garin, is it not?'' she asked quietly.

Mathilde nodded. "I should have guessed you would see.''

"If you wanted your feelings kept secret you shouldn't have given him your scarf as a favor at the tourney.'' Alaine's sympathetic smile took the sting from her words. "And all the week of the wedding—you were never in the hall or with the guests—I think you were spending more time with Garin than is seemly.''

"Alaine,'' Mathilde said in a soft voice, "Garin is the man I would spend my life with. Truly, I love him. We have pledged our troth to one another. In the eyes of God it would be sin to wed elsewhere.''

"Mathilde,'' Alaine pleaded. "What can I say? You had no right to do such a thing. The decision of who becomes your husband is not yours to make. And this thing with Garin—it is impossible. You know it is impossible.''

"How can it be impossible?'' Mathilde asked, tears beginning to overflow. "He's to be knighted at Christmastime. You yourself once told me you would only wed a man you chose. How can you not understand how I feel?''

Alaine sighed sadly. "It was a foolish thing of me to say. And as you can see, in spite of my bravado, I was wed without regard to my wishes.''

"But I love Garin. And he loves me.'' She dabbed ineffectually at the tears streaming down her cheeks.

Alaine tried to harden her heart and say the sensible

thing. "Even after he is knighted, Garin will still be a landless knight, with naught but his arms and horse," Alaine reminded her. "If he wants what his brother owes him, he'll doubtless have to fight for it, and even if he won that small patrimony, it would not be enough for Rorik to consider him as your husband."

"Oh, Alaine!" Mathilde cried softly, trying hard not to attract the attention of the others in the room. "I do love him! I've loved him since I first saw him. Could you not speak to Rorik for us?"

Alaine sighed sadly. "Dear Mathilde. Love has little to do with marriage," she said, repeating the very words that Rorik had spoken to her. "And I have very little influence with Rorik."

"Please!"

Alaine recalled her debt to Garin. She was also beholden to Mathilde, who had stood by her as a faithful and loving sister since the first day she had come to Ste. Claire. She wondered if she would really be doing the two of them a favor by approaching the dragon with their predicament. Rorik could send either Garin or Mathilde away, and well might if he learned of their involvement.

"I can try," she conceded reluctantly. "But you must wait on when I think the time is right, and promise most faithfully to do nothing foolish."

Mathilde was ecstatic. "Anything! I'll do anything! Oh, Alaine, I love you beyond telling. I do wish you were my sister in truth instead of sister by marriage! You are the most wonderful person God ever put on this earth!"

Rorik and his party returned from the hunt late that evening. They brought with them a boar, two stags, a doe, and a multitude of game birds. Late as it was, Alaine set the servants to butchering and cleaning. They set some meat aside to be smoked, some to be salted, and a small portion to roast on the spit over the huge kitchen hearth.

Tomorrow's meal would be a sumptuous one to celebrate the return of Ste. Claire's lord.

Alaine retired late to her chamber, and to her surprise Rorik was waiting. His hair was still damp from his bath, and he had only a loose robe draped around him as he sat before the hearth polishing the blade of his huge broadsword.

"Where is Timor that you do such work yourself?" Alaine asked.

"The boy is snoring in the hall," Rorik answered. "He's done a man's work these past days."

"And you, my lord?" she asked with polite concern. "Are you exhausted from your hunt?"

He eyed her with masculine appreciation as she took the pins from her hair and let the golden mass tumble down to her waist. "Not so tired as I thought," he replied.

She moved into a dark shadow beside the wardrobe to doff her gown and chemise. Suddenly feeling shy, she quickly pulled a shapeless shift over her head and then wrapped herself in a heavy woolen dressing robe. Rorik watched her actions with raised brow.

"Are you cold?" he asked.

She shot him a suspicious glance. "Not so much now."

"Move over here by the fire."

"I don't want to disturb you."

She turned away from him and started to brush out her thick mass of spun gold hair. Smiling, he set aside his sword and moved over to where she stood.

"Let me do that." He caught her hand and pried the brush from her fingers. Then, gentle as any lady's maid, he worked on the heavy mass until it lay in shining waves that cascaded down her back. "You have beautiful hair," he said, and lifted a fragrant lock to his lips.

She pulled away and glared at him, knowing full well what he was seeking. "Since when do you try to slither your way into my bed with honeyed words, my lord? That seems not your way." She was determined to remember her vow. No matter how many times she had regretted it, the reasons for rejecting his attentions still stood. She'd been a vacillating fool over the past days to wish her denial never spoken, and she despised such feminine weakness.

"Is that not what you want? Sweet words to soothe your ruffled feathers?" His dark brow furrowed in a frown, and the shadows cast by the fire gave him a particularly ominous look.

"Sweet words are for fools," she returned coldly, ignoring his frown, "which is what you think me, as well as being wily, cunning, and dangerous as a boar." As she recalled his words her anger grew. "I said you could seek your pleasures elsewhere till the time comes that you regard me as more than a necessary evil in your life. I meant what I said." She whirled away and stared angrily into the fire.

He followed her. "And do you not regard me as a necessary evil in your life, madam? I recall that you have been free in naming me usurper, villain, knave, snake, or whatever other creature came to your mind at the moment!"

"I at least have some respect for you, for all that you can be a fool at times!" she shot back. "I admit to your integrity and strength even when they hide behind your pigheadedness. But you condemn all women as perfidious, self-seeking, weak-willed, and traitorously cunning creatues, and me along with them. Well, I'll show you how weak-willed I am!"

He turned her to face him. "Don't think your will can stand against mine, Alaine. I know you and your desires better than you think."

She tried to push away his hands as they slid under her robe. "Keep away from me, you knave! I said you were no longer welcome in my bed!"

"And I said I'd take you whenever I pleased. It pleases me now."

She twisted away, but left her robe behind in his hand. Still the linen shift hid her from his gaze, but it did nothing to dim his appreciation of the sight of her, hair tumbling in a shining mass around her shoulders and small, firmly rounded breasts heaving under the thin cloth.

"You are beautiful, little rebel." He smiled and shook

his head in admiration. "Willful, hot-tempered, shrewish, disobedient, and childish. But still beautiful."

She was amazed at his cool demeanor. His face showed neither anger nor passion, and if his eyes gleamed somewhat at the sight of her, that might well be a reflection from the flames on the hearth. It seemed he had dispassionately made up his mind to conquer her, and was single-mindedly going about the task he had set himself.

"I will not yield to you!" she declared hotly.

"Aye, you will," he replied with calm to match her agitation.

He reached out and pulled her toward him. For a moment she was lost in the deep recesses of his emerald eyes, and when she remembered to struggle it was too late. She was firmly in his grasp. He lowered his mouth to hers and almost teasingly caressed her lips with his. She pulled away, surprisingly breathless after such a seemingly casual kiss.

"You said you never forced a woman! Do you mean to add rape to your talents?"

"Rape?" One brow angled upward in cynical amusement. "Nay. Never that. The man who must resort to rape is nowise a man, I think. There are far better ways." He proceeded to demonstrate.

Alaine was determined to remain stone cold during his assault. When his warm lips trailed soft fire over her brow, her eyelids, her nose, and down the slim column of her throat she shut tight her eyes, clenched her teeth, and stiffened her spine as though enduring torture. When his mouth descended on hers she knew not why her lips so readily opened to his demand, or why his sweet exploration of her softness produced such a burning need in the core of her womanhood. She thought she was still in control when he lifted the shift over her head and with one callused, warm hand cupped a sharp-peaked, tingling breast. She wanted to cringe from his touch, but her body seemed to flow toward him with a will of its own. His hand on her breast seemed so right, so natural. It took all her determination to muster the will to slap it away. He just smiled at her weak resistance. Twisting out of his gentle grasp, she bent down to retrieve her shift from where he had dropped it. Patiently he took it from her and tossed it to the other side of the chamber. Seconds later his own robe joined hers in the pile.

That he was ready to bring this game to its natural conclusion was all too obvious as he stood naked and unashamed in the firelight. She moved quickly to put the bed between them. She was afraid more of herself than of him. The sight of his arousal made her body remember the joys that could be had in submission, and the demanding ache of her traitorous body grew to torture. But pride still fueled her defiance. She had made her vow and was determined to keep it. She was no weak-willed, vacillating female who could be seduced so easily by a strong, well-shaped male body. To give in now would prove herself no better than a mare in heat who stood willingly when penned for the stallion's coming. And Rorik had no more regard for her than the stallion had for the mare.

He moved away from the fire and around the bed. She retreated until the cold stone wall was at her back. The chamber was too small for her to escape, she realized, and he was too fast. He would have what he wanted whether she willed it or not. But she would be as cold stone under him, she vowed, and in that way she would remain unconquered.

"You've lost, Alaine." He smiled as she stood stiff-backed and proud against the rough wall. "You've much too passionate a nature to deny me. And though you won't admit it, you want me as much as I want you. In spite of ourselves, you and I are well-suited in this mating game. You give me such pleasure as no woman ever has, and I would give you joy as well, if you would let me."

She glared at him in stubborn silence, and he was hard-pressed not to laugh at the look of righteous martyrdom on her face.

"All right, then, wife," he said with a knowing grin. "If you wish to be sacrificed on the altar of my lust, then I'll be happy to oblige you."

He picked her up and gently laid her on the bed. His eyes roved appreciatively over her supine form, lingering on the pert rounded breasts, traveling slowly down the firm abdomen, the slender, shapely legs, pausing at the soft, down-covered V that secreted her womanhood, then coming to rest on her fine-boned oval face with its golden halo of tumbled shining waves. Alaine felt herself grow alternately hot and cold at his bold assessment. A fire was building inside her, and she desperately tried to quench it with cold indignation.

"If you must force your lust on an unwilling victim, then be done with it. I would have this chore over and done so I can rest."

He smiled tauntingly. "Are you so anxious for my touch, my love? Don't you know that one such as you rates slow, careful attention, not a hasty and heedless mating such as beasts are wont to do?"

Chuckling at the look of outrage on her face, he stretched his long muscular body out beside her. The bed tilted under his weight, bringing her to rest firmly against him, and before she could escape, he circled her with a possessive arm and fit her even more closely to his form.

"You are a beast," she said scathingly. "So I would expect you to mate as one."

Her words failed to anger him, and the fire she tried so desperately to douse built to a raging inferno as he proceeded with his careful attention. Every fiber of her being cried out to cradle him in her arms as his mouth sought out each breast in turn and gently teased until she finally could not stifle a sigh of contentment. Then his lips moved to graze on the flat plain of her abdomen while his hand teasingly brushed and tickled the soft skin of her thighs, coming finally to rest in the nest of downy curls that hid the heated, throbbing core of her. When his mouth replaced his hand in the most sensitive of spots, she jerked away and cried out in protest.

"No! Rorik! This is surely a mortal sin!"

He laughed, low and throaty. "No motral sin, my innocent. Just mortal pleasure."

She had no more strength to protest, and he did with her what he would. His gentle, expert caresses sapped the last of her resistance, and she thought no more on vows and dignity. When he finally sheathed his aching manhood in her softness she was already riding the crest of her passion. Unashamed, she clung to him, desperately trying to bring him into her deeper and faster. But he gently kissed away her desperation, holding her against him until her breathing calmed.

"Patience, sweet Alaine," he breathed, himself stiff and needful with desire. "We take this trip together."

And they did. He took them to the high jagged peaks and then beyond to the sweet warm valley of fulfullment and perfect union. As her body pulsed with the ecstasy of release and she felt her husband's arms close tightly around her in possessive fervor, an instinct as old as time awoke in her soul and told her that more than lust had fueled the fire that was now burning slowly down to embers.

Long after Rorik had fallen into sated slumber, Alaine lay awake and stared into the dark. Without even looking she could picture the man beside her—the dark face that could look so gentle in sleep, so fierce when he must face the waking world, the superbly muscled body that could cause such pleasure, and such pain, the large callused hands that could wield a broadsword with killing skill, yet so gently caress a woman's sensitive body. Rorik was a fit master for Ste. Claire and a fit husband for herself, hard though it was for her to admit. But would he remain a true husband after he had his coveted Brix, after Ste. Claire had reverted once again to a minor fief among his many estates?

Alaine sighed and turned so that her head rested in the hollow of her husband's broad shoulder. Rorik stirred and drew her closer with one arm, still sound asleep. A brief, sad smile touched her face. How different her problems were now from when she had fled to the forest weeks ago. Then she'd been set to drive the invader away. Now she must fight to keep him. She couldn't hold herself from him on principle. He knew his power over her. He fascinated her, overwhelmed her. His simplest touch ignited her. She supposed if there were really such a thing as love between a man and a woman, she just might love this man.

But how to make him return her feelings in kind? It wasn't in her to accept being a mere adjunct to Rorik's life—a vessel for his lust and the key to Ste. Claire's support. She had to show him she was better than his bitterness painted her. No easy job, considering their relationship up to now. Her behavior certainly hadn't been a model of wifely propriety.

She raised herself on one elbow and looked down at her problem. He looked so peaceful when sleeping. How could he be so contrary when awake? She smiled in spite of herself. She was Alaine de Ste. Claire. She had never backed down from a challenge. She would fight not with the silly men's weapons she had always been so proud of, but with the new weapons she was just learning to use. She would prove she could wield these women's weapons with skill equal to her talents with bow and sword.

Poor Rorik, she thought with a smile. He had a bigger battle than Brix ahead of him, and he couldn't even see it coming.

CHAPTER 16

The hawking party left a mid-morning. Hawking was not a popular winter sport, and most ladies and gentlemen much preferred to ride out when the weather was fine, but Alaine convinced Rorik that the inhabitants of Ste. Claire would appreciate the jaunt. The noble men and women who rode to the hunt would benefit from the fresh air and exercise, and the serving people and common folk who were left in the castle would be given a much-needed rest by their absence. More than two weeks had passed since the last of the wedding guests had departed, and left to themselves, with only the work of girding the castle against the full onslaught of winter, the folk of Ste. Claire were getting a bit snappish. Even sweet-tempered Mathilde was heard to scold sharply a serving girl for some imagined clumsiness, and Alaine herself was growing restive within the dank walls of her home. She was accustomed to being out-of-doors in all kinds of weather, and having to play the proper lady and stay within the damp and gloomy keep did not sit well on her spirit.

These days past since Rorik had returned from the hunting lodge, Alaine had faultlessly played the proper wife. No more did she resist her husband's lovemaking. She openly enjoyed herself, and his ardor seemed to grow apace with her enjoyment. More than once as they lay entwined in each other's arms she thought she detected a warmth of eye or gentleness of voice that bore witness to a softening of Rorik's heart. But always when daylight appeared the magic was gone. His guard would snap back into place, and she despaired that the stone wall he had built around himself ever would crack.

If she allowed herself to be wanton in the late hours of the night, during the day she tried hard to act the proper lady. She groomed herself with a care she had never used before, and though she couldn't quite bring herself to relegate her men's garments to the fire, at least she no longer scorned the fine chemises, gowns, and cloaks of her trousseau. The only thing she refused to alter was her manner. The perfect lady was soft-spoken, gentle-mannered, coy, and mildly flirtatious—traits that did not fit well with the outspoken and straightforward person her father had raised her to be. She refused to change her inner self, even to win her husband's regard.

The day was going to be bright and fine, she decided as she rode beside her husband on the spirited little mare he'd given her on their wedding day. The morning fog was burning off, and the pale but determined sun was breaking through more and more to warm the land and melt the rime of frost that covered the grasses and trees. The sharp hooves of their mounts struck the hard-frozen path in an almost musical rhythm, ringing through the chill morning air. Alaine's heart sang like a bird released from an iron-barred cage, so glad was she to escape the gloomy confines of the keep.

"You look in rare spirits this morning, wife," Rorik said. His smile was unusually warm. Indeed, he was having difficulty pulling his eyes away from his wife's glowing face. She was like a child released from chores, like a bouncy pup escaped from its kennel. The brightness of her sea-blue eyes recalled the look of her in the forest when she'd challenged him, all confident and sassy and bent on rebellion. But now some of the sharp edges were gone. The image was softer. She had the look of a woman, no longer a girl. Rorik wondered if he could take credit for that transformation. Had he stirred the woman in her and produced that glow? He was reluctant to think so, for that would produce one more tie between them, and this little golden-haired maid had already made too many inroads into his carefully guarded heart. He had vowed with good reason to let no woman past his defenses, and here he'd married the one female who seemed to melt his stone shell with her smile and disarm his wariness with her innocent and forthright manner. He shook his head, wondering at his own foolish blindness. It had seemed such a smart idea at the time.

"You are pensive this morning, Rorik," Alaine commented. "That frown is not suited to so fine a day."

He started guiltily, wondering if she could detect how completely she filled his thoughts. "I was thinking on the band of miscreants that raided Bethune two days ago," he lied. "It nettles me that they've eluded my grasp. I should be running them to ground, not trotting off on gentle sport such as this."

"Even the lord of the castle deserves his day of relaxation," she said with a bright smile. "You will deal with the outlaws before they do much more mischief. You are more clever than they, and they can't hide from you for long."

He regarded her with lifted brow. "You are most confident in my abilities."

She laughed, and he thought how the merry sound seemed to lighten the air around her. "I should know your abilities well. You were clever enough to outsmart me, and I know that I am wilier by far than these common outlaws."

"You did give me a fair run," he said with a grin. "I appreciate you and your comrade-in-arms Garin much more now that you're on my side."

"Do you?" A momentary shadow darkened her face, but Rorik failed to notice. He was staring into a copse to the side of their path.

"What's this?" He reined the chestnut stallion to an abrupt halt. "We may yet have some sport from this day."

At that moment the two hounds that had been running in and out of the forest all morning, celebrating their release from the kennel, burst out of the trees next to the low, thorny copse. With great rustling and twig-cracking, three game hens rose from the briars and stretched for the sky. In a trice the fine falcon William had given Rorik as a wedding gift was unhooded and released. Quickly his powerful wings lifted him high above his prey. The hen that caught his eye didn't have a chance as cruel talons descended upon her. The whole drama was over in less than a minute.

"Go ahead and release your bird," Rorik told Alaine.

Alaine had kept her little sparrow hawk hooded and quiet, not wanting him to compete with the more powerful falcon. Now she released him after the other hens. She had trained the bird herself, and took pride in his steady and determined pursuit and his clean kill. The other members of the party applauded as the birds returned with their prey.

Morning wore into afternoon. The sun was shining steadily now, and when the party stopped to refresh themselves with bread, cheese, and cold meat, all were in good

spirts. Everyone had had at least middling luck, and they
would bring home enough birds for a modest meal. Even
Gunnor seemed in a rare good humor. She had curbed her
tongue over the last days, and Alaine chose to believe it
was because of a change of heart rather than her threat of a
few days past. But whatever the reason, she was grateful
for the small measure of peace her stepsister was giving
her.

When the meal was consumed and the party mounted up
to continue the sport, Rorik gave his falcon to Sir Guillaume.
Alaine saw him say a few words to the knight and gesture
toward the west. She nudged her mare until she was next
to the two of them.

"Is aught amiss?" she asked with a little frown.

"Nay," Rorik assured her. "It's just that I've a thought
to scout out part of the route to Brix this afternoon, since
we've come this far north. The sport can continue without
me."

Alaine's brow furrowed in irritation. Always his mind
was on Brix and what had been done to him there. Spring
and the time for war was months away, but he could not
rest from the thought of it. He must take himself away and
set his mind to routes and strategies and logistics.

"I would ride with you, if you'll have me, husband."

She could not yield him completely to his war games on
this fine afternoon. On this day more than ever before she
sensed a softening in his demeanor toward her. Almost
could she glimpse the real man who hid behind the stone
wall. She wouldn't let him escape now.

The crease in his brow told her he was annoyed, but he
couldn't rebuff her openly in front of retainers and family.
"If you wish." He yielded with only a slight edge of pique
in his voice.

For an hour they rode a course parallel with the sinking
sun, then they veered to the north. Finally they crested a
hill that gave them a clear view of the rocky coastline. The
gleaming ribbon of the Ste. Claire cut the hills to the west,
and in the far distance turned broad and sluggish and
joined itself with the sea. North of the river mouth the hills

grew higher and more rugged. And beyond the hills, Alaine knew, lay the village and castle of Brix.

She had seen Brix only once, on that desperate ride for help when Rorik had first surrounded Ste. Claire and Gilbert had squatted within. Before that day she had never been as far as the mouth of the Ste. Claire, which lay a good five miles from her overlord's castle. Suddenly she was gripped with a feeling of foreboding. She didn't want to see Brix ever again. Not ever. She wanted to run back to the safety of her own keep and drag her warring husband with her, where she could keep him safe. Strange feelings, she mused, for a maid who had always prided herself on her proficiency with the weapons of war.

Rorik's eyes followed the winding river to the end of its course. "There ends our easy path." His comment was aimed as much at himself as at her. They were the first words he'd spoken since they had left the group behind. He had ridden beside her but barely acknowledged her presence, as if thoughts of Brix and his final revenge had dredged up bitter reminders of the reason for his caution around the fair sex. "From there on we must traverse the hills."

"It's a rugged path," Alaine said. "But the roughness of the way over those last hills might hide your coming."

"No need to hide. I intend to give Fulk plenty of notice of my coming. I won't sneak up on the man like a thief in the night."

Alaine looked at him curiously. "Did he do you and your family such courtesy?"

A cynical smile twisted Rorik's mouth. "Nay. That he did not. But in spite of what you think, wife, I am not the knave that he is. Come." He set heels to his stallion and turned him to the west. "I've a desire to see if the seashore here is the same as I remember it."

The country grew rockier and the hills steeper as they approached the sea, but the way grew easier when they found a narrow path that wound between the rocks and the scree-covered slopes.

"This is the path I remember," Rorik smiled, reminiscing as he looked out over the half-remembered landscape.

"Did you venture this far south when you were a boy at Brix?" Alaine asked.

"Here and farther," he answered. "Several times I visited Ste. Claire with my father. Even once was I introduced to Sir Geoffrey's daughter, a little yellow-haired maid of six years. Though from her dress and manners one would not have thought her a baron's daughter."

Alaine had the grace to blush. "I don't remember you."

"You paid me little heed at the time," he smiled, "so I don't wonder. Sir Geoffrey seemed right proud of your wildness, and my father remarked on our ride home that you'd doubtless grow up to be the devil's own handmaid unless some good woman took you in hand. So I wasn't much surprised to find you running around the forest like a common woods-thief when I arrived at Ste. Claire and learned your father was dead."

Alaine sniffed indignantly. "I was not running around the forest like a common thief. I was defending my land."

"From its rightful warder."

"I didn't know that at the time."

"Well now that you know, don't forget again."

Alaine frowned. His tone was half-jesting, but there was an underlying hint of warning in his voice. What brought on the sudden reminder of their contentious past? Now there was peace between them, or what passed for peace. When would he stop thinking she was ever set against him?

"I would not turn on you again to fight, Rorik. I don't take my vows so lightly."

Rorik's answering smile had a cynical twist. "And as you said this morning, you are smarter than those miscreants in the woods. Come. We'll have to dismount here. These beasts can't climb down the rock face to the sand."

They secured their mounts and made their way along the path to the drop-off that led to the beach. Alaine followed Rorik in tight-lipped silence. Why must he persist in such a stubborn attitude? What must she do to prove herself worthy of his regard? This morning he had seemed to thaw, and now in the afternoon he was ice-cold and frozen once again. Her pride stung. Why did she even try? she asked herself. The stubborn jackass wasn't worth it. Let him go through life rejecting the love and companionship she could offer! Someday he would regret that he had treated her thusly!

The way down to the beach was more a series of precarious handholds and footholds than a footpath. Alaine's gown hampered her agility, and she finally set foot on the sand some minutes after Rorik was already at the water's edge. She impatiently flicked her skirts aside and descended the last few feet.

The wind from the sea was cold and filled with stinging, salty spray torn from the foaming water. The rocks and beach seemed to vibrate with the power of the roiling surf that alternately sucked and pounded at the land. Standing where high water could lap at his feet, Rorik stood with legs slightly apart and arms folded across his chest, looking out to sea. His tall form was reflected in the wet, smooth, mirrorlike sands where he stood.

Reluctant to get her shoes wet, Alaine set them by the rocks and, hiking up her skirts to her knees, went to stand beside her husband. If he noticed her presence he didn't acknowledge it. For a long moment they stood, each with their silent thoughts. Then his gaze swept slowly to the north, where stood Brix beyond the reach of their eyes. His face grew granite-hard, his eye sharp and stony as the green flinty rocks they had just climbed down. Alaine felt him begin to drift out of her reach.

"Is it the same as you remember?" she asked, grasping for his attention.

"What?" He turned toward her with a frown.

"The beach. Is it the same as you remember?"

He sighed and abandoned his brooding concentration. "It has changed." He looked around as if for the first time. "There's less sand, and more rock. It's been nearly twelve years since I've set foot on this beach."

"When were you last here?"

"My father and I stopped here once on a trip between Ste. Claire and Brix. My father caught a fish in the surf—I don't know what it was. But it tasted good."

Alaine sighed. "Most everything changes in twelve long years."

Rorik looked again in the direction of his family home. "Aye. Things change. But some things can be brought back again."

A few yards along the beach the dark flinty rocks reached down to the water's edge. They had been scoured smooth by countless years of thundering waves, but this time of day they were well above the tide. Alaine took a seat on a polished surface, grateful for the warmth of the sun-baked rock against her as the cold breeze continued to blow off the water. Rorik followed her and leaned against the jutting outcrop. The raucous cry of a seagull on wing punctuated the silence that grew between them. Alaine watched as Rorik's thoughts flew once again off to Brix.

"What will you do in the spring, husband, when you take Brix back again?" There was no doubt in her voice that he would retake his home. Rorik's whole life was war, and he was as skilled a fighter as Alaine had ever seen.

"What mean you—what will I do? I will take back what is mine and rule it as my family always has."

"And how will you revenge yourself on your lady mother who betrayed you? Will you put her to the sword?"

He shot her a surprised look.

"Sihtric told me the story of what happened," she explained.

"Sihtric goes beyond his bounds."

She smiled wryly. "He thought to explain why you act such a fool at times."

"Did he now?"

"But you haven't answered my question," she insisted.

"I doubt my mother long survived Fulk's rule." Rorik's voice was bitter. "He wanted her for one thing only. Fulk's avarice is for land and power, not for women."

"But she's still there," Alaine told him. "I met the

Lady Theoda myself when I rode to Brix for help against you.''

Rorik was grimly silent, his brooding eyes fixed on the sea.

"She's aged beyond her years. I don't think Fulk has been kind to her.''

"Why do you concern yourself with her fate?'' Rorik frowned.

"I would hate what it would do to you, should you vent your hatred on her,'' Alaine said in a thoughtful voice.

Rorik smiled cynically. "And you think I would harm my own mother, the dame who gave me birth?''

Alaine was not to be put off. "Considering what she did, I think you might.''

"And you would champion her?''

She was silent.

"Aye,'' he continued in a dark voice. "I see you would. Do women always excuse so lightly one another's perfidies?''

"I excuse nothing,'' Alaine told him evenly. "My concern is for you.''

Rorik turned toward her, his eyes like green chips of ice. "You needn't concern yourself for me, madam. I've been seeing to my own affairs since I was far younger than you. Rather concern you with yourself.''

With that he turned his back on her and the sea and started to climb up the rocks to the cliff top, leaving her angry, frustrated shout to be blown away by the wind.

When Alaine gained the cliff top, Rorik was no longer there. Her mare was waiting restlessly where she was tied, but the stallion was gone. Alaine suppressed the urge to kick the nearest tree, angry both with Rorik for being stubborn, pigheaded, and broody, and at herself for allowing her unruly tongue to once more rouse her husband's displeasure. The day had started out so well, and now had ended in disaster. When Rorik's men named him the Stone Dragon, they surely knew whereof they spoke!

She had spent more time then she'd thought brooding on the beach below, and now the sun was only two fingers above the surface of the sea. The shadows were growing long as Alaine guided the mare along the path. Earlier the way had seemed so bright and open. Now, with the day rapidly drawing to a close, the craggy rocks and looming trees took on ominous shapes, and the merging shadows harbored dark night imaginings. Alaine jumped as a rabbit darted suddenly out of a shadow and into the path, making the mare skitter to the side. She took a deep breath as the rabbit scurried down the path, willing her heart to resume its normal pace. She was as skittish as the mare, Alaine scolded herself. Though perhaps she had some reason, for the forest harbored wolves both animal and human, and the hours of dark, Father Sebastian so often said, were when Satan's own demons came forth and did their mischief. She had never believed his stories, of course. They were just fabrications to frighten children into being good. But with the gloom gathering so rapidly around her and the lonely silence of the hills pressing in on her imagination, she wondered if the old priest hadn't been telling the truth after all.

She rode through the gathering dusk, cursing Rorik for leaving her behind in his fit of anger and scolding herself for not following immediately on his heels. Had she thought he would wait patiently while she took her time sulking on the beach? More likely he would be glad to see her snatched up by some evil ghost or torn limb from limb by a pack of wolves. Then he would have her lands and her people and could take a wife more to his liking, if any woman could be to that man's liking.

She continued on to the spot where they had left the group early that afternoon. She almost expected to find Rorik awaiting her there, but the meadow was empty. The sun had sunk below the western hills and the sky was darkening. But now she was only an hour from the castle, and her overactive imagination was giving way before her innate practicality. She hoped Rorik was properly worried when he found that she was not following just a few minutes behind him, and she hoped Joanna gave him a thorough tongue-lashing when he returned without her. That usually soft-spoken lady feared no man when she was angry. She smiled at the thought of Rorik having to endure one of her stepmother's scoldings. And well did he deserve it!

She turned the mare south and followed the path they had traveled that morning. The creatures of the night were beginning to stir, and the mare snored warily at the rustlings and chitterings that accompanied their progress through the forest. Alaine grew jumpy again. She had lived in the forest for many days when Rorik had first come, but always she'd had her men around her and the comfort of a fire close by. Strange how loud and alive the forest was when one was alone. One set of rustlings especially seemed to be dogging her path, though Alaine tried to tell herself it was merely her imagination. Still she wished she had her sword at her side, or even her bow. With her weapons at hand she feared neither man nor beast. But alone and unarmed in this darkening wood she felt more vulnerable than the little rabbit that had earlier fled from their way.

Then up ahead two dark forms stepped into the path. They seemed as big as trees, but they weren't trees. They were men afoot. Alaine's heart speeded its pace and thumped heavily in her chest. Likely these two were not friendly woodsmen come to invite her to sup at their humble hut. No indeed! Much more likely they were part of the pack of scoundrels that Rorik was trying to run to ground.

She turned the mare right around and set her heels to the horse's sides. The mare sprang forward willingly, but whinnied in fright as four more shapes shot from the side of the path to grab at her. Alaine urged the horse forward with voice and heels, but the mare was no steed of war. One man had hold of her bridle and others crowded in front of her. She reared once and tried to back away, but others were approaching from the rear. Shivering, she stood and merely tossed her head as the outlaws swarmed around her.

Alaine slapped away the hands that grabbed at her. Her foot connected with one man's face, and another howled as

she whipped the loosened reins across his shoulders. But
there were too many of them, and in moments grasping
hands pulled her to the ground. The mare bolted as she felt
her rider's weight slip off her. A man grabbed at her, but
the wild-eyed horse sidled away, lurched free of the crowd,
and galloped down the path.

Alaine grunted with pain as she was pushed roughly to
the rocky ground. Hands groped at her, ignoring her kicks
and struggles. Above her was a sea of faces, indistinguish-
able in the gloom, but her imagination filled in the brutish
details.

"Damn!" one voice cursed. "If she had a purse, must'a
been on th'orse! Gilly, you run after that mare!"

"Run after t'damn 'orse yerself, damn yer arse!" Gilly
returned. "She's 'alfway t'Ste. Claire by now!"

Alaine attempted to rise, but was pushed roughly down
again.

"Well, we got somethin' fer our work. She's a right
pretty piece."

She felt multiple pairs of eyes turn on her, and sensed
the direction of their thoughts. Once again she struggled
against the hands that held her. This couldn't be happening
to her! Not to Alaine de Ste. Claire, who could outride any
man in the barracks and hold her own with a sword against
most of them! Not to Sir Geoffrey's tough little daughter
who had listened to the soldiers' stores of lustful play and
felt only grudging sympathy for the females forced to
endure their attentions. Now she was about to become a
plaything for men of a far rougher cut. This couldn't be
happening to her!

"She won't last long, from t'looks of 'er," one offered.
"She'll last long enough fer me!" another chuckled. "I
spotted 'er. I get first go at the goods!"

Already his dirty woolen hose was down around his
ankles, revealing long knobby legs and much more that
Alaine didn't care to see. He knelt and, ignoring her
frantic struggles, pushed her skirts up around her waist.
With no preliminaries he forced her legs apart and prepared to take his ease with the same casualness that a man

might relieve himself against a tree. Alaine bit her lip hard to hold in the scream that was pushing at her throat. She wouldn't give the slimy toads the satisfaction of hearing her agony!

"Wait!" The voice came just in time.

"What do ya mean, wait?" The man who knelt between her legs looked up in annoyance.

"Go stick it in something else, Erland! That there's the lady of Ste. Claire. Do you know what that dragon knight'll do t'us if'n we mess with 'is lady?"

"So who's to tell 'im, Alan? We throw 'er in a hole in t'woods. Or give 'er to t'wolves to gnaw. 'E'll never find the twit. Now leave me be! I'm fair ready to bust!"

"Crap for brains! What do ya think 'e'll give t'git 'er back? You were the one griping 'cause she 'ad na gold. Her ransom'll make us all rich men!"

Erland settled back on his bare skinny haunches and cast one regretful look at the feast spread before him. Then he reluctantly pulled Alaine's chemise back down over her knees.

"Git 'er up!" Alan ordered.

Ungentle hands pulled her to her feet and pushed her toward her unlikely savior. Alan confronted her with a sneer. He was a burly man and loomed huge and ominous in the dark.

"Yer 'usband better be prepared to pay well, my lady. 'Cause I wouldn't mind meself 'aving a bit o' what I saw down there. An' it wouldn't break my 'eart none to slit that pretty throat an' leave ya fer the wolves. I've 'ad my fill of fancy barons and their ladies."

Alaine was tempted to tell this arrogant swine that Rorik had had his fill of Alan and his band of cutthroats, also, but for once she wisely held her peace.

The journey to the band's camp was a nightmare Alaine doubted she would live through. Someone tied a filthy kerchief around her face and made it almost impossible, and certainly unpleasant, to breathe. Then her hands were bound and she was hefted facedown across someone's bony shoulder. The walk was long, and she thought her stomach must be ripped fairly in twain where the point of the man's shoulder dug into her gut. And frequently during the ride an exploring hand worked under her skirts and paused to crudely caress the contours of her rear. If she got out of this alive, she vowed, she would herself help Rorik to hunt these wolves down. She would note well the face of this particular tormentor so she could send an arrow through his throat.

Finally the torture was over. She was dumped abruptly onto the ground. Someone cut the rope that bound her hands and she pulled the filty cloth from around her face. She was in a small clearing. In the middle of a makeshift ring of logs, a blowsy woman tended a fire and occasionally stirred a pot sitting on the coals. A younger woman with faded red hair and a petulant mouth roasted birds over a spit. Except for the trash that littered the place and the dirt that liberally decorated all of its inhabitants, the camp could have been her old hideaway in the forest.

She got up on stiff legs and moved toward the fire. The blowsy woman regarded her with some sympathy in her face. She shoved a mug of something hot into her hands. The liquid almost spilled when Alan and one other man walked over and pushed her closer to the firelight.

"She's th'one, I tell ye!" Alan's companion peered intently at her face. "I was there. 'E wanted her bad, 'e did! 'E might pay better than Sir Rorik!"

Alaine looked at the man without recognition. A dark foreboding clouded her already exhausted mind. Could she possibly be in worse trouble than she thought?

"I was there when de Prestot took Ste. Claire, an' I tell ya 'e was about t'wed and bed this here very lass when Rorik comes roaring up. I tell ya 'e'll pay!"

"All right!" Alan said. "We'll send word to both Gilbert and Rorik. Then we'll just see who wants 'er most!"

Alaine shivered as a chill traveled down her spine. She was in far worse trouble than she thought!

Alan turned to her with a malicious grin. "We'll see 'ow much these gentlemen think yer worth, my lady. And then, when the money's in hand. . . .'' He laughed unpleasantly. ''Could be I'll change my mind about deliverin' the goods when the price is paid. I've never 'umped a fine piece like you in all ma cursed life. Ya just might be worth the risk. We'll see what these great and mighty bastard barons think then, when they see their plump little pigeon plucked by the likes of us!''

Alaine turned abruptly and walked away from the fire, away from the mad and leering face that mocked her. But his evil laughter followed her into the flickering shadows at the edge of the clearing. As she sat herself down against a tree and wrapped herself in her cloak, the blowsy woman came up to her to refill her now-cold drink. Alaine saw the glint of pity in the woman's eye, and it roused her ire. She was Alaine de Ste. Claire. She didn't need anyone's pity, and she wouldn't be bested by a slimy madman who wasn't fit to spit in a worm's eye. She would show them all just who it was they dealt with. Somehow she would think of a way to best these ruffians.

As the fire died and one by one the outlaws collapsed on the ground and wrapped themselves in their cloaks, she sat, cold, angry and bound by harsh and chafing rope. She was too furious to be fearful as she sat and stared into the dark and planned a glorious escape.

CHAPTER 17

The day was a dismal one, with heavy clouds shrouding the tops of the trees and a cold rain drizzling down from the gray sky. The morning was as gloomy within the keep walls as without. In the hall Rorik paced back and forth in front of the hearth. Joanna and Mathilde fretted at the high table, and even Gunnor looked distressed as she sat beside them and toyed distractedly with her porridge. Knights and squires and men-at-arms murmured among themselves and shook their heads.

Sihtric strode in, his pale yellow mustache beaded with frost.

"We're ready to ride—again." He held his hands out to the fire to drive away the numbing chill.

Rorik picked up his helm and threw a heavy cloak over his broad shoulders. His face was pale under its usual bronze, and shadows made his eyes seem deeper and darker than they were. But his hand was steady as he settled his sword in its scabbard. Sihtric, too, looked almost as pale as his hair. His mouth was a white slash in his face, and the only color in his cheeks came from the cold north wind that blew the rain against the stone walls of the keep.

Rorik and Sihtric had spent all the long night searching back along the trail the hawking party had taken. Other search parties combed the hills, meadows, and woods from the castle west to the sea and back again. But when night finally faded into the misty gray of morning, the only result of the search was a host of exhausted men and horses. Alaine had disappeared as if the wind had picked her up and blown her into another world—without a trace, without a clue.

Rorik had paused in his search only long enough to wolf down some breakfast and trade his spent stallion for a fresh horse from Ste. Claire's stables. His mind was haunted by a pert face with mischievous blue eyes and saucily curved lips, all flamboyantly framed with hair the color of sunlit gold. In a cursed fit of pique he'd left her to her own defenses, never dreaming she wouldn't follow directly on his heels. What other maid would be so bold as to linger alone when her protector left? Now she was lying hurt somewhere, alone and afoot. Her mare had been found an hour before the sun rose grazing in the village meadows, covered with scratches and dried sweat and mane tangled with brambles and thorns. Rorik couldn't believe Alaine had been thrown, not unless the worst had happened. If the horse had been terrified by a wild beast, or even worse, a band of cutthroats and rogues. . . . His thoughts shied away. He slammed his tankard down on the table and turned to Sihtric.

"Let's ride, then, if you say all is ready."

"Aye. There's ten lads from the village eager to go, though the lot of them have never sat a horse before. At least they had their rest last night, so I hope their eyes are sharper than mine this morn!"

Before they reached the door of the hall young Sir Robert burst in with a bedraggled, hollow-cheeked, and somewhat confused-looking youth in tow.

"My lord!" the young knight panted. "This varlet was caught trying to sneak into the keep. He says he has a tale for your ears, but I can't pry a word from him. It's about your lady, he says."

Rorik grasped the boy's shoulder in a bruising grip. "What is this tale you carry?"

The boy cringed at Rorik's frown. He eyed the fierce-looking knight with trepidation, then nearly choked when Sihtric's muscular bulk came in view.

"Get a hold on yourself, boy!" Sihtric advised in tones that were anything but soothing. "We'll not bite your head off. Say what you've come to say."

"I . . . I . . . !" the boy stammered.

"Gwyne!" Rorik roared. "Bring this lad a draught of beer. I think he needs something to liven his throat."

"I was down in t'west meadow," the boy croaked, then gratefully took the mug proffered by an amused Gwyne. "I looks after t'cows."

"Go on," Rorik commanded impatiently.

"This stranger came up t'me—some 'un I've not seen 'ereabouts. 'E says I was t'come ta the castle, an' tell the Lord Rorik that 'e an' 'is fellows 'ave yer lady."

The boy drew away, cringing at the look on Rorik's face, but Sihtric stayed him with a firm grip on his arm. "And . . ." the big Norseman prompted.

"An' you were t'bring two hundred gold coins to the Boar's 'ead Inn. Elsewise they'll deliver 'er 'ead''—the boy blushed scarlet—"an' other parts, ta t'church in Ste. Claire."

Rorik's eyes narrowed to fierce slits, and the boy swore he was facing the Devil himself. Desperately he vowed to never do another bad thing if God would only let him escape this keep alive.

"Was that all he said, boy?" Rorik asked in a tightly controlled voice.

"I swear, m'lord! That's all. 'E said 'is piece an' then gave me a kick in t'rear ta get me goin'. 'E was an evil sort, bold as can be!"

"You're a brave lad." Rorik's big hand landed on the boy's shoulder once again, making him jump with alarm. "Go to the kitchen and tell Mistress Hilda you're to have a good meal and a new woolen tunic. Take him, Gwyne."

The astonished and delighted boy almost skipped with joy as he went off with a smiling Gwyne. It appeared he was not only going to escape the keep alive but with considerable bounty as well. And what a tale he would have to tell his fellows when the cows were brought in this night!

Rorik's eyes followed the boy until he disappeared into the kitchen passageway, but his mind was miles away, at the Boar's Head Inn near the village of Bethune. So the worst had happened, but the uncertainty was over. His heart felt as though the tight band of tension that had been squeezing tighter and tighter all the night long had finally loosened. He had to be stern with himself to keep from shouting his relief for all to hear. Time later for celebration. Time later for anger and cursing himself for letting this happen. Now was the time for action. He had no illusions about the outlaws' intentions, and there was grim work to be done before Alaine would once more be safe. If they had harmed a hair on her fair head, Rorik vowed, they would every last man of them regret he had ever been born.

* * *

The Boar's Head Inn, set in the pine woods a short ride from Bethune, was a respectable place, as such places go. It served food and ale to travelers along the road from Cherbourg to Coutances, and for those who didn't wish to brave the forest at night, it had several rooms above the taproom that could sleep up to six on a reasonably flea-and lice-free mattress. The less affluent were always welcome, for a smaller price, to bed down in the straw with the horses or find their rest on a hard wooden bench in front of the taproom fire. The proprietor, old John o' the Woods, was a plump and good-humored fellow who in his younger days made his way as a woodsman, but an ill-placed branch on a falling tree had pinned him to the forest floor for three days and two nights. When he'd been found, his crushed arm had been black and swollen. A fellow axman had rid him of the festering limb and saved his life. But though old John was a good man with an ax even with only one arm, he had found it easier by far to wed the plump, comely widow who'd caught his fancy and retire to a less active life.

Together they built and ran the Boar's Head Inn. John and a hired boy tended the taproom while his wife saw to the kitchen. Two merry serving girls, Gillian and Rachel, helped in the kitchen and served the customers their drinks, food, and whatever other favors they might desire. It was a solid, respectable inn, and if John occasionally turned his eyes the other way when characters of dubious reputation met and talked over a bowl of his wife's venison stew, or if fellows with a cutthroat gleam in their eye came to swill his ale or give the girls a lusty tumble, at least no one could ever say he'd been set upon or robbed at the Boar's Head.

On this gloomy afternoon only a few souls had taken refuge from the damp and the cold in front of the taproom fire. But the coming night would be a cold one, and John thought with satisfaction on the number of villagers and farmers who would find his cozy taproom preferable to their own miserable huts. Rachel and Gillian were sitting at a corner table giggling at their own girlish conversation now, but they would be busy enough once the sun had set.

The inn door swung open. A gust of rain and cold air followed on the heels of the tall, scowling man who paused just inside the entrance. For a moment the new-comer's broad form was outlined against the glare in the doorway. Then he shut the door and moved inside the room.

Old John sat abruptly upright at his table near the hearth. He recognized the new lord of Ste. Claire even without his knightly regalia, for Sir Rorik had stopped at the inn some days back with the old lord's daughter, who he'd taken to wife. They had paused for a mug of cold ale and a taste of his Gertrude's good stew, and the lord had been most amiable while discussing the rents and duties the Boar's Head owed Ste. Claire, especially considering those rents and duties hadn't been paid in half a year's time. The lack of mail and helm, the proprietor noted, didn't make the man appear one whit smaller. Old John o' the Woods was a man who stood out among lesser men because of his size, but Rorik topped his height by a good two inches and matched his massive axman's shoulders in broadness.

Old John rose from his seat. "My lord, welcome to the Boar's Head once again. What may I do for you this day?"

It was passing strange, John thought, for a knight to be abroad without armor and a troop of men riding at his back, though, in truth, a whole army might be mounted outside for all he knew. There was a fighting look in Sir Rorik's eye, John noted, and decided wisely to keep his curiosity to himself.

"Will your lady wife be joining you as before?" John inquired politely. "My Gertrude has just cooked up some fine hot biscuits to go with sweet apple preserves. Perhaps your lady would care to sample . . ."

"My wife is not with me," Rorik said abruptly.

He gave old John a suspicious look, then swept the

room's other inhabitants with cold green eyes. Rachel and Gillian had ceased their giggling in the corner and were eyeing him with open invitation. One graybeard snored over an empty mug of ale at a table by the fire. Two burly young lads at another table were well dressed and well fed, and though they looked at Rorik with curiosity, they showed no signs of being the villains he had come to meet.

"Have you any other customers?" Rorik asked tersely.

"Nay, my lord," John answered quickly. "It is a quiet afternoon."

"Good," Rorik said.

He strode over to the table where the two girls sat, but instead of answering their smiles he ousted them from their seats and sat down at the table with his back in the corner and his face toward the door.

"Bring me a mug, John."

"Yes, my lord!" John hastened to obey.

For an hour Rorik sat nursing a mug of strong ale and waiting for the man who was to meet him there. He cast suspicious glances at the snoring greybeard, but before many minutes had passed, that worthy woke with a snort, eyed his empty mug and empty pockets with disgust, and staggered out the door. So Rorik settled back and continued to wait. The outlaw messenger had said to come alone, and alone he was, without armor and with a sword and a knife his only weapons. But he felt as though he could take on an army with the rage that he had dammed in his breast.

The innkeeper eyes him uneasily, not accustomed to glowering barons lingering for so long in his humble establishment.

"May I serve you another, my lord?

Rorik handed him the empty mug for a refill. "There's a man who'll come through that door this afternoon," he said as the full mug was placed in front of him. "The man and I have grave business, and whatever befalls I want no interference from you, or from your customers."

Old John's brow furrowed and his mouth drew into a grim line. He could not afford to have his inn broken up by a pair of heedless feuding knights, if that was what Sir Rorik was going about. But he held his tongue and satisfied himself with a resigned "As you wish, my lord."

But the man who finally appeared and strode with a cocky grin over Rorik's table was certainly no knight, John noted some minutes later. The innkeeper had seen his face before in his taproom, but certainly not in company with folk of the noble class.

" 'Ola! Sir Rorik!" The man greeted Ste. Claire's lord with contemptuous familiarity and sat himself down at the table. "Innkeeper! Ale here! And make it good and cold!"

John hastened to serve the newcomer, curious as to what was coming, but the stony hard look at Rorik's face inspired a quick exit back to the safety of the bar.

"I see ya got our message." The man grinned confidently. He wasn't smart enough to be afraid.

"Indeed," Rorik answered with deceptive mildness.

"An' ya' come alone?"

"Do you have eyes in your head to see?" Rorik replied. "Is a troop waiting without?"

"Never can tell, m'lord." The man sneered out the title. "But if you've got some lads 'id in the trees, the lady'll be the first to feel a blade."

Rorik smiled calmly. There was no hidden troop for this man's prying eyes to discover. Sihtric had ranted at his decision to come alone, and Joanna, for once in agreement with the burly Norseman, had joined him in naming Rorik a fool. But Rorik was loath to endanger Alaine's life any more than it was already. He could handle these cutthroats himself. If he couldn't, he had no right to call himself a leader of fighting men.

"And did your fellows trust you to come alone for all this gold?" Rorik asked, knowing the answer before the man replied.

The outlaw guffawed. "Me fellows don't trust no one wit' nuthin'. If you've tricks up yer sleeve, m'lord, think again and look at those two 'earties at the door."

Rorik glanced at the two who had just stepped inside the room. They were brawny and unshaven, with greasy hair hanging past their shoulders. One had an impressive scar running from scalp to neckline along the side of his face. What a shame, Rorik thought, that the good fellow who'd given him that scar hadn't taken better aim.

"Do ya 'ave the gold?" Rorik's unwholesome tablemate queried, impatient to get his hands on the glittering stuff.

"I have the gold," Rorik returned. "You'll get it when I see my wife here at the table with me."

The man laughed, spitting droplets into Rorik's face. "Do ya think us daft, m'lord? Yer lady's safe enough back at our little 'ideway. Give over the gold we asked for, an' she c'n find 'er way 'ome on 'er own. She's a right feisty lass, she is," he leered. "She'll make 'er own way."

Rorik longed to remove the man's mostly rotten teeth with his hard fist, but with an uncommon strength of will he managed to hold his temper.

"Then you have a problem, my man." He smiled a deadly smile. "For until my wife is safely in my hands, you get no gold."

The outlaw was made a trifle uneasy by the fierce light he saw burning in Rorik's eyes, in spite of the two sturdy fellows standing by the door.

"You 'ave the problem, Sir Rorik," he scoffed. "If'n we don't git back ta camp wit' the gold, yer lady's goin' ta be crow's meat, after the lads 'ave 'ad their fill of fun, o'course."

Rorik seemed undisturbed by the outlaw's threat. "Then by all means let's take the gold to your camp." With no hint of warning he unleased his big fist in the man' face, which met his oncoming knuckles with a satisfying crunch. The fellow didn't have time to be surprised as his eyes rolled back in their sockets and he crashed, bench and all, onto the rush-strewn dirt floor, dead to the world.

John o' the Woods, minding his business behind the bar, jumped and stared as Sir Rorik's table companion hit the floor. Rachel and Gillian screamed, the two well-dressed young men stared, and the two unsavory brutes by the door leapt forward into the fray, glad to be given an excuse to shed some blood. Rorik met them with sword in one hand and knife in another. The death's-head grin on his face matched their bloodthirsty grimaces as the two of the flew at him with blades swinging.

The outlaws' weapons were both sent flying by Rorik's first furious attack. Likewise were the confident grins wiped from their faces. Suddenly it seemed to them that two-to-one odds were not nearly high enough against this man. One grabbed up a sturdy oaken stool to fend off Rorik's deadly blade. The other ran to retrieve their swords from where they had slid to rest against the base of the bar.

The two young men at the fireside table stood up and drew their swords, eager to join the fun but uncertain which side deserved their help. Though it seemed a knavish deed for two to leap upon one man, it was painfully clear that the two were more than outclassed by the big man with the black hair. Before they could add their own sharpened steel to the battle, old John scurried cautiously across the room and urged them toward the door.

"A thousand pardons, young gentlemen, but my lord there wishes no interference with his . . . business."

He hastened to push them out into the cold afternoon, not even bothering to collect coin for their drink. He would be fortunate indeed, John thought miserably, if all he lost from this fracas were a few coins.

Rorik made short work of the two villains who had been so eager to cut his throat. By the time the inkeeper had sped the two wondering guests on their way and hastened back to the taproom, the two lay on the floor beside their companon. Their blood was soaking through the rushes onto the packed dirt of the floor. Rorik had sent a flustered Rachel for a bucket of water and was busy dousing his first victim. The man sputtered and choked, then sat up groggily and spit. Two teeth bounced over the wet rushes.

"Now, my friend"—Rorik ungently lifted the man from the floor and pushed him against the bar—"we will hear where this camp of yours is."

The man opened his bloody mouth to speak, but only moaned.

"Out with it, knave, or I promise you'll regret the day you laid eyes on my wife."

The outlaw gathered his courage and his hatred and spit full into Rorik's face. Rorik wiped the blood and spittle from his cheek as John and the two rapt serving girls held their collective breath. The knight's face grew hard and stony, and John recalled for an instant the evil-looking red dragon that Rorik bore on his shield. Did he see a hint of red glowing in the knight's eyes now? No. . . . Of course it was impossible.

Rorik deliberately drew out the long knife that was sheathed in his belt. He held it so the lantern light gleamed off the sharply honed edge. The outlaw's eyes grew wide as the wicked blade approached his face.

"There are many ways to die." Rorik's quiet voice was full of promise. "You can lead me to your camp and join your fellows in fighting me there. . . . Or I can make this a very unpleasant afternoon for you." Rorik's malicious smile allowed no doubt as to the truth of his words. "Not a very knightly way to kill a man," he acknowledged. "But I think I am not dealing with men who hold closely to honor."

The outlaw seemed to collapse in on himself. His mouth flapped several times as he watched the keen blade weave before his anguished eyes. "No!" The word came out in a strangled whisper. "I'll take ya, m'lord! I'll take ya straight to 'em. I promise! No tricks! I'll take ya!"

Rorik smiled and sheathed his knife.

Alaine sat on the wet ground and contemplated the teardrops of rain that dripped from the hood of her cloak. There was nothing else to occupy her attention, and had been nothing else this whole long miserable day. Every half-formed plan to escape had died aborning. Dull-witted as they seemed, the outlaws were sharp enough to know that escape for her would mean disaster for them. Every moment she had been watched. Even when she'd gone to attend to nature's needs a grinning member of the band had accompanied her. Not even their own women would they entrust with the task of keeping her with them.

So she sat watching the rain drip from the front of her cowl, watching and waiting and hoping for a miracle, for a diversion of the outlaws' attention, for some sharp edge left within reach of her bound hands.

The afternoon stretched on, and the watery daylight grew dim as the hidden sun sank toward the horizon. A cold fog settled in among the trees and gave the little clearing a ghostly air. Even sound was muffled, and the steady chopping of one of the outlaws splitting firewood sounded like a woodsman working far away in the recesses of the forest. Alaine's spirit was steadily sinking. Night was approaching, and even if the ransom were paid—by either Rorik or Gilbert—she knew she wouldn't live to see the morning. And the way she would meet her end did not bear thinking on. The outlaws had been eyeing her all day, like hungry wolves anxious to get to the feast and the kill.

"They oughta' be back by now," one man complained.

Erland laughed sourly. "If'n you 'ad a purse full o' gold and an inn full o' ale, would you 'urry out into the cold an' rain? I told ya we shoulda' all gone."

Alan spat into the dirt. "They'll be back. They know I'll find 'em if they take off."

"Don't know why we can't start without 'em." A man with a beard full of grease from the venison he'd been eating leered in Alaine's direction. "I could use a bit o' sport ta warm me bones. Don't know why we've waited this long!"

"You'll 'ave yer sport," Alan promised, "an' the gold, too. So quit yer squirmin'."

For a few minutes the dripping silence was unbroken. Then Alan cocked his head.

"I think they're comin'!"

He was right. Out of the drizzling fog a man's form materialized. The messenger's face wore a sickly grin. Blood was crusted dark red around his mouth.

"Did 'e come?" Erland asked eagerly. "Did ya get the gold?"

"He came."

It wasn't the messenger who spoke, but the dark form behind him—man and horse, hidden mostly by the dense fog. The horse stepped forward, pushing the hapless messenger into the clearing. The outlaws' eyes grew wide with surprise. Even through the fog the firelight glowed off the blood-red dragon on the shield and glinted off the sharp edge of drawn broadsword.

"Rorik!"

It was the glad greeting from Alaine that mobilized the outlaws into action. Alan, Erland, Gilly, and the big man with the greasy beard all drew steel. The two women by the fire fled hastily into the rain and fog, and, after a moment of hesitation, three more outlaws followed on their heels. The messenger bolted after them. Rorik let him go, concentrating on the four in front of him. He smiled unpleasantly, dismounted, and nudged his destrier—one of Alaine's famous Ste. Claire bays—into the safety of the trees. He spared only a moment to regret that his own chestnut stallion had been too exhausted after a day and night of work to be ridden into this battle. And he could not risk riding an unfamiliar mount toward the hostile blades of men afoot.

"Are you ready to die?" Rorik asked, still smiling.

Alan's grin was just as wicked. He noted the lack of mail and helm. And now the fool had given up the advantage of warhorse as well. "We won't be the one's adyin' today, Sir Dragon," he said with a sneer. "We'll be celebratin' with yer lady, I'm thinkin'."

"Then think again, swine!"

Alaine gasped as all five men leaped at once. She knew Rorik's skill, but doubted even he could stand against four of these hardened men. Any moment she expected to see Sihtric and a troop of men-at-arms crash through the trees, but the forest was silent save for the ringing of steel and occasional grunts of effort or pain.

Erland was the first to feel the bite of Rorik's steel. He

gave a liquid scream and crumpled in a heap, twitched a few times, then was still. As the knot of fighters moved away from the body, Alaine fastened eager eyes on the blade still grasped in the dead man's hand. Quickly she rose to her stiff knees, and shuffled to where she could lay the ropes binding her wrists against the edge of the sword. In moments her hands were free, and a few moments more her stiffened fingers managed to loose the bonds from her ankles. Her heart swelled with a fierce joy as she grasped the hilt of the dead's man's sword. Rorik would have help in this battle whether he wanted it or not.

Gilly laughed out loud as Alaine joined the fight, but his laughter ended abruptly when Alaine's sword tip scored a scarlet line across his cheek. Rorik's breath caught in alarm when Gilly broke off from the group to engage Alaine in a private duel, but he had his hands full with Alan and grease-beard. He returned his attention to his own battle and redoubled the fierceness of his attack.

Gilly's skill could not match Alaine's, but her strength was sorely snapped by her long ordeal. Her reactions were slow and her attacks clumsy. She had to struggle to hold her own. But when Gilly's blade scored a shallow cut on her thigh the pain shot new energy through her veins, and her next attack broke through his flimsy guard. He died with a look of stunned surprise on his face as her blade sliced through his heart.

Alan had fallen in a pool of his own blood, but grease-beard was still battling fiercely for his life. Alaine sagged against a tree and watched, seeing from the strong, confident swing of Rorik's arm that he needed no help. She winced as her leg began to throb. The cut was deeper than she had thought.

Grease-beard was no match for Rorik now that he stood alone against the knight. He was bleeding from a dozen cuts, and the death blow was on its way when he dropped his blade in a panic and ducked behind a tree, then ran into the forest with all his remaining strength. Rorik hesitated a moment, torn between following to finish the kill, or quitting this place and taking his wife to safety. He didn't hear the stirring of the man behind him.

But Alaine did. Alan's movement caught her eye as he struggled from the bloodstained ground with a knife clenched in his hand. His side lay open from shoulder to hip, and blood still poured from a long slash across his scalp. But his arm was still strong enough to lift a knife, and his eyes were fastened on Rorik's back.

Alaine yelled a warning and at the same time raised her own blade to divert the blow. But her weary arm failed her. Her blade didn't strike home. Instead, it opened a gash along the outlaw's ribs that just barely succeeded in sending the knife off target. With a maddened scream Alan whirled. His fist struck Alaine's cheek just before Rorik's blade pierced his heart.

Alaine sighed wearily as her mind insisted on swimming back to consciousness. She breathed in the scent of wet leather and blood, then opened her eyes to a close-up view of Rorik's heavy leather tunic as he bent over her.

"Ow!" She jumped as her husband gingerly examined the bruise that was darkening the side of her face.

"You'll live." He smiled and sat back on his haunches. Alaine tried to focus her eyes on his face, but her vision was swimming. She struggled into a sitting position, helped along by Rorik's arm at her back. Fire seemed to explode in her thigh when she moved her leg, but she could feel that the wound had been tightly bandaged.

"Ooooh!" she screwed up her face and groaned.

Rorik was unmerciful. His eyes twinkled. "Perhaps you're not as good a swordsman as you thought, wife. It was your puny blow that allowed the knave to turn and have at you."

Alaine lifted a cocky brow, though the effort smarted so that it was hardly worth it. "I was good enough to save your hide."

"So you were," Rorik conceded with a smile.

She staggered to her feet, leaning heavily on his strong form for support. It was full night. The rain had stopped, and the fire still glowed in the center of the clearing. The bodies were gone, and a fresh mound of dirt stood as the only monument to their remains.

"You must ride a little way," Rorik told her gently. "I've no wish to be here if any of these villains return."

"Aye," she agreed weakly. Her voice quavered in spite of her best effort to sound stalwart.

It was but a short ride to the Boar's Head Inn, where a surprisingly clean bed and a good bowl of hot venison stew awaited them. Alaine ate but little and paused only to wash off the worst of the grime before giving herself over to the soft straw mattress. She felt sick and dizzy, and gratefully snuggled next to Rorik's hard warmth when he snuffed the candles and joined her under the heavy quilts. She didn't want to think, only to feel strong arms around her and be grateful that this night would pass and she would still be alive and whole.

As she drifted close to sleep, lulled by Rorik's steady breathing and the rhythmic beat of his heart so close beneath her cheek, she smiled contentedly. He had come for her, she thought with satisfaction. For whatever reason, he had ridden into danger to fetch her back. He could have left her for those wolves to devour. He had her lands, and the men-at-arms and peasants had given him their loyalty and would not take it back. He really no longer needed her, but still he came. Perhaps there was hope after all.

CHAPTER 18

The coming of Christmas season brought the real cold. Mud froze to ice, and more than one knight's steed sliced his legs by breaking through the frozen surface and gashing himself on knife-edged frozen shards. A fuzz of white rime frosted the trees until well into the day, and fog and low clouds blanketed the land like a dreary cloak, wrapping the meadows and forests in cold, damp silence. The boundary between heavy fog and freezing drizzle grew dim, and always the inhabitants of castle and villages felt the damp chill.

Alaine didn't notice the dreariness of the days, however. She had too much reason for happiness to let her spirits go gray with the season. Christmastime, the most joyous season of the year, was fast approaching. Ste. Claire was safe and secure under the protection of a man whose might none would dispute; her people were content; loyal Garin was about to be honored with knighthood; her family and friends were all well and safe; and the mighty dragon was showing signs of domesticity.

Alaine smiled as she sat before the huge fireplace in the hall and wound the fine-spun wool off her drop spindle. A rosy-cheeked Thatch held the spindle as she twisted the wool into a skein. The boy's smile was especially bright these days. The hollows in his little body had filled out almost to plumpness, and under Father Sebastian's careful tutoring he had learned to speak intelligibly and acquire passable manners. Father Sebastian agreed with Alaine that the child who had been called a half-wit possessed not only normal intelligence, but also something beyond average. With a healthy diet and exercise, his spasticity had decreased and though he would probably never be able to run or fight or even walk normally, at least he could get from place to place efficiently and without assistance. The little redheaded tyke went in awe of Rorik, who treated him with the same mildly affectionate banter he reserved for all the castle children who were often underfoot in bailey and courtyard. He loved Alaine and followed her like an adoring puppy when given the chance. He liked the old grizzled priest, and threw himself with honest enthusiasm into lessons and prayers. But it was Judith whom he worshiped. Joanna's youngest daughter had instantly adopted the little cripple as her own and jealously guarded him from the sometimes cruel teasing of the pages, squires, and children of the castle villeins. They attended lessons together, since Joanna insisted against popular practice that all her daughters learn to read, and Alaine was amused to note that despite being two years younger than Judith, little Thatch picked up his letters with more facility than the older girl and often ended up helping her with their little tasks. He eagerly absorbed all the priest taught him, then begged for more. It was an odd sight to see the two children together, Judith's fair head and Thatch's shock of carroty hair bent together over a script, or the two restless little bodies kneeling side by side at their prayers in the chapel. Alaine was glad to see them grow so close, for Judith needed a companion close to her own age, and Thatch needed a friend in the confusing new world that Alaine had forced him to join. Alaine was determined to approach the priest about a possible future for the boy in the church, but it was bit early for that, she admitted. God willing they had years in front of them before she had to worry about finding the little cripple a secure place in this savage world.

"It's about time for you to be off to bed," Alaine told the boy as she wound the last of the wool from the spindle.

"Father Sebastian promised us a sweet," John declared. "I can't go to bed without a sweet."

"Did he now?" Alaine smiled and glanced at the priest,

who was absorbed with Rorik in a game of chess. "Well, then, run into the kitchen and tell Maudie you and Judith are to have one of the pastries that were baked for today's dinner. Then off with you. Michael and Stephen will be up in a bit."

John slept in the loft above the buttery with two of the younger boys who served knights of Rorik's retinue. Rorik had refused to have the boy sleep in their chamber with them, as he'd clamored to do, and Alaine had refused to have him sleep in the barracks with the squires and pages who were wont to tease him so unmercifully. So they had compromised, bringing two of the youngest pages from the barracks and putting them with Thatch in the loft.

The boy shuffled off toward the kitchen with Judith at his side, and Alaine got up and strolled over to observe the chess game. Rorik glanced up and gave her a smile as she rested a hand on his broad shoulder. The smile was a trifle reserved, perhaps, but Alaine could feel a genuine warmth that it sent her way. The warmth had been growing in the days since they had ridden back together from the outlaw's forest camp. For her part, there was no more mention of Brix, no more bedchamber rebellions, and no more flashes of childish temper. In turn, he no longer treated her with icy civility, and seemed to look at her with new respect after seeing her sword divert the fatal blow that had been meant for his back. The frost had burned off their relationship. Slowly and cautiously they were each exploring the limits of a new bond that was growing between them. In the dark hours of the night, with Rorik sleeping against her breast, warm and satiated by the heat of his passion, Alaine allowed herself to hope that what was growing between them was love and trust, and sometime in the future Rorik could truthly tell her that, apart from all considerations of land and power and politics, she was the woman he would choose as mate for himself and mother of his children—she was the woman who had washed the bitterness from his soul.

Christmastime brought a host of guests to Castle Ste. Claire, for Garin and two other squires were to be knighted the day after Christmas. In the doldrums of winter the folk of the countryside, serf and lord alike, were eager for an excuse for gay celebration. Once again the chambers below the hall were cleaned and fires laid on the hearths. Once again Maudie and her helpers labored to do Ste. Claire proud by turning out the best that the meagerly stocked storehouses could provide. This time though, in view of the season and the scarcity of the last two years' harvest, the guests came laden with bounty from their own larders. So there was no danger of anyone going hungry this season, and to make sure the villages could also celebrate Christ's birth in gladness, Alaine dispatched riders with gifts of food for each village and farm beholden to Ste. Claire.

In the bustle of preparations for Christmas and the knighting ceremony that would follow, Alaine scarcely had time to think of herself or her own family. But she did notice Mathilde's rosy-cheeked happiness as Garin's big moment approached, and, with mixed feelings she also noticed a blooming glow that shone from Gunnor. She knew well from whence came her eldest stepsister's unusual lightheartedness, for Gilbert de Prestot was among the castle guests, and he had been obvious in paying court to the comely young widow. Alaine didn't begrudge Gunnor her happiness, but she had serious doubts as to the honor of Gilbert's motives. The man wasn't the sort to be beguiled by Gunnor's wiles unless he thought Rorik might settle a handsome dowry on the widow. And Rorik was months away from even thinking about settling the future of Joanna's daughters. A word of caution to Gunnor had simply brought a bitter accusation that Alaine was jealous, seeing that Gilbert was such a polished, attentive man and Alaine's own husband was such a surly brute. And a passing remark to Rorik about the impropriety of Gilbert being their guest after what he had done at the tourney merely made Rorik smile and repeat that he wished to avoid war with his neighbor, at least for the time being. Time enough, he assured her, for Gilbert to be put in his place should he need it. A wise man did not make war on two fronts if he could avoid it. Besides, Rorik assured her, Gilbert was on his best behavior. Sir Guillaume, an aging knight who knew Gilbert's father quite well, echoed Rorik's sentiments and assured Alaine that the bastard knight was really not such a bad fellow, all things considered.

So Alaine let the subject drop. She was busy enough entertaining their guests and seeing to the holiday preparations without worrying about what Gilbert was up to with Gunnor. Her stepsister was a grown woman and had made it clear she wanted no help or interference from anyone, especially Alaine.

Christmas Eve was cold and clear. All the folk at the castle, noble and serf and villein alike, rode or walked in gay procession to the parish church across the river, where they joined the village of Ste. Claire in celebrating the birth of the Savior. The night flickered with a myriad of torches, and great fires were lit upon the hills. Groups of villagers and peasants from the surrounding farms marched about dressed as shepherds led by pipes and viols and singing:

> "Good Sirs, now hark ye!
> From far lands come we,
> For it is Noel!

An ox, heifer, and ass were installed in the church as symbol of Christ's humble birth in a stable.

The church was overwarm, smelling of the animals and the tight crush of bodies, but Alaine was happily content as she joined the crowd in singing the long responses that told the Christmas story. A year ago her father had been alive and standing beside her in this church. She remembered his strong voice singing out the responses as Father Sebastian led the service. And she had been restless and petulant because Joanna had insisted that she act the lady in entertaining the few guests that had come to spend the season with them.

She stole a glance at Rorik, standing tall and straight beside her. How things had changed! She thought that Sir Geoffrey would be pleased could he see the man who had claimed Ste. Claire, for all that he had recklessly boasted that Alaine could hold the castle and its lands for her own. Rorik was a man who gave other men pause, who made greedy neighbors cautious, and who made rash adventurers think twice before trying their luck on Ste. Claire lands. And yet for all his fierceness, he was a man capable of mercy, of justice, and even, at times, gentleness. She had much to be thankful for this Christmas season, Alaine thought. And she was determined not to lose any of it.

Christmas day dawned in fog and cold, but the hall was a place of bright warmth. Servants, lords, and ladies alike enjoyed a sumptuous meal topped off with toothsome confections of pastry and honey, and basketsful of leavings were collected to feed the poor that gathered at the court-yard gate. Alaine proudly presented Rorik with a fine ermine-lined cloak she had been secretly working on since their wedding, and was breathless when in turn he placed on her hand an exquisite ring of gold and sapphire. She had never worn jewelry, finding that it hindered her grasp of sword and bow. Even since her marriage she'd worn only the plain gold band that Rorik had placed on her finger at their wedding. But this gift from Rorik seemed the most beautiful thing she had ever seen, and stood also as a symbol that he deemed her worth adorning with this beauty.

Judith and John were delighted with the wooden sailing ships that Rorik had carved for them, and clamored to be allowed to immediately launch them in the half-frozen pond in Alaine's garden. Joanaa sternly told them they could wait until spring, and if she saw them tramping in with wet clothes and frozen hands she would sit them in the corner with the hounds and give them nothing more to eat all day. Alaine concealed a smile behind her hand as they promptly headed off toward the kitchen to beg Maudie for the use of one of her big buckets. She was amazed that Rorik had gone to such trouble to make gifts for the youngsters, and held it close and warm to her heart that he truly had become one of Ste. Claire's family.

Christmas night the festivities became more sober as Garin and two fellow squires were led into the chapel to ready themselves for knighthood by standing a night-long vigil before the altar. Alaine's heart swelled with pride as she watched Father Sebastian give Garin his blessing and his admonition to watch through the night and ask God's help to be worthy of the great honor that was about to be bestowed. She knew Garin would be standing just as straight and tall when his sponsors, Rorik and Sir Gunnulf, came to fetch him with the dawn's light. Rorik's generosity in taking Garin into his service would be more than repaid by the young knight's staunch loyalty. And Alaine vowed that it was her debt also, that Rorik should never regret dealing so rightly with her loyal friend.

The next morning Alaine stood by Mathilde and held her hand as Garin received the honor of knighthood. He looked so manly and solemn in the new mail and helm that Rorik had given him that Alaine understood why her stepsister was so smitten. Proudly he bore the new arms, as yet unbloodied by battle, that Rorik had provided him. And after the ceremony was complete and he wore the spurs of his new rank, he pleased the onlookers by successfully making the unassisted leap to the back of his destrier while fully mailed and armed, a traditional feat that young squires worry about and practice for months before their knighting.

Mathilde glowed with pride as the three new knights demonstrated their fighting prowess in mock battle with one another. It took a nudge from Alaine to remind her that such public demonstration of her favor was not seemly. But nothing she did could prevent Garin, after triumphing over both opponents in the fray, from saluting a sighing Mathilde with his new mud-spattered lance. Alaine caught Rorik's slightly surprised glance and smiled proudly, hoping her husband would believe it was she to whom Garin paid homage, not Mathilde. Then she gave Garin a frown that drew only a reckless smile from the new knight. Soon, Alaine acknowledged to herself, she was going to have to do something about these two fools before they got themselves into more trouble.

The festivities stretched on through the celebration of the new year and none of the guests even thought about leaving. The weather continued cold and damp, and the hall was crowded from morning until night with noble folk restless for diversion and serving men and women hurrying to avoid their masters' displeasure. Tired of the constant demand for her attention and wearied by the confusion in the hall, Alaine managed to spend several afternoons in the pleasant seclusion of her chamber, quietly busying herself with mending and working on the small loom that was set up beside the hearth. On these occasions Joanna willingly took on the role of hostess, understanding her stepdaughter's need to be away from the crush in the hall.

It was the last day before the new year, and Alaine once again sought refuge on the bench beside her own hearth. In the hall below, wine was already flowing freely, and she herself had drunk one too many goblets. Her head was swimming and her skin was hot. Joanna had declared that she looked in need of Hilda's special herb tea that was reputed to cure everything from the croup to a hangover. She had sent her bustling up the stairs and sent Gwyne straightaway to fetch the herbal potion. Alaine smiled as she thought of her stepmother's fine pretense at concern. In truth, Joanna enjoyed the hours Alaine abdicated from her role as lady of the castle and left the entertaining to her stepmother. And never before had Alaine appreciated so much that lady's expertise at the social graces. Joanna would molder from boredom when her daughters were wed and she retired to her dower estate near Valognes. Alaine wondered if her stepmother might be happier if Rorik found a husband for her also. Her comeliness still drew men's attention—it certainly drew Sihtric's whenever that worthy was in his cups, much to Joanna's loudly voiced disgust. But Joanna claimed that widowhood suited her well, saying that two husbands were enough to lay in the grave during one lifetime, but Alaine thought her far too lively to retire to some dreary pile of stone walls and rot away playing the lonely widow. With a dawning domestic happiness of her own, Alaine wanted those she loved to feel just as content.

A tap on the door signaled the arrival of none other than Hilda herself, carrying a kettle of steaming tea.

"You drink this, my lady." Hilda smiled comfortingly and set the kettle over the fire. "My tea will set you right in no time."

"Thank you, Hilda." Alaine took the mug that the plump woman offered. "You can tell Lady Joanna I will be down before the evening meal."

When Hilda had bustled happily out the door, Alaine sighed and settled herself on the bench beside the fire. The steam that rose from the mug carried a fresh aroma that already hushed the thrumming in her head. She did feel a bit rocky, she admitted. She should know better than to down two large goblets of wine in such a short time, but the hall had been so stuffy and hot.

She glanced at the loom as she finished the last of her cup, then decided against working on the piece she had started there. She was not yet good enough at weaving to work the loom without a great deal of thought and effort, and she didn't feel like going to that trouble this afternoon. Instead, she got out from the clothes chest the new material she had hidden away in the bottom. She was planning to make Rorik a fine new tunic for an Easter gift, and what better time to design and cut the garment than this afternoon. She had seen Rorik and three guests headed toward the stables not long ago, talking bloodlines and trainability and endurance. She suspected he wouldn't be back in the keep until the evening meal, so there was little chance of him happening into their chamber while she was cutting out his gift.

In only a few minutes of regarding the spread-out length of fine red wool she had well in mind what the new tunic would require. But before setting her scissors to the material a footstep outside the chamber door startled her. Could Rorik have returned early after all? Hastily she bundled up the wool and stuffed it back into the clothes chest before the door swung open.

But the tall form that stood framed in the doorway was not Rorik. Alaine stood up stiff and straight with indignation as a smiling Gilbert shut and barred the heavy door behind him and stood regarding her with a proprietary air.

"Good afternoon, *ma chère*."

Alaine's finely drawn brows knit together in a scowl. Her eyes flashed angry blue fire. "What are you doing

here, Gilbert? Begone from this chamber before I call for
someone to throw you out!''

Gilbert was undisturbed. ''No need to get upset, *cherie*.
I only came on a friendly visit. Besides, think of the
damage to your reputation should you scream and bring the
guests below to your rescue. You might claim innocence,
but none would believe you.''

Alaine shut her mouth in a tight line of exasperation.
Gilbert spoke the truth. Always the woman was blamed for
luring a man astray. Women were temptresses seducing
poor helpless men into the sins of the flesh. If Gilbert were
found in her chamber, even against her will, everyone
would assume that she'd been too free with her smiles and
had in some other way lured him into believing she would
welcome his advances.

''If you had the sense God gave a pig you'd be worrying
about your skin,'' she said acidly, ''not my reputation. If
you are found here, Rorik might believe me at fault, but I
doubt that would stop him from killing you. He's a
possessive man who doesn't like his property tampered
with, and you are no match for him, you know.''

Gilbert chuckled. ''Ah yes, the brave Rorik. Such a
shame I wasn't allowed to skewer him when last we met.
An impulse on my part, but rather clever, I thought. I
could have claimed it was an accident of the games, and
Ste. Claire would have been in line for a new master.''

''You will never be master here,'' Alaine assured him
with icy contempt. ''Not as long as there is life left in my
body.''

Gilbert merely smiled at the scorn ringing in her voice.
''That remains to be seen,'' he said mildly. ''But why all
this talk of fighting. I've seen you take to your chamber
these past afternoons, and I merely come to inquire if you
are quite all right. Are you . . . ill?''

She merely regarded him with cold-eyed impatience.

''Perhaps . . . with child?'' He cocked a knowing brow.
''Could it be the dragon has bred himself an heir already?''

Her eyes narrowed to angry slits as her temper snapped.
''Certainly not! Not that it's any of your affair! You're

being impertinent as well as annoying. Now go! Or I will go instead."

Alaine made a move to leave the room, but Gilbert easily blocked her way.

"So the great Sir Rorik hasn't yet done a man's job on you." He smiled with lazy satisfaction. "It would not have been so had I been the one in your bed, *cherie*."

Alaine's face heated with both embarrassment and fury. "Had you been the one in my bed, villain, that man's weapon you strut about would have felt the blade of my knife. Your blood would have stained the sheets that night, not mine. And you would have never again forced yourself on an unwilling maid. You can be sure of that, you puny peacock! Now leave! You foul the chamber with your presence."

Gilbert shook his head with tolerant amusement. "Such spirit. I can see the dragon has not yet tamed you. It's well known he despises the fairer sex. I'm surprised he hasn't beaten you into submission. I'm even more surprised he was willing to pay to get you back."

Alaine's eyes widened. "What would you know about that?"

"Nothing much, other than the message some varlets sent me offering to sell you for a ransom of some two hundred pieces of gold." Gilbert's eyes warmed as they roved over her stiff, indignant form. "I was well willing to pay, *cherie*, and rode myself to collect you. But the morning I arrived at the outlaws' camp, we found nothing but mounded graves and blackbirds pecking at the remains of crumbs. My villain of a guide straightaway ran for his life, like the devil was at his heels. It seems your Rorik got there before I did."

"You should learn from what you saw," Alaine said with a smirk. "Rorik will deal the same with you if you don't leave me alone. So begone before he returns."

Gilbert smiled confidently. "Don't fear, *cherie*. A squire waits in the hall and will warn of the dragon's coming. Do you fear him so much?"

Alaine turned away in disgust, but Gilbert placed a

heavy hand on her shoulder and turned her back to face him. "Is he so hard with you?" he said softly. "I would have taught you the joys of womanhood with none of the pain. I can be gentle as he cannot."

"What do you know of gentleness?" Alaine scoffed angrily. "Your mind is too crowded with greed and vainglory. You know nothing of gentleness, or of honor either!"

Gilbert shook his head sadly, but a quirk of a smile played at the corner of his mouth. "This bitterness does not become you, Alaine. Where's the innocent little girl I watched grow up at Geoffrey's right hand? I asked for you in full honor more than once. And eventually your father would have consented to our union."

"But I never would have consented!" Alaine shot. "Take your hand off me!"

Gilbert backed away deferentially. "I don't blame you for being bitter against men, Alaine, having to take that surly oaf to husband. But I honor you still, and would still have you to wife."

"You're mad!" Alaine almost laughed. "I am wed by vows taken in holy church."

"No vows are so binding they cannot be undone," Gilbert declared with a knowing grin. "The bishop of Cherbourg is my uncle. He would arrange to have your marriage annulled and I would make you my wife in full honor. I want you more than anything, Alaine, and I have since you first grew from a spindly girl."

Alaine muttered an unladylike oath. "You want Ste. Claire, not me. Is that why you've been hanging on my stepsister like some smitten swain? Do you think somehow you could get to Ste. Claire through her?"

"The land means much," he admitted with a casual shrug. "But you are worth just as much. I would sooner have Ste. Claire with you than without you. You are more appealing than your stepsister."

Alaine looked at him with eyes grown violet with anger. "Remember this, Gilbert, and remember it well. Ste. Claire is Rorik's, and I am Rorik's, and if you are not careful, it will be Rorik's hand that drives steel through your heart.''

Gilbert merely smiled that infuriating, confident smile. ''I think not, *cherie*. I think you and Ste. Claire are more than that bumpkin knight can handle. And think what a woman you will become under my gentle tutoring. You will bloom like the flowers in spring, and I will bring all of Normandy to do homage to my imcomparable wife.''

''You are mad!'' Alaine repeated. ''You haven't listened to a thing I've said.''

Gilbert's smile turned into a smirk. He saw no reason not to prove his claims here and now. Rorik was off playing host with his guests and had left his pretty wife to sit alone. Fool he was not to know better! The wench would sing a different tune once he'd shown her how it could be with a real man.

Alaine despairingly recognized the look in his eyes. She had seen it often enough in Rorik's. Swiftly she glanced around the room for something to use for her own defense.

''Don't flee, my love,'' Gilbert said huskily. ''You will soon stop whining about that fool Rorik and start purring about Gilbert de Prestot.''

He grabbed her arm before she could dart away and deftly avoided the knee she aimed at his groin.

''Soon you will not want to fight.'' He grunted with the effort of holding her as she tried desperately to twist away. She dared not scream for help, for anyone witnessing this debacle would surely bring disgrace down upon her head, and Rorik's wrath along with it.

He twisted her arm behind her and pushed her down on the bed, landing on top of her with his full weight. The pain of her wrenched arm drove the breath from her body and temporarily left her limp and helpless beneath him. He drove his hips against hers in excited frenzy. She felt him hot and swollen and ready against her and guessed that as soon as he could rid himself of his chausses the foul deed would be accomplished and she would be skewered as thoroughly as any pig on a spit. She had to think of something fast, but her twisted arm held her immobile. One move on her part and surely it would break.

Gilbert held her down with one hand and with the other fumbled at the clothing that impeded him. She heaved up under him, ignoring the hot pain that speared through her shoulder and arm, but his weight was too great to dislodge. He disregarded her struggles, pushing her skirts up around her waist. She felt his icy hands on her thighs and couldn't help the cry of distress that escaped her lips. Then a muted thump outside the door brought reprieve.

"What the hell?" Gilbert rasped.

With a crash that splintered the wooden bar, the chamber door slammed open and Rorik stepped calmly through the opening, his face a study in carved ice.

Gilbert's eyes grew wide, but he had no opportunity for words. In two long strides Rorik crossed the chamber and had the older man by the throat. A choked scream tore from Gilbert's throat as he was dragged ignominiously from the bed, his chausses halfway down around his knees. Rorik threw his victim against the stone wall and drew his sword.

"Pull up your chausses, you bastard," Rorik said in a stony voice. "Then find your weapon."

"Do it!" he thundered as the silver-haired knight hesitated. "Or I'll run you through where you stand."

Watching Rorik warily, Gilbert hitched up his pants and sidled over to where he had propped his sword against the wall. His eyes darted here and there around the room and at the gaping doorway, reminding Alaine of a cornered weasel. She looked at Rorik's stiff, straight back and the muscles bunched tensely under his tunic. His face was stony hard, but cords stood out in his neck and a muscle jumped in his jaw. There was a cauldron of rage seething just below the surface, and rage made men careless, Alaine knew. Suddenly, she feared for her husband's safely. Gilbert was a capable fighter, and was not above having some dirty tricks up his sleeve. And he would like nothing better than to see Rorik dead.

Alaine hastily straightened her skirts and slid from the

bed. "Don't kill him, Rorik," she cautioned. "It would be a dreadful sin to kill a man during this holy season."

Rorik turned on her, and it seemed to Alaine that the fires of Hell itself burned in her husband's eyes. "You're hardly the one to be talking of sin, slut! If you must beg mercy, beg it for yourself."

Alaine cringed as though he'd hit her, and at that moment Gilbert struck. But Rorik was ready. He beat back the attack with ease, and as Gilbert was forced back against the wall, a ghasty killing grin distorted Rorik's features, giving him the look of a demon bent on destruction. He was fury personified, and the older man could barely manage to fend off the blows that seemed too powerful and too fast for a mortal man to deliver. Gilbert's face was grim and pale, his mouth stretched into a tight line of desperation.

"No, Rorik! Please!" Alaine cried. She didn't care if Gilbert lived or die, but she didn't want Rorik to bloody himself in this insane fury—a fury that was directed more at her imagined betrayal than at the man who was now backed against the wall with Rorik's sharp steel at his throat. All color drained from Gilbert's face as he stared down the length of cold steel into the eyes of death. The scene suspended for a moment, then Rorik smiled unpleasantly.

"If I see you again within my borders, you foul pig, I'll kill you. You can be sure of it."

Rorik lowered his sword and Gilbert sagged forward, right into the iron-hard fist that swung toward his face. Before he could hit the floor Rorik grabbed him by the tunic and tossed him out the door. He fell in a heap beside the unconscious body of his hapless squire. Rorik slammed the door shut and turned to Alaine, whose thoughts turned abruptly from Gilbert's fate to her own.

CHAPTER 19

Rorik's face was carved stone. Only the eyes had life, and they flickered with a fire that was half pain, half anger, and all bitterness. Alaine read the accusation in his eyes before he could bring it to his lips, and she denied the charge before it was out of his mouth.

"I know what you're thinking." She held up a hand as if to fend off his anger. "But you're wrong."

"Am I?" he sneered and took a step forward. To Alaine he seemed taller and broader, and more threatening, than he ever had before. Even when she had held him trussed and helpless in the forest he had not looked so angry.

She tilted her chin and refused to back away from his rage. "This is not my doing!" she insited. "Gilbert tried to force himself on me."

"I heard no screams from that pretty mouth of yours while he was climbing under your skirts!"

"Do you think I wanted every guest in the hall running up here—to think exactly what you're thinking? I didn't need help. I could have taken care of it myself!" Alaine asserted with a challenging gleam in her eye.

Rorik laughed cynically. "You were taking care of it indeed! And with a fine bit of enthusiasm. What met my eyes was a woman having a fine time. You looked anxious enough to taste what he had to offer. Is that what you call taking care of it yourself?"

Alaine's volatile temper flared. "You . . . you are a pig-headed, pickle-brained fool!" The words sounded to her ears like an undignified, indignant squeak. She felt like a field mouse defying a hungry eagle. "You've already made up your addled mind. I vow you're delighted to have something like this happen so you can pat yourself on the back and tell yourself you were right all along!"

"Do I look delighted?" His voice was dark with a hint of physical violence held barely in check. "Do I look well satisfied to find my wife heaving and bucking under the bare buttocks of another man?"

"I was not . . . I was struggling!" she labored to explain. "Do you think I'd willingly make love to Gilbert, who foully attacked my home when my father died and almost forced me to the altar?"

Rorik laughed bitterly. "You were accommodating enough to me, who did much the same deed. I was disinclined to believe Gunnor when she told me how you and Gilbert had longed to marry when your father was still alive. But now I see it explains much—the hasty wedding ceremony after your father's death, and foul attack on me during the tourney."

Alaine's face went blank with amazement, and Rorik credited her at least with being persistent in her fabrications. "Gunnor told you . . . ?" Alaine would have laughed had she not been so close to crying. "Oh, you pickle-brained fool! Your mind has truly flown from your head."

"No fool I!" Rorik denied. "But I should thank you, madam, for I was about to make a fool of myself indeed— by believing you a cut above other females. I should be grateful that you've taught me the final lesson!"

"You're a bigger idiot than I thought," Alaine commented bitingly.

"Is it so?" he replied icily, stepping closer and taking a viselike hold on Alaine's arm. "Not idiot enough to let my wife play slut behind my back to every man who strikes her fancy. If you wish to play the whore, madam, you will play it for me, and me alone."

Thoroughly out of patience, Alaine lifted a saucy brow. "Well, right now, sir, prancing fool of a knight, you don't take my fancy."

"Don't I meet with your lovers' standards?" Rorik

pulled her up hard against the solid wall of his chest. "This time, my dear, you'll just have to suffer through."

She struggled to push him away. "What are you doing, you great oaf?"

Rorik ignored her squirming. "It was badly done of me to cut your love-play short at such an awkward time. Allow me to finish the job that Gilbert so hastily abandoned."

"Get away from me!" she demanded hotly.

The fire in his eyes had turned to angry lust, and Alaine knew the fight was hopeless. She would have to fight herself as well as Rorik, for something in her had turned molten at the touch of his hand on her arm.

But for pride's sake she fought anyway. This hot anger was a side of her husband she had never before seen, and she hoped never again to see. The bitterness in his breast rose up and deafened him to her demands for release, and he simply repeated again and again that if she behaved like a slut she should expect to be treated like a slut. Ignoring her pummeling hands and kicking legs, he pushed her down on the bed and pinned her with the weight of his hand-muscled body. He took her quickly and without preliminaries, thrusting into her with an intensity that branded her his possession, his and his alone. Just when Alaine's anger melted to desire she didn't remember, nor when his rage mellowed from violence to passion. His desperate intensity slowed to purposeful desire as her legs wrapped around his hips and she met him thrust for thrust. Together they strained in violent and aching need to ride the burning current that blazed within both of them. Anger and passion flowed together in one hot, demanding river of molten desire, until finally the universe shattered and they spiraled slowly, inevitably back to earth, drifting with the flaming fragments of the explosion.

When the world had settled back into place Rorik disentangled himself from Alaine and from the bed. Without a word he donned his hastily discarded clothing, then stood looking at the wall as if a scene from his mind was being played out on its stone surface. When he turned back toward the bed he regarded Alaine as if she were indeed a sorceress who had cast a spell on his soul. Alaine turned away from that hostile regard and felt bitter tears burn her eyes.

"I hate you for this," she told him tonelessly, not knowing quite what she hated him for but sure that she needed to hate him for something.

He didn't answer, and she wanted to turn and strike out at him, hit him, kick him, do something to make him react to her anguish. What shame that she had actually lost control and enjoyed his violent, punishing lust! She should have lain cold as stone beneath him, even when his punishing had turned to loving. How dare he think such things of her! How dare he treat her in such a way!

"Are you quite through?" she asked, putting all the bitter chill of winter into her voice.

"Quite," he answered in a flat voice. "For now."

"Then leave." She turned toward him with a face set in ice. "I feel like washing myself."

He smiled a twisted quirk of a smile. "Wash all you want, my lady. You'll not rid yourself of the stain on your soul."

She almost hissed, she was so mad. "You're no better than an animal." She knew she was including herself in the accusation, and it made her hurt all the more.

"A fit husband for a whore," he returned evenly. The rage had disappeared with the lust, and now was left only a bitter cold void where a blossom had been growing. "If you ever betray me again, Alaine, I will cage you in your chamber and the only person you'll see is me, when I come to do the duty of getting an heir on my legal wife. Pray to God that your courses come on time this month, wife. For I doubt this is the first tryst you've had with your lover, and I won't give my name to Gilbert's bastard."

Alaine speared him with a look of contempt. "So sure you're right! So certain everything is the way you see it—crooked and soiled. I'll tell you once more that you're the only man I've ever been with—God pity me!—and Gilbert has never been anything to me but an enemy. Ask Joanna if I went willingly to the altar with him, or if I welcomed him with open arms when he came and knocked down my crumbling gate.''

"Save your stories, Alaine," Rorik advised in a chilly voice. "I'll punish you no more for this, and I accept you as you are. Just know that from now on you will be watched. As long as your behavior is acceptable, you have nothing to fear from me." The threat he left unspoken hung between them. He buckled on his sword and stepped toward the door.

"Ask Joanna," Alaine tried once more, vowing it was the last time she would humble herself.

He shook his head and smiled. "Why should I ask Joanna? His eyes were blank and cold as the glinting snowfields on the southern mountains. "Of course she would lie for you. Is she not a woman also?"

"Keep going, my lord, and you'll drink the cellar dry. The winter ahead is long. Leave some for the rest of us poor souls who like to warm our bones with a bit of good wine."

Rorik fixed Sir Oliver with a jaundiced eye. He had grown to respect the old knight since coming to Ste. Claire, but right now he had no tolerance for anyone breaking in on his surly mood.

Sihtric came up behind the old man and clapped him on the back. "Is the boy here well in his cups?"

Rorik curled a lip. "Can I get no peace, even from the men of my own household?"

"Why so morose, boy?" Sihtric flashed his white teeth in a grin. "Tomorrow we'll have peace again, since most of this crowd is leaving. It is time they went home and cleaned out their own larders instead of ours." He sat himself down on the bench beside Rorik and stretched his feet out toward the fire. "In fact," he continued, looking at Rorik closely, "that rat's ass de Prestot already left. Saw him slink out with his squire before the sun was well down. Better count the gold and silver."

"Gold and silver is not what he stole," Rorik grumbled bitterly. He buried his face in his tankard for a good long moment and came up with a bitter eye. "Sir Oliver!" he growled. "You're a good man and a true knight. From you I would have the truth."

The grizzled old knight quirked one brow in question. "What truth would you have, my lord?"

"What truth indeed?" Rorik slurred. "I would know . . . was Alaine a willing bride for de Prestot before I came charging at the walls?"

"Willing?" Sir Oliver asked in a surprised voice. "I think not. The knave had to batter down our gate for admittance to Ste. Claire."

"You gave only token resistance, from what I can see."

Sir Oliver nodded agreement. "Aye. We had only a token force."

"And she told you to surrender." Rorik's lips curled in a cynical smile.

"Aye." Sir Oliver was forced to agree again. "But . . ."

"Ah! I had it right, then."

"The Lady Alaine meant to spare lives that would have been wasted in futile defense."

Rorik chuckled knowingly into his beer. Sir Oliver huffed indignantly.

"I'm an old man, my lord, and know little of maids and what they think, but if Lady Alaine wanted de Prestot she hid it well. He threatened to take the life of every fighting man and varlet in the castle before she went with him to the altar. And when he rushed away to defend the walls, I do believe our lady shocked the good Father Sebastian with the fate she wished upon that knavish knight."

"A prettily enacted scene, I'd wager."

"It was no mummery, my lord. Had the swine succeeded in wedding the lass I've no doubt she would have carved him like the pig he is before she became his wife in truth."

Rorik stared morosely into the fire. "Well, she's certainly changed her tune since then."

"Bah!" Sihtric scoffed with a laugh. "You've always been a fool where women are concerned. If all this moaning is because you think there's something between those two you're a bigger fool than I thought!'' He cast Rorik a sidelong glance of exasperation. ''Good thing for you that your guests are out of earshot. If you were fool enough to insult that sweet lady within their hearing I'd have to thrash you before the eyes of all.''

''Would you indeed?'' Rorik asked, his lips twisting in the hint of a smile. ''It is true the lady's name is not for just any tongue to defame. The little vixen is my wife, and her honor and mine are one and the same. More shame that she has dirtied it within so little time of our wedding.''

Sihtric cocked a disbelieving brow in Rorik's direction. ''Your tongue runs away with you, boy. Perhaps you should pause in your prattle and let your brain catch up.''

Rorik gave the big Norseman a scornful look. ''Aye! I know you are taken in by her virtuous airs—and you also, Sir Oliver. But I have seen with my own eyes what an unfaithful slut that winsome little girl is.''

Sir Oliver looked indignant at this insult to his mistress. ''Whatever your eyes have seen, my lord, you must be deceived. I'll grant the Lady Alaine has ever been a wild maid, but a more honest and straightforward lass was never born.''

''A witness of character from a doting old man,'' Rorik snarled. ''And a besotted Viking who should know better.'' He had consumed another half skin of wine. ''She's a wild one, all right. She has the charms to raise a man's eager lusts, and a winsome body to ease them. And if I don't take care to watch her every moment, I'll never know if the children she bears are mine or sired by some fellow plowing where I have lately been.''

Sir Oliver drew himself up with an angry look. ''I will bid you good night, my lord. It seems the conversation has got beyond what I would hear.'' He nodded briefly to Sihtric then stalked ff.

Sihtric shook his head sadly. ''You've an intemperate mouth, lad. You defame an innocent.''

Rorik snorted. ''You didn't see . . .''

''Whatever you saw,'' the Norseman interrupted impatiently, "I cannot but believe the maid was blameless. I've a knack of knowing a person's worth, and I'd wager my good steed, and yours also, that there's not a false bone in her body."

"Bah!" Rorik scoffed. "All women are deceivers at heart."

Sihtric made an impolite noise. "You've clung to that stupidity too long. Only a fool lets a hurt fester through the years until it clouds his vision with bitterness. I wouldn't blame the maid if she did turn to someone else for affection and comfort, being wed to a pigheaded varlet like you. Believe my words, if I had such a wife, I would not handle her in such careless wise!"

Rorik stood abruptly and slammed his mug down on the bench. The few guests who had not yet retired looked up at the racket. Rorik swayed on his feet and glared at his old comrade.

"The company here is not fit for drinking with. I'll make my bed in the stable. My horse is a better companion!"

Sihtric followed him with thoughtful eyes as Rorik stalked out of the hall. Poor Lady Alaine, he mused. In these past weeks it had truly seemed she was bringing the dragon happily to heel, with Rorik being very content to have it that way. But perhaps, after all, no woman was a match for the bitterness that ate away at Rorik's soul.

The winter wore on, wet and gray and cold. Alaine and Joanna together made the rounds of villages and farms with gifts of food and Joanna's pack of healing herbs and remedies. Alaine was gaining skill in seeing to the needs of her people, and becoming accomplished, also, in directing the domestic affairs of keep and baily, storehouses, and workshops. She wondered why she had ever believed women's work less demanding than her silly playing at war. Her days were filled from dawn until sunset with managing her home and seeing to the needs of the people who depended on her.

But late at night, when the demands of lands and people quieted and she was left alone with her own thoughts, she had to admit her life had become a dream gone nastily awry. Rorik was ever on her mind, and grief that the regard growing between them had died in such bitterness did not diminish with the weeks. In their public lives Rorik was icily polite, giving at least the respect due the lady of the castle. In private he had little to say to her, and if she tried to prod him from his glacial silence, his words were harsh and bitter.

Every night in the dark warmth of their bed, Rorik would turn to her and claim his husband's due. His lovemaking was thorough and intense, but so lacking in anything besides lust that it came near to breaking Alaine's heart to remember how gently and lovingly he had taken her in the first weeks of their marriage. Her body no longer responded to his caresses, and though he never caused her any physical hurt or forced himself on her in violence, she endured his nightly attentions with discomfort and embarrassment. She could not enjoy this mating of bodies while having no part of his soul to call her own.

Two weeks after the incident with Gilbert, Rorik appointed a comely serving girl, a wench newly come to the keep from the village across the river, to be Alaine's personal serving maid. He ignored Alaine's protest that she had no need of such a luxury, and russet-haired Lorraine became her shadow wherever she went. She helped her dress and bind up her hair in the morning, accompanied her on her rounds of keep, bailey, farms, and villages, sat by her side in the solar when she wove or spun or sewed, and slept on a pallet outside the chamber door when she retired. Alaine thought the girl a nuisance and told Rorik she would have none of it. Rorik replied coldly and politely that she was now a lady of rank, and it befit her to have a maid to see to her needs. The old nurse Hadwisa was a good woman, but she was getting on in years and deserved a rest. Lorraine would stay, and that was the end of the conversation.

That the voluptuous Lorraine was a watchdog for her husband Alaine did not for one moment doubt. She was certain that her every activity was reported directly to the lord of the castle. That the girl might have another function as well didn't occur to Alaine until a few days after the girl entered her service. She was sitting before the hearth allowing the wench to brush the tangles from her hair when Rorik strode into the chamber. The dawn was just breaking, but already he had ridden with a troop of men to inspect a farm that had been raided by some undisciplined men of a neighboring baron. Timor had stayed at the stable to see to the horses, so Lorraine helped Rorik pull off the heavy mail and leather arming tunic while Alaine finished her own hair. The smiles and glances that sparked between the two of them were difficult to miss, and Alaine got the feeling that the little russet-haired whore wanted her mistress to see how things stood between lord and servant. Her temper flared, and with narrowed eyes shooting ice-blue sparks, she peremptorily ordered the girl from the chamber. Then, taking the servant's place in pulling off the padded leather arming tunic, she jerked the garment with such violence that Rorik almost tumbled to the floor.

Rorik shrugged himself free of the tunic and scowled. "What was that all about?"

"That was about your cavorting with that overstuffed cow of a whore right here in front of my eyes, you vermin!"

Rorik for a moment looked genuinely surprised. Then he smiled. "We weren't exactly cavorting, my lady. The girl was simply . . ."

"I know what the girl was doing!" Alaine cried. "And no doubt she's been helping you off with more than your armor since she's been here in the keep. I'm surprised you don't have me sleep on the pallet outside the door and bring her to your bed at night."

Rorik's eyes almost twinkled. "That would hardly be seemly, now, would it?"

"Oooooh!" Alaine picked up her brush and threw it in his direction. He adroitly dodged the missile. "If you must take a mistress, you rutting boar, must you flaunt her before my very eyes? I will not have you in my bed after you have . . . have been grunting after that over-plump sow!''

Rorik calmly went to the basin and splashed water on his face and hair. Dripping, he turned back to his wife. "You will have me in your bed whenever I want, madam, as I've told you before. We both have our duty to do, and whatever else I do for pleasure is none of your worry.''

Alaine longed to strike him, but knew the consequences would be disastrous. "You are lower than the worms," she spat venomously. "How noble and true are men, as opposed to treacherous women! And yet how is your dallying with that slut more excusable than my entertaining Gilbert?'' In her anger and need to hurt she didn't even bother to deny her involvement with the silver-haired knight.

But Rorik refused to rise to the bait. Much to Alaine's annoyance, he almost appeared to be amused. He shrugged off her vehemence.

"That is the way our world works, my lady. You must bear my heirs, and thus be chaste. But no one would expect a man to cleave to one woman only.''

It was the truth and Alaine well knew it, but it stuck in her craw like bitter bile.

"Then I hope I am barren, Sir Stone Dragon!'' she replied with a frightening intensity. "If you must spread your seed among the lowborn wenches of Ste. Claire, then I hope your only harvest is a crop of bastards! If you insist on behaving like a rutting boar, then may you end up with nothing but a batch of piglets!''

She was perilously close to tears, and cursed herself for being weak. There was a strange light in Rorik's eyes, and he almost looked like he wanted to cross the chamber and comfort her. But he stood where he was, his face an unreadable mask.

She stalked stiffly toward the chamber door, but turned before pulling it open. "I'm beginning to understand how you can think all women faithless whores. I myself am beginning to believe all men are arrogant bastards.''

* * *

And still the winter wore on in shades of dismal gray. Lorraine fell by the wayside and was replaced by pert, ebony-haired Freida. A few weeks later Freida's place was taken by a statuesque girl from Bethune with hair of velvet brown and eyes of deepest amber. Rorik never denied sporting with any of them, but, Alaine noted with a hint of confusion, he never came out and admitted it, either. She flung no more accusations in his face, and set herself to show the infuriating brute that she could be as cold and uncaring as he. She tried her best to hate him, but found that she didn't fall out of love that easily. She had always been a person of stubborn passions, and from that misguided moment she had admitted her love for Rorik, her heart's course had been set in stone. Bitterness at his betrayal gnawed at her soul, but still every day she saw too many qualities of good, too much she admired, to be able to nurse the deep and abiding loathing she sometimes felt he deserved. She couldn't hate him, no matter how hard she tried. So she settled for ignoring him.

Alaine tended to her duties as though Rorik were not a constant presence in her life. If he were in the same room as she, she would give him her back, pretending that she was unaware of his presence. She ignored Joanna's frowns and lectures, chatted with a worried Mathilde as though nothing were wrong with her life, and tried to ignore the constant irritation of Gunnor's sulkiness.

Only days after Gilbert's ignominious departure from her bedroom, Alaine endured a volcanic blast of temper from her eldest stepsister, who had been seething since Gilbert's hasty exit and could no longer contain her venom. She told Alaine that Gilbert had contritely admitted everything to her before he left—how Alaine had lured him to her chamber and sluttishly offered her charms, how he had succumbed to temptation in the heat of the moment. Gunnor did not blame Gilbert, she told Alaine in furious tones. He was only a man, after all, and Heaven knew that even saints could be weak when it came to fleshly pleasures so wantonly displayed. But she wanted Alaine to know that Gilbert loved her, and had promised one day soon to marry her, whether Rorik willed it or no. And if she ever again caught Alaine lusting after that noble knight like a bitch in heat she would throttle her with her own two hands.

Alaine halfheartedly denied the story, but she knew before she opened her mouth that Gunnor's mind was set. She wondered if Gunnor had told Joanna and Mathilde Gilbert's version of that terrible afternoon, and Alaine wondered what they believed of her.

As the days lengthened and an occasional warm afternoon cheered the countryside, Alaine's spirits stayed mired in dismal winter. She made a few halfhearted attempts at rebellion, thinking she would feel more her old feisty self. But when she appeared on the exercise yard one morning dressed for battle play, she found to her distress that none of the boys or men would take up her challenge. They knew too well their lord's displeasure should they be seen in such unseemly wise with the Lady Alaine. Even the occasional comfort of a private visit to her father's grave was denied her by Rorik's order that she be accompanied by one of his men whenever she left the bailey. For her own good, he insisted, citing outlaws and ne'er-do-wells that still intermittently troubled the country, but Alaine thought silently that the rogue she needed protection against most was her own husband.

As the days lightened with the first hint of spring Alaine's mood sagged even lower. Since reaching an age where she could think and do for herself she had enjoyed her father's affection and respect. Rejection had been a stranger to her until she had come up against the solid wall or Rorik's displeasure. She wouldn't have guessed that the constant, unspoken contempt that radiated from him would put such a burden on her heart. But it did.

What was he to her, anyway? she asked herself in disgust. No man was worth the agony she was enduring, the dragon least of all. She should be grateful that her life was well ordered and safe, and that she still had her precious Ste. Claire. She shouldn't be mooning after a maiden's dream like some witless ninny. So what if Rorik's eyes had once been a warm summer green, and now they were glacial in hue whenever he looked at her? So what if his voice was harsh and clipped when he spoke, unlike the mellow tones he had once used in a passionate marriage bed? At least he didn't beat her, didn't abuse her verbally in front of others. Many a wife would be grateful for only that. And besides, she chided herself, if she was so determined to break down the wall between them, she should stand up and fight for what she wanted, not hide herself behind her own barrier of ice. When had she ever ducked a challenge? Where was the old Alaine de Ste. Claire who was afraid of nothing?

Where indeed? thought Alaine as her spirits sank even lower. Of late even her appetite had failed, and she'd been unforgivably snappish with Joanna and even sweet Mathilde. She'd lost weight, and to her own critical eyes her cheeks had taken on a most unattractive hollowness. How could she sink so low as to let a mere man do this to her?

One afternoon Alaine dragged her depression out to the kennels, hoping a good heart-to-heart talk Mallie would lift her out of the pit. The warm mustiness of hound closed around her as she pulled the kennel door shut behind her. Mallie had been kenneled to deliver her second litter of pups, and Alaine had missed her sorely.

The soft-eyed bitch thumped her tail in glad greeting as Alaine stepped into her run. Six squirming bundles of brown crowded at her teats, making mewling sounds of protest as brothers and sisters climbed blindly over each other in search of a nipple. Alaine smiled. She felt a little weight lift from her heart at the hound's affectionate welcome.

"There, now Mallie girl," she crooned. "What fine babies. They should all grow into good trackers like you, my girl."

Mallie's tongue lolled in a doggy grin.

"Aye," Alaine laughed. "And you're proud, I can see. Though how that raunchy lop-eared Diable sired such a fine litter is beyond me. It must be all you, my Mallie. And look how he struts about in the hall while you lie here in the kennel doing all the work!'' Alaine laughed softly. ''Males are all alike, the arrogant bastards.''

Mallie's tail thumped enthusiastic agreement.

Alaine stole the time to sit a while longer in the soft straw of the run. The pups stuffed themselves and promptly collapsed together in a furry brown pile from which tiny snores emerged. Alaine gently picked one up and laid the warm little body on her lap. Remains of Mallie's milk outlined the little mouth. Stuffed as it was, the baby hound looked like a round belly with four legs and a head added as an afterthought. Gently she touched the little red tongue tip that protruded from the mouth. Instantly the pup started sucking, latching on to the tip of her finger with an appetite that belied its full little belly. Mallie looked on tolerantly.

In the warm musty silence of the run, the vague undercurrent of thought that had muddied Alaine's mind for the past week suddenly crystallized into clear diamonds of certainty. Of course, she thought. It was so simple. She was an ignorant twit not to have realized it before now. Her unnatural depression, loss of weight, lack of appetite. . . . True, she hadn't been sick, but some women weren't. And her courses hadn't come except once after Christmas. Rorik had been zealous at his dutiful planting, and now she was going to reap the harvest. She was going to have a child—the dragon's heir, and future master of Brix and Ste. Claire.

She set the pup back into the pile with its brothers and sisters. She should have known before now the way things stood with her, but lately she had not given herself time to think, for all her thoughts were dark and angry. Now perhaps she could deal with her low spirits, realizing they were not due solely to her unspeakably pigheaded husband.

Rorik would be delighted, she thought with a tinge of bitterness. He had proved himself a virile male, done his duty as society deemed it, and now could concentrate all his energy and effort to the warfare that would come as spring drew closer to summer. Alaine was shocked at the stab of pain that shot through her heart. Now she would lose even the small part of Rorik she still had, and she was shamed at the knowledge that she was still so in love with the jackass that she would cling to even the unfeeling attentions of his body. She no longer knew the sweep of passion that had colored their earlier unions, but sometimes in the dark of night, lying close beside her husband's long body, enfolded in the cage of his hard-muscled arms and legs, Alaine could pretend that she was loved. Her longing imagination would conjure a different life with a fond and softened Rorik. Now even this would end.

No, she thought. Nothing would end. Not yet at least. Soon Rorik would ride for Brix. Who knew if he would return? Even if he didn't fall in battle, he might well decide to leave his troublesome wife in her own lonely keep and dwell at Brix with a constant parade of mistresses to ease his manly needs. Especially if he knew he had an heir safely on the way. She would steal what time she had left. Pigheaded and stubborn as he was, Rorik was still the man she loved, and there would never in her life be another.

She simply wouldn't tell him about the baby.

CHAPTER 20

Tender buds swelled the naked branches of the trees, and what had been just a hint of green on the meadows was becoming a verdant carpet of new life. The apple trees were laden with blossoms, and every morning Alaine woke to their sweet perfume floating through the air. Early dawn was now greeted by the caroling of birds, singing as though their voices alone could lift the sun above the horizon to begin a new day.

Spring was Alaine's favorite time of year. She delighted in waking to early morning birdsong and the fresh smell of new life. With the sun rising earlier and earlier, she no longer had to drag her protesting body from its warm cocoon in cold darkness. Even Father Sebastian's early morning masses were no longer a chore to be attended for duty's sake only.

The chapel was flooded with sunlight by the time the priest would begin his service, and the rising glory of the sun added life and substance to rote responses. Even the damp and dark corners of the keep seemed to warm a bit with the new energy of the season.

With the coming of spring Father Sebastian was truly in his element. Christmas was a joyous festival of hope, but Easter was the holiest season of the year. He enlisted Alaine's aid in exhorting the common folk to participate in the Mystery Play that he was planning for the great holiday, and was delighted when both Judith and Thatch begged to be given parts in the production. Joanna balked at having her young daughter rub elbows with serfs and peasants in such a display, but Alaine and the priest together convinced her that there could be no harm in such a holy undertaking.

While Father Sebastian went about planning for ways to honor the Prince of Peace, Rorik and his men girded themselves for war. Workouts in the exercise yard took on a new and serious intensity. The smith worked day and night turning out new weapons. Everywhere mail was being polished by industrious squires and pages, and swords sharpened to razor edges. Rorik and Sihtric had managed to draft the best of the young village men for their army, yet still leave sufficient manpower to handle the spring planting. Sir Guillaume took on the task of training the eager but green youngsters in how to defend themselves and how to hinder the enemy with such crude weapons as they would be provided. Some of the best he turned over to Sir Gunnulf to mold into archers.

Every day from the solar window Alaine was afforded an excellent view of Sir Gunnulf and his fledglings letting fly at straw targets set against the bailey wall. Something in her stirred with longing to be down among them and rebelled against her complaisant acceptance of her woman's role. She was a better archer than Sir Gunnulf, and a more patient teacher. But she knew better than to approach Rorik with the idea. He would merely look at her with those eyes of green ice and politely tell her that her talents were much more needed elsewhere.

And he was partly right, Alaine admitted as she set her sewing aside and went to the window. She sat herself down on the wide window lip and soaked in the warmth of the sun-baked stone. In the days since the air had warmed and freshened, she had everyone in keep, courtyard, and bailey scrubbing and sweeping and beating and washing. Even the stables and kennels received their due attention, and every workshop in the bailey was put in good order. The great ovens where village and castle wives gathered to bake their loaves were cleaned, and all refuse was swept from courtyard and bailey alike.

Alaine directed all these efforts with an energy that made her feel like a new person. Part of the urge to clean and freshen and make new came from a need to clear the castle of the stale dankness of winter. But part was due to the new life growing within her. Suddenly she felt wise and worldly and motherly and . . . needed. She was slim as ever, and feeling well and happy once again. But there was the constant feeling of having the child inside her, of nourishing a life other than her own. She wanted everything around her to be fresh and new and orderly.

In this new and lightened mood, she could even consider the child's father with some degree of tolerance. Their relationship had settled into a polite, reserved, watchful duel of strangers. If occasionally he murmured her name in his sleep, Alaine was certain that he was having a bad dream. And if occasionally his eye rested on her with something less than his usual reserve, she knew better than to hope for a real thaw in his manner. The stone wall he'd built between them had become an impenetrable barrier, and though Alaine hadn't exactly given up the fight, she had not yet thought of a strategy to breach his defenses.

She wondered briefly if news of the babe might be the key to releasing the man she knew dwelled inside the stone wall, but uncertainty made her cling to her earlier resolve. It would serve the fool right, she thought, to ride to battle not knowing his heir was on the way. A hard-hearted and petty revenge, but then, Rorik had done little of late to deserve mercy from her. And now the babe had grown into a secret joy that she hugged to herself in hidden delight. Likely Rorik would find a way to destroy her happiness if he knew, so she would keep her secret until it could no longer be hidden.

Still, in Alaine's newfound joy she could not find it in her heart to wish Rorik ill. The continued preparations for war weighed on her mind. Rorik had sent formal notice of war to Brix, for he was nothing if not honorable. But Alaine doubted that Fulk held so much to the forms of feudal niceties, and a niggling worm of doubt made her fear for her husband's safely. Fulk was a trickster, and Brix was strong. Taking it would be no easy matter even for Rorik, and what had been taken as a certainty in the safe months of winter now seemed more perilous as spring advanced.

And if Rorik were successful in his war, what then? Would he deal with Theoda as revenge demanded? Would he leave Alaine in her lonely keep and snatch their child— his only heir—from her breast to raise at Brix? So many questions, and no answers to any of them. Sometimes Alaine simply wanted to sag under the weight of such uncertainty.

Alaine allowed herself another moment to watch Gunnulf's inept students stick the target in all places but the center. Farther along the wall Garin leaned on his sword and shouted at future footmen who were pummeling each other with staffs. He spied Alaine in the window and waved. She waved back, then sighed and went back to her sewing.

Men and their wars, and their notions of honor and killing and revenge! And she had once thought women fools!

The great day had come. The army was assembled in the bailey and was ogled with interest and appreciation by castlefolk one and all. Small boys looked on with envy and staged mock battles with stick horses and lances. Wives and mothers looked proud and frightened at the same time. Knights were gruffly businesslike, seasoned men-at-arms openly impatient, and young men from castle and villages proudly hefted their staffs and blades and bows and looked with sympathy on the men not fortunate enough to be marching with Lord Rorik this day.

Alaine offered Rorik the stirrup cup and wished him good fortune. He took her offering and drank, then thanked her politely and formally. His mouth tightened into a tense line as he looked down at her, and his eyes flickered with unreadable emotion. His helm was still mounted on his saddle in front of him, and an errant breeze ruffled the short-cropped ebony locks that curled in disarray around his brow. Alaine thought she had never seen him look so fierce, so magnetic, and so vulnerable. A knot of foreboding squeezed her heart.

"Take care, wife," he said finally. His voice lacked its usual frosting of ice. "When the situation is stable I will send a messenger from Brix to tell you how we fare."

She smiled unwaveringly, as a good wife was expected to do. "Guard yourself, husband." She tried to mask the worry in her voice, but was not entirely successful. "I will pray for your victory. And for your safety."

For a moment he looked like he would say something more, but he held his silence and simply regarded her with a steady, intense gaze. Then their time was at an end. He gave her formal salute, then wheeled the chestnut stallion

and trotted away, raising an arm to signal his men to
follow. Of a sudden she regretted her pettiness in not
telling him of the child. But now was not the time. She
smiled and played the brave and confident wife as the
army filed out the gate.

Rorik breathed deep of the cool spring air and looked
back to see the last of his men pass through the gate and
over the drawbridge. He noted with satisfaction that the
bridge was immediately raised and the gate and portcullis
closed, a precaution he'd ordered since the day he had sent
formal notice to Fulk. A sense of freedom set his spirit to
flight. At last he was headed straight and true toward his
goal—the purpose that had driven his life since that bloody
night ten years ago when he had fled in ignominious defeat
out the postern gate of Brix. Now he would taste revenge.
Now he would redeem his family's honor in Fulk's blood.
His mind held no doubt of victory, and every fiber of his
being strained north toward the sea-swept cliffs that were
crowned by Brix's mighty fortress. Soon the castle would
bow before its rightful master, and perhaps then his mind
would be at peace.

But Brix was not the only burden that rode his mind as
he trotted through the meadows that bordered the rain-
swollen Ste. Claire. Part of him still lingered with the girl
who had bidden him farewell in the bailey, who had stood
haloed in the morning sunlight as she watched him ride
away, who had smiled in so wifely a manner and told him
she would pray for his safety. Her image would fade,
Rorik assured himself. A day's ride away from Ste. Claire
and Alaine would seem only another woman, comelier
than most but just as devious, fresh and alluring, but just
as untrustworthy. How he had prayed all winter for spring
to come, as much to ride away from her as to ride toward
Brix.

All the winter long Alaine had haunted both his waking
hours and his dreams. His body craved her, his soul longed

for the solace of loving her. Truth be told, he did love her, curse him for a fool. It had been weeks since he had stopped denying it. Even at times he had been tempted to forgive her and try to pick up again the thread of tenuous happiness they had been weaving together. But the vision of her in Gilbert's arms stayed to haunt him, causing him to lash out at her again and again, even though every time he saw the hurt in her eyes he felt the pain himself. It was so tempting to forget her deceit. In the cold, lonely hours of the night he would look down at her sleeping in his arms. The pale glow of the single candle that burned by their bed gave her a quality of childlike innocence. Even during the waking hours she had a guilelessness, a forthrightness, that was unlike any woman he had ever known. Almost he was tempted to believe her story of the Gilbert encounter. But the evidence was piled too high against her. Even her own stepsister said that Gilbert had been an ardent suitor when old Sir Geoffrey was alive, and that Alaine had always favored him above all other men. Mathilde and Joanna he hadn't apprised of the incident, and old Sir Oliver was obviously too besotted with the girl for his denials to be believed.

If only he could end this foolish infatuation. If only he could be indifferent to his wife and ignore the siren song he heard everytime he saw her. Then would life be so much simpler. He tried to solace himself elsewhere, to no avail. The voluptuous curves and eager charms of other women didn't move him. The parade of pretty chambermaids attending his wife was merely a ploy to raise her ire—a petty revenge, and one that had come to irritate him as much as it annoyed Alaine. It was Alaine he wanted, and Alaine he returned to each night. She'd bewitched him indeed! But he didn't dare reveal the tender passion she inspired, or he would indeed be lost. If she turned the full blast of her charm on him, welcomed him with that radiant smile lighting her face, or responded to his touch with the natural sensuousness she had shown during the first weeks of their marriage, then would his desperate hold on good sense slip and he would fall completely under her power, fool that he was! And he had vowed long ago, with good reason, that no woman would ever have such a hold on him. Hopefully, in the heat and blood of battle he could exorcise Alaine from his mind.

The army marched on all that day and well into night. There was no need for stealth, as Fulk had been purposefully forewarned, and the foot soldiers laughed and talked and joked and bragged at what rewards would befall them once Brix was theirs. The knights and older men-at-arms were quieter and marched or rode with businesslike mien. They knew what war was, and faced the coming battle without fear and without the bravado that marked the young green lads from the villages. They had faith in Rorik. If the day could be won then he would do it. If not . . . ? Well, who knew the vagaries of battle?

They set up camp under a moonless sky, three arrow's flight from the walls of Brix. The woods around them and the thick damp mulch underfoot muffled their movements, but all knew what they were about. Several times during the night the guards on the walls called out obscene greetings and ribald comments. Frequent laughter floated through the air. Fulk's men were confident. As were Rorik's. No fires were built, in case Fulk had a mangon on the walls that could throw stones into their encampment. Fires would make them too easy a target. So, cold and damp, Rorik's army set themselves to work constructing movable defenses for the morning's assault, checking weapons, armor, horses, and trappings, and swapping tales of other battles, sieges, heroes, and villains. Finally they ate an unappetizing meal of cold salted meat, hard bread, and beer, and wrapped themselves in their cloaks to sleep out the night.

Morning crept over the land in muted, foggy tones of gray. The towers of Brix were barely visible through the mist. Tiny droplets of water beaded everything that had been exposed to the night air—trees, grass, skin, hair, swords, lances, bridles, saddles, clothing. Men pushing through the trees to answer the call of nature got unwanted cold showers and woke their fellows with their loud curses.

Rorik stood at the edge of the woods, watching the fog swirl around the shadowy turrets and battlements that climbed the slope in front of him. He could feel the thunder of the sea beating against the cliffs and hear the raucous cries of gulls. Home at last. This little part of the world belonged to Rorik Valois, and to his children and his children's children. Once he had taken it back, he would hold it firmly in his hand and defend it with his life, if necessary. While he was still alive, he vowed, no one would wrest it from the Valois family again.

Brix was strong—built by warriors to withstand anything an army could throw against it. It crowned an east-sloping triangular corner of the land that jutted westward into the sea. Twelve-foot-thick stone walls outlined the entire triangle, and on the seaward side rocky cliffs dropped from the foot of the walls hundreds of feet to jagged rocks pounded constantly by the surf. At the seaward apex of the triangle the walls met in a great square tower—the great keep. Smaller towers strategically placed along the battlements put every inch of the walls within bow-shot of the castle defenders. Brix was almost impossible to attack effectively from either sea or land.

On the wide slope that spread out toward the land to the east, a line of palisades, ramparts, and moats fronted the wall. If one succeeded in storming the outer wall and crossing the outer bailey, there was still a stout inner wall and moat to be taken. If that could be accomplished, access to the keep was still blocked by the stone mass of the Great Hall, which was a large building separate from the keep and stretching almost the entire distance across the inner bailey, leaving only a narrow path to the keep—a path that was well defended by a tower on the adjacent wall. Then when all other dangers were surmounted, there was the keep itself, built to withstand a siege of months, possibly even years. Only by treachery had Brix been taken throughout its entire history. But as Rorik stood in the morning fog and gazed up at the battlements, he knew that victory would be his, or that he would die in the attempt.

Rorik's plan was simple, effective, and nasty—nasty particularly for the two lean lads who had volunteered to climb out over the surf-sprayed rocks, ascend the treacherous cliff, and shinny up the garderobe shaft behind the kitchen, which abutted the main hall of the keep. Brix was as invulnerable as any fortress could be, but castle inhabitants rarely thought to block the vertical shafts leading down through the thickness of the walls from the toilets. Seldom does anyone want a castle badly enough to take advantage of that mode of entry.

But Rorik did. And Miles LeBlanc and his own faithful Timor, both with lean and wiry builds ideal for worming their way up the noxious tunnel, had eagerly volunteered for the unusual assignment. Once inside the castle, they would mingle with the enemy as best they could. One would make his way to the gatehouse in the outer wall and open the iron portcullis, leaving the wooden gate vulnerable to the attackers. The other would station himself by the inner gate, ready to drop the bridge and open that gate should the defenders manage to shut themselves in the inner bailey before Rorik and his army could fight their way across the outer yard. The boys knew they would be well rewarded once the castle was taken, and looked forward with zestful glee to such an adventure.

The two lads took off with reckless grins on their faces. The morning was ideal for such a ploy, for if they were quick they could gain their objective before the warmth of the rising sun could burn off the blanketing fog. Rorik said he would start his attack on the walls when the dim glow of the sun had climbed two handspans above the eastern hills. Thus when the boys emerged inside the keep, the population of the castle should be well distracted and their presence should go unnoticed.

At the appointed time Rorik mounted and gave his signal to advance. There was virtually no chance of taking the stout walls by storm, so he ordered his men to waste no lives in foolish heroism. Until the gates were opened, their purpose was distraction and nothing more.

The appearance of Rorik's army in the open space before the walls brought on a hailstorm of stones and arrows from the defenders above. The knight made umbrellas of their shields and rode on. The foot soldiers moved through the deadly rain under cover of the mantelets—stakes wattled together and covered with hides—they had made the night before. Cautiously they crossed the unguarded outer ramparts and ditches. The barbican in the outer palisades was in such sorry disrepair that no one even bothered to defend it.

The barrage of deadly missiles doubled as the first wave of attackers reached the outer wall, but even the greenest of the foot soldiers continued steadily forward. A great show was made of propping ladders against the stone walls, and the soldiers on the battlements thought themselves clever indeed to dislodge every ladder before the enemy had ascended even halfway up the rungs. Rorik's men laughed among themselves as they jumped nimbly from the toppled ladders. They were glad enough not to have to face the swords and spears waiting for them at the top.

Rorik concentrated his knights and most of his experienced men close to the gate and left the green boys to the less dangerous positions along the walls. So when a great commotion rose from within the gatehouse and the drawbridge suddenly plummeted down as though abruptly cut loose from its moorings, he was ready. The crash of the bridge was followed immediately by the rattle of the portcullis being raised. Rorik mounted a silent prayer of thanks and signaled for the battering ram to be brought forward. Then his attention was suddenly drawn by a shout from the gate. A figure leapt from the top of the wooden barrier into the crowd of footmen below. Timor landed with a jolt and took several of his comrades with him to the ground, but all got up with grins on their faces. The squire waved a grimy arm and flashed a grin of victory. Somewhere in his journey he had lost his sword, and someone quickly threw him another. He saluted Rorik with a flourish entirely incompatible with the streaks of filth on his clothes and countenance. Rorik laughed. Even from a goodly distance away he could smell the stench. He wondered if any of Fulk's men would deign to get close enough to his squire to fight him.

The battering ram made short work of the gate now the portcullis was up, even though the defenders poured out arrows and stones from the gatehouse towers. Rorik was first to spur his horse through the opening, followed closely by Sihtric, Sir Guillaume, and Sir Robert. Then Rorik's whole army poured through the shattered barrier. The defenders fell back at the unexpected onslaught, then rallied bravely.

Rorik fought as though possessed by a demon. And indeed he felt possessed, not by a demon so much as by the fury he had held in check all these long years. He didn't feel the sharp pricks of the spears and arrows that rained on his mail. The yells and screams that echoed off the walls didn't register on his brain, nor did the muscle-cramping effort of hefting sword and shield again and again, and still again. Squatting arrogantly above the fray, the great stone tower that had once been part of his home now protected those who had taken his family, his honor, and almost his life. It beckoned like a siren, and he heard only its call.

Soldiers on both sides of the fray swore later that a mortal man could not have wielded a sword as the Stone Dragon did that day. A crusty veteran who had seen a dozen of William's own skirmishes vowed that an unholy green light glowed from the recesses of Rorik's helm-shadowed eyes, and a youngster who himself felt the bite of the dragon's steel babbled to his fellows that some force other than human guided the knight's sword. The blood-red dragon that reared and clawed on Rorik's shield had looked him full in the face when the knight had withdrawn his blade from his shoulder, the boy vowed. He'd closed his eyes then, waiting for the death blow that was sure to come, for his sword arm dangled useless at his side. When he opened his eyes again both knight and dragon had disappeared.

At long last the inner wall was reached. The gate was shut tight, but before Rorik could signal for the battering ram once again, the heavy, iron-studded wooden doors creaked on their heavy hinges and swung open. Rorik grinned as he spurred through the opening. Twice in one day the trick had worked. Fulk must be getting old and addled.

The fighting in the inner bailey was no less vicious than in the outer yard. Rorik strained to catch sight of the face he most wanted to see. Even after ten years he knew he would recognize the heavy jowls and coarse, sandy hair of the man who had slaughtered his family. But Fulk was nowhere in the heaving, jostling, struggling throng. Rorik cursed and prayed that the man had not already fallen. It was his sword that should deal the fatal blow. Fate owed him that much at least!

The weary sun was sinking toward the sea when the last of Brix's defenders lay down their weapons. Rorik's attack had surged through the castle so quickly that the keep had not the time to barricade itself effectively for siege. A bitter-eyed seneschal surrendered his sword before the entrance to the great hall. The family was within, he said.

Rorik stared past the seneschal in contempt. He had not guessed Fulk to be a coward to hide with the women and children while his men died to defend him. But the dead littered the yard around them, and Fulk huddled in the hall with his family. A sick, sour tide surged from Rorik's gut up into his throat. The man wasn't worthy to meet in honest and open battle. He was a stain on the honor of knighthood. But he wouldn't escape his fate by this cowardice.

Rorik dismounted and signaled a foot soldier to take his stallion. Sihtric and Sir Guillaume did the same. Together they strode into the Great Hall.

The interior was much as Rorik remembered it. He spied the balustraded walkway that led to the little hall and chambers where his family had conducted their private lives. Farther along, the walkway opened onto the loft where he and his brothers had slept. The large hall where they stood now had been used only on grand occasions, being hard to heat and almost as drafty as the open bailey. The hangings and tapestries his father had installed long before Rorik was born still hung on the walls, but they looked faded and dustier than Rorik remembered. The place looked as though it could use the touch of a capable housewife, Rorik thought, then wondered with sudden distraction how Alaine would feel about moving from her own beloved home and putting his in good order once again. Then his mind turned grim. That could happen only after he had first cleansed Brix from the vermin that had infested it these past ten years.

They were waiting for him on the dais at the end of the hall. The walk across the dirty rushes seemed a mile at least, and with every step Rorik's heart beat a little faster. The castle was taken. No threat lowered. Yet all was not as it should be. Rorik didn't know how he knew, but he knew. He loosened his sword on its scabbard, and the others with him did the same.

Rorik's heart seemed to freeze within his chest when he stopped before the raised platform. For a moment he didn't notice Fulk's absence. He saw only Theoda. He hadn't really believed she would be here, in spite of Alaine's words. He had dared not think on what he would do if she were.

He hardly recognized the woman on the dais as the mother he had once worshiped. His mother had been tall and straight, full-bodied and strong. This woman was hunched and thin. Her face was lined, her hair a dingy gray and escaped from the careless coil at her neck in scraggly strands. Dim, watery eyes rested on him, drifted to some empty corner of the hall, then passed over him again without a sign of recognition. Almost Rorik conceded a twinge of pity. Almost but not quite.

"Where is Fulk?" he demanded in a harsh voice.

"Who are you, sir?" The bitter question came from a

lean, daggerlike man at Theoda's right. "Who are you who wages war on us for no reason?"

Rorik grinned unpleasantly and ignored the young upstart. "Do you not know me, Mother? Not know your own son?"

A spark of life lit the old woman's eyes, but faded again just as quickly as it had come.

"Lady Theoda has no sons," the young man sneered.

Rorik's mouth twisted with bitterness. "Once she had three. She may yet regret that she still has one."

The young man's eyes widened, then he frowned in disbelief. "You can't mean . . . !"

"I am Rorik Valois, rightful Vicomte of Brix, and," he added with a hint of maliciousness, "Duke William's count over the entire Cotentin. I've come to take back what Fulk so treacherously stole."

The man turned pale, but Theoda raised her hand. Sanity returned briefly to her eyes.

"Fulk is gone," she said. To Rorik's surprise her voice was still as low and mellow as he remembered. He had expected the cackle of a witch.

"Gone where?" Rorik demanded, thinking that here was the reason the castle was so poorly defended.

"Fulk is dead." The young man's voice resounded with the ring of challenge. "I am Phillip, his son and heir. I am lord of Brix."

Fulk dead! The words echoed through Rorik's skull. He was robbed of the ultimate revenge. Fulk dead. What a bitter twist of fate. He looked at the young man on the dais. He could see the resemblance now. The same coarse, sandy hair, the same hawk nose. When Phillip was older he would probably develop the same jowls, too. He would be the image of his father, if he lived that long.

"You are no longer lord of anything," Rorik told him flatly. "And if you had a scrap of guts you'd have led your men in defending what you claim as yours. Only a coward hides in comfort and safety and sends others to die for him."

"Who are you to speak of honor?" Phillip flung in

angry defiance. "You who send boys to slither into our midst and treacherously breach our defenses from within?" He gestured with disgust toward Timor and Miles, who had joined the throng in following Rorik into the hall. The two boys had made a swipe at cleaning off the filth, but their method of ingress into the castle was still pungently obvious.

Rorik smiled. "I am not a fool to waste my men's lives in useless effort. If you look for conventional attack only, then you deserve to lose, just as you have lost. You may keep your miserable life, son of Fulk, and count me generous in granting it. And you may take your stepmother with you when you leave my lands."

Rorik turned toward Sihtric to give orders to make the hall secure. He didn't see the hate twist Phillip's face, didn't see Theoda's hand reach out to claw at the young man's wrist as he grasped his belt knife. Even Sihtric didn't see before it was too late. Phillip shrugged off Theoda's staying hand and flung the blade with deadly accuracy. At the same time the glinting steel flashed through the air, Sihtric cried out warning. Rorik turned, but was knocked to his knees by the meaty shoulder that rammed into his chest. The blade sank to the hilt into the Norseman's broad back.

CHAPTER 21

"Duel?" Alaine's eyes went wide with alarm. "What do you mean, duel? Is Brix not taken?"

The messenger sagged with exhaustion. "The castle is taken, my lady. Casualties were very few, and even Sihtric's wound will soon mend." The boy made a visible effort to gather his faltering wits. "The duel—I know not the details. I am but a squire. But I believe you need have no fear on that score, my lady. This upstart Phillip could be no challenge for our lord."

The youngster swayed precariously on his feet, bringing his condition sharply to Alaine's attention. She was immediately repentant of her badgering.

"Master Eric, forgive my rudeness. You're dead on your feet, and here am I harping at you with no regard for your weariness. Do get something to eat and then take your rest. We will be ready to leave by tomorrow morning."

"Thank you, my lady." The squire breathed a sigh of relief and stumbled off toward the kitchen.

Alaine turned to Joanna with a frown. "What can this be about a duel? If the castle is taken, and Fulk is dead, why not just boot Phillip out the gate, or hang him from the nearest gibbet for his treachery? Rorik was once quick enough about threatening to stretch my neck when he thought it needful!"

Alaine had been so anxious in questioning the messenger that she hadn't noted the ashen color of her stepmother's face as the squire had related how Sihtric had saved Rorik from Phillip's blade. But Joanna recovered herself quickly and met Alaine's questioning gaze with her usual cool demeanor.

"Men are strange creatures," she commented with slightly raised brow, "and seldom very practical when it comes to war. I suggest you wait for your answers until you can question your husband directly."

"Indeed! It appears I shall have that opportunity with little delay. The battle is barely done before he sends an armed escort to collect me. Rorik does not trust me long at Ste. Claire without him. Does he think I'll bar the gate against his return?"

Joanna's brow puckered in a vexed frown. "Curb that bitter tongue of yours, Alaine. Why would you say such a thing?"

"Why else would Rorik summon me so soon on the heels of his victory?"

"You are his wife, dear. And Brix is his home. Why would he not want you there?"

Alaine could think of several reasons Rorik might not want her there. She had truly thought he would leave her at Ste. Claire to live out her life apart from him, but apparently he had different plans for her future. Though a part of her rejoiced that she would be at his side, another part of her quailed at the thought of leaving her beloved home and living among strangers with a husband who despised her.

"Who will see to Ste. Claire if I am gone?" she objected halfheartedly. "This place is my life. I have no wish to leave."

Joanna sighed impatiently. Her stepdaughter was an enigma. She had done nothing but pace and worry since Rorik had ridden out the gate, and now she declared she had no wish to join him in his victory.

"You will always have Ste. Claire, Alaine. But your place is with your husband. I will be here to see to the running of the household, and Sir Oliver will command the men who are left behind. Rorik will keep us safe, I'm sure. Ste. Claire is still under his charge."

"But . . . you mean, you aren't coming with me?"

"It is not I whom Rorik summoned."

"I'm sure he meant that all of us were to come."

"I'm sure he didn't," Joanna said with confidence. "It's time you learned to manage your home . . . and your husband . . . without my help."

"Manage Rorik?" Alaine snorted. "Impossible. Even with God's help!"

Joanna smiled wryly. "And of course you yourself are such a model of wifely behavior."

Alaine had the grace to look sheepish.

"I would take Hadwisa with you," Joanna suggested. "She's still spry enough to make the trip with ease. And Hilda and Gwyne to help you organize the household."

She smiled with a rare flash of humor. "And if you could take Gunnor it would surely be a great relief to us all."

"Nay to that!" Alaine laughed shakily. "Mayhap I'm glad you're not coming after all."

"I thought you might see it that way."

The afternoon and evening were spent in a frenzy of packing and preparation. But even in the rush Alaine worried over the messenger's story of events at Brix. Rorik attacked by Phillip? That perhaps was not so hard to credit. She had heard rumors that the son was a smaller and more petty version of the father. Thus she was more than ready to believe Phillip capable of any sort of perfidy.

And Sihtric—bless him!—interposed his broad back between Rorik and the knife meant to foully take his life. It was hard to picture that huge Norseman vulnerable to any kind of harm. Pray to God that he recovered. And what of this silly duel? What harebrained notion had entered her husband's head to give Phillip another chance to kill him?

By the time morning dawned and the small cavalcade was ready to leave, Alaine's head hurt from all the questions running circles in her mind. She had forgotten her reluctance to leave her home. Her thoughts were centered on Rorik, who somehow over the past few months had replaced Ste. Claire as the center of her existence. She was anxious to see with her own eyes that her husband had taken no hurt in the battle—and almost as anxious to fill his ears with reasons why Fulk's spawn should be denied another chance to take his life. But the small troop that Rorik had sent as escort set a slow pace, and for the sake of the other women in the party Alaine curbed her impatience. She spent the day fidgeting in her saddle and wondering what she would meet at Brix. The messenger had refused to divulge anything more than what Rorik had charged him to say, and he was now beyond her prying questions. The exhausted youngster had developed overnight a hearty case of the grippe and would be unable to leave his pallet for several days. So now she was reduced to pestering the long-suffering captain of their escort for what he knew about circumstances at Brix.

The captain was respectful, polite, and very close-mouthed. She could almost read his thoughts by the look in his eyes. He didn't expect that she, being a woman, could understand the fine points of battle, strategy, or honor. And he did not want to be bothered answering her annoying questions. Even Alaine's determined persistence was not enough to break through his polite reticence, and finally she gave up and left the man in disgruntled peace.

The sun was well down by the time they arrived at their destination. Brix loomed as a dark blot that rose from the sea cliff and blocked the stars from view. The dour captain hailed the guard and Alaine heard the word being passed down from the walls about their arrival.

To her surprise they bypassed the main gate and finally halted on a flat stretch of ground between the outer ramparts and the wall. Here she could see the dark shapes of several large tents outlined by the ruddy light of a roaring campfire. Separated from the tents by a small space, several smaller fires were ringed by the dark figures of men sitting or standing in relaxed postures. She looked at the captain quizzically, but he ignored the question in her eyes.

"A tent has been set up for you and your ladies over there," he said gruffly, gesturing to a sizable shelter close to the wall. "I'll have the men unload your baggage."

"Wait," Alaine ordered as he moved away. "Is Sir Rorik staying out here also?"

"Yes, my lady," the captain said tersely.

"Which is his tent?"

The captain pointed to the tent nearest the main fire. "He's bound to be occupied right now, my lady," he warned, "for tomorrow he fights that snake Phillip. I'll tell him you've arrived, but I doubt . . ."

"I'll tell him myself." Alaine's tone made clear that she would brook no nonsense. She wondered how long the captain had been fighting under Rorik's command. The two of them certainly shared their attitude toward women.

"Go ahead and put the women's baggage in that tent over there, but leave mine here. I'll see to it later."

The captain opened his mouth to object, but the look in Alaine's eyes changed his mind. "Yes, my lady." He sighed, hoping he wouldn't reap the blame for letting Sir Rorik's wife disturb him when he didn't want to be disturbed. The lord had enough on his mind without an annoying woman rattling around his tent. Why Sir Rorik had been so quick to send for the woman he failed to understand.

Alaine allowed the captain to hand her down from her mare. She brushed the wrinkles from her gown and screwed up her courage, then started toward Rorik's tent, stopping abruptly as the captain started to follow.

"The baggage, Captain," she reminded him firmly. "I'm sure it requires your personal attention."

The captain frowned mightily, shook his head, harrumphed, and stalked away. Alaine stiffened her spine with more courage than she felt and strode with unladylike determination to the tent entrance. A low murmur of masculine voices carried through the canvas flap. If Rorik was occupied, Alaine thought with relief, at least it was not with one of the castle harlots. She took a deep breath and pushed aside the flap.

Both men looked up as she stepped through the entrance. Rorik had been minutely inspecting his mail for flaws, and Alaine was surprised to see Sihtric sitting at his side working on a mug of beer.

"I thought you had a knife in your back, Sihtric."

Sihtric grinned. "The shoulder, my lady." He shrugged to show how little he regarded the injury. "I've too much meat up there for one little knife to do much harm."

"I expected to see you flat on your back." She smiled with relief, realizing suddenly how distressed she had really been when she'd learned of Sihtric's wound.

"It would take a far better man than that sniveling snake to put me on my back," Sihtric snorted.

Alaine could no longer keep her eyes from Rorik, whose

scowl would have sent a woman of lesser heart scurrying for cover.

"Did you not send for me, my lord?" Her smile was saucily impertinent.

"I did," Rorik admitted.

"Then why the look of surprise?" His look was certainly more annoyance than surprise, but Alaine was feeling bold. "Did you not expect us to arrive tonight?"

"Aye." Rorik turned his attention back to his mail. "But I did not expect you to walk unannounced into my tent like some squire on a petty errand. Did Captain Holberg not show you the tent that was erected for the ladies?"

"Indeed he did," she admitted pertly. "And I have sent my ladies to it."

Sihtric cleared his throat and downed the last of his beer. "Think I'll wander around a bit and see how lively the guards are," he mumbled. "If you'll excuse me, my lady."

Sihtric winked at her as he lifted the flap and stepped out the door. She smiled at his impertinence, then frowned at Rorik, who was studiously ignoring her. She wasn't about to be put off by his gruff mood. He had brought her here, so he was going to have to put up with her. She wanted to know what was going on. In matters concerning Brix, she didn't trust him to be either wise or canny. His bitterness ran too deep. For the sake of his stupid pride he might well dive into waters too deep for any man to handle, leaving her and her lands up for grabs to any knight strong enough to take her, and their child an orphan before it was born.

"What is this duel I'm told about, Rorik?"

"'Tis a simple affair." He didn't take his attention from the task at hand. "Fulk is dead—probably drowned in the River Orne with the other traitors at Val-es-Dunes. Phillip is his son."

"I know who Phillip is," she snapped impatiently. "He's been following in his father's shadow since Fulk came to Brix."

"Phillip has challenged me to personal combat for the right to hold Brix."

"Personal combat?" Alaine set her mouth in a tight line of exasperation. "Will you put that down and pay attention to me?"

With a heavy sigh Rorik set the mail aside. "Alaine," he said. "Why don't you retire to the ladies' tent and get some rest? I've much to do. And once the contest is fought, so will you. The whole of Brix is in slovenly disrepair. 'Tis why I sent for you. A woman's hand is needed to set things aright."

It was the reason he had given himself for bringing her to Brix in such haste. But now that she was here, standing before him with the familiar gleam of challenge in her eyes, filling his tent with lure of her femininity, he knew that he had been fooling himself. He had wanted her beside him. Curse himself for a dimwitted idiot! He could never trust her, but neither could he purge her from his soul.

Alaine stuck her chin out in stubborn determination. "Why are you fighting this contest? Did you not take Brix by fair combat? Is it not yours already by the Duke's law?"

"It is," he admitted.

"Then why fight?" she asked in amazement.

"It is a matter of honor," he explained, as if to a slow-witted child. "Phillip attacked me after formally surrendering. And he injured Sihtric with his foul deed. He deserves a thrashing. Can you understand that?"

"And what if he thrashes you?" she asked archly.

Rorik sighed, stood up, and dipped himself a beer from the keg at the far end of the tent. "I fail to see why you're so upset. This matter doesn't concern Ste. Claire."

Alaine began to pace with exasperated fury. "But it does concern my husband," she asserted. "Is this why you sent for me, to watch you die in such a foolish gesture of honor?"

He sipped his beer, then chuckled. Even in her anger she was a delight to the eye, lifting his spirits from the

gray doldrums where they'd lain since he had discovered
Fulk was beyond revenge. He was strangely moved by the
concern she was hiding behind all that indignant bluster.

"Would it grieve you to see me laid low?" He grinned.
"Somehow I can't picture it."

"It would grieve me to see any man cut down in such a
needless prank," she retorted acidly.

He regarded her momentarily with an almost affectionate look on his face. In a flash of understanding Alaine
realized how empty her life would be without this impossibly
stubborn, pigheaded, exasperating man. An unreasoning
but certain knowledge of danger dissolved her anger and
made her acknowledge her fear.

"You needn't worry about this duel, Alaine," Rorik
finally said. "I doubt that Phillip is a match for me."

He said it with the easy assurance of a man who knew
his abilities well. But she didn't feel reassured.

"Don't be so confident," she warned. "Phillip is a
trickster. His lack of honor matches his father's and is well
known in the country hereabouts. If he challenged you
then there's some reason he thinks to win. Please, Rorik.
Be sensible. Take what is already yours and point Phillip
down the road, or imprison him. I have a bad feeling about
this contest."

Rorik was silent a moment. He was surprised by the
note of real concern in her voice, and he almost allowed
himself to think she was truly afraid. Perhaps in spite of
everything she harbored some regard for him. He suddenly
had an unreasoning urge to please her, to see her smile, to
wipe the frown of worry from her features. But he set it
aside. He itched to fight Phillip and have this whole affair
settled for all time. Whatever Alaine's motivation, he
would not duck a fight just because of a woman's weakness.

Alaine saw his resolve harden and pulled out her last
weapon. "Listen to me, Rorik. What if you fall tomorrow?
What of your heir? How long do you think your child
would live should Phillip triumph? And even if I escaped
from here, how do you expect me to hold Ste. Claire
against the ambitious men who would come to claim it?

Are you willing for your son to live on the mercy of such men?''

Rorik looked at her in stunned and baffled surprise. Then his face melted into a smile of delight. "Alaine! You are with child?''

She flashed him a look of challenge. "Your son should be delivered along with the harvest," she said proudly. "And no matter what you think of me, Rorik, the child will need a father.''

For a moment she thought the shell was cracking. He placed both hands on her shoulders and smiled confidently. "Our child will have a father. Never fear.''

There was pride in his eyes, pride and a warmth she had thought never to see again. She hadn't expected this powerful reaction. Who could have guessed such a man as Rorik would soften so to hear the news he had bred a child? Could this have been the key all along?

"Are you well?'' he asked almost anxiously.

"Of course I'm well. I'm as healthy as a . . .''

The warmth was igniting to something else equally unexpected. Abruptly he stepped to the doorway, opened the flap, and spoke to a guard outside.

"Is that your baggage out there?'' he asked.

"Yes.''

"I'll have it brought in.'' He smiled. The fire was still burning, warming his eyes to summer green. There was no doubt about what he wanted.

Alaine couldn't keep a traitorous smile from her face. Typical male pride. He was proud of sowing his seed so well, no doubt, and now looked to recap the event. She ought to say no and stalk off to the ladies' tent. It would serve the big oaf right to stew in his own juices. For months he had acted the ice king and treated her like a piece of cold meat to be used at his whim. And now another whim was on him and he expected her to warm up to his pleasure. She ought to walk out of the tent and leave him to roast in his own fire.

But she didn't.

A soldier pushed through the tent flap and set her trunk

in one corner. When he left, Rorik laced the flap behind him.

"Is that all you brought?" Rorik asked, eyeing the small trunk in surprise.

"I didn't know how long I would be staying."

"You're my wife. This is your home."

"I thought perhaps . . ." Alaine let her voice trail off. She wouldn't explain her notion that she would be left at Ste. Claire to molder in isolation. Conversation was not really what Rorik had in mind. His hands had moved to the laces of her gown.

"It's been a long time." His voice vibrated with need.

"Only three days," she answered with a hint of a smile.

"You know what I mean."

She knew too well what he meant. His hand slipped inside her gown and cupped a tingling breast. Feelings that had too long lain dormant in her young body rose up with a sudden ferocity that was overwhelming. She felt her heart pound against his hand, and saw the lazy smile of triumph spread across the rugged features of his face. He slipped the gown from her shoulders and just as rapidly untied the lacing of her chemise. Soon all her garments were pooled around her ankles.

"No more ice maiden," he whispered as his hands found and surrounded her bare breasts.

She caught her breath as he pulled her against him and let his hands drift down over her back, hips, and buttocks.

"It was all you wanted," she said in a soft voice.

Then her eyes were caught by his and she saw the maelstrom of desire that was building within. "I wanted more," he said.

His face was taut with desire, and she could hear the drum of his heartbeat above her own. Without a word he picked her up and carried her to the rough soldier's pallet that served as his bed. For a moment he only looked at her as she lay there, then he gently touched the slight mound of her abdomen.

"I should have known a child would grow this soon," he smiled. "No matter what else we are, together we are fire, and earth, and lightning. I have never desired any woman as I desire you."

Quickly he divested himself of his clothing and laid his long, naked form down beside her. His mouth found hers and took it by storm. His hands cupped her buttocks and pulled her hips tight against his, letting her feel the strength of his arousal. There was no gentleness in him, and Alaine wanted none. The fire storm of his passion pulled at her, sucking her into a hot whirlwind where his pride and hers were both burned to ash. She wrapped her legs around his hips, urging him to fill her and end the sweet agony building within her.

Rorik needed no urging. Their cold and emotionless matings of the past weeks had left him hungry, and like a starved man he greedily devoured the feast spread before him. Her ardent response to his first thrust inflamed him even further. He buried his hands in her hair and held her willing prisoner while he devoured her lips, eyes, throat, shoulders, and breasts with his mouth. All the while he buried himself in her soft depths with an urgent, demanding, primitive rhythm. When finally she shuddered beneath him, he saw nothing but red and felt nothing but a hot, throbbing demand for release. He took her soft cry into his mouth and held her against him. He drove once more into her warm body and felt the universe explode around him.

Later that night gentleness returned. Desire softened and made way for tenderness as husband and wife lay in each other's arms and explored the mysteries of their passion. No words were spoken. Alaine thought no words were necessary. It wasn't until the beginnings of dawn paled the eastern sky that she found she was wrong.

She woke as Rorik gently untangled himself from her and rose from the hard pallet. Fighting the temptation to drift back into the warmth of sleep, she watched as he pulled on chausses and donned shirt and padded leather arming tunic.

"You can light the lantern," she said softly. "I'm awake."

"Go back to sleep. You need your rest."

"And you got so much sleep last night?" she asked pertly.

She stood and brushed away the straw that clung to her skin. As Rorik moved to light the lantern she wrapped the rough woolen blanket around her nakedness.

The lantern's dim light seemed bright in the confines of the tent. Rorik looked at the blanket and smiled.

"It's a bit late for modesty, my lady."

He hooked one finger where the corners of the blanket were tucked between her breasts. The wrap slithered to the floor. He stared at her openly and without shame.

"You're beautiful, Alaine. You're the most beautiful woman I've ever seen. Don't ever hide yourself from me."

Alaine's mouth quirked in a crooked smile. "You won't say that some months from now when I'm round as a sow."

He laughed. "I'll say it even more then. And I'll mean it." Leaning forward, he placed a kiss on her forehead. "You might as well get dressed, now that you're up. There are some things to see to. We'll be moving into the hall this afternoon."

He paused as she moved toward her chest.

"Right after the contest," he finished softly.

She halted mid-stride. "What?"

"We'll see to moving after this affair with Phillip is done."

"But you said . . . !"

"I said nothing, Alaine. I will fight Phillip in the lists this morning."

Alaine sputtered with indignation. She had just assumed, as happy as he was with her announcement, as loving as he'd been all through the night, that he had seen the reason of her arguments. Nothing more had been said about the duel. He had let her believe she had won, the swine!

"You . . . !"

He held up a peremptory hand for silence. "Hold that sharp tongue of yours. I don't want to hear any more about it. I want no man alive to question my right to hold Brix and all its beholden lands. Have more faith in me, Alaine. I know what I'm doing.''

She saw the hopelessness of swaying him. And she saw the old grim wall building again. Last night had been a reprieve, not a pardon.

"Be careful," she warned morosely. "Watch Phillip. He's a snake."

He smiled with a hint of the warmth he had shown the night before. "He may be a snake, but I'm the dragon. Remember?"

A hastily erected fence cordoned off the area where Rorik and Phillip would fight. It was a flat area of trampled grass and mud that stretched between the eastern curtain wall and the outer ramparts. The men that gathered there to watch their leaders duel were sullen and tense. On one end of the temporary arena flew the dragon banner, and on the other side the crossed swords and dagger of Phillip's blazon. The men-at-arms that gathered under each banner eyed each other with suspicion and distrust.

Alaine stood at Sihtric's side and shivered in the May sunshine. The morning chill had long since burned away, but there was a coldness deep inside of her that no amount of spring warmth could dispel. Rorik had suggested she not come, and she had considered staying in the tent and hiding her head under the blankets, but at the last minute she realized it would be a public shame to Rorik if his wife refused to watch him battle for what was his.

A raucous cheer rose from the gathered men as the two combatants appeared. As Rorik entered the arena the sun glinted off newly polished mail and helm. The dragon clawing and snarling on the black shield looked alive and hungry for blood. Alaine remembered suddenly the first time she had seen Rorik, before the tumbled-down gate of Ste. Claire. She'd never seen a man wield a broadsword with more strength or skill. Then the sight of him had chilled her blood. Now it warmed her very soul. Why did she fear? With a weapon in his hand Rorik was as formidable as the dragon his men had named him. It would take a better man than Phillip to cut him down.

But Phillip also looked like a prince of battle. If he was truly the coward Rorik's men had labeled him, it didn't show in his demeanor. The black stallion he rode pranced and crow-hopped in restless energy as he moved into the arena. Alaine wished she could detect some looseness to Phillip's seat or some fault in the carriage of his lance. But she couldn't. He sat his eager black stallion with careless grace, lance balanced easily on one foot and grasped loosely in his right hand. From where she stood Alaine couldn't see his face, but she imagined an evil grin pasted to a coarse, ugly countenance. Only an unscrupulous ogre would commit his honor in formal surrender then turn and foully attack his conqueror. Alaine was surprised that horns didn't grow from Phillip's helm and a tail sprout from beneath his hauberk.

Sir Guillaume limped to the center of the field and raised his hand for silence. He had taken a spear thrust to the thigh early in the battle for Brix, Sihtric whispered to Alaine, but would soon be right again. Alaine nodded impatiently and strained to hear the knight's words as he outlined the rules of combat. Finally, he asked both contestants if they agreed to abide by the results of this private battle. When both nodded assent, he limped off the field. Rorik and Phillip whirled their destriers and trotted casually to opposite ends of the arena. Simultaneously they turned to face one another, and as if by invisible signal, spurred their stallions into a thundering charge.

Alaine held tightly to Sihtric's arm as the two knights met in a crash of splintering wood and scraping steel. Phillip's lance bounced off Rorik's shield, but Rorik's splintered against the crossed swords and dagger, almost lifting Phillip from his saddle. With a curse that could be heard by the onlookers, Phillip managed to regain his seat before Rorik could use his advantage. He spurred his stallion out of range of Rorik's broken weapon and made ready to charge again.

Alaine cried out objection as Phillip turned and galloped once again toward Rorik, who held a useless and broken lance in his hand. Sihtric hushed her with a frown.

"Be still, lass. It is not a tourney here, but a war with life and property as the prize. Never fear. Rorik can take care of himself."

And he did. In the last instant of Phillip's charge, Rorik nudged the chestnut stallion aside. The tip of Phillip's lance slid harmlessly off the dragon shield while Rorik swung his own broken weapon to connect with Phillip's undefended back. With a pained grunt, Phillip bent forward. His lance stuck tip down in the mud and twisted from his grasp. By the time he recovered his balance and turned to face his opponent, Rorik had his broadsword out of the scabbard that lay across his back and was closing fast.

They met with a clash of metal on metal. The heavy broadswords were ponderous weapons, and each blow seemed to travel in slow motion. Rorik opened a gash on Phillip's face, and Phillip managed a telling cut to the ribs, but neither man showed signs of weakening. The morning air seemed to shiver with the power of their hammering blows, and a tense expectancy hung heavily on the watchers at the fence.

The minutes marched by like hours. Phillip was showing more skill than Alaine had expected, and a niggling worm of fear was beginning to eat away at her confidence. Phillip's black stallion, though, was being hard set upon to match the strength of Rorik's chestnut. Both destriers were aggressive, vicious beasts, as any good warhorse must be. But the chestnut was in the prime of fighting trim. His bulk of muscle outmatched the black's, and the unrelenting pressure he was applying to the lesser horse was beginning to tell. The black was game and eager, but finally faltered under the relentlessly driving weight of the heavier horse. In a scramble of legs and hooves he went down, carrying Phillip with him.

Rorik immediately broke off his attack, jumped from the saddle with a litheness that ignored the 150 pounds of chain mail on his body, and advanced toward his opponent on foot. The watching men gave a cheer for his knightly behavior, but Alaine breathed a silent and most unladylike

curse. Honor was all very well and good, but it would
have been perfectly acceptable for Rorik to stay mounted
and use the advantage he had fairly won. Then would the
contest be over sooner and Alaine's heart could stop
battering at her chest.

Sihtric grinned down at her with unholy glee. "Now
we'll see a fight worth watching, I'll wager! Enough of
playing around on horseback! Now for some good honest
swordplay!"

It seemed to Alaine that Sihtric was mightily overconfi-
dent of the outcome of the duel, and getting far too much
pleasure out of watching her husband poised on the edge
of a violent death. Men! And to think she had once
thought she understood them!

Phillip wasted no time in aiming a vicious slice at Rorik's
neck, but Rorik met the blow with his shield and countered
powerfully with a slash that cut through the mail at Phillip's
chest. Phillip grunted with pain but struck back with a swift-
ness that brought shouts of admiration from the onlookers, all
except for Alaine, who was gripping poor Sihtric's arm with an
intensity that threatened to cut off all blood below the elbow.

"Oh, sweet merciful God!" she groaned in a low voice.
"Why doesn't it end?"

Sihtric patted her hand in awkward comfort. "Don't
bother yourself, lass. Our Rorik's not a man to be beaten
by this swine."

It appeared that Sihtric was right. As time dragged on
and the two men hacked and hammered and battered at
each other, Phillip's responses were slowing, but Rorik's
arm seemed as strong as ever as he forced his opponent to
slowly retreat from the rain of his blows. Both men's mail
was spotted by creeping stains of scarlet. Both men could
hear blood pounding like the hammering of mallets on the
insides of their skulls. But Rorik's arm never faltered, and
Phillip's was growing less and less sure. The mud sucked
at his feet. Sweat stung his eyes and clouded his vision.
His lungs labored painfully in his chest. He knew that
Rorik must be laboring also, but the man seemed inhuman.
He kept coming, knocking away Phillip's weakening at-

tacks and forcing him back and ever back, his deadly blows falling with never-ending power on the retreating knight's faltering defense.

With a shuddering groan Phillip collapsed to his knees.

"Enough!" he cried in a low voice. "Quarter! I ask quarter!"

Rorik immediately lowered his sword and stepped back, as honor demanded, but not in time to avoid the slice Phillip aimed to cut his legs out from beneath him. The blow was poorly executed. Phillip's sword scored a shallow cut through the mail covering Rorik's thighs. And Phillip promptly found himself flat on his back looking up the length of Rorik's deadly steel.

"I should kill you for that," Rorik told him in a deadly calm voice. "But I've a distaste for dirtying my good steel with your foul blood. I'll let you choose, coward. Death here—or life, and dishonor. Which?"

Phillip's eyes grew wide as Rorik's blade pressed against his throat. "Life!" he choked. "I choose life. Take the blade away."

Rorik's lips curled in contempt as he lifted his sword from the other's neck. Then a white-hot thunderbolt struck him in the back. His senses swam. Blood welled up into his throat. He saw Phillip smile as blackness came up and sucked him to the earth.

CHAPTER 22

Alaine screamed as the crossbow quarrel tore through Rorik's mail and into his back. Before Rorik hit the ground she had pulled out of Sihtric's restraining grip and bolted toward the arena. Men crushed around her as she broke through the fence. She desperately elbowed through the crush. Everywhere there were shouts, curses, orders being flung back and forth. Alaine paid no heed to any of it. Sihtric, sword in hand and a ferocious scowl on his face, was hard on her heels. He grabbed her arm in a bruising grip and abruptly halted her progress, shouting above the noise of the crowd that she should get herself back to the tent. Without bothering to answer, she pulled away from his grasp and pushed forward to Rorik's side.

The crowd of knights and squires who had rushed to their lord's fallen body made way for her with glances of uneasy sympathy. She knelt in the churned-up mud, not looking at any of them. One distant corner of her mind noted that Phillip was gone. Dimly she hoped he was dead, but it didn't really matter. The only thing that mattered was the ash-colored face of her husband and the blood- and gore-stained tip of the crossbow quarrel that stuck obscenely out below his collarbone. A flicker of hope lit her eyes when she saw that his chest was still rising and falling in shallow, uneven breaths. Gingerly she reached out and touched his cheek. His eyes blinked open, closed, then opened again. They were glassy and dim.

"Rorik! Oh, Rorik! Damn you!" she gritted in a low, desperate voice that only he could hear. "Don't you die on me, you toad! I'll make you sorry if you do! I swear by all the saints I will!"

He closed his eyes, but one corner of his mouth lifted in a smile. His lips formed her name, and then he was gone.

Alaine cried his name in desperate plea, heedless of the ring of onlookers. But Rorik lay still and unmoving. Gone. Her senses registered the fact in a numb haze. For a moment she felt nothing. The only thought that occurred to her stunned mind was that she'd not ever told him that she loved him. Then her blood turned to ice. The world crashed in around her. She couldn't breathe, and blackness was crowding the edges of her vision.

A harsh voice cut into the cold black fog and folded it back. "What are you jackanapes doing standing around gaping?" Sihtric roared. "Give the man some air, by God!"

"Sihtric . . . !" Alaine choked, grasping at the bearlike claw he laid on her shoulder. "He's . . ."

Sihtric pulled her to her feet. "No he's not, lass." The Norseman's confidence brooked no denial. "He's just had his daylight snuffed. You might say he's resting. We'll have that little arrow out in a trice, and before you know it he'll be making all of us miserable again. Now, this time you do as I say and go back to the tent. We can see to him there."

Alaine swallowed her sobs and followed behind as Sihtric, ignoring his own recent injury, hefted Rorik over his shoulder and carried him from the field as if his weight were nothing. He laid him out on the pallet where they'd come together in such hungry passion the night before. Then with businesslike aplomb he cut away both tip and tail of the arrow.

"Send someone for the smith's pincers," Sihtric commanded. "And see that water is heated over that fire out there. Get someone to build it higher. We'll be needing that water in here sooner than later." He looked up abruptly. "You're not going to swoon on me, are you? I thought you helped Lady Joanna with the healing at Ste. Claire."

Alaine forced down the sickness that was rising from her stomach at the sight of her husband lying pale and still as death with a gore-covered arrow sticking from his breast.

"I helped with the serfs, and the peasants." Her voice shook disgracefully, despite her effort to keep it firm. "But they . . . they don't get crossbow shafts stuck through them."

"Sometimes they do," Sihtric commented matter-of-factly.

"Oh, Sihtric! He looks like he's hovering at the very mouth of death! Are you sure . . . are you sure . . . ?"

"Go do as I've told you," Sihtric ordered gruffly. "He'll still be alive when you get back. This lad's made of iron. It takes more than a little stick like this to kill a dragon."

The Norseman shook his head as Alaine backed reluctantly out of the tent. Who would have guessed the lass would react like this? In consideration of how Rorik treated her, any other woman would have been glad to usher him straight to the gates of Hell. But then, women were fools, and who could understand them? Men were fools, too, he thought, looking down at Rorik's limp form. And smart and tough as this lad was, sometimes he was more the fool than any other.

No one could pry Alaine from Rorik's side when Sihtric went to work with the smith's heavy pincers to pull the shaft from muscle and bone. She gritted her teeth and fretted and took her husband's limp hand in both of hers. The patient came abruptly and unpleasantly awake as Sihtric yanked the gory shaft out of his body. His screech of agony practically lifted the tent from its moorings, and Alaine's hand was bruised for days after from his desperate grip.

Sihtric grinned and held up the bloody shaft before Rorik's wide-open, swimming eyes. "I see you've still the use of your lungs, boy. Might be you'll survive after all."

Rorik did survive, but his recovery was slow. Two days after the contest they moved him to the lord's chamber in the Great Hall. Much of the time he was unconscious, and when he woke he raved at visions that beset him from the very depths of his soul. Alaine allowed no one else to nurse him, and only when she collapsed and Sihtric picked her up and bodily carried her to another chamber was an anxious Hadwisa allowed to take her place.

As Rorik lay in the lord's chamber, hovering between this world and the next, Sihtric and Sir Gunnulf consulted together on how best to set Brix in order. Phillip had somehow slipped through their fingers in the confusion following Rorik's fall. The unfortunate squire who had been Phillip's tool in wielding the crossbow had been caught and hanged on the spot. Rorik's men were not pleased at seeing their lord cut down by such a cowardly blow, and the squire's death hadn't appeased them. Bad feelings abounded between Rorik's army and the surviving men of Brix. Fights were frequent. There had been at least three deaths—one of Rorik's men and two who had served Fulk and Phillip.

Sihtric and Gunnulf clamped down hard. A messenger was sent to William with the story of what had happened and a request that Phillip be formally outlawed. The fights ended instantly when Sihtric promised to hang the next troublemakers who were caught brawling, and promptly did. The survivors of Phillip's men-at-arms were given parole on the condition they recognize Rorik as their lawful lord. Most of them would have recognized the Devil himself as lord for a chance at continued life and freedom. Most took service at Brix. Only a few disgruntled diehards chose to seek their fortune elsewhere.

Alaine was only marginally aware of what was going on around her. Rorik's chamber was her world. She took her meals there, slept there, and spent endless hours sitting beside the huge canopied bed praying for her husband's recovery. She held him down when he flailed at fevered visions, suffering a black eye, swollen lip, and sprained wrist in so doing. She bathed him in cool water when he sweated and wrapped him in blankets when he shook with chills. When he lay quiet, she simply sat by his side and stared at his face—that rugged, uncompromising face that somehow, in spite of all their difficulties, had become so beloved.

Twice a day she changed the poultice on his wound, cleaning away the dead and rotted tissue. Five days after he had been carried to the lord's chamber she lifted the poultice from his breast and found naught to clean way. The skin had taken on a pink and healthy tinge, and a scabby crust was seeking to cover the injured tissue. His breathing was easy, if shallow, and his brow cool. Alaine knelt and offered a tired prayer of thanks. Then she rang for Hadwisa, retired to her own ajoining chamber, and slept the clock around.

From that day forward it seemed to Alaine that the sun shone more brightly and the birds trilled more sweetly outside the chamber window. She took a perverse delight in having Rorik helpless and under the care of her hands. For once in his life the dragon needed someone, and that someone was Alaine. Most of the time he still spent in heedless sleep. She could baby and pamper him to her heart's content without risk of being sent away by an angry scowl or cold, forbidding glare. She could smoothe the riotous black curls back from his brow, trace the sensuous line of his lips, and lovingly admire the velvet black sweep of thick lashes against a chiseled cheek. All this she could do without his seeing and pouncing on such womanly weakness, and she took full advantage of it. While he was safely muffled in healing sleep, she dared to tell him exactly what she thought of his arrogance, his pigheadedness, and his stubborn bitterness. In the same breath she cursed herself for a fool in loving him. She didn't see, during one of these soft-spoken tirades, when she turned from regarding him to gazing out the window, that Rorik turned his head in her direction, his mouth lifted in a secret smile.

In too short a time Rorik no longer needed Alaine's full-time care. When her husband began to spend his days in restless wakefulness, Alaine became uneasy under his constant regard. She turned her energies to Brix, acting the lady of the castle as though she were sure Rorik would keep her by his side. In truth she was not at all sure of this. Rorik had said that Brix was now her home, but she never dared to predict her husband's mercurial temper. When she was with him his eyes showed a hint of warmth, his smile a secret happiness. He never mentioned their night of desperate passion before the contest. Neither did he bring up her small deception about the child, or her supposed betrayal with Gilbert de Prestot. She couldn't fathom what was going on in his mind. It made her uneasy. And she took her uneasiness out on Brix.

Brix's defenses were in good order, but the living quarters were a mess. Theoda was a mere shell of a woman, and for the last years she had let the servants do as they wished. The buildup of dust, grime, and filth was incredible. Alaine set the serfs to scrubbing and cleaning the Great Hall, the smaller family hall, the sleeping chambers, the kitchens, the stones of the inner court, and the chambers, barracks, and small hall in the keep itself. Fresh rushes were scattered over floors and sprinkled with scented herbs to drive away the mustiness. Animal refuse and litter were cleaned from the baileys, shrubbery cleared from the moats.

Sihtric and Gunnulf were too busy girding up the castle's defenses to tend to the other aspects of bringing a great estate under control. Guillaume had taken to bed with the wound in his leg starting to fester. So Alaine took the authority upon herself. She collared Fulk's bailiff and pored over the ill-kept accounts, inspected storerooms, inventoried food, drink, clothing, yard goods, and untended fleeces. She inspected stables, kennels, workshops, and craft shops, and made a cursory inspection of the villages nearest the castle. Between these chores she saw to Rorik. She slept on the cot she had set next to his bed when he was at his sickest. Somehow she was reluctant to take up quarters in her own adjoining chamber, even though her patient no longer needed constant attention.

After a particularly trying day and evening spent with Hilda in the storage vaults, Alaine slipped silently to her cot and collapsed in a weary heap without even removing her gown.

"You're working too hard," came a whispered voice from the canopied bed. Rorik shakily swung his legs over the edge of the bed and sat regarding her with a smile. "You look too feeble to move."

Alaine eyed him blearily. "I look feeble?" she snorted. "What do you think you look like?"

He grinned. In the milky moonlight that flooded through

the window he looked like a tall ghost as he stood and moved toward the cot. She sat up in alarm.

"You shouldn't be out of bed!"

"I've been walking around on my own two feet for a week now. I'm probably healthier than you are."

He was stark naked, and indeed showing blatant signs of renewed vigor that brought an unexpected rush of blood to Alaine's face. "Get back into bed!" she ordered in her best don't-give-me-any-nonsense voice.

He ignored her and sat down on the cot instead. "Why are you still sleeping here?"

Startled by his abruptness, she was at a loss for an answer. "I . . . my quarters are cold," she improvised.

He arched an amused brow. "I meant, why aren't you sleeping in the big bed with me? I'm not so delicate that your tossing about is going to maim me."

She slanted him a wary look. "Is it so? I think you have ideas beyond your reach."

He laughed softly, stood up, stretched, and winced. Regretfully he regarded the impetuously eager tool of his manhood. "Nay." He grinned, "Though parts of me are feeling alive again, I'm not yet up to feeding your wildcat appetites, little Alaine. But the sweet feel of you next to me would be a soothing balm."

He cocked an eye to gauge her reaction, and for a moment she put on a stern face. But it wouldn't stay in place, and dissolved into a laugh.

"You're playing on my sympathy, you brute."

"Give me something else to play on, wench, and I'll leave your sympathy alone."

They slipped together under the covers and lay side by side, each drinking in the unusual peace between them. Finally he took her hand in his and guided it to the stubbornly insistent arousal that refused to listen to reason.

"Do you think we might do something about that?" he asked.

"Don't you know you're still sick, and weak?" she chided.

"Am I?" He smiled a smile that would melt a heart of flint.

"Aye, you are," she replied. "And you're the very Devil himself, to be thinking such thoughts when you're scarcely back from death's door."

"And you're a witch who could make a man hard with desire on his very deathbed."

She sent him a siren's smile, feeling powerful, womanly, and most of all, desired. Wordlessly she got to her knees, straddled him, and took the hard length of his manhood deep into herself. He sighed and grasped her hips, moving her gently as she allowed herself to sink forward onto his broad chest. His hands moved to the silky expanse of her back, stroking up and down in relaxing rhythm. Together they lay in silent communion as nature took her course. When she once more cuddled up to his side he dipped his head and pressed his lips to hers.

"Alaine," he whispered. "You're a good woman."

She smiled and dropped instantly into slumber.

The next week was a difficult one. Rorik was surly and restless. He was well enough to feel energy seeping back into his body, but had not the strength to do much more than pace up and down the confines of his chamber, or lie abed and grill poor Sihtric and Sir Gunnulf on what they were doing to safeguard Brix and its beholden lands from attack. He was sharp with Alaine about the haggard hollows below her cheeks, accusing her of heedlessly exhausting herself and endangering both her own health and the welfare of their unborn child. He suggested she send for Joanna and her daughters to help with the chores of putting the castle in good order, and straightway himself ordered a messenger to Ste. Claire.

"And will Sybil also come, my lord?" Alaine asked sharply, referring to the latest in the string of personal serving maids that paraded through their chambers in the pretense of serving her needs.

"Sybil?" he asked innocently.

Alaine glared at him through narrowed eyes.

"Do you need her?" His grin was wicked. "I don't. Never did."

She declined to ask his meaning. She had been treading on eggshells ever since the night she'd joined him in the big bed. Every night since they had lain together, mostly in quiet companionship, sometimes in gentle passion. She felt once again like the world had turned and she'd been slow in turning with it. This man was not the same Rorik who had left Ste. Claire on a mission of war and revenge—not the same Rorik who had used her nightly in cold passion and ignored her daily in icy contempt. It was as if Rorik had died there in the arena with Phillip's treacherous quarrel in his back, and the merciful Lord had sent in his place a Rorik with the bitter blackness cut out of his soul. It was a dream too good to last, and she didn't want to question it. But inevitably she did.

"I've not changed," Rorik denied with a wry smile, looking down at her where she lay in his arms, the light of a single candle touching her features with haunting shadows. "I've come to the end of a long and bitter journey, and now I want peace—peace for Brix, peace between us. I want to wipe away the past and start again."

She was silent. That was not the answer she hoped for. Had she thought by some miracle that he'd come to love her and would declare his undying passion? Might as well wish the stars down from the sky. She told herself to be satisfied with peace, but still she was disappointed.

He picked up a strand of golden hair and idly twined it around his finger. "I've been harsh with you," he admitted. "Maybe you deserved my harshness. But sometimes I think not. I'm not an easy man with a woman, and you were young, inexperienced. Could be I forced you into Gilbert's bed."

She opened her mouth in protest, but he placed a finger over her lips.

"Don't say it," he ordered. "I don't want to hear another lie or another excuse. The deed is forgiven. What I want now is peace." He longed to say more—that he loved her in spite of everything, that knowing she cared for him made his world complete. But he could not bring himself to place that weapon in her feminine hands. Old hates die hard. Some, he supposed, never die at all.

His face loomed above her in the dim candlelit intimacy of their bed. She wanted peace, also—so badly she could almost taste it. She was tired of strife and tension. The price was great—a tacit admission of deception and unfaithfulness, a meek swallowing of her disappointment that this man she loved could still believe her capable of such sordid behavior. But right now, held close by his strong arms, hearing his heart's strong beat against her bare breast—right now it was worth it.

She smiled and brushed her hand along his cheek. "For the sake of peace," she agreed. "I'll hold my tongue."

He chuckled softly and nuzzled at her neck. "A miracle, by God!"

Playfully she pushed him off her, but already he was serious again. He gently took hold of her dainty chin and turned her face toward him. "For one moment more I'll play the monster," he warned. "Then both you and I will not speak of this again."

Alaine lay in silence and waited. How did she ever come to love this man? she wondered. Even when he was breaking her heart she wanted to kiss him.

"My feelings toward women are laced with bitterness," he admitted. "You know why. Maybe I'm unjust. But I will not have a wife I can't turn my back on. If you betray me again, Alaine, I promise you this. If I don't kill you, as is my right, I will at least lock you in a cloister for the rest of your days."

He almost weakened at the hurt he sensed. Her face was an unmoving mask, but he could feel the wound he had dealt in the rapid beat of her heart against his chest and the spasmodic tightening of her hand on his arm. He wondered silently if he would really have the strength to lock this woman away from his sight for all time. He didn't want to find out. A tear tickled his shoulder where he cheek rested against him. Cursing both himself and her, he drew her body closer against him.

"Alaine," he whispered in a voice that was almost a

plea. "I love you as much as I can love any woman. Don't ask me for more than I can give."

"I won't." Her voice was laced with tears. She raised a hand to wipe the traitorous moisture from her face. "I won't ask until you can give it."

Spring warmed into full summer. The meadows were gaudy with wildflowers. Fruit ripened and hung heavy and lush on the trees. The whole earth bloomed with life. And so did Alaine. Joanna and family were prompt to arrive, and, together with Hilda and Hadwisa, that inimitable lady set the servants back on their heels and had castle and hall humming with order and organization. Alaine was quick to regain her energy. Her gently rounding shape didn't hamper her from riding out daily to inspect the ripening crops, chat with the villagers and farmers, and keep a sharp eye on the welfare of these people who had become her own. Sometimes Rorik rode with her. His strength was returning. The circles had disappeared from under his eyes and the pallor of his skin was warming once again to sun-browned bronze. He spent hours every day in the exercise yard with Sihtric, or Sir Gunnulf, or even Garin. The frame that had wasted to gauntness once again rippled with taut muscle. His stride regained its coil-spring litheness. And his spirits soared into the blue summer sky. Brix was his. Alaine was his, and soon the future of his line would be assured by an heir. Rorik was ready to forget the past and look to the future—except for one nagging problem.

Theoda. Rorik's mother haunted the castle like s skittish ghost. She drifted in and out of rooms, a dried-up will-o'-the-wisp with scraggly gray hair and darting, birdlike eyes. She was frightened to death of her one surviving son and scurried ratlike to shelter whenever his voice was heard. Rorik ignored her, turning his face away whenever he happened to catch sight of her cronelike figure. But Alaine found it in her heart to pity the woman. Servants' gossip had it that she had suffered mightily under Fulk's rule. And from Sihtric's account Theoda had tried to stop Phillip's unchivalrous knife attack on Rorik. Alaine couldn't help but think that Theoda had loved her sons. Her desperate attempt to rid herself of an abusive husband had turned into tragedy. And for all these years she had lived with the burden of their deaths weighing down her soul. It was no wonder the woman was more than half mad.

But Rorik would not confront the problem of his mother. Whenever he looked at the woman he felt the old rage building and when Alaine dared to bring up the subject of Theoda his face grew shuttered and cold. The bitch had food and a place to sleep, he snarled. She was lucky she didn't have his hands around her throat.

So Alaine took it on herself to pluck the thorn from the dragon's paw. She arranged for Theoda, along with a sizable amount of coin, to enter a well-to-do nunnery at Cherbourg. The sisters were practiced at caring for those with overburdened souls, and Rorik would be spared the daily trauma of having Theoda within his sight, and within tempting reach of his hand. When she explained her arrangements to the old woman, the round birdlike eyes instantly flooded with tears. Theoda snatched at Alaine's hand and kissed it, then dissolved in a fit of weeping.

When Alaine informed her husband of the authority she had taken upon herself, he merely grunted a bare acknowledgment. Taking this as consent, Alaine hurriedly assigned a suitable escort for the former lady of the hall and saw her on her way. For one brief moment before leaving, Theoda took Alaine's hand in hers. Sanity had returned to her eyes, for however short a time.

"My son's wife," she whispered hoarsely. "I am an evil woman, and my hell has already begun. My dead sons must curse me from their graves, and the one who remains will never think of me as his mother. But for his own sake, I pray that someday he may learn to forgive, and to understand, a little." She shook her head as if to clear away the cobwebs of madness. "Tell him, I beg you, that I never meant any to die."

Alaine simply nodded, and Theoda lowered her eyes to

the ground once again. When she rode out the gate, she didn't bother to look back.

The golden luck of summer held. The crops ripened and thrived as they hadn't in two long years. The walled garden behind the Great Hall burst forth with cherries and pears, peaches, peas, onions, turnips, and cabbage. No one would go hungry in the coming winter, in either castle or village. The earth had become giving once more. The summer rains were gentle and warm. Even the sea seemed benevolent as it surged against the cliffs of Brix.

As Rorik grew in strength and health, he eagerly took up the reins of command. A messenger arrived from William congratulating his victory, confirming his lordship over Brix and all of Brix's beholden fiefs, and charging him with bringing the Cotentin from Cherbourg to Coutances under the firm rule of Normandy's rightful sovereign. Almost as an afterthought the messenger added that Phillip had been decreed outlaw. Anywhere the man showed his face he was to be hunted down and brought to justice.

With Brix set in order and firmly under control, Rorik set about solidifying his regional support. He paid unannounced visits to all castles, towns, and villages that owed homage to him as Vicomte of Brix. Most of the minor barons who held castles under his overlordship he allowed to retain their lands and position. Those he felt unsure of he replaced with his own men as reward for their loyalty. Ste. Claire he gave over into his wife's control, but suggested strongly that, since she was busy fulfilling a chatelaine's role at Brix, she appoint a capable castellan to look after her interests. To her delight he put forth Garin's name for her consideration.

Garin was stunned when Alaine made the announcement. He'd not expected one piece of good fortune to follow so swiftly on the heels of another. Alaine couldn't help but notice that Mathilde was ecstatic also. She made a mental note to speak to her stepsister and remind her that Garin had a long road to travel before he could be considered a candidate for Mathilde's hand. She hoped the girl had the patience to wait. But it was not long before she discovered how little patience her younger stepsister had.

One evening as dusk approached Alaine made her way to the upper stables that housed the destriers of the household knights and a half dozen or so milder-mannered palfreys. Her mare had pulled up lame with a swollen tendon on the day before, and Alaine didn't trust the stable boy to see to the proper changing of the poultice. But in truth she needed an excuse to escape the small "family" hall where they had taken their meal. Judith and Thatch were being cross and loud. They missed Father Sebastian, who had stayed at Ste. Claire, and right now Brix had no priest to take up their education where Father Sebastian had left of. The serving maids were sullen and slow, having run afoul of the head cook, who had a temper to rival Alaine's own. Mathilde had not come down to table at all, being confined to her chamber with a headache, and Gunnor's brittle complaints about the quality of the food had added one straw too many. Alaine had made her excuses and fled to the comparatively fresh air of the stable.

Only one tallow lantern was alight as she slipped through the stable doors. Its faltering glow did little to dispel the gloom. Alaine promptly lit another lantern and carried it before her. Her little mare whickered as she came near, and Alaine smiled and crooned a soft greeting. At the sound of her voice, a sudden thump in the hayloft sent bits of straw raining down, spinning like gold in the flickering lantern light.

"Who's there?" Alaine demanded, thinking with considerable irritation that the stable boy had lured some wench from her duties to entertain him in the hay. She'd never had such problems with laziness among the servants at Ste. Claire.

The only answer was silence. Alaine's temper began to rise. She spotted a ladder propped against a stone upright. If that stable boy was shirking his duties again she would have his head.

"Who's there?" she repeated. "Answer or I'll come see for myself."

A rustling and bumping that sent more straw showering from above was her only answer. She hung her lantern from a ring at the wall and climbed. A feminine squeal greeted her as her eyes rose above the level of the loft, but the only thing she could see was a man's broad back decorated liberally with bits of hay. She raised a brow. Dillon the stable boy had never boasted shoulders that broad.

She stepped onto the loft floor, hands on hips and one foot tapping out an impatient cadence. "Who the devil . . . ?"

With a sigh the man squared his shoulders and turned. Garin! Out playing games in the hay! Poor Mathilde's heart would be broken if she knew. Then poor Mathilde's white face peeked around the shield of Garin's body. Alaine's mouth fell open.

"Oh, Alaine!" Mathilde wailed. "This isn't . . . this isn't . . ." Her words got lost in a flood of tears.

Alaine glared at Garin. Her true friend! Brother of her heart! Lusting after poor innocent Mathilde in a common hayloft!

"You sorry knave!" Alaine hissed. "I wouldn't have believed it! How could you . . . !"

With surprising ferocity Mathilde threw herself in front of Garin. The blow that Alaine had aimed at his face halted in midair.

"Don't you lay a hand on him, Alaine!" Mathilde squeaked furiously.

"Get back to the hall!" Alaine ordered, pointing an imperious finger toward the ladder.

"I won't. We were just . . . !"

"I know what you were doing! Get back to the hall!"

"No!" Mathilde jutted out her chin defiantly.

Alaine hadn't suspected her sweet, soft-spoken stepsister had so much nerve. She shifted her glare to Garin, who at least looked suitably sheepish. "Do you know what Rorik would do to you if he caught you like this? Mathilde is his ward. She's under his protection. How did you dare . . . ?''

"I would sacrifice all I have for Mathilde," Garin sighed. "Life would be meaningless without her."

"Drivel!" Alaine replied. "Get back to the hall. I'll deal with you later. And brush the straw off your clothes."

Garin had the good sense to obey, and in his absence Mathilde's defiance dissolved into a puddle of tears. Alaine's anger softened in the face of the girl's misery.

"Oh, Mathilde," she sighed. "What have you done?"

"We didn't do anything!" Mathilde sobbed. "I love him so much! And I wanted . . . I wanted him to do whatever it is a man does with a woman. But he wouldn't!" she wailed. "He said we have to wait!"

"Well at least Garin has some sense, even if you don't!" Her estimation of Garin climbed back up several notches. "Do you have any idea what you were risking?"

"If I'd gotten a baby, Rorik would have to let us wed!"

Alaine snorted. "Don't be foolish. If you'd gotten a baby, there are any number of things Rorik could have done besides let you marry Garin! And none of them is pleasant!"

Mathilde collapsed onto the straw, hiccoughing loudly and making no attempt to wipe the tears streaming down her face. "You promised!" she accused. "You promised to speak to him for us."

Alaine felt a twinge of guilt. She'd had problems enough on her mind. She kept putting off Mathilde's. But Mathilde was right. She had promised. "I told you we had to wait until the time is right."

"The time better be right now!" Mathilde sniffed loudly. "I'm going to be old and barren before you decide to help!"

"Oh, Mathilde!" Alaine said with a touch of impatience. "You know I want to help. But if I ask Rorik and he says no, then all hope is gone. I just want to wait until he's in the right frame of mind."

"If he says no I'll kill myself!" she declared hotly,

casting Alaine her best martyred look. But a runny nose and swollen eyes spoiled the effect.

Alaine just laughed. "No you won't, goose." Her temper had cooled as quickly as it had risen, and now she could see the humor of the situation, and the pity. "Come on now. We'll have to sneak you into your chamber without anyone seeing that face of yours, and that gown. You look exactly as though you've been trysting in a hayloft. And I've a few more things to say to you, sister mine."

Alaine sighed as she followed Mathilde down the ladder. As if she didn't have trouble enough winning her own husband, now it appeared she had to win one for Mathilde as well.

CHAPTER 23

In two days' time, Garin rode off toward Ste. Claire to assume his new duties, and Mathilde stayed behind at Brix, eyes swollen and mouth drooping with misery. The problem was solved temporarily, Alaine thought without much satisfaction, but very soon she was going to have to take the bull by the horns, or rather, the dragon by the tail, and try to convince Rorik to let Mathilde wed a landless and unproven knight—all for the sake of love. Love was something Rorik didn't believe in, so how could she make him understand that Mathilde could be happy with no man other than Garin? How could she convince him that Mathilde's happiness was of any consequence at all? She told Mathilde to be patient, that all would work out to the best. But the words rang hollow in her own ears.

Mathilde was the only one drooping at Brix, though. The great fortress hummed with energy. The castle servants, at first resentful and suspicious, found that having the watchful eyes of their lady follow them as they went about their duties was not such an awful fate after all, for she was as quick to reward a job well done as she was to scold the slacker. And the standards she demanded of them made a difference in the quality of life for all. The Great Hall had become a pleasant place to live. The air in the halls and chambers smelled of fresh herbs, the walls were no longer black with the soot from the fireplaces, the trestle tables and benches were scrubbed, and linens, bed curtains, and tapestries were cleaned and free of dust and grime.

Brix's vassals, also, found themselves pleased with the changed situation at Brix. Rorik was a hard man, and news that Brix was once more in the hands of the Valois family set the barons in a fine state of pessimistic uncertainty. But they soon found that, while Rorik was quick to demand homage, he was also quick to ride to their defense. Those who defied his overlordship felt his swift wrath, but those who admitted his rights were assured that their lands and families were part of the honor of Brix, and would be defended as such.

Guided by Rorik's strong hand, the world around Brix, its lands, and its people, fell back into order. The world within Brix also began to settle down to harmony. As summer warmed, so did the relationship between Rorik and Alaine. With Theoda gone, no one remained to call to mind the bitter past. Rorik smiled often, frequently in the direction of his wife. Joanna and Sihtric grinned at each other behind the couple's backs, saying that they knew all along such a likely pair would eventually fit together into a happy union.

Alaine was happier than she had ever been. Despite his words to the contrary, Rorik had changed. The deep green of his eyes no longer froze to icy hardness when he looked at her. He warmed her nights with passion, and brightened her days with gentle regard. It rankled that he still believed she'd been unfaithful. The brightness of her days was dimmed somewhat by the knowledge that his affection did not run deep enough to trust. But she allowed herself to bask in the glow of this new warmth. Even though she sensed that Rorik still held much of himself in reserve, the wall was crumbling, slowly, but steadily.

Alaine's slowly ripening shape didn't deter Rorik from taking full advantage of their tentative reconciliation. Alaine kept her own chamber, where she could seek privacy if she felt the need. But most of her belongings were in the lord's big chamber, and most of her nights were spent in the lord's big canopied bed. Even though her pregnancy had not yet reached the point of discomfort, he was unfailingly considerate and gentle in his loving. Knowing now of his past, she was amazed that such gentleness could win through the bitterness of his life, and she loved him all the more for it. More than once she woke at night to the feel of his hard-callused hand splayed out over her stomach. She would open her eyes to see him grinning with irrepressible joy as he thought on the child growing in her womb. Then he would kiss her forehead, and her nose, and her mouth, which more often than not led to other pleasant doings. The closer he let her to his heart the more she loved him—and the more her heart ached with the thought that never would he love her as she loved him. The seeds of hate and distrust had been planted deep and strong. The leaves and stem of the noxious weed might be severed, but the root remained festering in his soul. Only a miracle could burn it out. And Alaine was in short supply of miracles.

But one bright, warm morning she decided the time had come for one minor miracle at least. Rorik had returned the night before from successfully putting down a small rebellion at St. Sauvear, one of the largest and richest fiefs in his domain. Sir Corwin had been a thorn in his side since he had returned to Brix, and now he had justification for replacing the troublemaker with a man loyal to himself and to William. He offered the rich fief to Sihtric, who to Rorik's surprise accepted the honor, contingent on William's approval. Always before Sihtric had shunned lands and keeps as something that would bind his free spirit within stone walls. But now it seemed the Norseman felt that being bound would not be such a dismal fate after all. If Rorik was going to settle in one place, he had mumbled with a half-embarrassed grin, best that Sihtric stay close to keep him out of trouble. His decision delighted Rorik. So when the dragon descended to the hall for the morning meal looking well satisfied with himself and with life in general, Alaine decided there was no better time to cast the die for Mathilde's future.

Rorik seemed pleased when she suggested he take the day off to ride up the beach with her. She had the cook pack a hearty dinner of venison pasties, fruit, cheese, beer, and portions of Rorik's favorite pies. They were on their way well before the church in the village had rung the bells for Tierce.

For an hour or more they rode along the sea trail in companionable silence. A gentle breeze blew off the sea and filled the air with the fresh tang of salt and seaweed. Occasionally the trail hugged the beach. At other times it climbed over the green-carpeted bluffs that rose behind the rugged sea cliffs. Alaine was enthralled by spectacular views of waves dashing themselves to foam against jagged rocks, and equally thrilled by glimpses of quiet stretches of sparkling sand slipping into the blue of the sea.

It was on one such protected stretch of beach that they stopped for their meal. The tide was at low ebb. A good way from the water's edge, surf roiled and foamed over a shallow sandbar, but the water that lapped onto the beach was quiet and warm, almost cut off from the main sweep of the sea. It sparkled and glinted in the bright sunlight— an irresistible invitation on such a warm day.

As Rorik gently lifted Alaine down from her mare she noted a rare twinkle of merriment in his eyes. "Yon beach would offer the chance of a cool swim, my lady, but with that extra load you're carrying you'd sink to the bottom like a stone." He smiled mischievously and eyed her slightly rounded shape.

"You expect me to sit sweating on the beach while you cool yourself in the water?" She arched a saucy brow.

"It would be the proper thing to do," he advised, setting her gently on her feet.

"Think again, my lord!" She began unlacing the fastenings of her gown. "There never was a more improper female than I, as you keep reminding me."

Alaine peeled down to her thigh-length linen shift and Rorik shamelessly peeled down to nothing at all. They raced toward the beckoning water, and though Alaine wasn't as light on her feet as she once had been, she managed to splash into the salty water right behind Rorik.

The water was pleasantly cool as it washed around her bare thighs. Without a moment of hesitation she followed Rorik's lead in diving headfirst into the brine. She had been swimming like a sleek seal since infancy, and pregnancy was not going to hold her back from enjoying herself on this rare outing.

"You look like a beached whale," Rorik commented as she surfaced and turned to float on her back. Her shape was not yet that ponderous, but he never missed a chance to nettle her with such comments. Her reactions were so delightfully predictable.

She sputtered and sent a fountain of water his way, then dove out of reach of his revenge. A hand closed around her ankle, yanking her back. They surfaced together like two cavorting dolphins, laughing and gasping for air. Alaine barely had time to fill her lungs when Rorik's hand landed on top of her head and pushed her back into the cool blue.

She stroked away and dove deeper. It was another world, this sun-warmed ebb tide lagoon, a world where the unaccustomed heaviness of her small extra load didn't weigh her down, where she could move as gracefully as any sea nymph through oscillating strands of kelp. Tiny fish regarded her with round-eyed blank fishy stares then darted away with a flick of their fins. A crab scuttled sideways through the rippled sand. She surfaced, breathed deep, then dove again. Rorik glided up beside her, a sea god with muscles rippling smoothly under sun-dappled skin. He wrapped her with powerful arms and legs, holding her prisoner as his mouth came down on hers. Alaine's loosened hair drifted around their slowly spinning bodies, wrapping them in a web of tangled gold. Slowly, thoroughly, and insistently he plundered her willing mouth as a hand glided over her smooth hip and worked its way under her shift and between her thighs. She felt a gush of hot liquid welcome him, and suddenly her veins ran with liquid fire. A quiver of desire rippled through her body like a tidal wave. Passion swelled, elemental as the sea. Every nerve ached for him to take her—here, in midday, on the warm sands and under the open sky where God and all nature could witness their joining. She wanted him. How she wanted him! All shame was burned away by scorching desire.

They broke the surface gasping for air. Without a word he gently pushed her toward the water's edge, and without a word, when the water splashed around their ankles, he pressed her to the smooth sand. Kneeling between her open thighs, he gently, slowly filled her with himself. His flesh was hot, burning its way within her, plunging to the core of her and driving all thoughts from her mind but the sweet, agonizing pleasure of their union. Warm lips played at the nape of her neck as Rorik moved urgently within her welcoming depths. Alaine surrendered to ecstasy as the primitive rhythm of Rorik's loving merged with the ebb and flow of the sea. The world shattered, then came together in a new pattern. She was no longer just herself. She was a new creature, a flowing together of man and woman, as big as the world, as small as the tiniest grain of sand that shifted and danced beneath her. Rorik filled her and seemed to flow within her. The savage intensity of his passion intertwined with her aching desire, carrying her on a low and joyful spiral into a universe where the two of them were the world, the two of them were all that mattered. The sea tumbled around their joined bodies, flowing with them in their tide of ecstasy. With iron will Rorik held his passion from the final crest, determined to linger, to draw out the pleasure, stretching the time of escape from the world of duty and distrust and hate and confusion. Until finally nature drove him to the aching limit. With an explosive shudder he spent his seed, and she accepted his offering with a cry of joy.

The sea surged around them in foaming chaos. The tide had turned and was rapidly reclaiming the quiet lagoon. They stumbled onto the warm sand and collapsed in each other's arms. When the advancing sea once again tickled their toes Rorik lifted his head from its sandy pillow and looked down at his wife. Her eyes were closed, her mouth curved into a contented smile. A dew of seawater spangled her thick lashes. He plucked at the soggy shift that outlined her breasts.

"Why do you keep this on?" He chuckled with amusement. "Did you think to protect yourself against ravishment by your beast of a husband?"

She opened one reluctant eye. "Perhaps I don't want to shock the fish with my ungainly body."

"We've done our bit to shock the fish today," he snorted. "Here." He pulled her up and lifted the soggy material over her head. "Let us be rid of this."

She flushed and turned away, but the firm grasp of his hand turned her back.

"Don't hide yourself from me, Alaine. How can you show such maidenly shame, after all the times I've taken you as my own?"

"It's not shame, my lord," she laughed. "It's just. . . ." She gestured with an embarrassed wave to her no longer slim figure.

He pushed her down on the sand and regarded her with a steady, unabashed gaze. "You're beautiful," he finally said. "Every bit of you is beautiful." He laid a hand on her slightly swollen belly. "Especially here, where my child is sleeping. I tease you only because you react so well."

She laughed, still half-embarrassed, and twisted away. "I doubt the child is sleeping, my lord. Not after the visit you just paid him."

Rorik grinned wickedly. "I'll pay him another if you don't distract me with some food, wife."

They splashed once again in the water to wash the sand from their skin, then found a nook against the bluff that was shaded from the sun and set out the feast the cook had packed. Alaine laid her shift out on the rocks to dry and wore Rorik's soft linen shirt, which covered her from shoulders to knees. Rorik was content to merely don chausses and cross garters and leave his chest bare to the salt wind and sand.

The venison pasties, cheese, fruit, and apple pie disappeared with appreciative haste. As Alaine gathered up the remains and packed them in their saddlebags, Rorik leaned somnolently back against the hard wall of the bluff and regarded his wife with a knowing gleam in his eye.

"So, wife," he began, "tell me why you lured me out here and seduced me."

Alaine sat herself down beside him and raised a doubtful brow. "I seduced you?"

"Indeed you did."

"You were the one who insisted on prancing around naked in the water."

He grinned. "And you followed right behind with that silly shift clinging to every line of your body. You knew I couldn't resist those flashing legs and white flesh."

She hadn't known, but was glad he hadn't resisted. Certainly she had never planned to soften her husband's temper by such underhanded and womanly means, but it might indeed prove to her advantage.

"So what do you want, wife? Goodwife or whore, when a woman gets soft and cuddly it's always for a price."

"Nay, Rorik," Alaine denied quickly. "It is true I have a request, and I sought to be alone with you to plead my case. But I had no mind to...to use such a ploy to achieve my desire. Rather did I so eagerly yield to you because I...because I am your wife." A puckish smile played around her mouth. "And being a good wife, I am always anxious to do my duty."

Rorik snorted in disbelief. "There's nothing in the

world so dangerous as an accommodating woman." But he softened his words with a smile. "What is this request?"

Alaine took a deep breath. Tact had never been her strong point, and she didn't have the talent of gently easing into a difficult subject. So she dove in and hoped for the best. "My stepsister Mathilde . . ." she began.

"Yes?"

Best to blurt it right out, Alaine decided. The news would not be softened by shilly-shallying around the meat of the matter. "She's in love with Garin. And he returns her affection full measure. They've asked me to speak for them, Rorik, in hopes you will consent for them to wed."

Rorik lifted his brows in surprise. "Garin and Mathilde?"

"They've loved each other for a long time. Even before my father died, I think."

"Did your father intend for them to marry?" His voice was skeptical.

Alaine wished she could say yes, but as she thought of the iron-hard man who had been her father, she knew that he would set even less store by the young couple's feelings than would Rorik. "I don't know what he planned," she compromised.

"I had Mathilde in mind for Sir Guillaume," Rorik said flatly.

"Sir Guillaume?" Alaine laughed unbelievingly. "Guill-aume is old, and a dull fellow with a surly cast of mind. They wouldn't suit, my lord. You would do them both a disservice."

Rorik grunted. "Sir Guillaume is a bold knight and a loyal follower. He likes the maid well enough and would treat her kindly. I've a keep near Falaise that needs a good man as castellan. I had a mind to send him there once he was wed, if William would permit it. I'd even thought of gifting him with a fief to be held under service to me, and in that case he'll be needing to breed an heir."

"Hmmph!" Alaine snorted in disgust. "All you men think about is breeding heirs to carry on your precious bloodline. You think naught of women and their needs!"

"And what needs have a woman other than a man's

good sword arm to protect her and a man's seed to give her children?''

"A man's love, perhaps?'' Alaine ventured with a bold stare.

Rorik frowned into the sand in ominous silence.

"I have asked for little in this marriage of ours . . ." she said.

"Seems I heard that same line when you begged me to take in that little half-wit child,'' he interrupted with a scowl.

"And what harm came of that? Even you enjoy Thatch's bright wit and sweetness. You have said yourself he's a likely lad.''

"Aye,'' he admitted. "But what is there in this request that will give me pleasure?''

"You will make two people very happy, and tie Garin to you with bonds nothing can break. Find another likely maid for Guillaume.''

Rorik looked at her long and hard. She didn't flinch from his gaze.

"And you, wife,'' he asked with raised brow. "What would you give to see this match made?''

Her mind went blank. There was a light to his eyes she couldn't fathom. What could he possibly want from her that he didn't already have? "My lord, everything I have you have already taken.''

"Is it so?'' He looked at her with brows knitted into a scowl. What indeed did he want that she had not already given? Something no woman could give, perhaps. Or if a woman could give the last ounce of loyalty, that gift of truly unconditional love, maybe, fool that he was, he would not even recognize it. And certainly he would not trust it.

She held her gaze steady, and his finally dropped. "It will be as you wish.'' Then he added with a smile. "This time.''

Rorik thought he had never seen the equal of the smile that lit Alaine's face. He didn't want to admit the power that smile had over his heart. He didn't want to admit that her gratitude wasn't enough, he wanted her adoration. He who had been so cautious and wily, crushing with disdain every tender trap that had ever been laid for his heart— now he was caught in the trap all unwilling and floundering like a raw boy. And still there was the sharp edge of distrust that told him he was running full tilt for disaster. This woman was like any other.

"Hold hard, woman!" He laughed as she threw herself at him in impetuous glee. "You've a battering ram attached, there!"

"Oh, I have not!" Alaine could swear she saw a softening in the deep green of his eyes as she hugged him close. She couldn't believe he had actually changed his plans to suit her. It strengthened her resolve. She was winning. The wall was tumbling down, and time was on her side. She would have him yet, this bold knight who dared to take all she had and give so little of himself in return.

The wedding was in midsummer, and all during the long bright days that preceded the ceremony Mathilde twittered and fluttered like a happy bird. The women of the castle busily stitched on a trousseau. The huntsmen labored to bring down boar and stag for a grand feast, and the scullery maids and house servants scrubbed and dusted and polished and cleaned under the sharp and watchful eyes of both Joanna and Alaine. Mathilde floated through the days oblivious to all except her blossoming happiness. Nothing could prick her on her high summit of bliss, not even Gunnor's sulky mood and stinging barbs.

And Gunnor was indeed in the foulest of moods. Like a dark cloud threatening to hide the sun on a bright day, she hovered around the fringes of gaiety with scowling eyes and downturned, pouting mouth. Alaine noted her gloominess with resignation, thinking it was envy of Mathilde's happy estate that drove her oldest stepsister to dark depression. But there was also a hint of smug superiority in her manner that struck a discordant note. Alaine uneasily recalled to mind the romance that had blossomed between Gunnor and Gilbert in the days before that treacherous knave was thrown out of Ste. Claire in fear of life and limb. And now that Gilbert could no longer show his face on any of Rorik's lands, Gunnor was having words with every jongleur, itinerant tradesman and traveler who passed through the gates of Brix. Alaine suspected she was sending lovers' messages to de Prestot, foolishness on Gunnor's part but certainly nothing to cause worry. But something in Gunnor's secretive smugness did cause worry.

Alaine's vague suspicions about Gunnor were swept away in the flurry of activity preceding the ceremony. The wedding of a minor knight and a landless maid did not rate attendance of the great barons of the land, so the guest list was small. But still everything must be done properly to honor Garin and his bride. The barons who did homage to Brix would all be in attendance at the Mass and the feast, and appropriate entertainments must be provided for both the noble guests and the serfs and peasants who would gather outside the church and enjoy their own feast and celebration after the ceremony. Alaine had little time to think on the possible machinations of her eldest stepsister.

With Joanna's skilled help, all was in readiness well before the sun had set on the day before the ceremony. Alaine and Mathilde enjoyed a respite from confusion and bustle. They stood together on the battlements ringing the inner bailey, watching the surf pound out its fury on the rocks below. Sea gulls wheeled and screeched above the foam. The golden orb of the sun hovered above the watery horizon, gilding a path of silver-gold brilliance across the surface of the sea. The golden warmth of the sinking sun seemed to kindle a similar glow in Mathilde's face.

"Happy?" Alaine asked with a smile.

Mathilde answered with a shy nod. "Happy... and a little afraid," she admitted. "When I saw Garin ride in from Ste. Claire last eventide, he looked so manly and handsome. I thought my heart would fair burst in my breast, Alaine. But I couldn't help but wonder how it will be with us . . . if I will be a good wife and pleasing to him. Suddenly it seems to me I am such a child. What do I know about pleasing men?''

Alaine put her arm around the younger girl and gave her a brief hug. "All a man need do to be pleased is look at you, sister mine. Nothing else is required.''

Mathilde gave a nervous little laugh. "It's my understanding that men are fain to do more than look. Yet in my foolishness I offered Garin all I had to give before the vows were spoken, and he refused me. And now I fear he might find me lacking in somewhat that men expect from women.''

Alaine laughed merrily, then immediately tried to soothe away the hurt look on Mathilde's face. "Garin refused you because he holds your honor dear. Don't worry that you won't be pleasing to him, sweet sister. I know he desires you above all things in this world. Certainly he has risked much for the right to hold you in his arms. If Rorik had not been pleased with this stubborn love of yours, he might well have sent Garin on his way to earn his keep in some far corner of the land as a landless and lordless knight.''

The sun was turning hazy red as it neared the surface of the sea. The tide was pulling the waves away from the rocks, and a silvery smooth stretch of wet sand mirrored the glory of the sunset. Crimson bathed the battlements and the girls perched on the wall walkway. Mathilde looked into the dying sun and breathed a pensive little sigh. Her last day of maidenhood was rapidly drawing to a close.

"I remember your wedding well," Mathilde told Alaine. "Rorik looked so grand as he met you before the church. So strong, so knightly. And you pale as snow. Were you terribly frightened? Everyone said you must have been, to be so white and silent.''

Alaine laughed. "I was numb. Rorik and I were not friends, if you remember. He had threatened to hang me only days before he decided to wed me. He took me to wife only to gain better control of Ste. Claire.''

''Nay,''—Mathilde demurred. ''It was more than that, I vow.''

Alaine was silent, and Mathilde slipped a sisterly arm around her slim waist. ''I don't know why I'm being such a goose. But such unruly thoughts crowd my mind on this night. Did it . . . did it hurt terribly when . . . when Rorik took you to bed?''

Alaine shook her head and smiled. ''Nay, Mathilde. Even though he loved me not, Rorik was gentle and kind. The way of a man with a woman is a thing to take joy in, not a thing to fear.''

''Gunnor said that when men lust they care not who they hurt.''

''Do not listen to that one!'' Alaine snorted. ''She sees the whole world in her own unhappy light. Garin loves you so well, he would sooner cut off his sword arm than do you hurt.''

Mathilde breathed a little sigh of confusion and leaned on the rough stone wall. The sun was a mere sliver glowing red above the darkening sea. A warm breeze whipped strands of chestnut hair around her pensive face.

''You need have no fear of sweet Garin,'' Alaine said. ''Even Rorik, who is a harsh man with anger boiling always right below the surface—even in the height of anger he has never raised a hand to me, or done me hurt in any way. Not always has Rorik been gentle with me, but never has he caused me pain other than in my heart. How much better will you fare than I, with a man who truly loves you.''

''I cannot believe that Rorik does not love you, Alaine.'' Mathilde's mind had readily turned from her own fears to her stepsister's plight.

Alaine smiled and shook her head. ''He received a mighty hurt from a woman's hand. The pain and bitterness run deep. Deeper than I can heal.''

''But you love him well.''

Alaine smiled sadly. ''Is it so plain to see?''

"Perhaps only to one who loves you like I do. And Rorik loves you too. This I can feel. Oh, Alaine, how selfish I'm being! How can I stand here speaking of happiness and love when you are unhappy?"

"I'm not unhappy, Mathilde. We have peace and understanding between us, Rorik and I. And perhaps the day will come when I can prove to him that women hold honor and loyalty as dear as any man. So don't let foolish thoughts of me mar your happiness. Believe me when I say I would have none other than Rorik as my husband."

Mathilde drew Alaine close in an affectionate hug. "You are braver than I would be, Alaine, but then, you always were. Perhaps I am hopelessly trapped in childish dreams, but thanks to you my dreams for myself have come true. I have faith that my dreams for you will come true as well."

Mathilde's doubts melted away with the morning sun, and with the warmth of the smile that Garin bestowed upon her at the church door. Never was a bride more radiant, or a groom prouder and more pleased with his fate. As the priest declared in a loud voice the dower gift and dowry, Alaine squeezed Rorik's arm.

"You dower Mathilde most generously, my lord," she said. "I am grateful, and Joanna also."

"I would not dishonor Sir Geoffrey's stepdaughter by setting a mean dowry. He was a loyal vassal to my family for many years. The lands I gift them with were granted me by William two years past. It is a minor fief without a proper castle, but it should provide them with some income, at least. I count myself fortunate to have found such a loyal man as Garin to see to it."

"Garin will not disappoint you," she assured him. "Neither there or at Ste. Claire."

The couple knelt for the vows. Alaine noted the special smile that crossed Mathilde's face as Garin took her hand. Her mind dredged up the memory of her own wedding many months past. She had not smiled as she knelt beside

Rorik. It had been all she could do to not turn and run. And yet for all of that disastrous beginning, she was well content. Especially since every day their cautious peace grew further and further toward genuine warmth. She wondered if Rorik was also thinking of their wedding day, and the stiff-faced and ashen-hued bride whose trembling hand he had held that day.

"Rorik?" She whispered so as not to disturb the onlookers around them.

He looked down at her inquiringly.

"Our own wedding sticks in my mind this day, and how the whole parish knew from my actions what a reluctant bride I was. I am shamed now to think I dishonored you, and would have you know I am. . . ." Dared she say she loved him? No, he would only despise her for such a womanly fancy, he who didn't believe in love. "I am well content with you as husband, Rorik."

He smiled down at her and squeezed her hand. "And I am content with you as wife, Alaine," he answered in kind. "I made a better bargain than I thought." Lukewarm words considering the intensity of emotion that bubbled in the cauldron of his soul. How sweet it was to stand beside this wife of his and watch the morning sun fire streaks of gold through her hair, and drink in the blue of her eyes that shamed the brilliance of the summer sea. How beautiful and kind her smile as she watched her stepsister kneel at the church door, she who had braved his wrath to see these two united. What man would have been as loyal to a brother or sister not truly of his blood? Rorik's throat ached to speak the words he felt, but the iron links of distrust and suspicion still chained him. He would never be free of the scar of his mother's treachery, he thought. And best that was so, for he didn't trust these soft new feelings that Alaine inspired. She thought herself in love with him. Such had she revealed when she thought he couldn't hear her words. But she had betrayed him once. Who knew that she might not again?

The day passed in a whirl of celebration. Two jongleurs and a troop of acrobats sang and danced and cavorted in return for good food and a warm place to lay their heads at day's end. Wine, beer, and food were plentiful, and even the lowliest of the serfs had more than he could eat set before him on this day. The morning would bring much moaning and groaning and holding of stomachs, Alaine suspected. The servants, farmers, swineherds, gooseboys, and milkmaids who made merry today wouldn't be fit for a day's work on the morrow. But she didn't begrudge them their celebration. She suspected it had been long since these people had known such generosity from the lord who ruled at Brix.

The day stretched into night and the candles and tallow lanterns were lit. The merrymaking threatened to last long into the night, but not many hours passed before Joanna, as mother of the bride, signaled time to put the new wedded couple to bed. The noble ladies who attended Mathilde made great show of escorting her upstairs, and for a moment the bride turned pale and breathless and grasped out for Alaine's hand. Alaine wrapped her arm about the girl's waist as they ascended to the chamber where the couple would spend their night. She gave a reassuring squeeze, and Mathilde rewarded her with a tentative smile.

Mathilde was duly disrobed, washed, set in her flower-strewn bed, and left to a bride's fate. As Alaine watched the raucous and joking men carry a nervous-looking Garin up the stairs toward the chamber, she couldn't help but remember how terrified, angry, and distraught she had been on this night in her life—terrified mostly because of Gunnor's vicious stories. And to think the witch had tried to poison the mind of her own true sister as well. But Mathilde would know naught but joy on this night, and Alaine was shamed by a small stab of envy. How happy was the bride who could greet her groom knowing she was cherished and valued above all other women.

Garin opened the door to the chamber and firmly blocked the way. The men gave disappointed groans, but finally allowed the groom to shut himself in with his bride. Bellowing loud jokes certainly not meant for a bride's tender ears, they descended once again to the hall. In a contemplative mood, Alaine did not rejoin her noble guests as they returned to celebrating. Instead, she headed toward her own chamber at the far end of the balustraded walkway that ringed the Great Hall. Before reaching her doorway, her footsteps slowed to a hesitant halt. Great sobs were coming from the dark chamber where Mathilde, Judith, and Gunnor made their beds—now only Judith and Gunnor. They were muffled, as if the weeper meant to stifle the sound of her sorrow. Alaine didn't have to peer through the half-open door to recognize who was shedding tears while the rest of Brix was rejoicing. She felt a brief stab of pity for her eldest stepsister. How sad that she could find only cause to weep on a day all others found gladness. She made a mental note to speak to Rorik. Gunnor should be found a husband who could fill the void in her life and keep her out of trouble. Otherwise, she thought with an impatient grimace, who knew what the witch would do?

CHAPTER 24

The Inn of Two Brothers sat on the eastern boundary of Brix's land, on the outskirts of the village of Gauchemain. It was run by one brother only, the other having met his fate in a fight over the buxom black-haired wench who still presided over the taproom, serving up ale, food, and nearly anything else a customer desired. Marie had lured the remaining brother into marriage shortly after the fatal quarrel. She enjoyed being the wife of a prosperous inn proprietor, and she enjoyed being queen of the taproom, reveling in the admiration of every lusty buck who stepped through the door. Her husband enjoyed the extra money she brought in from those who were willing to pay the price of her favors for a night, or an hour. He asked no questions of those who sought refuge or entertainment in the greasy taproom or musty loft chambers of the inn. As long as any who entered brought with them the jingle of coin, then he was well satisfied.

So no eyebrows were raised on the evening when a richly gowned, heavily cloaked and cowled woman stepped through the door. The rain-dark night swept in around her as she paused in the open door and looked around with uneasiness. At a growl from one of the customers she shut the door. Her cloak and cowl dripped with foul weather, but she didn't shed them. She moved hesitantly to the bar and made soft inquiry, at the same time setting a coin on its less than clean surface. The proprietor bit the coin, then gestured to the loft stairs.

Gunnor brushed aside the curtain that shielded the first chamber at the top of the stairs. She stepped inside the dingy room and with a little cry of joy rushed to the figure who stood in frowning disapproval by the single window. She coiled her arms around Gilbert like a clinging vine seeking anchor.

"My love, don't frown at me so!" she pleaded. "You know not what risk I take in coming to you, riding alone through the woods with outlaws ever about, and on such a foul night as this!"

Gilbert carefully rearranged his face. "Frown, my love?" He chuckled, but his voice held no amusement. "You mistake my impatience for you. Passion rides me hard as I sit here waiting, knowing I will soon hold your sweet body in my arms."

"I too," she breathed, shrugging out of the sodden cloak and helping him to unlace the damp gown and chemise. As he peeled her damp clothing away from her body, she stood stiff as a marble statue. Obligingly she stepped out of the pile of garments that slipped down around her legs, but her eyes darted away from Gilbert's as his gaze wandered through the landscape of her woman's body, pausing to appreciatively review the full curve of her breasts, the rosy splash of her nipples against the creamy ivory skin, the lush tangle that hid the joining of her legs. As if by rote she reached out, took his hand, and pressed it to the fullness of one soft breast. "I am yours, my sweet lord. Do what you will with this body of mine. Willingly I come into your arms."

Without preliminaries Gilbert pushed Gunnor down on the dirty straw pallet that served as the room's only bed. He knew better than to expect passion from this one. She ever regarded herself as a sacrifice to lust, and lay down like a martyred lamb awaiting the cruel impalement. He obliged her quickly, pushing his chausses down around his knees and shoving himself with callous abruptness between her obediently opened legs. She lay beneath him cold as ice as he thrust with his hips and kneaded fervently with his hands. In only seconds he grunted with satisfaction and stiffened, spilling his desire deep within her coldly cringing body.

As he untangled himself from Gunnor's stiff embrace, he didn't miss her sigh of relief. It was all part of a game, he knew. The twit thought to trap him with this cold use of her woman's parts, no matter that she cringed from him. She thought to be his wife and feed off his power and security, and he let her think so. If she was daft enough to believe he would honor her then she deserved whatever fate she reaped. He had a more winsome female in mind, once his purpose with Gunnor was done.

"Who knows you are here?" he asked, hiking his chausses up around his hips.

"None, my lord! I swear! They take no note of me, those fools, where I go or what I do. They think me sleeping in my chamber with Judith, and she will not wake to spread the tale of me being gone, for I saw to it that she took a hearty sleeping draught."

"Good," he approved. "You are a woman with brains. A fit mate for such as I." His eyes slid over her naked body in appraising regard. He reached out and fondled a heavy breast. She was a well-made woman, God knew!

Too bad she was carved from ice. What man wanted to nightly spend his seed on such a lifeless lump of cold flesh?

Gunnor raised her hand to Gilbert's and pressed him more firmly against the lush globe. "Oh, Gilbert! Let me go with you tonight! I long to be with you night and day. Rescue me from those who despise me and treat me cruelly."

Gilbert curbed an impatient sigh. "Not yet, my dove. But soon, I promise. Then will all the world know I love you. But first we must chastise Rorik for his arrogance, else he will never let us wed."

"The time is so long," she complained. "Take me from him, my love. He'll be angered, but he dares not move against you. Did he do aught when you attacked him at the tourney? Nay. He fears you, my lord. And what man wouldn't? Your skill is unsurpassed. Your strength . . ."

"Would you come to me without having your due from him?" Gilbert sneered. "Without your dowry? Where is your pride?"

"What need have you of a dowry, when you will have me to wife?" Gunnor asked sharply. "You have lands and coin aplenty. And now you have my love."

Gilbert pulled away from her clinging. "Be patient, woman! Rorik took what was rightfully mine. I mean to take from him more than one insignificant ward and her paltry dowry. My revenge is not so simple."

"Insignificant, am I?" Gunnor puffed up with indignation.

"Nay, nay!" Gilbert denied with a scowl. "To me you are the world. But to Rorik you are nothing. He cares little, I've heard, even for his own wife. How much less do you mean to him, merely the stepdaughter of a dead vassal."

"Aye," Gunnor agreed bitterly. "I am nothing to him."

Gilbert smiled and reached out to tilt Gunnor's face up toward his own. "Rorik will pay for his arrogance, my love. Never fear. I will have just revenge from the Stone Dragon. Mark my words. And you will help me."

Gunnor regarded her lover in wary suspicion. For all of

Gilbert's smooth charm and polished looks, at times he reminded her disconcertingly of a snake. She wondered momentarily if she were making the right choice. But then, nothing she could do was likely to deter the silver-haired knight from his course, and almost anything would be better than the treatment she was accorded under Rorik's rule.

She backed away from the touch of Gilbert's hand. "I will help, if that is your wish. Rorik has been no friend to me, and I would not regret whatever flesh you pulled from his hide."

"Then tell me what you have found," Gilbert demanded.

"Naught have I found," she admitted. Then added hastily in the face of Gilbert's scowl, "not from lack of trying, my lord. I have walked the walls both inner and outer, and no hidden entrance or secret gate is to be seen. And even if I got you within the walls, the keep can be closed on a moment's warning. Two sturdy, iron-barred doors guard the keep's hall, one at the base of the stairway and one at the top leading to the entrance lobby. The stairway is carved from the thickness of the wall, and is only wide enough for one man. For certain any enemies who risk that ascent will be showered with arrows or burned with oil poured from the murder hole above. Rorik is not the slacker that Fulk and his get were, to let the defenses slide from neglect and overconfidence."

"And the garrison?" Gilbert prompted.

"A full complement of fighting men," she replied. "Of course I am a lady and know little of these things. But Alaine boasts of such unwomanly knowledge and daily vaunts the fine army Rorik has assembled. Some of the Ste. Claire men have decided to stay on, and many of Phillip's men-at-arms have willingly sworn oath to Rorik."

"He is making it difficult," Gilbert commented in tight-lipped exasperation.

"What did you expect?" Gunnor scoffed. "The dragon is no gentleman. He knows naught but war. Brute that he is, he'll be as hard to oust from his den as a snake from his hole."

"Aye," Gilbert agreed, a thoughtful look on his face. "But there are ways, and there are ways."

"My lord, what is passing through your mind?"

Gilbert smiled cagily. "Patience, my love. I have resources you don't know about. With time all will be revealed."

Gunnor frowned petulantly. "The time had best be soon. Four days past my sister was wed, and now my mother plans to return to Ste. Claire with Mathilde and her husband. I am to go with them."

"Nay. You must stay at Brix."

"There is no place for me at Brix. Not while Rorik and my whey-faced stepsister are there."

"Think of some excuse," Gilbert instructed. "Women are experts at thinking up excuses."

Gunnor pursed her lips and knitted her brows. "It will be difficult, Gilbert. My stepsister and I thoroughly vex one another, and she's looking forward to seeing my back, I vow."

"You'll think of something, love. You're important to me at Brix. So stay there. You're of no use to me if you ride off to Ste. Claire."

"No use?" she queried sharply, her underlip protruding in a pout.

Gilbert raised a brow. He refused to placate her with comforting words. He was getting tired of this game, and only the high stakes held him to it.

"You're cruel, Sir Knight," Gunnor sulked. "If I were a less trusting lady, I would see cause to doubt you. Come, prove to me once more that you are mine and no other's."

For a frigid bitch the woman was insatiable, Gilbert thought. Did she think that his labors between her legs bound him to her with unbreakable ties? Aye, like that she did, stupid wench that she was. Still, he was not so old a man that he couldn't plow a good row twice in one night.

Her grasping arms pulled him down to the pallet. He lay on his back and suffered her ministrations as, like a distracted milkmaid churning butter, she grasped his limp member and worked to bring him up to his task. When he pushed her down and covered her soft body with his own, he closed his eyes and imagined another, slimmer form in her place. What pleasure he would have when haughty Alaine de Ste. Claire lay thusly under him with legs spread wide and body stiff with loathing. Not for long would she loathe him, he vowed. He would tantalize her woman's body until she ached for him with a passion that matched his. She would wrap him with arms and legs and heave and moan and cry and beg him to pierce her deeper and yet deeper. As he plunged violently into Gunnor's stoic flesh, Gilbert felt himself swell with power and unbearable passion, then explode with hot fury in the far reaches of his dream. The woman under him lay with eyes tightly shut in ladylike disdain, cold and unmoving and limp as a dead fish, but Gilbert saw only golden hair and laughing blue eyes, rosy skin chafed from his loving and lips swollen with desire. Thus would Alaine look after receiving his offering of passion, after he stole her and lands and honor from the dragon at Brix. What pleasure indeed!

Rorik opened his eyes to the splash of morning sun full on his face. Another lazy morning to end a lazy week. Seldom in his life had he slept to an hour that the sun could arouse him. Usually it was he that woke the cocks, long before even a hint of morning's glow had lightened the sky. But these few days since the wedding had been full of sloth. Today the last of the guests would depart, and life would return to the normal routine.

He turned his head and looked at his wife, still sound asleep with her face hidden in a pillow. Hair like molten gold tumbled over the sheets in glorious disarray. Rorik refused to let her braid it at night. He loved the feel of it sifting through his fingers, tickling his face, and coiling about his arms like silky tentacles when he made love to her. He lifted a strand from the sheets and pressed it to his face, inhaling the fresh scent of woman that clung there. How easily this little witch had slipped under his skin. He spent his days with thoughts of her constantly riding his mind, and his nights indulging himself in the comforts offered by her soft flesh. Even swollen with his child she still pricked him to a heady lust. He couldn't keep his hands from her, or his lips. By now most men would have left their wives in peace and sought to ease their needs on one whose shape did not so resemble a pear. But he could find satisfaction with no other. Long ago he had quit trying. And despite the nearness of her time, Alaine always welcomed him with a passion that was heart-stopping in its sweet fervor.

Even when lust was far from his mind this woman pulled him into her silken net. Never before had Rorik sought a female for aught but physical reasons, but Alaine had become companion, comforter, friend. She was not like most women of his experience. She knew of things other than stitchery and the concerns of storehouses and hall. She wasn't coy, didn't flutter her lashes or make pretty faces to angle for compliments. She could listen as well as talk, and her words were measured as closely as a man's. She had the comfortable straightforward manner of a boon companion, combined with the lush passion of a sensuous woman. What man would not be enchanted with such a wife? And he was enchanted. He was just as thoroughly enmeshed as his father had been with the treacherous Theoda.

The thought of Theoda brought a scowl that seemed to chase the sunshine from the room. His treacherous mother—how dearly she had paid for her crime! His first sight of the woman she had become haunted him still. All the years of his exile he'd imagined her just as she had been—beautiful, stately, with a laugh that could make the gloomy hall bright, though in truth she had not often laughed in those last years with his father. Suddenly Rorik knew beyond a doubt that Fulk had slain Theoda just as surely as he had slain Sir Stephen and his sons, only he had done it slowly, and with a less clean blow. Of all the victims of that tragedy, Theoda had reaped the cruelest fate.

Rorik untangled himself from the skein of Alaine's hair

and swung his legs over the bed. He hesitated, half wanting to wake his wife and bring the sunshine back to his mind by losing himself in the sweetness of her flesh. But she was tired, he decided, and needed her rest. His babe was growing heavy within her and weighing her down. Lying amid the spill of her golden hair, she looked small and fragile, too small to bear the burden of setting a castle back on its feet, too fragile to carry and nourish and give birth to the babe she sheltered under her heart— and too vulnerable to stand under the constant suspicion and distrust of her husband. Rorik shook his head in resignation as an unwanted spell of protectiveness and pride surged through his heart. What deceptive weapons were the face and form of a beautiful woman!

Hastily he rose, splashed his face and chest with cold water, and pulled on clean chausses and tunic. This one more day he must stay within walls and play host. But after this day the last of the wedding guests would be gone, and then he would be free to ride over the lands that had been his family's for three generations, granted to his great grandfather by Richard I, son of the first William. The numerous lands that were held from Brix were now firmly under his control, and it was time he rode out to the villages and farms on his own land and let them see his face. Too much he had let Alaine tend to his people while he rode about setting his vassals in order.

The small family hall was all but empty. Rorik was surprised that the one person who sat at table breaking the fast was his wife's stepsister Gunnor. He nodded to her briefly as he broke a hearty chunk of bread from the loaf by the hearth and cut himself cheese from the round on the table.

"Been riding early this morn, have you?" Rorik asked.

"Aye, my lord," she answered shortly.

In truth, Gunnor looked as pale and worn as if she'd ridden through the night. He wondered what plagued the woman that she rose from bed at such an early hour. It was her wont to linger in her chamber until the sun was high in the sky. Alaine had been at him several nights ago to find her stepsister a husband and see her settled, but he'd paid little heed. At the time his mind had been filled with Alaine and the desire she sent galloping through his body, not her sour stepsister and her constant whining. If the widow was hot to marry, she could speak for herself. She was no shy and cringing maid like Mathilde who needed her stepsister to intercede for her.

"You shouldn't ride from these walls without an escort, Gunnor," Rorik said gruffly, sitting himself down in the lord's seat and talking to her from across the dais. "The roads are not yet so peaceful that a lady can be safe without a defender nearby."

"I will remember that, my lord," Gunnor promised meekly. It was passing strange, she thought, that this man to whom she meant less than nothing thought of her safety, however fleeting the thought, while Gilbert, who claimed to love her, blinked not an eye at requiring her to ride long miles through the night-dark woods to do his bidding. But Gilbert did love her. Had he not proven it with the heat of his lust?

"Is my stepsister ill, my lord, that she does not come down to table?"

"She sleeps long and hard," he said. "The babe grows heavy within her, and the work here at Brix is always at hand to plague her. She does not rest enough."

"Perhaps it would be wise to ask my mother to stay at Brix until Alaine has safely delivered."

"Nay." Rorik dismissed her hopeful suggestion with a wave of his hand. "Your mother must needs help Mathilde, who I daresay has less of the housewife's skill than Alaine. There are ladies in plenty hereabouts to attend her when her time comes, and the old midwife from Ste. Claire— Ruth is her name—is coming to stay in a sennight's time. Mayhap I will send for Joanna when the babe is delivered, if it be my lady's wish."

"I would be glad to stay and help, my lord."

Rorik didn't bother to hide his frown.

"Aye, I know what is filling your mind," Gunnor said

with a bleak smile. "My stepsister would no doubt be more comforted by my absence."

"Truth," Rorik acknowledged, rising and tearing another section of bread from the loaf. "You two are not friends, I think."

Friends with that skinny little arrogant twit of a misfit? Hardly! Gunnor hid her grimace of distaste, smiled ruefully, and swallowed her pride. For Gilbert, she thought, and everything he could give her—only for that would she carry out this humiliating charade.

"I've not treated Alaine as a sister should," she admitted in a voice she hoped was appropriately repentant. "My temper runs away with me at times, and she always takes to heart words that she should let pass by. But still, the fault is mine and I'm loath to let my carelessness cost me a sister's regard. Now that she needs my help, I would fain make up to her the harsh words I've given her in the past."

Rorik looked at Gunnor over the rim of a mug of hot cider he was busily draining. What womanish fancy was this? Gunnor never had a kind word for any nor cared who she injured with her bitter barbs. Why all this silly whining about being Alaine's friend and true sister?

"If my mother must leave, sir, then I do beg your permission to stay. It would ease my conscience if I could make up in some small way the grief I have caused Alaine in the past."

Rorik grunted. He wanted no part of these woman's dealings. "Take up the matter with my lady. It's of no consequence to me."

As if summoned by mention of her name, Alaine descended the stairs. She was big but not yet so awkward that she'd lost her natural grace. Rorik marveled at how she could appear so light on her feet when her belly preceded her by a good six inches. He rose to meet her at the base of the stairs, took her hand, and escorted her to the lady's chair on the dais. She raised a brow to see Gunnor sitting at table with her husband, looking wan as a ghost and not nearly as happy.

"You look like you slept not at all, Gunnor," she commented in a bland voice.

"You look well enough this morn, Alaine," Gunnor greeted her cordially. "It appears that childbearing agrees with you." It agrees with cows and sows, also, Gunnor continued to herself.

Rorik grinned. "Your stepsister has a matter to take up with you."

Gunnor flashed him an irritated grimace. The man had no tact. She would have chosen a better time, after she had an opportunity to butter up the bulbous little bitch. Lord! She hoped she never got pregnant with Gilbert's child. Imagine month after month of looking like that. It was positively obscene!

"What is it, Gunnor?" Alaine's curiosity was piqued. Gunnor had few words for her that weren't barbed with sharp spikes, and now she craved a boon?

"I . . . I . . ." Gunnor stumbled over her words, damning Gilbert and his demands. How was she to eat humble pie in front of this oh-so-superior stepsister of hers? She couldn't abide the whey-faced little turd. When Gilbert was safely in marital bonds and she was mistress of Brix and Ste. Claire and Prestot besides, she would make the woman pay. Indeed she would!

"It has occurred to me, sister, that misunderstandings have set us sorely awry. I was telling your husband that my conscience plagues me for my part in this."

Alaine listened with one brow arched cynically toward the rafters. Gunnor was choking on her own attempt at sweetness as the words tumbled from her mouth. What did the bitch want?

When Alaine learned what her stepsister wanted, her brow inched even higher.

"I think you should go with Joanna," she answered without any concessions to pretense.

Gunnor did not have to be an actress to look genuinely dismayed. But Alaine was not impressed.

"In the years we've been together, Gunnor, you've had

naught for me but spiteful words. So why do you now crave to stay in my company?"

Gunnor struggled to maintain a bland face. She should have known the little witch would be hard to convince. Alaine always had possessed a disconcerting talent for looking past people's words to what they were truly thinking—an unseemly trait for a lady.

"I truly long to be friends, Alaine," she said with difficulty. "If you can find it in your heart . . . we can start over. Everyone deserves a second chance."

Alaine regarded her stepsister curiously. Gunnor had been given second chances by the dozen. She shouldn't let the bitch stay. She was looking forward to her absence. But no doubt the creature was up to something. Why else this patently false penitence? It might be best to keep her close at hand where she could be watched.

"I could use the help, I suppose," Alaine conceded, dangling a bit of hope before Gunnor's anxious eyes. "The harvest will begin soon, and the storehouses will have to be seen to, and there will be provosts' and bailiffs' reports to audit."

"Aye." Rorik laughed. "The fields will not yield the only harvest this season." He shot a playful glance at Alaine's swelling belly.

"That harvest I can handle by myself, sir," she quipped with a smile.

"See if you think the same when you are brought to bed with the pains of childbirth," Gunnor cautioned.

"And what would you know about birthing a babe," Alaine returned testily.

"When I was wife to old Osbern I attended several ladies at their lying-in."

"I will trust me to good Ruth when my time comes. She knows more about birthing a babe than God himself, I vow."

Rorik shook his head, heartily tired of this women's chatter. He drained the last dregs of his cider and slammed the mug down on the table. He was about to leave to find more entertaining company when the inner gate warden entered the hall and saluted briskly.

"My lord, a messenger from good Duke William begs leave to speak with you."

Rorik gestured for the man to be brought in. A lean youth walked to the dais and saluted respectfully. He was slump-shouldered from weariness and carried the dirt of the road with him, but the roll of parchment he handed to Rorik was clean and the seal was unbroken.

"His Grace, William, Duke of Normandy sends greeting, my lord," the messenger repeated. "He congratulates you on your progress in bringing this rebellious land to heel. He also wishes to inform you that Phillip, son of Fulk, usurper of the duke's rights as exercised by yourself, has been sighted in England. William assures you that should the villain return to Normandy he will be duly punished and brought to the duke's justice, however long it may take."

Rorik broke the seal and opened the parchment. The messenger had repeated almost verbatim the first part of the duke's message, but it was the part of least importance. The youth stood in respectful silence while he perused the document. Only when Rorik lifted his eyes did he continue speaking.

"How soon, my lord, can you ride?"

Rorik frowned thoughtfully. "A week," he said. "Certainly not less. I must call up a levy of men from my vassals, and they are widespread."

Alaine looked at Rorik in alarm. "What is it, husband?"

"William summons me to Castle Brionne."

Alaine swore she saw the light of joy in his eyes as he said it. Trust a man to take pleasure in riding off to war. Hard to believe that once she had longed to be a man so she could do the same.

"The traitor Guy of Burgundy has shut himself inside the walls of Brionne. William has laid siege to the castle, but it goes not so well. He wants a fresh viewpoint, and fresh men, I suspect."

Alaine frowned in confusion. "Guy of Burgundy . . . ?"

"Aye," Rorik said with a glint in his eye. "He who tried to murder William at Valognes, then was defeated by William's and Henry's forces at Val-es-Dunes. Most of the traitors fled to their death in the River Orne. Others surrendered and swore oath to William. But Guy, their leader, escaped the net. We didn't know it at the time, but he fled to his castle at Brionne. Now he cowers like a skunk in its hole."

"The battle where Fulk was killed," Alaine commented thoughtfully.

Rorik smiled. "Would that it had been me that met him on the field of battle."

The messenger hesitantly interrupted. "May I take the duke your answer, sir?"

"Tell William I ride as soon as my army is gathered. But take the message after you have supped and taken some rest, lad. A siege is a battle of weeks, not of days or hours. William would not have you kill yourself to rush to him with such paltry news."

The messenger allowed himself a smile of relief, and Alaine noted how much like a mere boy he looked when his face relaxed from its martial sternness. War could chew up such a young lad and spit him out in lifeless pieces. It could do the same to Rorik, a man full grown and in the prime of his strength. Why had she ever thought war and weapons such a glorious game?

Later she managed to catch Rorik alone in their chamber, sitting on the bench beside the cold hearth and inspecting in minute detail the chain links of his hauberk. She sat on the bed and faced him. Suddenly she was acutely aware of the familiar curve of his mouth, the errant way one eyebrow arched more than the other, the slight crook where his helm had smashed against the bridge of his nose in battle. His face had become a beloved part of her world. Would she ever see it again after he rode out the gate some days hence?

"My lord, how long will you be gone?" she questioned quietly.

He looked up from his task, his eyes meeting hers. "A

few months, perhaps. A year, possibly. Long enough, my sweet little rebel, to miss the coming of our first child.''

Her mouth twitched. No proper woman would send her man off to war with aught but a brave face. But why now, when for the first time things between them were halfway right? She struggled unsuccessfully to hide the pain in her eyes.

"Think you that Fulk is still alive in Brionne?" she asked hesitantly, knowing how the subject of Fulk or Theoda had made his temper flare in times past.

But Rorik simply smiled and shook his head. "I go because William calls me, and for no other reason. If Fulk escaped and is in Brionne he will die like the other traitors. All that is in the past, Alaine."

She wished it really were in the past—that the last barrier could fall between them. If she had the time, she might make it happen. But her time was being taken from her. For the days and nights that remained, Rorik would be readying himself and his men for war. He would have no time for her, a mere woman. And then he would be gone. God only knew when or if he would return.

"I will miss you," she said helplessly. "I love you, you know."

"I know," he said with a grin. "You said as much when you tended my wound after the duel."

She flushed red, feeling like a naughty little maid caught in a prank. She really hadn't meant him to know, for pride's sake. But now he was leaving and their future was unsettled, and somehow the words had slipped past her lips. At least he might be polite and say he loved her too! But he wouldn't because it would be a lie. Rorik didn't lie. And Rorik could never bring himself to really love a mere woman.

"I will guard Brix well until you return." She offered assurance in the thing she knew meant the most to him.

"I know you will." A glimmer in the deep-set eyes of summer green spoke of words left unsaid, words that still he could not bring himself to utter. "Of all the women in the world, Alaine, you are the fairest and best in my eyes. God help me but I don't want to leave you.''

On an impulse he rose from the bench and pulled her to him, and she soaked in the feel of his hard, warm body against hers, the sound of his heart beating strongly in his broad chest, the joy of his hands caressing her hair. There was this at least. He no longer despised her. He didn't want to leave her, took pleasure from having her near. His mouth came down onto hers with a sudden violence that sucked the breath from her pliant body, sending her off in a soaring spiral of desire. When he released her she couldn't still the trembling that shook her frame, so strong was his effect on her, breeding wanting, passion, fear.

''When I return, perhaps then, little witch, I can give you what you want.'' His voice was heavy with unaccustomed tenderness. ''Even the most stubborn men change with time.''

He wanted it too, she realized with surprise. He wanted to give the part he held in guarded reserve. He was as much a victim as she was. More.

''Whatever you give or can't give, Rorik, I still love you. Remember that. You are the very heart of me.''

He was silent. No more words came to either of them. Just a riot of feelings.

It was eight days later when Rorik led his vassals and their men through the outer gate to start on the long road to Brionne. Alaine stood on the wall walkway and watched him go, continuing to strain her eyes as the bright yellow scarf she had given as token faded into the morning haze. She had been brave in giving him the stirrup cup and repeated with fervor her vow to guard this home of his until he could return. And she thought she had seen a certain pain of regret cut through his eyes before he turned to trot off to the head of his troops. What it must cost him to recover his birthright then ride off and leave it in the hands of a woman he believed had already betrayed him once.

The bailey was crowded with castlefolk and villagers gathered to see their lord off to war. At the edge of the crowd, Gunnor also watched Rorik depart. Long after the crowd had dispersed she stood in her little shadowed corner of the wall, her face dark with thought.

CHAPTER 25

The bright heat of August slowly faded before the cooling breezes of September. The year was sliding slowly down into autumn, and activity was at a feverish pitch on farms, in villages, and in the great castle of Brix itself. The crops were thriving, and fields lush with ripe grains shimmered in the late summer sun. Harvest had begun, and every man, woman, and child of the farms and villages saw both sunrise and sunset from their backbreaking labors in the fields. Brix's provosts were kept busy collecting the lord's share of the harvest and making sure the serfs and free peasants paid their owed labor to bring in the crops on the lord's desmesne. Alaine also had tasks aplenty to keep her occupied. The provosts' reports needed constant scrutiny, and the new bailiff appointed by Rorik, though a willing and hard worker, was still somewhat unsure in his duties. As mistress of Brix it also fell to her lot to supervise the spinning, weaving, preserving, and candle-making that would prepare the castle for the winter to come. Without Joanna to organize the household tasks, the work seemed to triple overnight, and though Gunnor surprisingly made an attempt to be of some help, the womenfolk of the castle resented her constant scolding and harping, and more often than not flew to Alaine to bend her ear with complaints about her tyrannical and ill-tempered stepsister. More than once Alaine regretted her decision to let Gunnor stay behind when Joanna left with Mathilde and Garin. Though she had to give Gunnor credit for at least trying to assist in the multitude of tasks that were threatening to overwhelm her, there was a current of tension in the air whenever her stepsister was in a room, a sense of expectant waiting that made Alaine uneasy.

It was partly this uneasiness that prompted Alaine to each day take time out from her woman's work and tour the key points of Brix's defenses. Rorik had left Sir Guillaume behind to act as seneschal, but that good knight had been laid low with a fever since two weeks after Rorik's departure. He could hardly rise from his sickbed, much less climb to the walls and towers that watched over the comings and goings of the castle. And though Alaine's burgeoning figure made it difficult for her to manage the rounds of watchtowers, the daily tours were reassuring.

Rorik had left them well prepared for any eventuality. He had repaired the barbican that Fulk had left to rot, so now a sturdy gate in the outer palisades formed an outermost line of defense for Brix's walls. He had seen all dry moats cleaned of shrubbery, blocked any possible entry by the garderobe shafts, and reinforced all the heavy, iron-studded gates and doors of keep and bailey alike. In addition, he had left them with a full complement of men to guard the walls. Alaine and her people were as well defended as anyone could possibly be. But still a feeling of unrest dragged at Alaine's confidence.

Some of her unease Alaine attributed to homesickness. It seemed that every part of her life had changed. All that was familiar had been torn away. Joanna and Mathilde and Garin, the three people she loved and trusted most in the world, were gone. Little Thatch had pleaded to go with them, begging not to be separated from his friend Judith. Alaine had let him go. The depths of his velvet-brown eyes had shone with the longing for home. Alaine readily recognized the expression, for the pangs of homesickness occasionally swept through her own soul with the fury of a hurricane—the longing for dear, comfortable Ste. Claire rather than Brix with its new ways and unfamiliar, sometimes less than friendly people.

Rorik's absence made her homesickness more acute. There was no amount of pressing work that could keep her from missing him. Her bed was cold and empty. In the dark of night and confusion of sleep she would reach out for him and find no familiar masculine shape lying beside her. Thoughts of Rorik tantalized her memories. His presence had made Brix seem like home. His absence made her feel bereft of support in a foreign place. All she could do to keep the hounds of loneliness at bay was to lie alone in the dark and try to call her husband's image to mind.

Her intense longing for Rorik surprised Alaine. He had become the very life of her, the beacon star of her existence, the solid core of her being. What would she do, how would she cope if he were taken from her? She wondered if he thought of her often, or at all. And if he thought of her, was it with affection? Or was it with concern about how she would deal with Brix in his absence? What peace of mind it must have cost him to leave a mere woman with the welfare of his birthright in her hands!

Weeks turned into a month. The harvest was good, the storage vaults were full to bursting, and Brix was well set for the winter. Even Gunnor was attempting to be pleasant. Her mood had improved gradually over the past weeks, and Alaine dared entertain hopes that the girl was easing out of her bitterness. Ruth had arrived within a week of Rorik's departure, and now that Alaine's time was very near, the midwife scolded constantly for her to ease the demanding schedule that kept her going from daybreak until sundown.

Alaine was surprised when Gunnor stepped in to take some of the load off her shoulders. Indeed, her sulky stepsister seemed anxious to help. She even offered to take on the duty of checking the watchtowers and gatehouses, now that Alaine could no longer manage the strenuous climbs, but Alaine put her foot down firmly to squash that idea. Sir Guillaume was on his feet again, though shakily, and he could manage very well without Gunnor's interference. Gunnor had seemed inordinately disappointed at Alaine's decision, and had promptly taken to spending much of her time on the battlements, looking off into the distance as though she and not Alaine were pining for her lord's return. Alaine noted her behavior with confusion, and noted to herself that she must prod Rorik again to find Gunnor a husband who could give her what she needed, if such a man existed.

As the burden she carried grew heavier, Alaine took to spending most of her time in the big solar that opened off the southern end of the Great Hall. She busied herself with the spinning and weaving and sewing while Hilda supervised the kitchens and kept a watchful eye on the housekeeping. The days passed in contented industry, and as the first light rimes of frost greeted the early morning sun Alaine allowed herself to slip into a state of peaceful waiting—waiting for her child to be born, waiting for Rorik to return. It was tempting to put worries and problems and speculations aside as the days followed one after the other in peaceful progression.

But the lulling sameness of the early autumn days was shattered one bright and chilly morning as Alaine broke her fast with Gunnor and Ruth. Sir Guillaume usually joined them at the early meal, as did Brix's new priest Father Egar, but on this morning it was just the three women. Guillaume had left before dawn to check on one of his patrols that rode the borders of Brix's lands, and Father Egar had been called to the beside of an aged villager who was night to drawing his last breath. Alaine would have accompanied the priest to bring comfort to the family, but the awkwardness of her advanced pregnancy now prevented her from doing much more than traveling from hall to bedchamber to solar. Later she would think back and be grateful that on this day of all days she was in the castle, where she was needed.

Alaine was chatting casually with Gunnor when a whirlwind of commotion broke into the hall. At its head was Sir

Guillaume, breathless and beaded with sweat in spite of the coolness of the autumn air.

"My lady," he said, doffing his helmet and running hands through the graying hair that was plastered to his head. "I bring evil tidings, I fear."

The two men-at-arms with him looked exceedingly grim, and Alaine's heart began a painful hammering in her chest. Her first thought was of Rorik—Guillaume had intercepted a messenger from Brionne, a messenger carrying the tale of Rorik's death or injury. Her hands gripped the arms of her chair with desperate strength.

"What is it, Sir Guillaume?" She tried desperately to keep a level voice.

"The patrol that didn't report back last eventide, my lady—I found them slaughtered by the east quarry pond. One lad still lived, though barely. He managed to tell me before he died—they spotted an army on the move in the late hours of the night. It was Gilbert de Prestot's banner at the head, and the crossed swords and dagger of Phillip rides beside it. I scouted the area and spied them camped in the hollow a few minutes' ride from the pond. The camp was rousing when I came upon them. I've set a full complement to man the walls and ordered the gates shut."

Alaine's first reaction was relief that the news was not of Rorik, but her relief was immediately flooded over by a wave of outraged anger. She didn't note the breathless stillness that came over Gunnor as she listened to Guillaume's report.

"How soon do you think they'll attack?"

"It's any man's guess, my lady. They may well be following hard on my heels. Or, since they think they come undetected, they may rest a day or two before coming at us. It would be the more reasonable course."

"Gilbert and Phillip allied!" Alaine said wonderingly. "What can they hope to gain by attacking Brix? Surely they cannot expect to take the castle?" She speared Sir Guillaume with a sharp glance. "Can they?"

"Not unless they intend a very long siege, my lady," Sir Guillaume confirmed. "Unless they think we are as careless about our defenses as old Fulk was. The most they can hope to do is terrorize the villagers and slaughter the livestock. The crops are mostly in, so even there they can't do much damage.''

Alaine pursed her lips thoughtfully. "I'll wager Gilbert has something up his sleeve. Phillip might be fool enough to stage a useless siege simply for the sake of revenge, but Gilbert wouldn't join him unless he thought there was something to be gained.''

Guillaume looked momentarily uneasy, and Alaine wondered if he were as confident as he would like her to believe. Did he know something about the state of Brix's defenses that she didn't know? She dismissed the thought instantly. Had she not toured the walls herself and seen their readiness for battle? Brix would never fall to forces from without. Not unless a fool or traitor had charge of their defense.

She looked at Gunnor with unconcealed suspicion. "I don't suppose you know anything about this?''

Gunnor lifted an indignant brow. "Certainly not!''

"Gilbert was courting you not many months past,'' Alaine reminded her.

"Aye,'' Gunnor agreed bitterly, "but your Rorik put an end to that when you so unwisely lured that poor knight up to your chamber. I haven't seen Gilbert since.''

Alaine felt her face grow hot as Sir Guillaume's mouth tightened in disapproval. If the dour knight had not known before of her supposed perfidy, he did now. Gunnor tossed her a look of triumph. Every trace of amiability had disappeared from her face, and Alaine knew with instinctive and unreasoning certainty that Gunnor had something to do with Gilbert's arrival.

Gunnor smirked at the uneasy frown on Alaine's face. "I'm sure Gilbert hasn't forgotten his feelings for me, though. When he takes this keep it will be you begging me for favors and me ordering you to do this and that and go her and there like some miserable serf.''

Alaine ignored her gloating. She turned back to Sir Guillaume, who was shifting restlessly on his feet. No doubt he wanted to be out of her presence, Alaine thought. She had never liked the man, thinking him dour, unimaginative, and sulky, and suspected he returned the ill regard in like measure. Now that he had heard Gunnor's spiteful accusations, he probably respected her even less. But if Brix were to stand they would have to work together as a team, whether he liked it or not.

"Send a reliable man to my lord with a message of what is happening here. William will surely let him go to defend his own lands. And send other men to the villages and farms. Everyone is to gather as much of their livestock as possible and come into the bailey for protection."

"I have already taken that liberty, my lady," Guillaume answered with a strained reserve.

"Perhaps we should send to Ste. Claire for help," Alaine ventured.

Guillaume shook his head. "Young Sir Garin has hardly enough men to defend his own stronghold, my lady. We are more than capable of defending ourselves."

Alaine murmured agreement, but Guillaume's hearty confidence worried her. He was almost too confident. Her father had told her again and again that overconfidence had been more than one man's downfall.

When Guillaume and his men had left she turned with a scowl to her stepsister. The half-smile on Gunnor's face only strengthened her conviction that the girl was not to be trusted. "We're going to move the household to the keep, Gunnor, and once we're there, you'll stay within its walls. No!" she cut off Gunnor's half-uttered protestation. "Say what you will. You take no trouble to hide your sympathy for Gilbert, even if you didn't know his plans. I'm not fool enough to trust you. If you set one foot outside the keep while Gilbert is within a day's ride of this castle I'll have you dragged back inside by your ears. I swear I will! So heed my words!"

Alaine didn't give Gunnor a chance to retort, but hefted herself to her feet and made her exit. Gunnor stared after her in scorn, Ruth in bemusement. Finally, the old midwife cackled to herself and tore another wedge of bread from the loaf on the board. She turned to Gunnor with a gap-toothed grin.

"Ye'd best be listening to what my lady says," she warned with a malicious twinkle in her eye. "She's no gentle and simpering maid, ye know, and I'd not be surprised to see 'er stuff ye down into that great gloomy cell in the gatehouse if ye displease 'er, or better still, 'ang ye by yer thumbs 'til ye screech out what evil ye been doing with that knave out yonder."

"Oh, shut up, you old hag!" Gunnor spat. With a great show of dignity she flounced from the hall, the glow of triumph still in her eyes.

Gilbert did not attack that day. The villagers flocked like frightened geese into the bailey, driving their sheep, cattle, fowl, and goats in front of them and dragging their wailing children behind. The few who had wagons had loaded them full of their meager household goods. Others carried bundles of their most valued possessions on their backs or in their arms. The outer bailey became a roiling mass of people, beasts, and dust sent whirling from under the feet and hooves of the crowd. Wooden shelters were hastily erected against the outer wall beneath the overhang of the walkway. Raggedy, dirty-faced children cried and laughed and ran wild in everyone's way. Adults yelled and argued and complained. Sheep, goats, cattle, geese, and chickens added their comments to the cacophony. And everywhere were men-at-arms looking grim and impatient, chasing dogs and children and fowl from beneath their feet.

But by dawn of the following morning all was quiet. Only two or three cook fires glowed in the semidarkness as Alaine struggled to lift her body to the wall walkway. She knew well that she shouldn't be here. If Ruth saw her attempting to climb the ladder the midwife would give her a tongue-lashing she wouldn't soon forget. But sleep had eluded her all the night long. Visions of another attack by Gilbert preyed upon her mind. She had to go the wall to see for herself what was happening.

The nearest sentry started with surprise as she breathlessly heaved herself up the last rung of the ladder and climbed onto the platform. When he recognized her he saluted respectfully, then motioned to a bulky shadow that separated itself from the parapet. Sir Guillaume. She should have guessed he would be walking the battlements. He was nothing if not conscientious.

Sir Guillaume nodded stiffly as she moved to join him. "My lady."

"Sir Guillaume," she returned in a reserved voice. "Is all quiet?"

He motioned to the east. The glow of the rising sun tinged the horizon with dull orange. The morning was quiet and chill. No sound or stirring indicated that everything was not as it should be.

She squinted again to the east, growing suspicious. "That isn't the sun," she finally said.

"No," Guillaume confirmed. "Probably Gauchemain. A common trick, my lady. They set fire to a village in hopes of luring us out to fight, then they fall on us in great numbers when we leave the protection of the walls."

"Then you didn't send a patrol out to try to defend the village?"

"No, my lady," he confirmed. "That would not have been wise."

Wise or not, Alaine was still tempted to try. The sight of Gilbert wreaking havoc at will with Brix's holdings was almost too much to be borne. But she had to bow to Guillaume's greater experience. He didn't seem much concerned by the destruction.

"The bastard!" Alaine gritted in a most unladylike fashion. The villagers of Gauchemain were sleeping safely within the walls of Brix, but the wanton destruction rankled. Even more did it anger her that she could do nothing about it.

"Yes, my lady. It seems he means business, this . . . Gilbert of yours."

Alaine turned on him with a look that could have melted the armor off the old knight's back. "He is no Gilbert of mine, Sir Guillaume!" She'd had enough. She was in no mood for sly insinuations and veiled insults. "And you'd best remember your place! If you're fool enough to believe the sly mouthings of my stepsister then that's your choice. But keep your disapproval to yourself. I'll tolerate no more disrespect!''

Guillaume seemed little moved by her vehemence. "I meant no disrespect, lady."

"The hell you didn't!"

His eyes widened slightly at her profanity. He remembered suddenly that Sir Rorik's bride was not an everyday simpering female. She'd led that stalwart knight a merry chase like a common thief in the woods, and it was rumored among the men of Ste. Claire that she was better at wielding a sword than at plying a lady's needle, and better with a bow than most men. And Rorik seemed inordinately fond of her, considering she was a woman. Guillaume decided abruptly it would be wise not to anger such an unpredictable and highly placed female. He had greater problems to consider than the lady's morals.

"I apologize, Lady Alaine," Guillaume said with a sketchy bow. "My mouth ran away with me, it's true."

Alaine's flash of temper faded as quickly as it had come. If she was this touchy before Gilbert even attacked, she dreaded what a few weeks of siege might do. She would become a veritable shrew.

"Apology accepted," she said coldly. "We'll say no more about it."

A molten sliver of the sun appeared above the horizon, drowning out the meager glow of hapless Gauchemain in a vivid display of red and gold.

"He hasn't a chance, has he?" she asked. "This army of Gilbert's is not large enough to take us by storm?"

"As far as I know Brix has never been taken by storm," Guillaume replied with confidence.

But it had been taken other ways, Alaine reminded herself. She thought again of Gunnor, who had kept to her chamber and the hall as she was bidden, frosting Alaine with icy glares whenever they happened to meet.

"I'm going to move the household to the keep," Alaine told him.

"I hardly think that's necessary," Guillaume commented. "Even if Rorik cannot respond to my message for weeks, I doubt Gilbert will as much as take the outer wall. In fact I'm sure he won't."

"Just the same, I'll take no chances."

Alaine had turned to make the difficult descent of the ladder when a cry from the nearest watchtower snapped her attention back to the wall. Guillaume hurried to the nearest crenel to look down to where the sentry pointed.

"Alaine de Ste. Claire!" The call drifted over the wall in a familiar, hated voice.

"I am here!" Alaine called back defiantly, crowding beside Sir Guillaume in the crenel, a cut in the high wall that allowed defenders to fire at their enemies.

Gilbert sat astride his prancing gray destrier on the other side of the outer palisades, well out of bow-shot of the wall. Behind him in the shadow of the woods she could make out at least one troop of men. Probably there were many others hidden behind him where she couldn't see.

"My Lady Alaine!" Gilbert called in a ringing voice. "I come on behalf of the rightful lord of Brix, Phillip, who your husband foully attacked and drove from his home for no just cause. I demand you surrender Brix and all its people and lands immediately!"

A frisson of helpless and unreasoning terror shivered along Alaine's nerves. Once before she had stood on a wall and listened to Gilbert spouting demands for surrender. She had defied him then, and Ste. Claire had paid dearly for her defiance. The unnerving feeling of having acted this part before nearly robbed her of courage. But this wall she stood on now was Brix's, not Ste. Claire's, and it would not fall to the demands of this braying jackass!

"Begone, Gilbert!" she called down. "The one who's part you take has been outlawed by William for his unknightly treachery. Best leave while you can, before William deals the same with you, or Rorik serves you even worse!"

She could hear Gilbert's laughter float across the open

space between them. "Rorik is not here to defend you, my lady! And I doubt he'll come. There's a messenger I met along the road yestermorn and dispatched to his reward!"

Guillaume scowled in seeming puzzlement, but she smiled at him and shook her head. Not content with Guillaume's one messenger, she had sent two of her own. She had been surprised at his oversight. Guillaume knew well the ways of war and should not have risked such a vital message to a single man.

"You cannot take this fortress, de Prestot!" Guillaume roared with impressive volume. "You're a fool to try! When Sir Rorik returns he will dispatch you straight to Hell! And may Phillip be waiting for you there!"

Gilbert called back in a confident voice. "Think on this, fools! Each day until you surrender Brix I will burn one village. One and all in those villages will be put to the sword. Do you want your people to die?"

Alaine didn't answer. The villagers and farmers were all safe in the bailey below, and most of their livestock likewise. Villages could be rebuilt. But the senseless destruction angered her beyond words. The people of Brix would know naught but hardship in the winter to come until they could return to their own homes.

"Our people will not die, de Prestot!" Guillaume answered for her. "But yours will! Beware rousing the dragon!"

"Do not fear, my lady," Guillaume said solicitously when he had helped Alaine down from the steep ladder. "De Prestot doesn't have a chance against Brix's defenses, and all our people are safe within the walls. More fool he for testing so strong a fortress!"

"Gilbert is a swine. But he's no fool. Could Phillip be coming with reinforcements?"

"It would take more men than William himself could command to take these walls," Guillaume assured her. "I doubt that Phillip is with him. He's probably cowering safely behind England's shores and lending funds and his name to this venture. From what I've heard of the man, Phillip is not one to risk his own neck if he can get another to risk it for him."

"All well and to the good," she puzzled. "But I've known Gilbert since I was a child. He doesn't ride on foolish ventures. He fights only when he's sure there's something to be gained. Don't dismiss his threat so lightly, Guillaume. There's something here we're not seeing."

The next morning, another village was burned. Alaine wasn't on the walls to view the destruction, but got a full report of it from Guillaume, who was looking more worn with every passing hour. His fever had left him not strong enough to cope with the demands he was placing on his body. Alaine ordered him to rest, not knowing what she would do should he collapse. There had been a time when she thought she knew as much of war as any man, but now she realized how wrong she'd been. Guillaume was her bastion against a stupid error that would allow Brix to fall. Boor that he was, his experienced defense would allow Brix to hold firm until Rorik could ride to the rescue. If Brix fell—God forbid—people would die, she among them. For if Gilbert didn't kill her then surely Rorik would. He would never believe her innocent of conspiring with the man he believed had been her lover.

But Guillaume didn't have time for the rest Alaine commanded him to take. Late in the morning Gilbert's forces stormed the outer palisades. Heaps of bodies grew at the base of the spiked log barrier as bowmen from the barbican gatehouse took a deadly toll, but still the attackers kept coming. The numbers of Gilbert's army seemed limitless, and he was not at all reluctant in spending lives to achieve his aims. In the afternoon a wooden ram carried under a protective umbrella of stiffened hides pounded insistently at the barbican gate. It shuddered and creaked but did not give. Guillaume assured Alaine that no such attempt would succeed. There was no need to reinforce the troops manning the gatehouse, he told her. Gilbert was simply demonstrating his serious intent in order to scare her into surrendering.

But Guillaume's words were small comfort to Alaine as she presided over a gloomy evening meal in the keep. An unreasoning pall of doom held sway over her mind. She tried unsuccessfully to convince herself they were safe. Every exigency had been anticipated. Gunnor was well watched. Rorik had plugged every hole a snake like Gilbert might use to gain access to the castle. She told herself her fears were just a pregnant woman's fancies. Guillaume said the walls would hold, that it was foolish even to have moved into the keep. And Guillaume should know whereof he spoke.

The next morning the barbican fell to the ram.

There was no reason to fear, Guillaume insisted. No reason, even, for concern. The barbican was their weakest point of defense, and many castles did not even bother with maintaining one. Gilbert would never advance past the outer wall. But the look on the weary knight's face when he was uttering his assurances didn't make Alaine feel better at all.

Days passed, then a week. Gilbert threw men against the outer wall in endless attack. Hourds were extended to overhang the battlements, and the men of Brix greeted the attackers with hot oil, burning naphtha, a hail of deadly arrows, and human and animal excrement that was fast piling up inside the bailey. The dead and screaming wounded piled into mounds outside the walls. But still they kept coming. Alaine worried over where Gilbert was getting such a multitude of men. He had no such resources at Prestot. Her only thought was that Phillip was pouring in men and supplies from wherever he had found refuge in England. England was not lacking in powerful men who would like a foothold of power in Normandy. Some across the narrow sea regarded young William with wary eyes, and would grab at a chance to harass him on his own shores.

But days passed and the wall held. The ram was ineffective against the larger, stronger gate and portcullis, and the deadly fire from the watchtowers took a painful toll of even Gilbert's seemingly limitless fighting men.

Within the walls the inhabitants of Brix remained safe, if not happy. Crowds of livestock and frightened men, women, and children did not make for a congenial atmosphere. The stink from the filth accumulating within the bailey was almost as noxious as the stench from the piles of untended dead outside the wall. The cacophony of wailing children, squawking poultry, bleating sheep, and short-tempered men and women was continuous. Fights were becoming common, and more than once Alaine, as lady of the castle, had been forced to sit in judgment for petty squabbles and disputes. In one instance she gritted her teeth and ordered a public whipping of two free peasants, one from Gauchemain and the other from the village of Brix, who were bent on mutual murder over a woman. The ordering of even a light whipping turned her stomach, but without a firm hand the situation in the bailey was likely to turn into pandemonium. After she had shown her determination to keep order, the bailey was quieter, but the tension of fear and unrest still hung in the air like the heaviness before a storm.

With help from Hadwisa, Hilda, and Ruth, Alaine soothed ruffled tempers in the bailey, tended the hurts and sicknesses of the swarm of people who had taken refuge inside Brix's walls, and supervised the distribution of food from the storage vaults. She wanted to do more. She wanted to be on the walls with a stout bow in her hands and herself wreak some havoc on the enemy. It had even occurred to her to take a force outside the walls under cover of night, as she had at Ste. Claire, and try to pin down Gilbert's forces by an attack from behind. That was before she remembered that she could barely manage to waddle from hall to bedchamber, much less ride a horse or play a hit-and-run game with death the prize for the labor. All the same she itched to leap into action. The slow crawl of days drove her to distraction. She sat morosely with the women in the cold, gloomy hall of the keep, listening to the rattling of men in the barracks one floor below, wondering if Rorik had received her message, and if he had, could he ride to relieve the siege before Gilbert managed to find a way inside the walls. Soon she would be brought to bed with child, with Rorik's heir. What if Gilbert's persistence paid off? What would he do to Rorik's child, to her child? It did not bear thinking about. Gilbert could not succeed. Brix was too strong. And surely before too many more days Rorik would appear at the head of an avenging army.

But Rorik did not appear, and Guillaume's reassurances sounded more hollow every day. The sheer numbers that Gilbert was throwing against the wall was taking its toll. Alaine cursed Gilbert, cursed Phillip, cursed William, and even cursed Rorik. On the day that Guillaume collapsed from a return of his fever she made the decision to move the refugees into the inner bailey, just in case the unthinkable befell. There was only room enough for people. The livestock would have to take their chances in the outer bailey. She was being pessimistic, Alaine told herself. Gilbert's army would batter itself to death against the outer wall and never gain an inch. Even with Guillaume lying insensible in his bed, she herself could manage the defense well enough to keep Gilbert at bay. She didn't quite convince herself it was true.

Three weeks after the siege began, the outer wall was overrun. That same day Rorik arrived with his army.

CHAPTER 26

The curtain of a black and starless night hid Rorik's army in the dense woods just east of Brix. Only Rorik, with Sihtric at his side, ventured to the edge of the heather-carpeted moor that sloped up to the outer palisades, and farther on, to the outer wall. Campfires dotted the open space between palisades and wall, and hints of conversation and laughter floated across the moor to where the two men sat astride their destriers. The flickering light of torches illuminated the wall's main gate, still intact but gaping wide.

"Miles says the inner wall has fallen also," Sihtric reported. "Fell after only a couple of hours fighting in the outer bailey."

"I'd say someone in there isn't on their toes," Rorik growled.

"Aye. Guillaume should've known well enough to put a strong line of men around the inner bailey."

"It matters little," Rorik said in a quiet voice. "It's a useless victory for Gilbert."

It was true, Rorik thought, looking across the moor to the dark towering shadow of the keep. The keep could hold out indefinitely. With its own kitchen, hall, and a large barracks on the floor below the hall, there would have been room for everyone to take refuge when the bailey was taken. The windowless ground floor held naught but storage vaults of grains, salted meats, vegetables, and dried fruits. And the vaults were centered around a deep, reliable water well. The walls were twelve feet of stone pierced only by narrow arrow slits in the upper stories. No entrance to the ground floor existed except from the floor above, which held the barracks, and the entrance to all the upper floors could be accessed only by way of a narrow stairway built into the thickness of the wall and well guarded by two iron-studded wooden doors. Inside, the keep might be crowded, chaotic, and noisome—but it would be safe.

Rorik frowned across the moor to the torchlit wall. Come dawn, when Rorik made his move, Gilbert's army would be trapped between the keep, the walls, and the sea cliff to the southwest and northwest, and Rorik's advancing army on the east. They would have no choice but to surrender. The battle should be straightforward, surrender a certainty. But still there was something awry. In crossing the hills to the east, the advancing army had met no patrols, and only a single scout who they'd rousted from a tree perch along the only line of approach. Even in these woods so near to the castle, not a single sentry had to be silenced. Gilbert must know Rorik would come, but he was acting very much like he didn't care.

Rorik wheeled his stallion. "Back to camp," he said. "No fires, no noise. If they're stupid enough to be taken by surprise, then we'll oblige them."

Later, couched for the night on the cold ground, Rorik sought sleep. But sleep eluded him. His thoughts kept pulling him back to the torchlit walls of Brix, and to the dark tower of the keep. The besieging army was too at ease, too unwary. There was no way that Gilbert, if he had half a head on his shoulders, could not know that Rorik was here. If they had flushed one scout from his nest, there must have been others they hadn't seen. Gilbert could not be ignorant that Rorik was in the area. Any other commander who had a care for his life and the lives of his men would have retreated at the first hint of his arrival. Gilbert was no fool. If he was not retreating, then he had a reason. He must think that he could break the keep before Rorik could pin him down and crush him. And if Gilbert had the keep, then would Rorik be forced to lay siege to his own home And the country hereabouts was so ravaged by Gilbert's destruction that it could not support an army for nearly the time it would take to drive Gilbert from the tower.

All that was impossible, Rorik tried to convince himself. Like an untried boy, he was letting vague specters of fear rule his mind at the expense of solid logic. The keep was fortified well enough to withstand Gilbert for months.

Unless Gilbert had someone inside, someone he could use as a last resort should he be threatened from the rear.

The persistent thought chased away any chance of slumber. An image of Alaine swam into his mind's eye. Would Alaine take a cue from history and let her former suitor into the keep? Rorik thought they had been building happiness between them when William's summons had drawn him away. But who knew the mind and heart of a woman?

For all the long days and nights at Brionne Rorik's mind had been filled with Alaine. She'd been a constant shadow by his side, an unwavering image floating before his eyes. Too often he caught himself wanting to share the day's concerns with her understanding ears or laugh with her at some joke or trivial silliness that lightened the boring tedium of siege. And too often he thought his very soul would collapse from the emptiness within him when there was no Alaine to fill his arms in the dark hours of the night and no Alaine to smile at him with her special smile at the first light of morning. The woman had somehow invaded the very core of him. In the long, lonely hours at Brionne, he had come to realize that his mind could no longer hold out against his heart. If his love was what she wanted, he had decided, then she would have it. If his trust was what she longed for, then she would have that also. His instincts told him that finally he had found a woman who was true and straight and honorable as any man who ever lived—a woman he could trust with his life, and more important, with his heart.

Thinking back over their months together, he found that he could dismiss even her dalliance with Gilbert as being a fancy of his suspicious, automatic reactions. He should have listened to Joanna when she told him of Alaine's loathing for the man. He should have seen the evidence in Alaine herself. But he had been blinded by his prejudices, wanting, perhaps, some protective barrier to throw up between himself and the tender emotions he felt were threatening his well-ordered existence. At Brionne, with the insight granted by distance, he had come to recognize that his feelings for his wife ranged beyond simple passion to deep-rooted love. He had driven the uncertainties from his thoughts and determined to make a new start to their relationship the minute he returned to Brix.

But now all the doubts he had chased from his mind came galloping back to whirl in chaotic confusion around the inside of his skull. Gilbert thought he could get inside the keep. He must think that, or else have a death wish. Who else in the keep might favor him other than Rorik's enchanting, loving, treacherous wife?

Rorik cursed and sat up, brushing dirt from his heavy cloak. He just could not accept that Alaine would betray him, no matter how logical the conclusion. He walked over to where Sihtric snored and nudged the blond giant with his toe.

"Mmmmph!" Sihtric grumbled.

"Wake up, you great oaf."

The Norseman groaned and rolled over, opening one eye. "Why?" he croaked.

"Because you're to take over command here come morning." The grin that flashed across the younger man's face was wickedly malicious.

"And just what the hell will you be doing, come morning?" Sihtric growled, sitting up groggily.

"I'll be in the keep."

"The hell you say. And just how is that to come about? Going to skinny up the garderobe shaft with all that slime? I think maybe you're a bit too broad for that."

Rorik chuckled, and his white teeth flashed briefly in the night. "I had those blocked. There's a tunnel under the walls and into the keep that no one but I should know. My great grandfather had it built into the castle when it was first commissioned. It was passed on only to the head of each generation, but I found out about it by accident."

"I can well believe that," Sihtric snorted. "You were always prowling around that castle like you were going to own it someday, in spite of being the youngest. How do you know Fulk or Phillip didn't find this tunnel and have it blocked?"

"They might have. I'll find out soon enough."

"You'd do better to stay right here. Gilbert'll wait until morning."

"Maybe not," Rorik answered. "Now listen well. . . ."

*   *   *

Having the entire population of Brix's villages and farms penned up inside the bailey seemed like a picnic compared to having the same number crowded together within the keep. Children screamed, adults squabbled among themselves, women wailed, and men complained. Men-at-arms were everywhere, archers crouching before the embrasure of each arrow slot, pikemen guarding each entrance. The air was hot and ripe with the odors of too many bodies crowded into too small a space. Noise was constant, and most tempers were badly frayed. As Alaine moved among her surly people, she felt her own temper sharpen to a cutting edge.

For the third time this day she had been forced to a heated exchange with the chief cook. Yes, she'd told him as calmly as she could, all these people must be fed with supplies that were in the vaults, and yes he must tolerate the presence in his kitchen of the women serfs she had detailed to help with the meals. And he must dole out the supplies so that everyone stayed in reasonable health, but in amounts that would conserve for the future. No one knew how long they would be in this situation.

The cook was surly. He cooked for the lord and his household, not the horde that was milling like so many cattle in the hall and barracks. They could manage their own slop. At that point Alaine invited him to take his place on the battlements atop the keep if he didn't care to see to the distribution and preparation of food. Some man-at-arms who crouched behind the parapet dodging the missiles sent his way would be happy to take the cook's place in the kitchen. The cook grumbled and shot her a scathing look from beneath lowered brows, but afterward held his silence. Alaine made a mental note to see to his replacement if the chaos at Brix ever ended. The man was a free peasant and fancied himself above the common run of castle servants, continually bristling about the way Alaine ordered things done.

Alaine sighed wearily as she made her way through the press of bodies in the hall. At Ste. Claire she'd never had this problem with the serving people. They had known their worth and been diligent at their duties, but they had also known their place and were happy to be in it. Brix had not been a happy place for years, and a few short months of reform was not going to make so many problems disappear. Under the strain of these last days, all the festering resentments were floating to the surface.

"I want to speak to you, if I may." Gunnor's icily polite voice cut through Alaine's musings.

"Yes?" Alaine inquired reluctantly.

"Why am I not allowed on the battlements? The captain of the guard told me he has strict orders from you."

Alaine sighed. All she needed on top of the other problems besetting her was to hear Gunnor's complaining and whining! But she tried to be patient. She noted with some satisfaction that the little tiring woman she had assigned to watch her stepsister was hovering tactfully in the background. "Now that the battle has come to the keep itself it's not safe for you to be up there."

"I want to see what's going on!" Gunnor demanded. "I refuse to be stuck down in this sty with these . . . these pigs!"

More to the point, Alaine thought, she wanted to be where she could watch Gilbert ride back and forth exorting his troops. How Gunnor could still fancy herself in love with that villain was beyond reason.

"I'm afraid you have no choice, sister," Alaine replied calmly. "If you dislike the crowd, then retire to your chamber."

"A chamber crowded with six other women, all filthy serfs!"

Alaine sent her a narrow-eyed look of contempt. "If you're so put out by such inconvenience, Gunnor, perhaps you could use your influence with Gilbert to lift this ridiculous siege. Did he not once seek your hand? Do you think he would continue if he knew his beloved suffered so from his attack?"

Gunnor's eyes smoldered with resentment at the biting sarcasm in Alaine's tone. "Why don't you just surrender? Gilbert will have Brix in the end."

"And then you think to rule here as mistress?" Alaine snorted. "For a woman who's been married and out in the world, you know very little of its ways!"

"More than you, I vow!"

"Do you think so?" Alaine sniped, giving full rein to her frayed temper. "If he were to take Brix with all its wealth and power, Gilbert would not wed you, a dowerless widow with no land and no influence. He would go angling for an heiress who could bring him more power, more land, more wealth. Why do you let yourself be deceived?"

"Deceived, am I?" Gunnor spat. "I will see you eat your words when Gilbert walks into this hall! See if I don't."

"If Gilbert walks into this hall, Gunnor, it will be over my dead body, and possibly over yours."

"Bah! You are a fool. You should surrender while you can still crave mercy."

The spat with Gunnor left Alaine shaking with fatigue. She wanted nothing more than to retire to her chamber, close her eyes, and let sleep dissolve the worry and frustration from her mind. But there could be no rest for her this day. Sir Guillaume lay senseless on his pallet, and the captain of Brix's guard was looking to her for orders. She felt helpless and harassed, frightened of making an error or oversight that might break the defenses of a keep that should be able to protect her people for weeks. She knew more of war than most other ladies of her station, but she didn't have the expertise of Sir Guillaume—or Rorik.

Rorik. Where was he? Had one of her messengers gotten through? Should she risk someone else's life to send another plea for help? Could anyone get through Gilbert's forces to carry a message? The questions were too many, the answers too few.

The day dragged on, finally fading into night. After just one day penned in the keep the people of Brix were surly and restless. Alaine could imagine what the situation would be in a week, or a month. Exhaustion dragged at her feet as she climbed the stone stairs to the small wall chamber she shared with five other women. The burden in her belly seemed to be made of stone, and her back strained and ached with the task of lifting her awkward body up the stairway.

Alaine lay down on the straw pallet that served as her bed. She thought of the myriad campfires that surrounded Brix's walls, like an evil reflection of the stars that lit the sky. She was surrounded by enemies, penned in by forces that, given the slightest chance, would annihilate her before she'd even had a chance to truly live. With a pang of regret the image of Rorik floated into her mind. Perhaps he was still at Brionne. Perhaps neither of her messengers nor the man Guillaume had sent had made it through Gilbert's net. Rorik could be sleeping peacefully on this night with no idea that the home he held so dear was being clawed away by the forces of Gilbert's greed and ambition. She wondered idly if the unfortunate people shut up with Guy of Burgundy in the besieged castle of Brionne felt as helpless and frustrated as she.

The babe stirred restlessly within her. Alaine rested a hand on her swollen belly. No doubt he was upset by his mother's unease. Poor babe, to be born into a world so fraught with uncertainty. Would he ever see the man who sired him? Would he even be given more than a few weeks of tenuous life?

Alaine shut her eyes with determination. She should try to sleep. All her energy would be needed to face the morrow. She concentrated on wiping her troubled mind free of everything but the ever-present exhaustion. The breathing and restless stirrings of the women sleeping around her made for a harsh lullaby. The rough pallet pricked where the straw poked through the thin covering, and once again she cursed herself for not having more furnishings brought from the now deserted Great Hall. Now it was too late, and she had to endure the discomfort as best she could, along with everyone else.

Sleep finally came, but it didn't bring with it the comfort Alaine hoped for. Images out of the past assaulted her dreams. She saw once again Gilbert striding into the hall at Ste. Claire, threatening to put her people indiscriminately to the sword until she agreed to do his bidding. And then he was kneeling beside her in the chapel. But the figure in black who stood over them was not brave little Father Sebastian who had tried so valiantly to delay the ceremony. It was instead a dark-winged specter of evil. It pronounced the awful words giving her to the invading conqueror, then locked their hands together, its dark, clawed fist resting on their joined hands and sending icy shards of fear and revulsion shooting through her body. The specter laughed. And Gilbert laughed with the same evil, booming sound. Their laughter splintered into a scream. But no, the scream came from the arched doorway of the chapel where Gunnor stood, her eyes wide, her hair in tangled chaos about her head and shoulders.

"Alaine!" she screamed. "Alaine! He's mine! He loves me! Me!"

Alaine struggled to rise, to tear her hands from the fingers and the claws that held it. But she was weighted down by lead. Gunnor rushed at her, eyes ablaze. She grabbed her and shook her.

"My lady! My lady!" The shaking became real as Alaine struggled to wakefulness. "My lady!"

Gunnor's little tiring woman crouched above her. "Sorry I am to wake you, lady, but my mistress is nowhere to be found!"

It took a good many seconds for the servant's words to cut through the fog around her brain. But when they did an unreasoning pang of foreboding stabbed deep into her heart. "What mean you?" Alaine demanded.

"I was delayed in the hall, my lady, when my mistress retired to her chamber. When I went up to the chamber to sleep, the Lady Gunnor's pallet was empty. I checked in the hall and barracks. She is not to be found!"

Sleepy grumblings rose from Alaine's chamber mates at this middle of the night conversation, but Alaine paid them no mind. She rose shakily to her feet, the heaviness of slumber adding to the weight of her other burden. "We must find her," she told the cringing servant. "No," she said impatiently. "Don't be such a frightened mouse. I am not so angry with you that you need cringe so."

The hall was dark, with silence broken only by the snorings and rustlings of the people who made their beds on the stone floor, the hearth, and the hard wooden benches lining the walls. The flickering light from the candle Alaine carried was sufficient only to avoid stepping on the sleeping bodies at her feet. Beyond the pale circle of light she could see only dimly, but since no upright figure or movement caught her eye she guessed that Gunnor was not there.

They found her in the kitchen, polishing off the last of one of the loaves of bread that had been intended for the morning's meal. Alaine frowned in irritation and waved the little serving maid out of the room.

"I was hungry," Gunnor said without remorse. "I vow that cook of yours lets as little as possible go out of this kitchen."

"He does so on my orders," Alaine explained in a vexed tone of voice. "Food is a resource we can't replenish, so we must stretch what we have for as long as possible. Since you've gorged yourself with part of our breakfast, you can do without your meal come morning."

"I will do no such thing!" Gunnor retorted.

"You will, if I have to set guards on your chamber to keep you there. I will not see others starve because you won't tolerate a little rumbling in your belly. We all get enough food to stay well and healthy. And to be honest" —Alaine regarded her stepsister with a gleam of malicious humor lighting her eyes—"you should be grateful for an opportunity to lose some of that excess."

Gunnor dropped the last crumb of bread she held in her fingers and huffed indignantly. "Gilbert likes me just the way I am."

"No doubt," Alaine chortled. She should be angrier than she was, but her relief at finding Gunnor indulging in only minor mischief, rather than seeking to bring the keep and Gilbert down around their ears, made it difficult to work herself into righteous fury. She took Gunnor by the elbow and firmly steered her to where her watchdog was waiting in the hall.

"I don't want to see you out of your chamber until after the rest of us have broken our fast," she warned. "If I do it will be more than one meal you'll miss."

Even in the dark she could feel the seething heat of Gunnor's glare. No doubt her stepsister was counting off in her mind the miseries she would inflict upon Alaine once Gilbert had broken their defense. But that was something that wouldn't happen, not if she was still alive to prevent it.

Alaine waited until the last rustlings of Gunnor's departure were gone, then went back to the kitchen to douse the lantern. When she stepped back into the hall, she noted for the first time that the entrance lobby was dark, in fact it was black as the pit of Hell. Her heart began to pound. Something was not as it should be.

Alaine picked a path between the sleepers and made her way to the main fireplace. Taking a torch from its wall bracket, she thrust it into the dying coals of the fire to light it. As it flared to life, a few mumbled protests rose from the sleepers. She thought briefly of waking one of the serfs, simply to have a man at her side. Then she discarded the idea. There were guards enough within ready call should she need help.

The entrance lobby was empty. There should have been a guard standing by the heavy door at the head of the access stairway from below, but no one was there. The wall sconce that should have held a blazing torch was empty. Wherever the guard had gone, he had taken it with him. She moved to the door. It was shut but unbolted, an oversight that could be deadly in view of their situation.

She descended the dark stairs with cautious steps, the torch lighting her way. At the second stone archway she paused to look up into the murder hole, an opening carved into the postern stairs that ran above the archway, intended to let hot oil or scalding water be poured down upon attackers who had gained entrance to the keep. The hole was dark. Nothing moved in the postern stairwell above.

A few steps further on was the door to the barracks, which filled the entire second story of the keep. The torch by the door was in place. Since Gilbert had retreated from attack with the coming of dark, most of the men-at-arms were within getting much-needed sleep. Only a minimum patrol kept watch on the battlements, and soon they would be coming down to let others take their place. Alaine was thinking better of her decision to descend the stairwell alone. A pair of sturdy swordsmen by her side would be welcome if there was indeed mischief abroad.

The door to the barracks was not unbolted though, as Alaine discovered when she approached. The outside bar was lowered, so those within were locked inside. Alaine's heart began a heavy pounding in her chest. Something was very wrong here. First the missing guard. Now this. She threw her weight against the bar, but it wouldn't budge. It was well wedged in the lock, and it would take far more than her strength to move it.

She was about to return to the hall to fetch help when a shuffling sound from below made her freeze in place. Then came the unmistakable sound of wood splintering. Her heart leapt into her throat and stayed there. Almost without thinking she drew the dagger that she had taken to carrying at her belt and set her feet in a path down the stairs. She almost expected a ghost to appear from the leaping shadows that fled from her torchlight. But the one who stood at the base of the stairs, standing in the dim light of a wall sconce and hacking with his sword at the heavy crossbar that sealed the main keep door, was no ghost. The missing guard lay sprawled with his counterpart who had guarded the lower door. Their blood stained the stone floor a dark crimson.

Sir Guillaume turned as the light from Alaine's torch flowed into the broad chamber that led from the main keep door to the vaults. His surprise was as great as Alaine's, but it lasted only a moment before he lifted his blade for another blow.

"Sir Guillaume!" Alaine croaked when she finally found her voice. "You're supposed to be . . . !"

"Lying senseless in my bed," he continued for her. "Leaving the defense of this fair castle in your incapable hands."

She scowled angrily, suddenly understanding. "I thought you looked remarkably well the day you supposedly collapsed. What do you think you're doing?"

"What does it look like I'm doing?" he snarled, never taking his attention from his task.

"Well stop it!" she ordered uselessly.

He laughed, not sounding like the Guillaume Alaine knew. "Why?" It was a sneer of contempt more than a question.

"I'll show you why, traitor!"

She crossed the space between them with surprising agility and thrust the torch in his face. He screamed and pulled back, clawing at his face with his one free hand. But the damage was mostly singed hair and brows, Alaine observed with some regret.

"How fortunate that Rorik learned the lesson his mother taught him and replaced all the crossbars with ones only two men can move."

Guillaume's mouth twisted in a snarl. "A sword can do what one man cannot."

"But it takes time, does it not?" Alaine reminded him. "Time for the traitor to be found out, as you were."

"You will wish, lady, that you'd stayed above where you belong. You cannot stop me."

He held his sword at the ready, and she guessed rightly that he wouldn't hesitate to kill her now that she and her torch and her little dagger stood between him and the door. She had no doubt Gilbert and an army of men had filtered through the concealing dark of night and waited on the other side of that barrier.

"Why would you betray Rorik?" she asked, bidding for time. Soon the patrol from above would be descending to the barracks. Then she would have the help she needed to put this traitor in his place. "He was going to install you as master of one of his eastern keeps and find you an heiress for wife. And you've served the duke for years. How could you betray him?''

"Aye, I've served for years,'' he growled. "Twenty years and more I've served Richard then Robert the Devil and then his bastard whelp William. I've earned more than some paltry broken-down keep, much more. It's time to change masters. Gilbert offers me more than Rorik ever could.''

"And you think Gilbert and Phillip will reward you well?'' Alaine asked contemptuously. "I doubt there is enough of Brix to satisfy the three of you greedy hounds.''

"Gilbert's not going to share with that puppy Phillip,'' Guillaume spat. "And without Gilbert's support he doesn't dare set foot on Norman shores. He'll give me Sauvear and Ste. Claire and your Channel Isles besides. It is a promise I'll hold him to.''

"You'll never live to see them,'' Alaine predicted. "When Rorik comes he'll tear you limb from limb, and Gilbert too.''

"Rorik won't come,'' Guillaume told her with smug satisfaction. "I sent no messenger.''

"But I did,'' Alaine said calmly.

"So that was the man Gilbert intercepted,'' the knight frowned.

"I sent two.''

Guillaume's frown grew deeper. "Two?''

"Yes.''

Guillaume squared his shoulders and stepped forward, sword held before him pointing at her heart. "If Rorik comes, it will be too late. Now let me by, lady, or I'll end two lives with one cut.''

"It won't be that easy, Guillaume,'' Alaine proclaimed, hoping her voice didn't betray her uncertainty. A year ago she might have been able to best Guillaume, but in her present condition she doubted she could best a six-year-old page. Guillaume would kill her then finish his work on the bar. Gilbert and his men would be the victors and she would be cold and dead, her unborn babe with her. She thought of screaming for help, but doubted that her voice would be heard by those who snored in the hall, two stories above.

At the knight's first lunge her fighting spirit resurged. She dropped the useless dagger and blocked his blade with the heavy torch, using both hands to counter his strength. As he recovered and stepped back she waved the fire toward his face, but he was not to be caught by that trick a second time. Alaine was panting already, and at every movement her back burned in agony. She couldn't last more than a minute at most. It was doubtful she could manage to last that long. Now, she thought, was the time for a miracle.

Guillaume lunged again. Alaine caught his blade near the head of the torch then slid it down to sear his hand. He yelled in pain and retreated, and she followed up with another lunge to his face. Alaine thanked God that her father had defied convention and taught her the use of arms. But this time Alaine overbalanced herself, not used to fighting with her center of gravity out in front of her. In trying to recover, she stumbled back against the door, and the splintered bar cut painfully into her already throbbing back. For a moment nausea rose up into her throat and her limbs went weak with pain. Guillaume chose that moment to lift his blade again.

"Hold there!"

The voice rang out of the black shadows of the vault. Alaine recognized the imperious tone, the deep, rich timbre.

"What passes here?" Rorik demanded, stepping forward into the light of the torches.

Sir Guillaume turned, looking surprised but not at all discomfited. Alaine had no idea he was such an accomplished mummer. "My lord! How . . . ?"

"Never mind how," Rorik said curtly, looking with an ominous frown from Guillaume to Alaine. "What goes on? Explain yourself."

Alaine leaned against the door, numb with shock and with the pain still coursing through her back. What in God's sweet name was Rorik doing in the keep? How did he get in? And if he was here with an army, why was he not attacking Gilbert from without?

Sir Guillaume waved his blade in her direction and managed to look reluctant to speak. "As you see, my lord. The Lady Alaine . . . she . . . ah . . . I found her here chopping at the bar. I ordered her to stop, my lord, but she was determined, so I set about to stop her 'ere the enemy was within our walls. I managed to take this blade from her hands, and now she comes at me with a torch."

Rorik's eyes, like glittering shards of cold green glass, swiveled to pin Alaine to the door. She knew how it must look. Here she stood, looking guilty as sin. She knew exactly what Rorik must be thinking and feeling. Being what he was, how could he help but think her guilty?

"Lies," she denied breathlessly. "He lies. This time it is not a woman who brings betrayal to Brix. It is a man. He!"

She knew before the words were out that he wouldn't believe her. Sir Guillaume, in Rorik's own words, was a stout companion and a good man. And she—she was the one who had run and fought and harassed and hid when he'd claimed his rightful due from Ste. Claire. She was the tart he'd found writhing on a bed with Gilbert. She was a woman, treacherous, faithless, dangerous, and in Rorik's eyes, forever damned. But she prayed for a miracle just the same. *Believe me*, she begged in silence. *For Brix's sake, if not for mine, believe me.*

Rorik's measuring gaze swung to Guillaume, who stood in artfully contrived embarrassment at having to see the master witness his wife's perfidy. The silence was heavy, and Alaine could hear her heart pound a painful cadence in her chest.

"Give me the sword," Rorik finally commanded in a grating voice, holding out one hand while the other rested on the hilt of his own blade.

Guillaume's eyes widened slightly in surprise. He hesitated, gauging the worth of trying to play the outraged innocent. Then his mouth drew into a tight, determined line.

"Be damned!" he gritted, raising his blade.

Rorik's steel whispered from its sheath and easily deflected the vicious blow. With a twist of Rorik's wrist Guillaume's blade went spinning into a corner, ringing with a hollow sound as it met the stone wall.

Rorik smiled grimly. "You always were much better ahorse with a lance than afoot with a sword. I warned you often enough it would be your downfall."

Alaine's breaths came in joyous gasps. Her miracle had happened. Rorik had believed her, trusted her over the word of a valued companion. She wanted to shout for joy, to run across the room and touch her husband, to feel his arms around her, to feel the strength and security of his presence surround her. But right at the moment her body refused to move. She leaned back against the door and was engulfed with vertigo as a queer twisting pain invaded her body. The pain built itself into agony. A little cry she couldn't suppress escaped her lips.

Rorik turned, looked at her ashen face, and was instantly by her side. "Alaine, what . . . ?"

The agony faded as Rorik gripped her shoulders. She opened her eyes to see Guillaume's bulk rising behind her husband. The torchlight glinted off the knife in his hand, the knife she had so thoughtlessly dropped so she could swing her torch.

"No!" Alaine screamed.

She summoned all her strength and pushed a confused Rorik away from the path of the descending blade. The arc of the knife was unbroken, though now its victim was different. A tongue of fire licked her flesh as the blade tore into Alaine's side. She actually heard the rasp of it scraping along a rib and sinking deeper into soft tissue. The fire became an inferno that grew and spread in wave after wave, engulfing her in what seemed an arm of Hell. Rorik calling her name was the last voice she heard before sinking into oblivion.

CHAPTER 27

"It will be a while yet before this 'un makes 'is entrance," Ruth declared, regarding Alaine with the air of a mother hen brooding over her chick. Hadwisa loomed in the background, her face pinched and pale with worry. "It is no surprise that such a tussle would bring on the pains early, nor that they've stopped. When the water breaks, then's when we'll know that the babe's on 'is way. But whether that be this very hour or next week, you'll not move from this bed, my lady. You just lie 'ere an' rest. You'll need yer strength when the time comes."

Indeed, the pains and the gut-twisting cramps were gone. The only discomfort she felt now was the burning of the shallow groove that Guillaume had carved in her side, made even more painful by the neat stitches that Hadwisa had taken to close it. Still Alaine felt deserted when Ruth and her old nurse left the chamber, saying that they must see to preparations for the babe and promising to return well before they were needed.

How long had it been, she wondered, since Rorik had carried her up the stairway and laid her gently on the blanket-covered pallet? It seemed so long since he had fleetingly touched her cheek—a gesture out of tune with the grim lines of his face—and explained that he must go and see to Gilbert's fate. It had seemed hours, but might only have been minutes. Time for Alaine was measured only by the heavy beating of her own heart and the throbbing of the cut in her side. The dank chamber had no window, not even an arrow slot whose narrow view of the outside world might tell her it if was day or night. What was happening outside these chamber walls? Had Rorik won the day? Was Gilbert dead? Or fled? Or—God forbid!—perhaps even now gaining victory. And what of Guillaume, the traitor? Odd it was that all this time Alaine had looked to Gunnor to be the weak link in Brix's armor. Perhaps she had taken a cue from Rorik in believing only women capable of such perfidy. She had set a watch on her stepsister and completely trusted the traitor.

As if summoned by Alaine's own thoughts, Gunnor stepped hesitantly through the curtained entrance into the chamber. Her face was pale, and lines of strain seemed to add ten years to her age.

"Gunnor." Alaine greeted her in a wary voice.

"Alaine," she answered quietly.

She walked to the pallet and took a seat on the hard floor, looking everywhere but directly into Alaine's eyes. Several times she tentatively opened her mouth and then snapped it shut again.

"Rorik has returned." Gunnor's voice, when she finally found it, was flat and weary.

"Yes," Alaine confirmed.

"You are all right?"

"Well enough."

Gunnor looked hesitantly into Alaine's face. "I never meant that you should be hurt. Had Gilbert won, I wouldn't have let him harm you."

Deceived and deceiving to the bitter end, Alaine thought, and closed her eyes as a great feeling of weariness washed through her.

"The siege is over," Gunnor said reluctantly. "I was up on the battlements. I saw Rorik bring his men out of the forest and pin Gilbert against the walls."

"You weren't supposed to be on the battlements," Alaine chided. "It's too dangerous."

"What does it matter if something happens to me? I am naught but a stone around my mother's neck, and yours. One you would well be rid of, even more so when I tell you that . . . that it was I who sent to Gilbert and told him Rorik was called from here to Brionne. I stayed behind when my mother left so I could spy for Gilbert. He promised to reward me with marriage and wealth and position. But now it seems . . . it seems I have lost.''

Alaine merely sighed. It was what she had suspected, but it was strange to hear it from Gunnor's own mouth. Now it seemed to matter very little. Gilbert had been planning revenge ever since Rorik first came to Ste. Claire. Gunnor had simply been a convenient tool to be used and then, doubtlessly, to be tossed aside.

''Why do you tell me this?'' Alaine asked wearily.

''Better to tell you before your husband hears it from Gilbert's lips. Rorik will want me hanged, but from you I might hope for mercy.''

''Rorik need not know what you've done.'' Alaine gave her stepsister a crooked smile, thinking that Rorik did not need another woman's treachery to add to his list.

Gunnor looked at her with bleak eyes, and Alaine saw the quivering fear behind the solemn stare.

''I will not tell him, Gunnor, and I doubt that Gilbert will think to, either. If he still lives I would guess he has other things on his mind, like saving his own miserable skin.''

''Why would you do this for me?'' Gunnor asked suspiciously.

''I have my reasons,'' Alaine admitted. ''And my silence carries a price.''

''Of course,'' Gunnor sneered. ''I should have known. It is too much to expect a simple kindness.''

There was no sympathy in Alaine's face. ''You've done nothing to inspire a kindness from anyone at Brix or Ste. Claire, Gunnor.''

Gunnor turned her face away and stared morosely at the blank stone wall. The lines of bitterness etched in her face made her look suddenly to be an old woman, but when she turned back her features were composed.

''And what is this price?''

Alaine sighed heavily. ''You may not live at Brix or return to Ste. Claire to plague Joanna and Mathilde.''

"Then what, pray, am I to do?" Gunnor queried acidly.

"You must choose as any woman must choose. Tell me what you want to do, Gunnor, and I'll do my best to see that you have it. Do you want to marry?" she asked, wondering if Rorik could find a man willing to put up with Gunnor's sour temper. "Would you perhaps like to take to the Church? I will do my best for you Gunnor, if only to free myself and Joanna of your bitterness."

Gunnor was silent for a long moment, her face a mirror for the conflicting emotions raging through her mind. "It seems I have no choice but to do as you say."

"It's not so bad a sentence, is it?" For the first time Alaine allowed a hint of sympathy to color her voice.

"I dislike men," Gunnor stated without reservation. "Gilbert is no better than the rest of them, ever promising what they cannot achieve."

"A nunnery, then?" Alaine suggested hopefully.

"The Church holds no pull for me—to spend my life being ruled by autocratic, dried-up virgins."

"It must be one or the other, Gunnor. There is no other place for a woman in this world."

Gunnor sat a moment, staring at the wall. Then she drooped in sorry resignation. "Then it must be marriage, if Rorik will agree to find me a husband as he said before that he would."

"I will do my best for you, Gunnor," Alaine promised. "Truly I will." She hoped Rorik could find a man who by some miracle could make her stepsister happy—far, far away where she would never have to see or hear her again.

Gunnor finally left her in peace. Ruth returned to hover over her and force doses of bitter-tasting tea down her throat. After what seemed an eternity of waiting a warm flood of water between her legs signaled that the real thing had come at last. Time marched on, measured now to the cadence of the urgent demands nature was pressing on her body. The pain built and faded again and again, each time seeming a little stronger, a little less bearable. Hadwisa paced with her around the room, supporting and cajoling and encouraging. Ruth soothed and clucked and told her the time was not yet, that she must try to relax and save her strength. Alaine didn't remember the births she had attended with Ruth being such long and painful travails. Next time she would have more sympathy with the mother-to-be.

She no longer had the strength of will to stay on her feet, and Ruth finally allowed her to lie back down on her rough pallet. The midwife gave her cheek a comforting pat then dragged Hadwisa from the room, muttering about finding someone to build up the fire on the hearth.

The pain built again, this time harder than before, sooner than before. Alaine shut her eyes and clenched her teeth, trying to think of something pleasant, as Ruth had advised her, trying to drive away the hurting with visions of apple blossoms in spring, sun glinting off the waves of the sea, Mallie's puppies soft and brown and smelling of warmth and milk, and Rorik as he'd looked when she had sent him off to Brionne, proud and straight and so much the man she could hardly look at him and keep her breath in her body.

The pain faded and she opened her eyes. He was there, kneeling beside her, not as she'd pictured in her vision but stained with the dirt and sweat of battle and looking weary unto death. She found she loved him just as well this way.

"Rorik." Her voice was but a whisper. She halfway feared he would disappear like an image of her weary mind's imagining.

He took her hand and smiled down at her. His hand was warm and hard and real. "How goes it, my love?"

She attempted a brave smile. "It goes well enough. The fight is over?" she ventured hopefully.

"Aye. Gilbert will bother us no more."

"Is he dead?"

Rorik shook his head. "Nay, not dead. Turned tail and run for Prestot. I will deal with him in time," he promised grimly.

"And Guillaume?" she asked.

"He's thinking on his sins in the hole below the gatehouse."

"Will you hang him?"

"Not I," Rorik said, his mouth quirking in a cynical smile. "A knight can't be summarily hanged like a common felon, for all that he may deserve it. He's William's man, only lent to me. He'll be sent to William for judgment."

Alaine sighed. It was over. They were safe, and together. Her prayer for a miracle had been answered. She basked for a moment in her husband's presence and in the precious hiatus from pain.

"How did you appear when you did? How did you get in the keep?"

Rorik smiled mysteriously. "Old family secret."

"And why did you not just attack Gilbert and trust us to hold fast? How did you know . . . ?" She frowned, confused. Then the frown faced to a cynical smile. "You thought I was the traitor, didn't you? You feared that I would let Gilbert into the keep when you attacked."

Rorik shook his head. "Nay, wife. I knew you would not betray me. You have never betrayed me."

Dawning realization of what he'd said spread across her pale face.

"I've been a fool," he admitted with a smile.

"Aye," she readily agreed, quick to follow up her advantage. "That you have. And a beast as well."

"But you'll forgive me." His words were jauntily confident. His grin made his stern, hard-planed warrior's face look young and boyish.

She sent him a saucy grin. "You're allowed to be a fool from time to time, you know."

Rorik smiled. "Am I? It seems I've stretched the limit of late, I've been wrong about so many things."

"Have you?"

"You've told me so often enough."

"I suppose I have at that. I suppose you think a good wife should turn a blind eye to her husband's many failings."

"That she should," Rorik confirmed with a twinkle in his eye. "But you're hardly the model of a good wife, or a meek and gentle maid such as most men crave. So how is it that I find myself so glad that it was you who finally trapped my heart?''

Alaine's mouth curved in a mischievous smile. ''You say that only because I've saved your miserable life . . . what is it? . . . twice now? And because I'm about to present you with an heir.''

''I'd say it even were you barren as a stone—say it and mean it.'' He grinned wryly. ''Though I'll admit it would be difficult to declare my heart had you let it be cut out those two times.''

''And you'll not trade me for some gentle lady who would say you yea at every turn?''

''Would a gentle lady survive the assaults of such a boorish husband?'' Rorik chuckled.

''Aye, indeed you are more like the boar than the dragon—pigheaded and nearsighted and so set of mind. . . .'' She stopped abruptly. ''And I love you so much.''

Alaine's eyes caught at Rorik's, and he felt his entire world fall into place, everything where it belonged, everything as it should be. The silence that spread between them was warm and full of wordless communication. Suddenly she grimaced as another contraction built and shook her in its merciless grip. Rorik reached out and took her hand, wrapping it warmly in his own. Slowly the pain faded, but Rorik didn't release his comforting grip.

''I've sent for Joanna,'' he said with a worried smile.

''You needn't have. She cannot arrive before the babe. Ruth will see me through.''

''You will need help in the days to come. I won't have you wearing yourself to the bone. I should have summoned her before I left. Besides, there's a reason I must talk to her. Sihtric has asked me for her hand in marriage. Apparently he has reason to believe she'll accept him.''

''Sihtric and Joanna? They bicker like children!''

Rorik grinned. ''And of course a couple who begin by bickering can never end up loving!''

Alaine matched his smile. ''Of course not! Not in a . . .'' She grunted with sudden pain. Her eyes widened. ''Your son knocks at the door and clamors to make his appearance. Unless you would be the one to greet him I pray you call Ruth to be quick to attend me.''

The fierce Stone Dragon turned a shade paler than his wife. He who had never given an inch in bloody battle beat a hasty retreat. Alaine smiled at his back.

Stephen Geoffrey William Valois spilled into the world from his mother's womb the thirtieth day of October of the year 1047. From his father he inherited fierce courage, strength, eyes of summer green, and pigheaded stubbornness. From his mother he took an equal measure of stubbornness, along with humor, patience, and hair of burnished gold. And from them both, he and his brother and three sisters were gifted with a secure home full of the sometimes boisterous peace of two spirited and hardheaded people who were deeply in love.

Never again did Brix pass from the hands of those who could count Rorik Valois direct kin. And as years followed upon years, grandchildren and great-grandchildren thrilled to the stories of how the fierce Stone Dragon had ridden west from the River Orne to sow the seeds of war and reap a long-sought revenge, and how he harvested instead a lifetime of love with a woman who never learned the meaning of defeat.

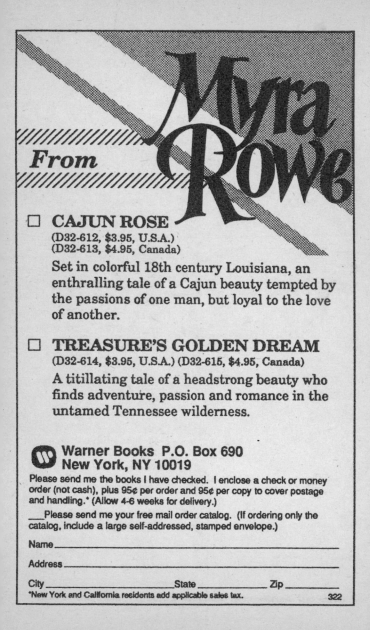